The Trees of Eden

Rebekah Tyne McKamie

Settings Christian Publishing, LLC
Calhan, CO

Cover Design and Book Design by Settings Christian Publishing, LLC

Author photos © RJ McKamie. All rights reserved. Used by permission.

Cover and interior stock images licensed from stock.adobe.com

Scripture taken from the New King James Version®. Copyright © 1982 by Thomas Nelson. Used by permission. All rights reserved.

Scripture from the King James Version (KJV) is public domain in the United States.

Settings Christian Publishing, LLC
Calhan, CO

ISBN (paperback): 978-1-7348040-6-5
ISBN (e-book): 978-1-7348040-7-2

Library of Congress Control Number: 2023909798

Printed in the United States of America.

For Chloe P.

I love who you are.
I don't know who you'll become as you grow in Christ,
but I know I will love her too.

Ephesians 2:10

For you, brethren, have been called to liberty;
only do not use liberty as an opportunity for the flesh,
but through love serve one another.

Galatians 5:13

A Note of Caution

Beloved Reader,

Just after finishing my first draft of The Snow Fence, I sat in the front room of a house I no longer live in and told some family members that I was going to start a new book that would be finished in seven months. I no longer remember the justification for that statement, as that conversation occurred over a decade ago, and it seems a different person said it. This book fought me, and I fought it. Among many other things in my life, God used this book as a place to challenge my perception of who He is and what His people look like.

My husband will recall that I asked him many times: If I write a book that explores the limits of Christian liberty, am I going to encourage people to push God's boundaries for them? Will people sin or stumble because of me? Will I offend people? What will my mother think? But those were not my actual questions. The deeper questions were desperate battles I was fighting in my own heart. God, will You teach *me* about liberty? At what point does Your grace end? Is the whole world black and white or do You really live where things are gray? Can I handle offending someone? Can I handle offending *everyone*?

A decade ago, I didn't live in a world that was so divided, even within the body of Christ, that there might be a need to explain the limits of the liberty we were given at the cross. But in recent years, Christ's model of unity in diversity (1 Corinthians 12) and of the way we should use our liberty to foster love and service (Galatians 5:13) have been corrupted and broken by the enemy.

It wasn't even hard. All the enemy did was help us forget one thing. See, there was *one* tree Adam and Eve needed to avoid in the Garden of Eden (Genesis 3). Because they ate of the *one* tree not permitted, sin and death, which didn't exist before, entered our DNA and corrupted our world until the end. They were given paradise and ruined it for a couple of bites of fruit.

But this book isn't about *that* tree. This book is about the *other* trees from which Adam and Eve could freely eat without consequence.

Even when we are in Christ, we all seem to have a specific fruit tree that we prefer when we know that all but one are acceptable, beautiful, and delectable. To condemn the sinless actions of another person is moralism, which can lead the whole world to believe that we can find our way to God without the cross. But there is no fruit that will reconcile us with God except the precious blood of Jesus Christ (John 14:6).

Don't worry, the Bible condemns sin and false teaching at every turn, so I will not waste my time brainwashing you or justifying sin to you. I am a Christian who lives by the Word of God, and I am married to Jesus, with an ongoing love affair with the Holy Spirit (and a guy named RJ). So, I am going to reverently speak the truth of God's Word while telling you a romantic story that will stay with you.

But fellow Christian, **I will still likely offend you**. You might even be heartbroken or disappointed or triggered. Yet my ultimate hope and prayer is that you are *challenged*. I aim to challenge your tree. I want you to vehemently disagree with something one of these characters says or does, and I want you to open your Bible to try to prove them wrong. And after you dive into Scripture and consider it all in your heart, I want you to look with love at a fellow Christian you hated yesterday.

I love you and the purpose God has for you within His will, my sister or brother in Christ. I can't wait to meet you in person or in glory.

Because of Grace,

Rebekah Tyne McKamie

Acknowledgments

Disclaimer (Updated 2026): A traumatic moment or season can change a person, even causing them to be broken and remade. God is faithful to teach us a new song, but we cannot carry many of the old tunes with us. This book was written "before" one of those moments, and these acknowledgments reflect that version of me. However, in reverence for the way that God uses our *whole* journey to shape us, and because even reading them to modify them is simply too painful for me today, I left them intact.

. . .

As a book editor, I often read the acknowledgments section in other books. Most are quick and to the point, taking about a page to mention a few important names. This time I promised myself I'd do that. People know I love them, and they know I am thankful for them. But I am just *so* thankful for them and I feel like everyone should know why. Books don't come from just one person. So bear with me just one more moment while I break the promise I made to myself. The best laid plans, as they say.

First, reader, I'd like to acknowledge you. Thank you for taking a chance on this book. I went through a lot to make this book a thing, and you holding it in your hands makes everything worth it.

Next, because he is also my proofreader, em dash hater/lover, cheerleader, coach, counselor, resident theologian, the person who reminds me of boundaries, and the person who has always been the first to breach them; I have to acknowledge the wonderful contributions of the guy I call Husband (or Hubberdind or Berdind or Pastor RJ or Dad or my Love, depending on my mood or request). This thing exists because of you, and you know it.

RMC Ellicott has been one of the greatest blessings in my life. I have forged so many bonds in this little church that it is unfortunately impossible for me to mention everyone's name. But somehow, years before I met any of you, I even named some characters "after" you. Most often, the character that bears your name will not match your personality, so I almost changed them. But because you are like my sisters, I decided to keep those glimmers there. Some names, though, I must mention. Because Jessie, you changed my life when I met you, and I never thought I'd find a friend so dear as an adult. I am so grateful that God saw how much our messes coordinated and put us on the same path together. But you're right, we still shouldn't sit together in church. The giggles that would ensue…Penny, you are just so cool and put together (and you probably think it's funny that I think that); Jessi, you're the most mature, responsible person I know, yet still more adventurous than I will ever be; Robyn, you're such a kindred spirit; Amy, I love your faith and our common disdain for moralism; Rebecca, I strive constantly to have your quiet spirit; Bekah, your smile is infectious; Hayley, you are a constant force of beauty and truth; Ruby, Glenda, Kris, Lisa, Pat, Missy, Gail, Dela, all the ladies around the table at women's study, and the list goes on. If you don't see your name here, there are a few reasons for that. One, this paragraph is already starting to annoy the readers and the editor in me. Two, you are male, and how do I get started on a whole other category of wonderful people? And three, it probably wouldn't be wise to mention the names of the few dozen or so young people in our youth ministry who have challenged me and lifted me up and sometimes broken my heart. But young or young-plus-experience, I treasure you all specifically and individually. I see you and God sees you.

I have to thank my three kids who somehow crept into the teen years when I wasn't looking—even though I'm basically always looking. Because when I'm not looking at you, I'm looking at this screen. You have given me so much grace as I write and edit. Caleb, you are also a gifted writer, and I can't wait to see what God does. Levi, your imagination and passion make me wonder if there is any color in my world at all. And Chloe, you have grown into such a beautiful young woman through and through. This one is for you, Angel.

I must always thank my sisters and brothers. Some by birth, some by marriage. But really, who is counting anymore? Also, you have amazing kids, and they are bringing amazing people into this family. God is so good, and I am so grateful that you all walk in step with Him.

Okay, so Momma, you get an extra special content advisory before this one. You're the reason the acknowledgments are first. And Daddy, I know you'll root for all the wrong people and all the right people in this book. But both of you? Thanks for rooting for *me* and for introducing me to Jesus.

Papa, thanks for raising the best man in the world and for spoiling the three hoodlums with your love, silliness, gifts, and your presence.

Acknowledgements

I simply cannot print this book without giving a nod to what will seem a strange source to some: The Duggar Family. To the world, they are a spectacle. To me, they were an inspiration. Yes, they did wrong sometimes, but there was so much good. The proof is in the fruit, and the overwhelming majority of their children walk with the Lord with their whole heart. Without this family, I would not have had the courage to stand against a world so contrary to a holy God. I wouldn't have my daughter, I may not have homeschooled, and maybe a dozen other very important things. I watched them grow up, and in the decade I have been wrestling with this book, some of their adult lives have eerily echoed the fiction within these pages. Jinger, your most recent book inspired me to get this one off my computer and out into the world. I know none of you will read this, and you don't know me. But thank you for being a city on a hill.

Father, thank You for being so patient to teach me the depth, height, length, and breadth of Your grace. Thank You for showing me the way You see people and for stripping me of legalism and moralism while I cling ever tighter to righteousness. I am not who I was, and that is completely because of You. Again. And always. The glory for this one is all Yours in Jesus' name.

One

Jubilee Monroe

"Do you think they'll grow if we plant them?" I whispered to my older brother through still-sweet lips. I was pawing at five dark, teardrop seeds, wet and pulpy from the snack we had just shared out on the front porch.

It was early summer then, in a dry, flat, arid valley of Colorado where the wind can uproot trees, and it rarely rains. But when it does rain, it comes down with the fury of a thunderstorm. The winter's rage is far different. The sky can be blue and the sun shining, but the air is so bitter cold that it takes substance as glistening flecks. It only warms up when it snows, and sticky seeds outdoors would invite frostbitten fingers even then. I was thankful, therefore, for the dawn of summer.

"Isaac says the apples we get from the store don't grow things." My brother Hakim shrugged his string bean arms.

"But we didn't get these apples from the store. We got them from the farmers' market, remember? McIntosh. Dad's favorite." My optimism sprouted. "He'd be so happy to have his own tree. And we could climb it, Hakim!"

"Jubilee, it takes years to get apples from a tree and decades to be able to climb it," Hakim resolved, ever the realist.

"Oh. I didn't think about that." I nearly tossed the seeds in the nearby garbage.

"But," Hakim started, perking up with a sense of adventure. "We won't know for sure unless we plant them. Worst-case scenario, you'll have to wait and watch your children climb it."

"We should ride until we find the tallest, greenest grass. We'll plant the seeds there." I revived the dream, skipping out into the horse corral where the chestnut Thunder and gray Lightning were already saddled. We'd received and named the horses late the previous summer, a day after we had been enthralled by the power of a Colorado thunderstorm.

The greenest grass turned out to be along the fence—our furthest dictated boundary at ten and twelve. Hakim suggested we venture just across it, where our neighbor had a miniature pond forming at the edge of his eighty acres from all the recent rain. They would likely never know if someone had breached the boundary, and Hakim said as much. Our father would also never know. Still, I protested.

"We're not allowed to go past the fence, Hakim. We'd have to do it all the time if we had a tree there. I don't even want to do it once."

Hakim did it with a roll of his black eyes, but he agreed. The seeds were planted with unskilled hands in sandy soil ten feet from the edge of our parents' property. We marked it with the largest rock we could find, then ventured back home, careful to make it back in time for supper, as instructed.

Our father met us at the porch. We could see him waiting there for ten minutes as we led the horses into the corral, unsaddled them, and dragged our feet to our father.

"Where were you?" Dad boomed.

"We were out by the fence. Jubilee wanted to—"

Our father interrupted. "You were out of your mother's line of sight. Anything could have happened, and she would not have been aware."

"But Daddy, you didn't say we had to stay in Mom's sight. You said we couldn't go past the fence, and we didn't," I pleaded.

"And we came back before dinner like Mom told us," Hakim appealed. He later told me he was glad for my choice to bring only obedience before our father.

But for our father, obedience wasn't always enough.

Adam Monroe, the man I call Dad, is a serious man. A great big, balding, gray-haired, wire-framed glasses around dark eyes, serious man. I supposed at the time that someone as wise as Dad would have to be that serious. He never spared us that wisdom.

"Children, never take liberty to the outermost limit. It should have been clear to you that you should not even venture *near* the fence and that you must stay within your mother's sight. I want you safe. I didn't bring you two from the furthest reaches of the world and love you as my own to have some evil befall you here. Understood?"

Dad's brief lecture left us stunned until we mumbled a *Yes sir* in unison. We had given up the fight with ease because Dad hardly, if ever, mentioned our adoptive origins. It meant he was making a grave point that should never be contested. Stay within Mom's sight. Never venture *near* the boundary. Otherwise, you are not grateful for escaping the "furthest reaches."

For a day or two, I was heartbroken that I'd never get to go tend those apple seeds. Within a week, I understood how foolish I'd been to have planted them in such a harsh climate anyway. Still, for a month, I wondered if they might sprout. Though the lessons from that day remained, like rings of a tree remember, those seeds eventually went dormant in the innermost gardens of my mind. I'd sown memories there before, but not all remain dormant. One does not forget the furthest reaches.

I remember the heat. In India, it's the kind that stays inside the bones and leathers on the skin and doesn't relent for anything but the rare mercy of a breeze. So, I remember the breeze; mostly the stench it brought in from those streets filled with people society had vomited out.

If I close my eyes during the right time of day and the right season of the year, I can also remember the paper lanterns, aged from sun and stench. If the scarlet and bright yellow beads swayed from those lanterns in that merciful breeze against that relentless heat, the sun would catch and scatter the light to the other baby cages like mine. So, I remember the cage.

The cage, probably a high-sided crib, was the best of my first two years. It was home. The adults would wear medical masks, but their enormous brown eyes would smile. I had survived a night on the step and was quiet enough that they almost left me there to die. I don't remember that night. But they say it was flooded with moonlight. And so, they would call me Chandra, for the moon in that country. I would draw sweet milk from bottles and grab hold of the great colorful cloths the women tied around their bodies. I'd look up at the spot of darkened flesh between their eyes. I am not supposed to remember all that, or that white families from faraway lands would come to stare at us children and pity us. They would hold us if we were lucky. I was often lucky.

When I outgrew the cage, I soaked in that heat with memories that sometimes awaken me in the night, though no one knows that I remember.

But if there is something a child does not ever forget about the furthest reaches—that thing is hungry.

I remember hungry best; the way it starts in the belly with empty, then moves to the arms and legs with tremors, the mind with fog and faintness. It falsely subsides for a time before returning to the belly with agony, the body with weakness. There is no way to cast away hungry from memories because I know that it is only a memory to me. But it is still a way of life for far too many, something impossible to forget.

As a child, I was more beautiful than all the others, or so I was told. My golden eyes stood out among the dark. When I met Adam and Leah Monroe on my first birthday, that beauty might have been what saved me from heat and hungry. It took them a year, but they fought hard for me. When I was two, I spent a long airplane ride trying to forget hungry as my mother braided thick black hair and prayed over me until they took me to a place I still call home.

Here, I am the seventh of eight children. They named me Jubilee because Dad turned fifty the year they brought me home. He likes numbers and rules and the letter of the law. But I was his Jubilee, and he was mine. He swept me away to the land of security and abundance where Jesus redeemed me deeper still.

This cool June evening, nine years after sticky seeds in sandy soil, we are celebrating birthdays. When there are enough children and grandchildren, it is practical for celebrations to be consolidated. I just turned nineteen, so my name will be mentioned in song this evening.

We are blessed to overflowing, and Dad prays it solemnly, wisely. During the prayer, Hannah's oldest child yells out, "Mommy, I'm *starving!*" Hannah, the fifth of eight, shushes him.

After the prayer, when forks begin to connect with plates, still-skinny Hakim addresses Hannah.

"Didn't he just eat a snack an hour ago?"

"Yes, but we had an early lunch today, so he hasn't had a meal since eleven." Hannah winces at some movement of the child still inside her.

James, Hannah's attentive husband, inquires of her well-being and sets a loving hand atop her belly. Hakim continues the previous inquiry, unfazed.

"You should still teach him the difference between *starving* and mildly uncomfortable or greedy." Hakim. Oh, Hakim.

4

"He's five, Hakim. He doesn't have a concept of that difference. But you're right. We are certainly working on Jonathan's manners," Hannah explains with tact, watching James place bread rolls on each of their two children's plates.

"I'm hungry too." Isaac's oldest son, the first nephew I ever held, speaks out. "I didn't get a snack like the little kids."

"You're fine, Lawrence." Isaac, first of eight, corrects his son.

"Seriously. That kid's never been hungry in his life!" Hakim comments.

"Hakim," I whisper. "Stop it." Because I know where he's going and where he came from. Hakim came from hungry too. From the furthest reaches.

"Lawrence has forgotten his lunch at home a time or two." Maren, Isaac's wife, chimes in. "But hunger like that will teach you pretty quick not to forget it next time."

"Maren, you could certainly teach him at home instead of sending him away. None of my children ever forgot their lunches." Mom leans, speaking encouragement to Isaac's wife.

"She's right, Maren. I love homeschooling. I don't think I could ever do anything else." This is from Noah's wife, Penny. Noah is the third of eight.

"I manage a bank, Penny," Isaac boasts. "Our children go to a private Christian school with a strong academic testing record. Maren keeps herself busy at home without having to homeschool."

"I'm sorry, Isaac, did my wife offend you in some way? She was praising homeschool, not condemning your kids' school," Noah defends his wife, who is sheepishly now looking at her plate.

"Oh, Penny. I apologize," Isaac says. Meanwhile, Maren seems distracted but is masking it by putting another spoonful of mashed potatoes on her child's plate.

"No harm done, Isaac," Penny forgives.

As a child, my deepest fear was to grow up and become like all of them. When I wanted to run and sing and scream and cry, they played out their wildest emotions in mere facial expressions and the red hair they all have and never talk about. When I wanted to mount my horse and let him ride into the wind until it stopped blowing, they would sit on the porch knitting and jewelry making, warning me to be careful and stay close. I would long for love in those younger days. They would condemn me to wait.

5

In our home, they do not raise voices without reprimand or become too heated in an argument without a call to simmer. I used to think that at some point, someone taught my parents and much older siblings how not to feel; how to be boring and do boring things and sing boring hymns without lifting their hands like they actually enjoyed it all and found meaning in it. I never received that lesson amid long division and long prayers. But as I grew, I came to understand that perhaps those wild emotions eventually wane into a deeper sense of sincerity. I even began to enjoy serving my sister by helping make jewelry, and I find hymns to be beautiful.

If I long, somehow I know that I can wait. From lessons planted deep inside, I know that I mustn't sing too loud or ride too far. There is only so much boundary-breaching that occurs before I go from serving at the homeless shelter to being served there. I am an adult now, and it isn't boring at all. I watched my siblings do it, and I watched myself become it too. They serve in the home and the community, honor God in all they do, and produce other children who have done the same. They are all successful and live lives of purpose.

That is, if purpose is what they are after.

"Would you listen to yourselves?" Hakim, sixth of eight, stands from the table, leaving half his food behind and finding a spot on the swing on the wraparound porch.

Hakim is the only person in my circles who has ever made me consider that maybe who we are as children is rooted inside still, not having withered at all. Hakim is known to fly off the handle, as my father labels it. But he's also willing to leave behind half a meal after working all day in the unforgiving sun roofing buildings. Because hunger, to him, is something different than it is for them. And since I'm the only other person in his world who understands hungry, I am also the one who joins him on the porch, leaving half of my meal behind as well.

"They never say anything, do they?" Hakim says, letting me sit next to him on the porch swing.

"What do you mean?" They were saying plenty, I thought.

Hakim laughs once. "It's like the second they start to feel like they'll have an emotion happen, they pretend they aren't and act like everything is always okay. Not exciting. Not devastating. Just okay."

"Well there's no reason to get excited over a little disagreement." I shrug, Adam Monroe exiting my exotic mouth.

"Those kids have never been hungry. None of them. But pretty soon, they'll be taught to ignore the thought that anyone ever is." And when Hakim looks out across the field, watching and smelling the June breeze wave through the natural, budded grass and prickly junipers and bring in a thunderstorm, I know he isn't saying what he wants to say. He isn't mentioning Africa. He isn't talking about the infant brother that starved in his mother's arms; the mother he loved, and remembers well, who gave him up, simply so that he could eat more than a morsel every three days.

Hakim's never said it. But I think he may have preferred to starve if he could have just been with his mother. I have nightmares about hungry. But I also have nightmares about what it must have been like when Hakim realized he was being left at that orphanage. He was told to forget about his mother at three years old. There are just some wilds too big to bury in sandy soil. They must be worn like sackcloth.

"You think they'll ever grow?" He whispers.

I don't answer because I'm not sure if he's talking about seeds or people. I'm less sure if it matters, and unable to comment further as Dad calls us back in from the rain to finish our meal.

I'd prefer to feast upon the memory of a shared apple and the sweet aroma of the first raindrops calling up the helpless dust.

But as a Monroe, there is no honor in hungry.

Two

Jubilee

"Jubilee, you have to come help me. The farmers' market is in a month, and I only have half of what I need," Hannah says over the phone on Wednesday morning. She seems agitated, which is rare for her. "Bethany dumped all of my seed beads last week, and I just now got them all sorted. Do you have any horsehair for me?"

"Yeah, I brushed Thunder this morning. And I have some feathers from Mom's chickens too. I have work, but then I'll come over. Do you need anything from the store?" As I ask, I look myself over in my full-length mirror—buttons to collarbone on a top tucked into a skirt that ends where my boots begin. Perfectly acceptable to be seen.

"Actually, yes. Some milk would be great. The kids go through it so fast. Thank you," Hannah says with grace.

"Alright. I'll see you at three with horsehair and feathers and milk." I say goodbye, set a reminder in my phone about the milk, then head downstairs.

"Take a look at *this*, Jubilee." Mom catches me at the bottom stair with elegant font on cardstock that I have seen plenty of in my life. Marriage is a norm still big enough to celebrate without consolidation.

I recognize the name on the wedding invitation: Peter Samson.

I glance over at the couch where he sat across from my father two years ago, asking if he could court me. As is the custom in recent times, Dad then brought the prospect to me for acceptance.

Peter is a tall, striking blond from a wealthy family of cattle ranchers. But though I had been taught to respectfully accept an offer for courtship and allow love to find its place later (hopefully prior to the inevitable marriage), I had been urged with greater fervor to pursue the will of God.

"I don't think he's the one, Dad," I whispered in the kitchen.

"That's a myth, Jubilee. The 'one'? There is no 'one.' You must *choose* to commit, and he is a worthy prospect. I thought you two were good friends," Dad whispered back.

"We are," I answered with a shrug.

"Then it's settled. Peter is a good man from a good family. It's a decent match."

"I know." I demanded the attention of my father's eyes. "But I don't think Peter and I are a part of each other's purpose."

I didn't tell my father about the prior week's conversation with Peter himself. He had confessed that while he longed to go away to medical school, he knew he'd be better off just settling down with a wife and running the ranch, as was expected of the only son of traditional parents. Yet he was mostly done with a bachelor's degree then, at age eighteen. He'd maxed out all of his college entrance exams early in his teen years and been accepted to two medical schools already. While there is no dishonor in raising cattle, and it suited my vet tech degree well, I knew exactly what Peter needed me to do.

Peter greeted me with a stand as I approached him from the kitchen that day. Dad stayed in the kitchen, giving me space to tell him the news.

"Stop this and go get your white coat, Peter. It's all you've ever wanted." And all he ever talked about.

"You know I can't do that, Jubilee."

"You *can*. There's nothing here for you. Go do what God has called you to do."

"And tell my parents what?" He sighed, already half relieved. "I really didn't think you'd say no."

"But you prayed I would?" I whispered.

His quick glance at my father over in the doorway to the kitchen, then his barely perceptible nod and his minuscule smirk were in direct contrast to his reddening cheeks and the tears in his eyes. But they spoke it all to me.

"Just tell your parents I turned you down, and you're so heartbroken that only escaping to medical school will lift your spirits." That called us both to a smile. "Someday you'll thank me."

Peter hasn't looked at me in years since that day—whenever he is in town, that is. Usually, he is away at school.

Today, I am holding a wedding invitation. My mother winks as she hands me another envelope with his name on the return address and mine as the sole addressee.

I open it to reveal just one item. It is a picture of the handsome young man with an equally beautiful young blonde embraced in a side hug. I look it over with a smile, then turn it over. The penned message is simple:

"Thank you. –Peter"

"Peter's mother says he met her at school. She's a bit older than him, but that's to be expected when he went to medical school so young," Mom supplies. "He'll be a doctor soon, and so will she."

I breathe a sigh of relief for Peter, then look to the clock. I'm glad that James comes out to pick up Judah for work, and Hakim has his own car now. But I'm not so glad that I'm running late and Judah didn't put the keys in the designated basket after his trip to the store last night.

Mom takes the picture and envelope from me and heads to the kitchen. I get Judah on the phone.

Mom stopped bearing after five children. Other women in our church continued to have ten or twelve children, so only five was a heavy blow. Dad never liked the idea of adoption until our pastor preached a sermon about our adoption into God's family. Because Israel stopped bearing fruit, we were grafted in by the blood of Christ. And because Mom stopped bearing at five, they adopted Hakim from Africa, then me from India. Shortly after we arrived home from India, Mom found out she was expecting Judah. He is the eighth of eight, and Mom's greatest treasure. He was the remnant of her strength, still fruitful after all. And Leah Monroe praised the Lord. She spoils my key-misplacing little brother to this day.

"Hello?" Judah yells over loud equipment in James's shop where he works.

"Judah, do you remember where you put the keys?"

"Oh! In the ignition. I apologize," Judah says. "I returned from the store late and my hands were full."

"Someone could have stolen the car, Judah." I give him all the politeness I can manage as I exit the house.

"Jubilee, we live half a mile down a private dirt road. I don't believe car bandits would make it near the garage undetected." Judah tends to belittle me. He tries it with Hakim, as well, but Hakim has spice on his tongue for anyone who tries. A submissive woman of virtue, I respond with:

"You're probably right, Judah. But next time, just tell me?" Then I sigh in frustration when I see the gas gauge is in the red after I start the car. "Judah, where did you go last night?"

"The store. In town. Mom asked me to get—" Judah's voice is covered by loud equipment again.

"Judah, I got gas the last time. Couldn't you have gotten some on your way back home?" I try not to become frustrated.

"I've barely driven the car in the past two weeks, Jubilee. I left you with half a tank. Why do you need gas?" Judah sounds frustrated as well, anxious to get back to work.

"I'm looking at it right now. I have less than an eighth, so now I have to get gas before work. I'll be late."

"Well, I'll pay you back for the gas. But Jubilee, I'm willing to swear you had half. An eighth will barely get you to the gas station. Why would I put you in that position?" A honking horn in the background. "I must go, James has a fair amount of business today."

"Sorry. Didn't mean to disturb you. Bye, Judah." I put my phone on the seat next to me and head out, praying I make it.

There is a gas station halfway between our house and the town. To some, it's in the middle of nowhere. But to all that live on our branch of the outskirts of town, it is often the only source of civilization, and certainly the first people see in a day. Good for gas, respite for travelers, and late-night ice cream, it is a bustling place sometimes.

Today, as I lean against the well-maintained little hatchback, listening to the fuel flow and running fingers along the end of my black French braid, the place is like Grand Central Station—not that I'd know. I smile at the toddler flailing about in a tantrum because he couldn't have a second popsicle. I glance at the road-tripping family in a beige minivan filled with pillows and juice boxes; the mother waking the preteen for a bathroom break. Then I spot the maroon extended-cab pickup truck pull into the pump right next to me. I wish I had a truck, so that I didn't have to get Thunder and Lightning's hay delivered. But I choose to be thankful, not covet.

I watch a man in his late twenties exit the driver's seat of that truck, set the gas to flowing, then say something into the open back window. "Stay put. I'll be right back."

When I was a child, my older brothers were a relentlessly disgusting, exasperating addition to my life. They were constantly reprimanded for both evils. For a long time, I had no understanding of why any girl in the world would actually want to *marry* one of them. Yet I watched them walk down the aisle, one after the other, even more disgusted with boys and men when my mother told me briefly how they were contributing to bringing all those babies into the world.

But then I watched Noah with his oldest daughter, nicknamed Leelee, named after Mom. Leelee was two then, and so enthralled by her grandmother's peony bush that she was practically in tears at the beauty and fragrance. And all Noah did was crouch down and help her smell the flowers and admire their loveliness. My brothers disgusted me until I saw them as fathers. Something is incomplete and raw in a man until he has a child. And then he is refined and honorable and gentle, even. But a warrior on short notice if need be. I saw it as their sister, and I watched their already dizzied, infatuated wives fall back in love with them, because they saw it too.

That's the reason for the smile I give the man who leaves his offspring in the truck. The man smiles back, then turns toward the gas station and walks slowly for about ten feet before swinging his head, then his whole body on swift heels to face me as he continues walking backward. People, especially at this station, are usually trotting along obliviously on the road to their next purpose. Rarely do they stop for a first smile. This man gives me a second, pearl teeth against ample brown lips, then a wink of generous eyelashes around sad, ebony eyes. His unexpected friendliness earns him an appreciative smile and a tilt of my head. His final move is to use a thumb and forefinger on his left hand to tip his cowboy hat with liquid ease. He turns again, and I watch him quicken his pace until he reaches the glass door of the building. My pump thuds to a stop, and I top it to an even number like always. As I replace the fuel cap, I hear a voice that startles my heart into a gallop.

"Hey!" The voice is coming from the child hanging out the window of the friendly man's truck. He has wild curls and black, shimmering eyes against medium skin, all of which remind me of my brother Hakim.

"Hey," I respond, waving to the beautiful child.

"I'm Bennett. I'll be eight in four days. My dad is taking me fishing today," he says in some kind of southern accent.

Apparently, this boy has no stranger danger training. I worry, having been taught that every stranger is a sinner, and there is no way of knowing what kind. But counting caution a feeble pursuit when it comes to children, I respond in the same way he began the conversation.

"Hi Bennett, I'm Jubilee. I just turned nineteen. I'm headed to work."

"Jubilee is a funny name," he teases. From the teasing, I wonder if he's a brother, though it appears he is the first of only one.

"So is Bennett," I tease right back.

"Yeah, I think so too. A kid in my class had a last name Bennett. He says I have two last names and no first name," Bennett shares.

I giggle—a bit of nonsense I'm sure to reserve only for children.

"Nineteen is old," Bennett declares.

"I suppose it is, compared to 'eight in four days,' " I banter.

"Shoot, I didn't stay put." Bennett's eyes snap to the opening gas station door.

Bennett disappears into the seat again and I smile to myself as I reclaim my driver's seat. I drive away just as Bennett's father returns to his truck, replacing a fuel cap without topping off. The man has chips, a bottle of apple juice, and an energy drink. I am running late and could have retained my frustration over it. But a seven-year-old stranger and a cowboy turning on his heels for one more smile had jarred my perspective. I am smiling still.

The most annoying thing about my job is that I find people to be good at proving what Dad has always taught me: Most people are ignorant. They come into the Mexican restaurant and speak to me in Spanish to be cute. And I answer them back, being fluent in three languages due to childhood boredom. After I seat them and walk away, they still haven't realized that I am so obviously Indian, not a Latina.

But other than that, it's a decent situation. I get to be kind to people while wearing a cross so they can see how happy people are who know the Lord. It's more effective at the soup kitchen, but I have to get paid for it somewhere. I even smile at the ones so obviously living sinfully. Christ is redeemer for all, I've learned at church. But so few come to Him completely.

I drive over to Hannah's after work, and spend much more time keeping her kids out of her way than helping her weave horse hair with straw and beads for bracelets or turn feathers and wooden beads into earrings. Hannah sells pieces online and at craft fairs and farmers' markets, making next to nothing but a lot of women happy and more beautiful.

Hannah's jewelry is all I wear ever since I was permitted to pierce my ears at age sixteen. I am the Indian girl who lives with a family of gingers. The Indian girl, who in all honesty thinks a pair of feather earrings looks out of place against Hannah's freckles. She's said the same thing. Much of the community is third or fourth generation Mexican and even some Native American. There is something about turquoise and silver and feathers and leather strands that speak to the beauty of black hair and caramel skin.

I catch Hannah staring at me remorsefully as I crouch on the floor and tie Jonathan's shoe.

"What's wrong?" I ask.

"We got a wedding invitation for Peter Samson today. He and James were always close," Hannah states plainly.

"We got one too. And he sent me a picture. The wedding is near their college and her family in California, so we probably can't make it," I smile at my nephew as he runs off with tied shoes.

"That doesn't bother you that he's, you know, moved on?" Hannah treads lightly.

"We weren't in love. He *thanked* me for turning him down."

"But you'd be married, possibly with a child or two. Peter's a good man that you always got along with as a kid. Trust me that love can wait just around the corner from something like that. And you would have loved living on that gorgeous ranch with all those animals."

Two years ago, everyone but Hakim interrogated me and condemned me for not marrying Peter. I can see the invitation is an aftershock from the once-calmed epicenter of shame. But I have two more years of perspective.

"Hannah, the only thing worse than settling for your backup plan," I shrug, "Is *being* the backup plan."

James and Judah come in the front door. Hannah lights up, rising despite the back pain that constantly plagues her throughout pregnancy, and she kisses James with a smile.

"Have a good day?" She asks in some low gentle tone I don't feel like I should be hearing.

"It was alright," James replies in the male version of the same tone, embracing his wife. Their love has always inspired me. They each give all of themselves continually, and in return, receive blessings and joys like flowers a gardener will reap from the same passion.

Judah stirs me from my musing. "Hey, Jubilee, may I have a ride home? James said you were here, so I thought I'd ask so as to not inconvenience him."

His speech is a contrived version of Dad's eloquence, and always has been. But he is serious, just like Dad, so no one corrects him or teases him.

"Yeah, sure. I was about to leave. I told Mom I'd make dinner tonight." I grab my purse.

"Thanks for your help, Jubilee. I'm feeling a little better about the farmers' market." Hannah pulls me into a warm hug she learned from our mother.

After the embrace, I address the family mechanic. "Oh! James. I got gas this morning and I feel like I've used too much gas today. Judah even swears he left me more than he did. What would cause my gas mileage to be so bad?"

"You probably have a misfire somewhere. Just bring it in if it keeps happening and I'll take a look," James says. I say goodbye to my niece and nephew and head home with Judah, who pays me for the gas, as promised, even though we both know it wasn't his fault.

Mom, a large woman with hair that has faded now to white from its fiery red of my older siblings' childhood, always cooks hearty meals. She uses fresh produce from the garden and greenhouse, chicken and eggs from the coop, and hand-kneaded bread. But tonight, on one of the nights I cook, we eat a little lighter, highlighting that same produce, but with less fat and carbs and more natural flavors. I try to remain healthy, and everyone complains at my lighter, more creative fare. But when it is in their just-as-full bellies, I am much more energetic and prompted to turn to the tired Hakim over the dishpan.

In a whisper, "Wanna ride?"

"You don't even have to ask," he whispers back.

We've trodden a path now through the eighty acres. Through bushes, around rocks, and not too close to the fence. We take the same path every time we ride. But the horses know it now, so we can just enjoy the ride without having to guide them anymore. Summer is my favorite, when warm dusk stretches right into night and the stars begin to come out before we need to head home for the darkness.

It's the one time my father permits me to wear pants. And jeans are the only pants worth wearing. I am at home in them under a properly brimmed hat, inside leather boots for western riding, and atop Thunder's weathered saddle. I'm annoyed by the way my braid slaps at my back like a whip when the horses gallop, but other than tied up hair, there is only the kind of freedom that seeps inside and makes us forget about rules and responsibilities. Hakim and I are siblings and fond friends, and we connect the best in this use of freedom.

"So, have you decided to quit your pointless job yet?" Hakim both teases and inquires again.

"No vets in town are hiring. I'll take what I can get for now," I explain yet again.

"Mom and Dad think it's weird that you want to work. Priscilla and Hannah have never worked a day in their lives."

"They work plenty hard! You try chasing around kids all day every day all alone while the other parent is off breadwinning," I correct Hakim's teased ignorance. "And I don't necessarily *want* to work, I just feel like I should know how to take care of myself. It's unjust that they never encouraged Priscilla and Hannah to do that. Sure, Elliot and James are both excellent providers for them, but what if they hadn't gotten married at eighteen? What if the girls married men who weren't yet financially established and they needed two incomes? What if something happens to one of their husbands, God forbid? I think it's practical for a woman to know how to work, and for a man to know how to manage a home."

"Jubilee, the feminist who doesn't need no man," Hakim takes on the world's dialect with laughter.

"That's ridiculous. I *want* to fall in love and get married and stay home with my children. I'm just trying to live life as it comes. And since God hasn't yet provided a husband…" I start.

"There was Peter…" Hakim teases.

"Can everyone just stop with the Peter thing today?" I shake my head in frustration.

"I kid, I kid." Hakim smiles. "And honestly, I think there are guys who are interested at church, but Dad is waiting for *your* interest first *because* of Peter. And Elliot, of course." He means Priscilla's husband. Priscilla is the second of eight. But her courtship with Elliot is a subject not even Hakim is brave enough to fully breach.

"It's stupid, I know. I just—"

"You want real love and God's best, or you want nothing. Trust me. I get it." Hakim's eyes narrow the way they do when he's done teasing and ready to say something. "Lest you forget, I am beyond our family's requisite marrying age, riding horses with my sister. I want God's best too."

Still, I defend it. "The Bible does say that without love, anything we do is meaningless. I know I'm odd for it, but I don't want to have any reason but love to get married."

"Obviously. You were about to inherit the Samson Ranch and said *no*." Back to the teasing Hakim. "And thank God. I would have cried if you'd married Peter 'Cottontail' Samson, the city boy who only ever talked about becoming a doctor while attempting to masquerade as a ranch hand. Not tears of joy, either."

After the ride, we leave our boots and hats in the barn, as our mom has always instructed, and put on the foam rubbery slippers she bought for the fifty-yard journey from the barn to the house, exhilarated from the gallop on the home stretch. We walk into the house after I shove Hakim aside, and while we're laughing about nothing or maybe more, like always, Dad's solemn stare from under his silver hair meets us at the door.

"Jubilee," he says, pointing to my shirt, which during the shove had raised above my beltline, showing an inch or two of my tanned side. "You know if a top will move when you raise your hands, you should wear another underneath or get rid of the top."

I pull down the soft fabric of my favorite riding top. "Sorry, Dad. You're right. I should change out of my jeans, too." And as I walk upstairs, embarrassed, I hear Hakim's defense.

"Tell me it glorifies God to make her deflate like that. She didn't do anything wrong."

"I'm not concerned about *her* sins," Adam Monroe grumbles.

"I'm her brother. I didn't even notice until you pointed at her like she's disgusting. You act like she was performing a satanic ritual in the nude or something," Hakim grumbles.

"Discipline, Hakim. Righteousness must not weaken, even at home. Modesty will keep her pure and respectable."

"And make her less beautiful? Who are you fooling with this?" Hakim takes to laughter.

"Do not question me about what you do not fully understand," Dad booms.

"Best way to learn."

Three

Elijah Bering

"All to Jesus, I surrender
All to Him I freely give
I will ever love and trust Him
In His presence daily live."

When I hear that old hymn at the end of a modern, upbeat set of worship music, it bounces around inside me, calling echoes from my soul's walls when all those songs are in the voices of a few dozen children.

One of those children is my son, who taught me the night he was born the origin of the idea of love at first sight. He's still so innocent and precious and wild. I hear his voice among the dozens, and it reminds me not to worry so much or be so hard on him. He's just a boy. Just a child. And if I've surrendered everything to Jesus, all that matters is that boy's voice right now. All those deep brown curls and that always-in-motion body wiggling and fidgeting make me wish this moment could live on as long as stars.

It is the last night of Vacation Bible School, and the children are performing worship songs for parents under the direction of the twenty-one-year-old pastor's daughter, Jessie. She's full of energy, bouncing around up there like she feels His freedom. Yet now, she is solemn and full of passion for the old hymn, using sweeping arms to lead the children to understand the meaning.

"I surrender all
I surrender all
All to thee my blessed Savior

I surrender all…"

There is no freedom on earth like surrendering everything to Him. That's what I'm reflecting upon while sitting next to Jessie's parents, Jordan and Lucinda Durant. Jessie's an only child, so when I arrived in town, they had room in their hearts for us Bering boys. The church is big for this town, so I don't know why the Durant family enfolded us so warmly and specifically. Maybe everyone at this church feels that way about their family. But they did come find me in the front pew, like always.

"He's so cute up there, Elijah," Lucinda says, turning to me. Pastor Jordan, on her right, nods.

"So is she," I whisper, nodding to their Jessie.

Lucinda sighs. "Beautiful, isn't she? Makes us so proud."

Then the nervous sigh of the young man to my left, and the far-too-fast-for-the-song tapping of his foot takes the notice of the entire row.

His name is Garrett. Tall, lanky, and just twenty-two.

"Don't get yourself all worked up, Garrett," I tease.

"But this is the last song, isn't it?" He asks. "I'm about to die right now."

"Seems that way sometimes," I tell him, chuckling. Waving to my son up on that stage.

Bennett. That little boy with those curls and that supernova-bright smile. In a life of darkness and struggle, only Jesus has been my vision at times. But my seven-year-old little boy has been a light for me. He was joy and heartache just when and how I needed them. I was fine without him, I suppose. If fine is anything. But now, Bennett dances with Jesus at the center of my world.

The song ends and the parents applaud. Most of the church congregation is present tonight. Pastor Jordan stands to make the announcement to adjourn us to the cookies waiting out in the front hall.

"Just about time, Garrett," Lucinda says across me, smiling at Garrett.

Garrett breathes. "Okay."

Garrett's parents and siblings on the pew behind him begin to jeer him, and then Garrett stands and walks to the right side of the stage. Jessie bows when her father thanks her for leading the children, and seems confused at the young man by the stage waving at her.

"Before I dismiss you, I think I have a young man over here who wanted to say something. Garrett?" Garrett approaches and Pastor Jordan hands him the mic.

Lucinda squeaks. "This is it, isn't it?" Then she sniffles, and I put my arm around the fifty-year-old woman. "You know, I'd hoped this would be you, Elijah."

"I'm a little old for her, Cindy."

"Nonsense. Seven years is nothing at all in the grand scheme of things." She sighs.

"That's Bennett's whole life, Cindy. But it ain't the years. Jessie's a kid to me," I remind Cindy. She was a kid when I met her and she'll be a kid when she's an old woman, no matter how narrow that seven years gets. When she met Garrett, that was the first time I even considered that she might also be a woman.

We watch as Garrett stumbles over some words and even squeaks a little when he talks. But still, when he drops to that knee in front of everyone, Jessie is streaming tears and nodding her head even before he's done asking. To her, he's the perfect man. She's loved him for two years and has barely gotten started.

When Garrett gives her a tender kiss once a diamond is glinting in the sanctuary light, Pastor Jordan clears his throat, delighting the crowd.

"Save that nonsense for the wedding," Pastor Jordan teases.

"Yes, sir." Garrett smiles.

They've never been together or with anyone else. Both raised in loving Christian homes and untouched by the darkness of this world. I wasn't gifted with much innocence, and I'm not sure I'd change that if I could, though I might have preferred a scenario that involved a woman. Still, I cherish the innocence in Jessie, who has called me her big brother when "friend" just didn't suffice.

Pastor Jordan asks us to bow our heads. "Lord, thank You for the children on the stage and the wonderful week we had. And thank you for my daughter to lead them in song. Lord, help this kid take care of my little girl and love her well. Remove the calories from the cookies in the lobby so that we can take joy in all Your gifts. In Jesus' name, Amen."

In the lobby, I'm pleading something familiar. "One cookie, Ben. One. We still got dinner at home," I tell my seven-year-old, then settle him outside on a bench where Jessie finds us.

"Elijah!" she says. "I'm engaged."

I hug her warmly after she shows off the ring. "I think the whole church knew that, Jess."

"Oh, hush." She smiles. "Hey, would it be okay if Bennett was our ring bearer? We're thinking the end of this summer for the wedding."

"Of course!" I tell her.

"Unfortunately, he'll have to represent you both. We wanted to ask you to be in the wedding too, but Garrett has so many siblings and cousins, and his mother insists that—"

"Jess, you know I don't need all that. Just provide me with some tissues for when your daddy walks you down the aisle."

"I will, 'Lijah. Thank you so much for supporting us and everything. I know you convinced Dad to tell Garrett yes."

She isn't wrong. Jessie is her daddy's joy, and Garrett has some growing to do. He works hard and has a decent job, but he isn't sure he likes the work he does. And because he grew up as one of ten kids, he has Jessie convinced they don't need babies even though she's a schoolteacher who adores children. But I reminded Jordan that God didn't ask us to grow into a masterpiece before He'd offer us salvation. When He folds us into His family, He sees the masterpiece through the blood of His Son and gets to work on the mess we are when we arrive. Marriage isn't exactly the same. But I know that some of the growing Garrett has to do he will have to do as Jessie's husband. He loves her more than he loves his own soul. He loves the Lord even more. So if fervent love is the standard, and it is, then he far exceeds it.

"I may have to talk to him again with this timeline, though. End of the summer? Seems…quick…"

"Well, we're ready. Garrett has a house, and the school where I did my student teaching hired me." She shrugs. Speaks in her sweet little voice. "I love him, Elijah. God made us for each other. And when you know, you know. You know?"

"So I hear." But I don't know. Not really.

"What's a ring bear?" Bennett asks, smacking on that cookie.

"I'll explain it later, Bud."

"Oh! I was sent with a message and almost forgot. Mom and Dad want to know what kind of cake you want for his birthday Sunday."

"Bennett's a chocolate man. Y'all are kind to give him a party, once again."

"It's nothing big, once again." Jessie bats her eyes.

The front door of the church opens. "Jess?" It's Garrett. "Mom wants pictures if that's okay."

Jessie smiles and heads inside with her new fiancé. Lucinda uses the open door to come outside while I am watching the love story through the window.

"Your time will come, Elijah."

"My time for…" I know what she means. But I've heard this far too many times from far too many people, especially this one. I know what's coming.

"*Love*, Elijah. You're handsome and you're still young. You just have to put yourself out there. Go on a date or two," she pleads.

"I don't have time for—"

"Elijah, you work four twelve-hour shifts a week. Which means you're off three days a week. Don't make excuses."

"Cindy, Bennett needs weekends to recoup. It took a lot for me to get Saturdays off. And Sundays we come to church," I try.

"What about Wednesdays?"

"We fish on Wednesdays when the lake isn't as crowded." She knows that.

"Even in the winter, Elijah?" But Lucinda catches me.

"It's June." I roll my eyes.

"It won't always be June!"

"Well, when it ain't June and I quit wanting to soak up every minute with my son, maybe we'll talk."

"Elijah Bering! You are a catch, love. Ask any girl at this church and you'd have a date. A wife. There are even some single moms. Like Sarah Walsh, maybe? You could handle a blended family, I think. Give Bennett some siblings. We'll be happy to watch Bennett anytime you go out." Cindy means well. She feels for her friend and sighs, glancing at Bennett. She whispers, "He needs a mother, Elijah. But that's not the worst of it. If this goes on too long, you'll start to resent him. Find a woman…for *you*. I bet a woman could find a way to do something about that scowl of yours."

"Ms. Lucinda!" I cross my arms defensively, scowling of course, but knowing exactly what she thinks would correct it.

"You know I'm right, honey. You're a darn good one, but you're still a man. Don't think God's forgotten that." Cindy. So encouraging and provocative all at once. I concede, but only in my stubborn way.

"Well, if God wants to give me a wife, He'll orchestrate it. I can't be taking that into my own hands anyway." I kiss sweet Lucinda's cheek as Bennett is throwing his napkin away. "Let's get home, Bennett."

"So, I dress nice and carry the pillow and then give the rings to Jessie and Garrett?" Bennett confirms on the ride home. He's not too excited. "I don't understand why that's a thing."

"I do wonder who the first person was that said, 'Hey, we have these tiny pieces of expensive jewelry that are supposed to last our entire lives. Let's tie them to a pillow with a ribbon and put them in the care of a little boy who is already restless because he's in a tux.' But it's an easy gig. You can handle it."

"Can we go see Jubilee?" He asks this as we pass the gas station.

"Who is Jubilee?" I am often unable to follow exactly what switch or junction led Ben's tracks to each point in a conversation.

"From the gas store."

"You're talking crazy." I laugh.

"You're talking silly," he banters.

"You're talking elephants."

"You're talking elephant poop!"

After the roar of laughter, I sigh with fatigue, shifting in my seat to stay awake. I'm glad tomorrow is Saturday, and that Bennett is giggling. He's a merry light in a lonely darkness.

After reading my Bible, I stare at the ceiling in bed tonight considering what I hate considering. I really am doing well for the two of us. Bennett knows the Lord. We are finally stable, maybe even happy. But I can't just shake off Lucinda's words. "Find a woman...for *you*."

I'm not opposed to women. In fact, at twenty-eight, I've become quite good at averting my eyes from the direction of a proper feminine physique. Sure, I'd rather look, but my relationship with God is much more important than looking where I ought not. Sarah Walsh has green eyes and a bratty son and petite little princess. She constantly talks about her ex-husband. That's as far as I've looked. At Sarah. But I have gotten lax. Something happened at the gas station the other day that I'm still working through. I'm glad Cindy doesn't know about it.

I pulled into the gas station and the Spirit whispered, *"Look."* I did.

She was a beautiful young woman that looked to be from India. That was glance one, as I pulled around the parking lot to find an open pump. Glance two was when the only open pump was next to her. That's when I noticed that her hair was long enough for the end of her braid to come around her shoulder and bend across her left breast. She was stroking the end of the braid there on her diaphragm, oblivious to my second glance as she looked around. There was some intelligence in her eyes that made me want to keep looking. I didn't. One look is good sense for situational awareness. Two was decent, considering God told me to. Three would mean I was asking for sin. The Spirit told me I'd seen all I needed to see. You'll learn that I don't question even the crazy from God.

The third glance wasn't my fault, though. I had to start the gas. Normally I stay there, but I knew I should flee. I had to remind Bennett not to get out and try to follow me into the store like he does, and when I turned, she was observing. That look in her eye had changed. It was…she was appreciating something with a coy little smirk. Oh. Just the kid. She was watching me talk to my kid. That's all. Women smile at that stuff. I smiled back, then planned to make a break for it. But it's like I was walking through sand, and I would never be right again if I didn't look at her one more time. Just one more glance.

God told me not to. He told me to bolt for the door of the store like the rest of the world was on fire and all was lost. But was she wearing green or blue? Did the skirt really go all the way to her boots, and the buttons all the way up to her eyeballs, or could I maybe catch a bit more skin the next time I looked? Were her eyes really that big and could I get her to smile at me again? I shouldn't have. I never have these problems. I'm a decent man.

"You have seen enough."

But like Lot's wife, I pivoted on my heels, and she was already looking at me. Blue. The top was blue. Her hair was black and reflecting the morning sun, and the skirt was far too long.

Glance four was too many. Like every playboy and scoundrel, I looked her over, then got one more friendly, intelligent smile out of her. And that was it for me. I stumbled right into lust. I folded, and she was completely unaware as she gave me a friendly little nod. She didn't know when I winked that I had her wrapped up with me someplace dark. I hadn't seen a woman that beautiful in a long time, or maybe ever. And for a full five seconds, she was completely mine.

The Spirit hollered into my soul down deep and He and I drove that adulterous image right into the pig I am and it ran over the cliff in my mind that leads to all the other darkness I work hard to ignore. She was an innocent young stranger, though she carried herself like she was older, and she was just minding her own business, pumping gas. And like the virtuous lady she obviously was, I apologized for what she didn't know happened with a respectful tip of my hat and a one-eighty on my heels.

I confessed and repented, and God forgave me. But I'm a mess. That's maybe what God was showing me. Thing is, because of that incident, I'm not sure how to look at or for a woman without compromising everything I'm trying to teach my boy. A seven-year-old doesn't need to watch his father fumbling and lusting trying to find the right fit of woman. That's God's job. And with God, being my kind of single father isn't a sin or a problem. Finding a woman might be. My carnal mind is still set on the one from the gas station.

Celibacy. That's probably the best course of action.

I pray tonight. I rejoice for Jessie and Garrett and thank God for all my blessings. For Bennett. I pray, as always, for the spouse no doubt already in the world for Ben. Then I sigh at wondering if there's one for stubborn, sinful old me. Would I even want a woman around? A manipulator? A nag? Gentle curves and soft skin like the woman at the gas—No. I'm closing my eyes with my palms until pain comes and the darkness speckles, keeping away the thoughts a man shouldn't think, digging deeper into prayer.

"God, can't You make it any easier to be a man? Why did you even make women? Don't You know they are the fall and failure of man? Why did You make me look at her?"

"Trust Me," God replies.

"Always, Father. Let Your will be done."

I do what I always do. I consider the size of my God. I think how my heart is more liberated with arms raised in worshipful surrender than during any impure hope for realized wilds. I consider that women are just a nuisance. Just a beautiful, interesting, mysterious nuisance that add something powerful and perfect to the world that man cannot. But since Bennett is my world, I assume I don't need that perfect power in my life.

I know that Jesus is the best Friend a man can have. He has shown up and conquered and healed in ways too wonderful for my own understanding sometimes. It's nothing for me to relinquish the notion of romance into the hands of that kind of Friend and Father. I'm fine for now. I'm fine with cooking and parenting and stretching out alone across this queen size bed and fishing on Wednesdays with my boy. Fine, even with scowling, if there isn't a wife in the world to correct it.

Four

Jubilee

Wednesday again, and I need gas, when normally I can go two weeks on a tank. This car has been faithful, a tradition almost, among my siblings. We all learned to drive in it. We maintain it well. But it has given me fits since I've been its main driver. I always tell my father it doesn't agree with me. Still, I follow tradition, even with the strange gasoline anomaly. But I'm delighted when that same maroon truck pulls in and the same man, in hat and boots and heather gray t-shirt comes out of the driver's seat and heads inside.

"Jubilee!" The same seven—no—eight-year-old voice.

"Hey, Bennett. How was your birthday?" Bennett is visibly ecstatic that I remembered.

"My cake was all chocolate!" He says in that accent. Texas. I hear it now.

"I love chocolate!" I connect. "Dad taking you fishing again?"

"Yeah. You have really big eyes. Are you from Mexico?" Bennett takes to a humorously creepy stare.

"I was adopted from India, but I'm American."

"Where is India? Is that in Mexico?" Bennett asks.

"No, it's in Asia," I tell him with a doting laugh, and my pump stops. I'm tightening my gas cap when Bennett's father returns.

"Dad, Jubilee is from India. India is in Asia," Bennett tells him.

"Jubilee?" The father narrows his eyes at me. "*You're* Jubilee?"

"Yes?" As if I'm someone famous or this man is some kind of stalker. Neither is comfortable. The man extends a deep brown hand. I shake it, and look up into sad onyx eyes below tightly curled black hair under the best kind of hat. He's clean-shaven with chiseled features. Not in the least bit unattractive if I allowed myself to see such things in men. Such would be vulgar. Unholy. I have worked my whole life for righteousness and a compromise would be unacceptable.

"I'm sorry. He, um…mentioned Jubilee a few times this past week. From the gas store, so I guess that's here. And I guess that's *you*. I'm Elijah Bering. This is my son—"

"Bennett. We're old pals now. He's a friendly one." I release the firm handshake.

"That, he is."

"It was nice to meet you, Elijah. Nice to see you again, Bennett. I'd love to chat more, but I am late for work. Have fun fishing." I open my car door and hear Elijah speak.

"You have a blessed day, Miz Jubilee." And he tips his hat like last week, handing his son some apple juice in the back window as I drive away.

Dad taught us that God only ever speaks through His word. Anything we ever need to know about life and trials and questions is already written, and if one cannot find what one is looking for in the Bible, one has not been granted the wisdom to learn it. So, throughout my life, when I have not known what to do, I've combed the Bible and prayed for wisdom. And since the Bible says nothing about whether I, Jubilee Monroe, should say…get a nursing degree or a veterinary technician degree…marry Peter or let him go to become a doctor…I also use a lot of logic in my life, since I suppose I've not been granted wisdom.

Right now, driving away from the gas station, my logic tells me that my gut is flipping and knotting and tensing because I need some ginger or peppermint oil. But I can't use logic to describe why the feeling is connected to a thought of Bennett. It is not like nerves or excitement, but like a call that has yet to be put to words. That's impossible, though. The Holy Spirit only moves through the words of the Bible, I've been told. That's my dad's answer every time I have a feeling about something. If I wind up following that feeling, I'll never tell my father. But I can't help but have them.

"Hakim, do you think God calls us to things through feelings?" I ask during the portion of our ride this evening while the horses walk side by side.

"Feelings can be pretty untrustworthy, Jubilee," Hakim answers.

"Yeah, I guess you're right," I admit. Men are granted a lot of wisdom, I'm told, and Hakim's sometimes makes a lot of sense.

"Then again, feelings are really just a reaction to observations your brain put together without you noticing," he analyzes.

"So, Dad says that the Bible gives us the answers we need. Is it possible that my brain is able to apply what I've always read to my life without me knowing and it comes out as...as a feeling?" I ask.

"Yeah, I think that's very possible. And don't forget about the Holy Spirit. He has a way of translating things so we understand...what do you have a feeling about, Jubilee?"

"Just this kid I met at the gas station a couple times. Him and his dad. I don't know. I just can't stop thinking about them and I don't even know them. It's weird."

"God isn't subtle for long, Jubilee. If He wants to tell you something or lead you somewhere, the road will bend under your feet. I don't know why a *feeling* surprises you." He charges ahead to a gallop.

I lie in my room tonight, thinking about a feeling that will not relent, but only grows. My head spins enough for me to finally fall asleep.

"I can't find anything wrong, Jubilee. Are you sure you didn't change gas stations or let Judah use the car and forget?" James asks, wiping grease off his hands with a pink-brown rag in the front area of his shop.

"I double checked the mileage. He's as baffled as I am," I tell him on Thursday morning, knowing I sound like *that* stupid girl talking to the mechanic, just like always. "And I've always gone to the same station. The one outside town? I haven't changed a thing."

"Don't know what to tell you, Jubilee." James shrugs his powerful arms.

I'm suddenly remembering the day James made Hannah a Martin. James grew up in our church, and the family is conservative and righteous, just like us. Still, much of the family had considered the choice borderline. James is the first brown face among us—except for Hakim and me, of course. But the adoptions had been in service to God and Hannah had no other tangible excuse to *marry* James but love. He was adopted into a white family as an infant, but still bears the face of a Mexican. For the sake of love, eventually, he'd been accepted. Well, it was that *or* his ability to rescue the car's brakes from Hannah's too-careful driving.

"Thanks, James. What do I owe you?"

"Let's see…after I add in the discount for helping my Hannah with her sanity and my babies so much…I'll put it on your tab." He winks. That tab, of course, is covered by familial love.

Another Wednesday, and another tank of gas later, and I laugh aloud when a feeling transforms into that maroon truck pulling up right next to me, yet again. The man, Elijah, gets out.

"Howdy, Miz Jubilee," Elijah says with a smile, starting up the gas pump right away instead of going inside.

"Hi!" Bennett says, hanging out the window.

"Well, hey, you two!" I cheerily move my braid over my shoulder and lean against the car. "Where you headed today?"

"Fishin'." Bennett says. "Dad caught a big one last week. He says we're gonna save 'em up and have a big ole fish fry."

I smile at the boy's enthusiasm. "Where are you two from? Accent sounds like Texas."

"Yes, ma'am. We rolled in here about five years ago and loved it. So, we stayed," Elijah shares. What kind of life can allow for rolling any place with a then three-year-old? He continues, "You seem like you were born and raised here."

"Well…born in India. Raised here from age two. That's when my parents adopted me." I smile, and Elijah nods with compassion. Passion, even, with some powerful brew of understanding.

"Are we grateful to be adopted or…?"

"Extremely." I nod.

"In that case, God is good."

"God is good in *any* case," I correct.

"Amen to that," he replies with an appreciative chuckle.

But everyone knows that, right? Because otherwise, the fact that this man is also a God-fearing man just made pretending not to be attracted to him a tad bit harder. My gas pump thuds, signifying that the tank is full. I replace the nozzle, screw the cap back on, and close the fuel door, all the while feeling him staring, but taking the opportunity to look away.

"I'm young, Dad. Jubilee told me," Bennett says.

"He also told *me* I was old," I share with Elijah, who winces when I look up. He's embarrassed at his son's lack of tact, like a gentleman would be.

"She is! I told her I was almost eight. Which I am now. She said she was nineteen. That's a lot of years, Dad," Bennett reasons, resting his arms on the window frame.

"Well how old am *I*, Ben?" He cackles.

"I don't know, like quintillion?" Bennett guesses. I smile, knowing a giggle would be out of place.

"Not quite. But if Miz Jubilee is old, I'm practically dust. You stay put." Elijah tips his hat once again and bids me goodbye on his walk to the gas station. "Miz Jubilee."

"Until next time, you two."

Five

Elijah

I close my eyes and listen to the wind leap across aspens and evergreens, catching the clean yet rustic blend of pine and mountain air. All is peaceful with the light zip of the rod and the almost imperceptible way the lake cleanses the rocky shore. I think there is some deep, cosmic reason Jesus chose a few fishermen as His disciples.

Bennett sighs in boredom. "I'm dying here, Dad!"

"I thought you liked fishing."

"Yeah, when we catch the fish!" Bennett proclaims. "But waiting is boring. Are you sure we're using the right bait?"

"We ain't using bait. I told you that."

"A worm is bait."

"But that ain't how we catch the fish." I lower my voice to just above a whisper. "You can use the most expensive bait in the world, but they'll come to the quiet anyway." I give my son a side glance. "So, shhh."

"Quiet ain't even a *thing*," Bennett grumbles.

"Exactly."

On the way back into town, having gotten skunked with fishing today, Bennett begins groaning in the back seat.

"You alright, Ben?" I'm father *and* mother to him, so concern comes quickly.

"No. My legs."

"Swollen?" I'm thinking of the steep rocky slope we'd had to hike to get to a new spot at the lake today.

"Yeah, n'red." Bennett sighs.

"Don't worry, son. I'll stop for some ice at the drug store. We need a couple more packs, anyway."

I leave the windows down and tell my son to stay put, as always, heading into the drug store in the small town. I rush inside for ice packs and catch sight of a familiar face down one of the aisles, having to back up a few steps before she notices.

"Well, hey there, bride-to-be." I beam. But Jessie is in distress, fretting and sighing over the vast makeup section. She is holding a little paper bag from the pharmacy, cradled in crossed arms at her chest.

"Hey." She's almost in tears, smoothing her nearly boy-short dark hair, then re-crossing her arms.

"What's the matter, kid sis?" A label we both claim, even playing to strangers' ignorance and confusion at times.

Jessie got her mother's sass and dark hair, but with her father's curls and emotional vulnerability. She sniffles her freckled little nose. "I bought my wedding gown."

"That's a big step, right? You excited?" I try to brighten her mood.

"Yeah, it's beautiful. But the ladies at the bridal shop were teasing me about how young I look and how the dress might swallow me up if I don't cover my freckles. I've never bought makeup before. I have no idea where to start."

My eyes widen. "What's their names? I'll teach 'em a thing or two."

Jessie giggles. "Daddy wasn't pleased, don't worry. He let them know they were being unprofessional. They were right, though. Can a twenty-one-year-old with freckles be taken seriously in a wedding gown? Garrett and I are so in love we didn't even consider the opinions of other people."

"Well, you shouldn't. Don't do what people expect you to do. Do what you're *meant* to do according to God's will. Leave it at that. I can help you with the makeup." I see the tool I need out of the corner of my eye.

"I'm sure," Jessie scoffs at what she knows is going to be anything but me knowing something about makeup.

I grab a handheld mirror and wink at Jessie, then put it up so she can see herself. "This is the makeup you were wearing when that boy fell for you. Someday, maybe you two will have a little boy, and you'll raise him in a house where there's a wedding photo of his momma with her freckles showing. That boy will eventually go out into the world and fall in love with a girl for her kindness and love for Jesus and her *natural* beauty. He'll end up with someone like you, Jessie. And that's what you want. Don't you *dare* hide behind makeup."

Jessie sniffs at a tear, and hugs me full on in the drug store, that paper bag crumpling at my back. "I can't *believe* you haven't wooed a woman yet."

"I will when it's time."

Jessie releases the embrace, then cradles that bag again. I smirk and nod to it.

"That what I think it is?"

"What?" But she knows what, given the sudden blush in her cheeks. Birth control. She rolls her eyes and sighs. "Yes. I had an appointment this morning. I want to be on it long enough for it to actually work when we get married."

"I told you a month is plenty. Some of them say a week is enough. You have two months, right?"

"I think you underestimate our desire to not have kids."

"Never? You'd be a good mom, Jessie."

"Definitely for now." She shrugs, leaving that subject on the ground with her gaze. Then she looks up with the mischievous little smile of a Sunday School teacher and picks up another subject from nowhere. "Bennett says you have a crush on some girl."

I scrunch my eyebrows, baffled. "Uh…what?"

Jessie giggles. "Some girl named Jubilee?"

My heart tremors in panic. I hope Jessie didn't catch that before I sober and laugh a little. "Jubilee is a young woman we've talked to at the gas station two or three times. I've spent a total of five minutes of my life with her."

"Uh huh." Jessie winks. "She's from India, I hear. She pretty?"

I laugh, too loudly, or stutter, or something. I turn and walk to the checkout, Jessie in tow, teasing like the little sister God never gave me.

"Wow! That pretty, huh?" She asks, in line with me now. "Bennett sure seems to like her. Is she like…*from* India? I hear they have gorgeous red wedding gowns."

I raise an eyebrow at Jessie. "She was raised in the States. Jessie, I hope you're not actually considering this a prospect. She could be married for all I know."

"She wearing a ring?" Jessie prods. Swimming her own ring through the air.

"No," I answer too quickly.

"Which means you looked," Jessie teases. "So, you've considered—"

"I haven't considered anything." I pass the ice pack across to the checker. "Except that Bennett's legs are giving him fits."

Jessie sighs. "My mom's right. You'll be a grandfather before you consider being a husband. See you Sunday." She kisses me on the cheek and exits the store with only her youthful beauty and that little white bag.

Bennett is asleep when I return and set an ice pack on each leg. I want the best for him, and suddenly don't really know what that is.

"I'm giving this to You, God." I whisper, then head to the outskirts of town as the wind picks up and thunder teases the distant sky.

Six

Jubilee

I spend Wednesday at work and then at Hannah's getting her ready for next week's farmers' market. The market shuts down Main Street, and takes place on the last Saturday of the month throughout the summer. Hannah has already asked me to help man the booth since James has to work on Saturdays. It's a week and a half away, but she's concerned already. So, I rush to her aid all week, without hesitation.

On the Saturday evening before the week of the farmers' market, my gut begins speaking again, especially while I paint my toenails a subtle pink so I can wear some new sandals I bought to go with a sundress my mother conjured from the sewing machine. Sunday at church, the congregation fumbles their way through robotic songs with powerful lyrics as our old and oblivious piano player stumbles through the musty hymnal. Then the reverend gives a message on the importance of obedience.

After the final hymn, life restarts. The plan, as usual, is to have a big family dinner at lunchtime, but Mom forgot to plan dessert, which is a necessity for after dinner chit chat, and we are all the way at home when she realizes it. No one volunteers to go get dessert, but only because they know I will go without being asked, like always.

"Popsicles sound okay?" I head to the hand-me-down hatchback.

A few of them agree fervently, the mercury topping ninety today. Then I set off toward the gas station, hoping I can find enough popsicles there. Sadly, there are only picked-through individuals, and there are far too many overheating sweet-tooths back home. So, I head into town, hoping they don't start the meal without me. Well, town is the plan. But all the "reliable" little hatchback does is gurgle and sputter, no matter what I do in the oppressive dry heat of the gas station parking lot.

Frustrated with James's promise that everything is alright, I get out and pop the hood. I know how to check about three things in my engine. When the oil is fine and the transmission fluid is red, I'm at a loss and feeling like a stranded fool. Noah, who owns a towing company, is on the other end of my phone within minutes. Well, his voicemail at least.

I lean against the side of the car, earning a modest tan line for a half hour while I call various family members. Most of my ginger siblings would earn a hefty sunburn in the same amount of time. Therefore, even stranded, I am thankful. I'm in a below-knee-length sundress with cute sandals and subtle pink toenails, and I'm broken down on the side of the road. No one will answer their phones. And all I can do is laugh. Just once. Because I'm worried that all my father's protective rules and honorable statutes have failed me today. I should have made Hakim come with me.

I'm startled by a honking horn. Oh great, a catcaller too, despite modesty. But I glance up, though taught to ignore such nonsense, and see that the horn belongs to a sight more soothing than a popsicle. It is, of course, a maroon pickup truck.

Lord, please don't let this guy be a stalker or a serial killer, I pray.

"Listen," I hear, or feel, throughout my being, which is impossible. I don't detect it with ears, so I know the command must not be for my ears. It's all insane, but the call is clear. I'm to listen with all that I am.

Before I can ponder further, that truck parks three spaces over, headlights facing the road, just like mine. Bennett leans out the window waving, and Elijah makes his way over.

There is a painting in *Los Arboles,* the restaurant where I work, that portrays a classic western scene. It's a perfectly formed cowboy, leaned up against a fence. He fittingly adorns a cowboy hat, boots, and jeans, with not a care in the world but the horse tied up next to him. I love that painting. There's an ease about it—a snail's pace of life that helps me combat lunch or dinner rush at work. It's like all the universe across time has it wrong, except for that cool, confident cowboy with the crooked smile on his face, his eyes on something in the distance that the painter didn't capture.

So, when Elijah walks—make that "moseys"—over and I feel the peace and pace of that painting, cowboy hat and all, mixed with something terrifying...something new. I know exactly what God, if that's Who called me to listen, wants me to hear.

"Howdy, Miz Jubilee." Three deliberately silly words, and my ears hear them one way, but the rest of me awakens, experiencing them another.

Something happens. It's as if my panic over this situation never existed—or couldn't exist. Like even though I'm stranded and overheated, this moment fits me like my weathered boots. I'm with a cowboy's crooked smile and perfect physique that surpasses that of any beloved painting. Every fully grown, confident step he takes drives the comfort deeper into my soul in a way Peter Samson didn't accomplish with thousands of steps and conversations. The eerie calm is almost unpleasantly pleasant, like the earthy essence of rain when you know a devastating thunderstorm is coming. It's certainly a sin, at the very least. I clear my throat, already confessing and repenting and looking away as I answer.

"Hello, Mr. Bering." My peace wavers when I realize I'm nothing more than a helpless teenager to him.

"No thank you, ma'am. Let's stick with 'Elijah.' You in trouble?" He asks as he stops six feet in front of me.

"Uh..." A predator. That's all he is. Yeah, that theory will help when I look at him next.

"You just gassed up on Wednesday." He moves to the still-popped hood after the wink.

"Darn you, Elijah. You too, sinful flesh. What is happening to me?" I think. But what I actually say is: "Well, I'm not out of gas. But my mileage has been pretty bad, so I took it to my brother-in-law, the mechanic, last week, and he said nothing was wrong. But it just died. So weird. It was fine when I left my house." I hip my hands, frustrated. But I'm more frustrated with the pleasant prickly feeling in my lungs than the plight of my car. "I've been trying to get a hold of my family. One of my brothers owns a towing company, so if they'd answer, they could help."

"I see. So...what were you looking for under here?" Elijah smirks like Hakim does just before he sets Lightning to a gallop or cracks a joke. Is he teasing me? It's hard to tell, since he is checking this and that under the hood, not looking at me. He appears to be far more adept at mechanics than I am.

I go with a self-deprecating joke. "Well...the engine is still there, so I thought that was a good sign."

He laughs in a way that makes me feel uncomfortable and safe all at once.

"Where you headed? Let me give you a ride," he says at the conclusion of the laughter.

"No, I can't let you do that."

I know better. A man and woman should never ride in a vehicle together alone unless they are married to each other. It doesn't do well for appearances and invites undue temptation…or something. Which is silly in this case. It's an emergency, and he's a first-name-basis acquaintance, not a stranger. My dad couldn't get mad about that, right?

He gives me some sort of scolding look he probably gives his son often. There is practice and decisiveness behind it that makes my gut do a full somersault.

He repeats the offer with warmth and gentleness. "Where are you headed, Miz Jubilee? I would like to help you get there."

"My family is having this big dinner, and I was headed into town for popsicles. But I think just getting home would be sufficient at this point, since they won't answer their phones. I bet they are worried." I clear my throat. "But you have to promise you're not a serial killer. My dad is a well-respected judge with lots of connections, so it wouldn't work out well for you." Which was mostly unintentional, and completely satirical.

"Not that I recall. I keep people *alive* for a living." He laughs, his voice softening even further, especially after the dry-heat cough that had accompanied the laughter. "But you can't go to a family dinner without popsicles on a day like this. Let's get you into town and then to that dinner. Keep trying to reach your family on the way."

"Miss Jubilee!" I barely hear Bennett over the roar of the traffic. That's right. I'm not alone with this man. Does an eight-year-old count?

"This is embarrassing as it is. Home is a lot closer than the store. You could just—" I smooth back slightly sweaty stray hairs as I smile at Bennett.

"God wants you to get popsicles or He wouldn't have sent me." Elijah smiles and walks backward to where his truck is. "Hop in, Miz Jubilee. Truck is nice and cool. Don't keep your family waiting."

There's the rules—the things I've been taught. They protect me from what I know to be dangerous, according to my father. And then there's this call that seems to overrule everything. It's enough so I climb up into the truck and see Bennett is bouncing with excitement in the back seat. I have more confidence in the choice than even the dire relief of air conditioning could explain.

"The supermarket is closest to this edge of town. We'll head there," Elijah says, pulling into a break in the traffic.

I have a sickening realization or two. "Elijah, I am probably ruining your Sunday. Does your wife know where you are? You should call home."

Elijah chuckles. "It's just me and Bennett, Miz Jubilee. No wife to worry. We were headed home from church for a lazy afternoon, but who doesn't need a popsicle adventure every now and then?"

Which would explain why the woman would never, ever go fishing with them on Wednesdays. I always just thought it was a father–son thing. I suppose it is, but only because it has to be. So many questions emerge. So much pity and fear too. Bennett breaks though the frantic thoughts.

"My mom is dead," Bennett says, rubbing awkwardly at his thigh and yawning.

I gasp, feeling more awful still. "I am so sorry. This is not my day. I didn't mean to stir up anything."

Elijah smiles. "No harm, no foul. He never knew her."

"Dad," Bennett whines. "My legs are sore. Can I take them off?"

"No! They'll stink." Elijah protests as a friend might. "Not polite in front of a lady."

"Take his shoes off? I don't mind. I sometimes drive without shoes on," I allow, looking back at Bennett.

"No, my legs," Bennett corrects.

Elijah laughs at the obvious confusion that probably cascades across my face. "He usually doesn't travel with his, um…prosthetics on. That's why I make him stay in the back seat at the gas station when I go in. I had him put them on when we stopped a minute ago in case he needed to get out."

"Oh…" I feel silly, like I missed when I was told that Bennett is missing body parts. Or worse, that I was supposed to notice on my own. I think about the gas station, trying to remember if there was some awkward way in how Bennett would hang out the window, holding onto the door frame like he does. But I cannot find such an anomaly in my memory. The awkward is all happening now. I don't even know how to react. This is the strangest day of my life.

"I was born with no legs, Miss Jubilee. And seven toes in all. But I don't have those anymore," Bennett shares.

That is both nauseating and intriguing to imagine, though it isn't something that changes my fast fondness for this little boy.

Elijah winces, embarrassed, and begins the mumbled explanation. "It's uh…a birth defect. Lower limb reduction. But that's enough, Bennett. What did I tell you about other people and your legs?" Elijah glances in the rear-view mirror a few times as he speaks.

"Sometimes other people can get freaked out so I shouldn't tell them everything." Bennett sighs, rolling his eyes at what he likely is called to recite every day.

"But...?" Elijah uses a tone that my mother may have used during school lessons.

"I am fearfully and wonderfully made," Bennett mumbles.

"And?" Elijah's tone softens with gentle passion.

" 'The Spirit Himself bears witness with our spirit that we are children of God, and if children, then heirs—heirs of God and joint heirs with Christ, if indeed we suffer with Him, that we may also be glorified together. For I consider that the sufferings of this present time are not worthy to be compared with the glory which shall be revealed in us.' Romans eight, sixteen through eighteen." Bennett recites, mumbling begrudgingly at first, then by the end, he is speaking enthusiastically and clearly. Then he sighs. "I still don't understand that, Daddy."

"You will, son, someday when you need to," Elijah promises.

Suddenly, in a truck with near strangers, everything I ever believed about single parents and disabled children is transformed. I dare not even mention aloud what I believed before. This young boy has no legs. He was born that way, which would mean that it could be considered a curse from God for his father's sins, according to what my father has said. But Elijah does not seem to have ever sinned enough to deserve a disabled child. And even so, Bennett would be a weak punishment for *any* sin. He seems to be a delightful blessing of a child, and I know many children. To what extent he is damaged, I am not privy, nor does it matter. Elijah seems to be aware that others look down on the two of them, and makes his son aware too. But he also tells him that others are irrelevant, because Bennett is a child of God.

How can a father be as wise as mine but so vastly different?

I sit in silent awe a moment, then smile and look back at Bennett. "You can take off your legs if you want, Bennett. I have five stinky brothers. I can handle seven stinky toes you don't have anymore."

Bennett happily removes metal rods attached to shoes and some plastic assembly, and the pants now hang freely against the seat from bumps of legs under them that stop about mid-thigh. I smile at his smile as he places the legs next to him and the truck pulls into the supermarket.

"I'll be right back." I grab my purse, practically run inside, and buy five massive boxes of popsicles and a bag of ice to keep them under on the way back to my house—if Elijah decides not to abandon or kill me instead. Just after I check out, Noah returns his ten missed calls.

"Jubilee, you okay? The signal was all weird. None of our phones rang and then suddenly we all had missed calls from you." Which is odd, since we have a cell phone tower on our property. But from the concern in his voice, I believe him.

"It's alright. No, I uh…the car is stuck at the gas station. It died on me. I'm in town. I got a ride to get the popsicles, but I still need my car fixed. Can you tow it?" I ask as I reach Elijah's truck with my treasures.

"I'll tow it tomorrow. But we'll have someone…Hakim probably, meet you at your car in a half hour. We started dinner without you, sorry. The kids were starving," Noah admits. "Saved you plenty, though."

That's when I see Elijah has a cooler at the tailgate of his truck.

"Oh good, you bought ice," Elijah says, then winces when he sees I am on the phone. He silently loads the popsicles into his cooler, and I pull one out of a box just before he finishes. He covers the cooler with a tarp, then straps it down to secure it all. The process of juggling cold items in the heat, a cooler with a phone, heightened situational awareness, and two conversations should be awkward and frustrating. But we somehow manage it smoothly.

"Alright. I'm just fifteen minutes from the gas station, so I'll wait at my car," I tell Noah during the process.

"I can take you home. No problem for me," Elijah says quietly, opening his passenger door for me to enter.

"Oh…nevermind. I have a ride home. I'll see you soon with the popsicles." I am disappointed that they didn't wait for me but understand the needs of the children. Though I'm betting Hakim is livid.

"Tell me you weren't dumb enough to take a ride from a stranger?" Noah scolds gently on the phone.

"After you tell me you trust me." I sigh. Noah sighs. "See you soon." And then I hang up as Elijah rejoins us in the cab. "I am so grateful for your kindness, Elijah. Can he?" I am handing Bennett the popsicle I saved for him. Elijah nods and Bennett happily opens the wrapper and starts licking away at the treat. "I got an extra box for you to take home with you, too. As a thank you. I'd have given you one, but driving with a popsicle doesn't always turn out well."

"Thank *you*, Jubilee. Most people don't give my boy the time of day without his legs on," Elijah says quietly. Then he starts up the truck again and fills what would otherwise be silence. "So…five brothers?"

"Yes. Five brothers, two sisters. I'm number seven of eight." Just small talk, I assume.

"Jubilee." He laughs once. "The fiftieth year was the year of Jubilee for the Israelites after seven weeks of years. And you're the seventh kid. Your parents name you that on purpose? That's pretty clever."

"They did! Very few people catch that." I'm astonished that he did. "And Dad turned fifty the year they brought me home. His year of Jubilee."

"That's great. I did the same kinda thing with Ben. His middle name is Mephibosheth. People look at me all crazy when I have to tell them, and spelling it is a nightmare."

Suddenly, sung from the back seat amid slurps of a popsicle, in a tune that I think is a hymn, we hear, "M-E-P-H-I-B-O-S-H-E-T-H, I know!"

"That is adorable! Mephibosheth was Jonathan's lame son that King David allowed to sit at his table, right?"

"Exactly!" Elijah is delighted that I knew. "It was unheard of then to have a disabled man at the king's table. But David was never all that orthodox."

"Well, I think he just had different priorities than being culturally correct," I surmise.

"He was a man after God's own heart. Tends to run deeper than culture, I've found. Deeper than ritual or man-made rules or anything," Elijah agrees.

My heart pounds as I connect with an acquaintance over the thing I know and love best.

"Yeah, David tended to do things differently. Eating the show bread, not wearing Saul's armor, using a sling not a sword…"

"The, uh, dancing thing," he adds with a chuckle.

"Exactly. And caring for Mephibosheth. That's a good name."

"Thank you. It's nice to hear it appreciated." He clears his throat. "So, all these brothers and sisters are at this family dinner you're late for?"

"Most of them. Priscilla lives three hours way, so she only comes sometimes. And Aaron is in Seattle, so it's just Christmas for him. But the ones who live here bring spouses and kids and Isaac has a dog, but it terrorizes my horses, so he leaves it home now." I wince at the over-share.

"Horses, huh? You ride?" Elijah relishes the extra information.

"Yes, with one of my brothers. No one else was interested when my father was given the horses."

"The one on the phone?"

"No, that was Noah who owns the towing company. I ride horses with Hakim."

"Hakim. *That's* an interesting name. I mean, next to Priscilla and Aaron and Noah and Isaac, was it? It seems more, um. . .what language is that?"

"Amharic. Hakim was adopted from East Africa. Our parents were going to call him Samuel, but he was old enough that he didn't want to change his name. He's stubborn like that. So Samuel is his *middle* name."

"I see. Are all eight of you adopted from all over the world like that?"

"Nope. Just me and Hakim. Everyone else has freckles and bright red hair."

"So you both have an *Irish* last name, I assume?"

"Monroe, yes. It isn't spelled the Irish way, but Dad says it's Irish." I smile at his interest, reluctant to use that information to get us back to business. "We live five or ten minutes past the gas station and Monroe Road is our driveway."

"Oh! I know Monroe. I pass it twice a day. Always thought it was a road, not a driveway."

"Well, it's both. The county made my father name the road since it crosses the frontage road and it's an easement. It was either County Road 223 or our last name."

"Monroe is a much better name." He nods. "We live in the little subdivision off Blanca on the other side of the highway. Just about a mile further out of town than y'all."

My parents feared that subdivision would be a trailer park when the county zoned it about seven years ago and a developer advertised "luxury modular homes" out in the middle of nowhere. I didn't understand why a trailer park would be a problem, but I digress. We have a few friends from church who live out there in that subdivision of about seventy-five homes, and most people can't even tell the homes are "modular." They just look like regular one-story homes with detached garages, and even have porches. It is also a covenant community, so all the houses are attractive and well maintained, each on a quarter-acre lot. It turned out to be quite an addition to the outskirts of town.

"Oh yeah, I know the one," I tell him.

"First house me and Bennett ever owned. Maybe the last." Elijah winks back at Bennett, who smiles. "He likes that there's no stairs."

"My dad thinks you're pretty, Miss Jubilee," Bennett blurts.

I don't let on to the sudden thunderclap of fear, except with the silence. Elijah doesn't know what to do except laugh nervously. Bennett fixes the situation.

"I asked him when you were in the store. I said, 'Do you think she's pretty?' He said, 'I suppose.' 'I suppose' means yes. And 'we'll see' means no. Dad talks in code like a spy." Bennett's speech is animated and confident, like he's much older than just eight. And since children are the easiest thing to fall in love with, I am already smitten with this one.

They are almost strangers; good Samaritans that use the same gas station that everyone does on this side of town. That's it. So, I can't explain why the clear and living call I felt has suddenly morphed into only peace. It's like riding in this truck, staring out the window as home nears is natural, like I'm out riding Thunder. I shrug off the feeling. Nothing can feel this way, it just…it doesn't work that way. Then again, I'm riding in a truck with a black cowboy and his legless son. The world is new.

The truck crackles up my driveway to the familiar clinking of rocks in the undercarriage on the dirt road. Halfway there, Elijah instructs Bennett to put his legs back on, which he does. We arrive and the children are playing in the front yard, and Hannah is on the porch with Dad. Hakim and James walk over, looking confused as Elijah exits and heads to the back of the truck to release the cooler.

"Jubilee?" Hakim reprimands in a whisper, likely fearing more for my fate than discouraging my behavior. "Explain."

"James," I tease our brother-in-law. "Didn't catch whatever it is that means the car is stuck at the gas station. I told Noah. He's towing it tomorrow. But Elijah and Bennett here gave me a ride. I got the popsicles, don't worry."

"You broke down?" James asks, concerned now about the car.

"Nevermind that. You accepted a ride from a stranger? A *male* stranger…I mean…I totally trust your judgment, but *they*…" Hakim nods in warning for the approaching Noah, Judah, and Isaac.

"Well, he's not exactly a stranger. I've spoken with him a few times. Remember? The gas station guy and his kid. I mentioned them." By now, my other brothers have arrived, and Elijah is carrying the cooler over and setting it on the ground at my feet, looking at the scowling company.

"Miss Jubilee said one of y'all could tow the car? I'm Elijah. Bennett and I were just driving past when we saw Jubilee checking to see if her engine was still there."

Hakim's mouth curls into a smirk and he shakes Elijah's hand. "Nice to meet you, Elijah. I'm Hakim. Noah here is the tow guy."

Noah steps forth and shakes Elijah's hand next. "I'll get it first thing tomorrow."

"I'm James. I must have missed something in my diag, so just tow it to me, Noah," James says, then shakes Elijah's hand.

"Why would a man be so eager to help a young woman?" Isaac asks, not shaking Elijah's hand when he offers it.

Elijah narrows his eyes. "What does it say about the body of Christ when a man *isn't* eager to help a young woman?"

Which silences everyone. Because Elijah isn't aware that no one crosses Isaac so directly. Ever.

"I was wondering how you convinced her. Jubilee, just because a man says he is a Christian, that doesn't mean his intentions are pure," Isaac teaches.

"Isaac…" I say to the ground, not willing to cross him either.

"No, he's right. Don't take my word for it. Christ is in the fruit, not the words. You can go ahead and hold onto the cooler and I'll get it back from you the next time we cross paths." Elijah nods, backing up to his truck, tipping his hat. "Nice meeting y'all. You take care, Miz Jubilee. Have a blessed day."

"Wait!" I quickly pull an unopened box of popsicles out of the cooler and hand it to Elijah. "Thank you so much. I'd still be baking in the sun if you hadn't come by."

"Not a problem at all, Miz Jubilee. Until next time."

I wave to Bennett in the back seat as Elijah drives off, leaving me with that nagging call again. The peace leaves with them.

Hakim nudges me a little, speaking into my ear and out of the perception of our other brothers. A common practice between us. "You didn't mention…"

"Didn't mention what?" I shoot Hakim a look.

"Um, tall, dark, and handsome? You didn't actually mention *any* of that."

"So?" I whisper.

"He married?"

"No. But why would you—"

"So you really don't know why you can't get him out of your head?"

"What is that supposed to mean? It's the same with his son."

"Well, it seems to be a package deal. I wouldn't mind a brother-in-law and nephew all at once."

"Hakim!" I'm blushing at his gall, pushing him back as he laughs and the brothers scowl.

"Jubilee, a word," Dad calls from the porch.

"Yes, sir." I walk with my head down, passing an especially bratty Judah as I go to receive the reprimand.

"Not a wise move, Jubilee."

Seven

Elijah

"God, why do You keep doing this to me? Just let me live my life in obedience. Why must I fight so hard not to sin? When will You deliver me?"

Bennett is in bed. Another Sunday is over, and I'm in the living room, sipping at my nightly two fingers of whiskey. I am out a hundred-dollar cooler. But God has an odd response to my pleading.

"Trust Me."

"You're funny," I say aloud, then allow my mind to wander back to the reason for the prayer.

She's not just pretty. Bennett thought he'd caught me in a tight spot there. But I know he has no idea. Jubilee, the young woman I've met just a few times, and usually just for a few minutes, is one of the few mysteries in this life I feel obsessively compelled to solve. She's not "pretty." That word up against that woman is a few dictionaries short of truth.

Well, maybe with one glance she's just "pretty." But we all know I've done more than glance just once. I'm convinced that Jubilee Monroe is doing her level best to conceal beauty in a capacity I've never encountered. Like she's hiding some deep ancient magic in those enormous eyes. Something wild and free and sexy, even. And she's covering it up with skirts below her knee and shirts at her collarbone. She's mysterious enough for me to lose myself in, but respectable enough for me to know I shouldn't do anything of the sort—especially since she's barely nineteen and I'm pushing thirty.

Still, I imagine Jubilee's hair would reach her backside if she let it out. It makes no sense that a woman would grow her hair so long and silky and then tie it up like no one should see it. That's how I know that deep down she's crying out for something she doesn't even know she's missing.

I lusted that first chance meeting, and foolishly. I sinned, considering and reconsidering every God-crafted curve, soft feature, and sparkle in her eye. She was a treat for the eyes that took me, a God-fearing man, a full week to get out of my head. God told me to look, so I looked. But I don't think I saw what God intended.

To my dismay, God gave me a second chance to look the moment I'd been free of her unwitting enchantments. Since then, I have kept my heart from lust, but now I'm now imprisoned by the enticing mystery of Jubilee Monroe. And since her brothers counted me a threat to all that purity on her surface, I'm likely out a cooler now. But at the time, all I wanted to do was make sure she had what she needed when and how she needed it. Obsessively. And I'd been happy to tell her that I'm not married.

"Lord, please cure me of this woman."

"Dad?" Bennett comes scooting out on his bottom, disrupting my mumbled-aloud thoughts. I imagine that as Bennett grows, his arms will be twice the muscle mass of his peers'. But for now, he's just a little boy.

"Yes, son?"

"My legs hurt. Will you rub that stuff on 'em?" He scoots over and climbs up onto the couch beside me. I abandon my mostly empty glass and retrieve a balm one of his doctors recommended from a drawer in the coffee table.

God made him a different version of perfect. But the world wasn't made for him. He has to wear man-made legs because of what the world requires of him. They chafe and rub and bruise Bennett's version of perfect so that he can fit into theirs. So I rub the legs that seem to have started to grow in the womb and then just stopped long before they should have. He has thighs that are half the length they "should" be. He was born with ankles with boney little globs of flesh to which toes seemed randomly attached, but the doctors recommended we amputate them to better accommodate his prosthetics.

I have seen nurses and therapists hide disgust behind their smiles. I'm glad Bennett only sees with his eyes for now—the same way I first saw Jubilee. Jubilee had barely flinched at learning of his legs, and only in confusion. After the shock, Jubilee had treated him just like she might any other child. Jubilee adores Bennett. She'd make a fine mother. I snap my mind back from straying once again.

Instead, I'm watching the perfect little boy fall asleep on the couch as I rub the sores and callouses on his legs. I'm remembering the nurse at the

Neonatal Intensive Care Unit who told me that Bennett probably wouldn't make it.

"But they said his vitals are fine," I argued.

"They are. Especially for a baby born at twenty-seven weeks. But he's deformed. Mom didn't make it, and Dad…All I'm saying is that someone like him as an orphan in this world doesn't have much of a chance. That's *if* he makes it out of the woods." She tried to be compassionate. But I had been visiting the tiny baby daily for three weeks solid. I was already smitten.

"He's an orphan, but he's not alone. He has me." I was just twenty-one then, and fresh out of nursing school.

The NICU nurse laughed. "Son, this baby, if he survives to be released from the hospital, will require a lifetime of dedicated care and support. We don't know yet if the swelling on his brain after the crash caused permanent damage. He could have cognitive difficulties, as well as obviously never being able to walk on his own. You're a kid. No one would blame you if you couldn't handle the burden."

"I'm aware of the situation." I don't appreciate being talked down to. "But I guess I'm the only person alive doesn't think he's a burden. *When* he is released, he's coming home with me."

With help from some social workers, I'd been able to arrange everything before Bennett was released. My little two-bedroom apartment that I shared with a roommate had been inspected for a home study. I'd taken required foster parent classes during weekends and an overnight shift in the pediatric psych ward of the hospital that no one else wanted. It was a stretch and a reach, but that judge saw something in me, and granted me emergency custody of the infant Bennett.

I took him home after doing research and buying whatever I could for him whenever I could. The other nurses in the psych ward threw a baby shower, where I learned a lot about parenting. I paid my barely-scraped-past-the-home-study roommate to listen for Bennett, then covered that baby in prayer and went to work all night while he slept, save the half-hour lunch when I sped home to check on Bennett and gave him a bottle so that I didn't have to entrust the task to my roommate.

One morning while arriving home exhausted to my roommate and a scantily clad woman on the couch, both high, Bennett was screaming. I rushed to get him and made him a bottle while my roommate stared at the wall. That roommate startled me by managing to form words.

"Elijah, what kind of an idiot twenty-one-year-old decides it is a good idea to take in a deformed baby that ain't his?"

I didn't think he actually required an answer, so I didn't give him one. I simply moved out of the apartment the following week and hired a professional nanny to spend the night at the new one-bedroom apartment while I worked. It cost me more than I could afford. I knew the whole thing was insane. Really anything is if you don't know the circumstances.

But I belonged to Bennett before Bennett ever belonged to me. All I did was obey the call. I watched him learn to crawl in that apartment after I quit the night shift for him. I watched him try to stand, which broke my heart and one of Bennett's "ankles." It was not a choice whether I'd have the amputation done and then pay the thousands of dollars for the first set of prosthetics, and every set after. It was not a question whether I'd legally adopt Bennett when he turned two.

Few are privy to Bennett's special circumstances; both his missing legs and the adoption. But under pants and his big wide spirit, most of Bennett's classmates don't even know just how he walks into school. And unless he tells them, they are not aware of how he was born, or exactly the circumstances that led to me calling him my son. He is not a burden. Not a mistake. And no choice of mine would have led us elsewhere. I imagine that if Bennett were acquired the conventional way, it wouldn't make him any more meant to be my son.

We all have a similar story. We all veil our miracles with the mundane. We all pretend as we go out into the world of strangers that it is all just ordinary. We pretend that grief is something to be coped with. Joy is to be stifled and stored in a neat little box for births and weddings and Christmas Day.

I know better. As I carry my son, who isn't really my son, back to his bed, I know that there is far more depth to each of us than we are acceptably allowed to convey as we live our lives. We are all imprisoned by what is acceptable. We're all hiding not just something, but quite nearly everything. We all fool the world with prosthetics.

Therefore, after a few slip-ups of pure sass when I watched Jubilee Monroe stare out my passenger window today and play with that long braid she pairs with modest clothing and cautious steps and words, that's when I knew that wanting to help her break free and stop hiding has nothing to do with lust and everything to do with obedience.

I just wonder if someone like her learning to ride bareback in the wind could release some sense of freedom into the rest of the world.

Eight

Elijah

"Up!" I pull the covers off Bennett and he groans, drawing what limbs he has into a fetal position.

"Do I really have to go back to that place?" He mumbles into his pillow.

"Mrs. Parker is all I could afford to take you twelve hours a day, four days a week, all summer. You know that. Get up. Don't make me late for work." I coax my son out of bed.

"Just lemme stay home. Staying home is free."

"Eleven. That's the age for being home alone, and certainly not for twelve hours. You're barely eight. They'd take me to jail." I go back to the kitchen and set up Bennett's nutrition bar and milk breakfast as he gets dressed.

I drink coffee and Bennett sips milk. Then randomly, he asks, "Are you gonna marry Miss Jubilee?"

"Marriage requires a little more than giving someone a ride home, son. I found out the woman's last name *yesterday*." I laugh, a little irritated that Bennett provoked those thoughts so early in the day. More irritated that I didn't just pass Jubilee yesterday. Why am I always the sucker who stops?

"But ladies change their last name when they get married! So, it don't matter what it is *now*," Bennett reasons.

"Get your legs on, Ben." I finish my breakfast, hoping the caffeine kicks in soon, and we carry on with the day.

Driving along and trying not to think about big brown eyes, I startle at Bennett's voice.

"Look, Daddy! A tow truck is taking Miss Jubilee's car. And there she is with that man. Was he a man from yesterday? One of her brothers?"

"Stop, Elijah."

I suppose *that* is why I'm always the sucker who stops. I sigh and pull into the gas station.

"Be right back, son." I walk across the parking lot half expecting the man I recognize as Noah, Jubilee's brother, to take out a pistol and shoot me. But all negative thoughts dissipate when Jubilee smiles and walks to meet me. She's wearing a denim skirt and a cotton top that cinches in at the hip and has a drawstring on the top. I saw her horses and she mentioned riding them, so I know the brown, worn-in cowboy boots aren't just for show. She's about five foot five and heart-poundingly beautiful. Like the Indian cowgirl version of heaven, if you ask me.

"Morning, Elijah. I wish I'd brought your cooler." She is not alarmed at all by my presence.

"It's alright. You need a ride somewhere? I'm headed into work."

She looks me over uncomfortably and responds to the question with another.

"Who works in jeans, a scrub top, and cowboy boots?"

"An RN in clear violation of the dress code," I admit too quickly, wincing. I forget every time before I say it that the image of my job includes a funny hat and a skirt for most people.

A male nurse. I wanted to serve sick people and do it with skill. I love a hard day's work as much as the next guy, and some days I'd much rather turn wrenches than change bed pans and be on my feet listening to whining and watching people die. I've done my time in hard labor. Held a job, usually a tough, dirty one since I was fourteen. These days I prefer to do time in everything from operating rooms and emergency rooms, psych wards and clinics and morgues. I have finally found my peace at a nursing home here in Colorado. There is simply nothing like the flirtatious cheek pinch of somebody's great-grandmother after she gives you the best advice you'll hear in ten years—every single day you introduce yourself to her like new.

"Of course! You did mention keeping people alive for a living. I should have inferred." Jubilee's voice cuts through my conflicting career satisfaction and cultural unease.

"Most people would infer 'doctor' for a man."

"A doctor would have *said* he's a doctor. You said you keep people alive." Jubilee smirks. "And you always stop to help, regardless of my obvious lack of medical need. That's service, not pride. Nurse. A good one, if they allow you to break the dress code." She is unfazed. Impressed, even.

"I enjoy my work."

"It shows. Anyway, um, Noah's giving me a ride. I really shouldn't have accepted the ride from you yesterday. It was very kind of you, but I should have found another way and I apologize if I acted inappropriately. I didn't see that clearly yesterday. I do now. But thank you for your generous offer." She suddenly takes to programmed, robotic speech like she's a different person entirely, without the caliber of mind that could "infer" what someone does for a living.

Brainwashed. I should have known from the excessive modesty heaped on such a lovely figure, and the overprotectiveness of her brothers. Ultra-conservative, fire and brimstones, honor unto death kind of family, I'm betting. With an overbearing father to oversee it all. I'm stuck for a fraction of a thought between allowing the prison she likely doesn't see and proposing to her and breaking her free right now. I want her free to take rides in my truck and infer as she pleases. But before I allow all that, I decide there must be a middle ground and take a stab.

"So…what channels does a guy have to go through to be kind to you, Jubilee?" I check my phone, realizing I'll be late for both work and day care if I don't leave soon.

The question takes Jubilee off guard and she isn't sure how to answer. I try again when I see I just offended everything she stands for.

"That probably sounded rude. Let's try…when can I come get my cooler?" Which sounded coarse again, when I meant for it to sound charming. Maybe I should have asked Jessie or Lucinda to help me form these words before delivering them.

"I'll clean it out when I get home from work tonight. There was a popsicle incident with one of my nephews…Anyway, I work until eight, which is okay since I won't have a ride home until about then anyway." She's all business as the cars whoosh by on the highway.

"I get off at eight too. Where do you work? I can take you…wait…no rides from strange male nurses. Just keep the cooler." I wince at the awkward. Then she smirks. Not at the awkward, but like she thinks I'm funny…or adorable. I can't seem to stop failing at this.

"God…help."

Help comes in the form of Bennett calling to me. Noah calls to his sister. Jubilee offers the parting words.

"If we run into each other again, let's talk about the cooler. If not, I'll keep it," she suggests with a shrug. I nod before I turn and use every ounce of energy to not turn back and watch her walk away. I succeed this time. No more extra glances for me.

"Dad, can I have a brother?" Is the first thing I hear when I reenter the truck.

"What?"

"Don't babies come after marriage? I want a brother. Not a sister. Girls are annoying." I'm not sure whether Bennett is way ahead of me or just reading my deep soul aloud.

"Jubilee is a girl. Is she annoying?" I challenge as I pull onto the highway.

"Jubilee is a lady. Girls are okay once they grow up. But not when they are little. Becky at Mrs. Parker's doesn't do anything but color rainbows and unicorns all day. That's stupid, Dad," Bennett complains. I just shake my head in laughter, adoring my little boy.

When I pick him up from his daycare after a twelve-hour shift, Bennett is the last one to leave, like always.

"Dad, Mrs. Parker made nasty pea soup for dinner, and I was polite and didn't tell her it was nasty, but I'm starving," he says the second we hit the truck.

"Alright, let's grab some food. What do you want?" I am famished myself after spending my lunch hour watching generations of a family say goodbye to their matriarch.

"Tacos." But all the cheering up I need is in this boy's smile.

We enter *Los Arboles* at 8:10 p.m., and I'm far too exhausted and not prayed-up enough when I hear the hostess's laughter of disbelief before I even see her face. Laughter is new with how in control she is, and equally as exhilarating for me.

"Miss Jubilee!" Bennett exclaims. And never having been shy, he runs and throws his arms around her hips. She hugs him right back. I don't suppose she's seen him standing before.

"Table for two, guys?" she asks.

"I thought you got off at eight. We could make it three," I suggest. Not realizing at all what I just said until she looks down and moves her braid aside.

"I actually get off at ten now. My relief called in sick." She smiles, hiding frustration somewhere under that cross around her neck, grabbing menus and leading us Bering boys to a table.

"We saw you just before eight this morning. Is this place a sweat shop?"

"Noah took me to our sister's house this morning, not right to work. I walked over here at two. I'm part time."

"Well, who is taking you home?" I don't understand why I'm so relentless or how she's possibly so beautiful.

"My brother Hakim is coming to get me." She nods, glancing back to make sure no one else needs to be seated.

Hakim was the one I liked, I remember. He seemed like a normal human among brainwashed robots.

I persist. "He have a job in the morning? Ten is late."

"He does, but my car won't be ready until Wednesday. It was a fuel pump, by the way. But um, Hakim will come get me."

"It's on my way, Jubilee. I'll take you," I plead. "Don't make your brother drive all the way into town at that hour. That's ridiculous."

"Minor inconvenience, I admit. But ten is late for this little guy too," she reasons, gesturing to Bennett.

"I'll stay up!" Bennett offers, of course.

"I agree. It's late. But someone in our corporate office who doesn't have kids decided to try a later shift time." I shrug. "It's alright. We adapted, and Bennett has gotten used to late suppers and later bedtimes. It won't even be a *minor* inconvenience if you need us to wait for you."

"I'll think about it. You two enjoy your meal." Then she walks away, unable to quench with that same modest skirt from this morning my enjoyment at watching.

"Dad...Dad?...Dad!" I *hope* Bennett only yelled for me three times.

"Sorry, Bennett. What do you need?" I blink my eyes and catch my breath.

"How do you say 'taco' in Mexican words?" He asks, bringing my impure thoughts around with doting laughter.

We eat crunchy tacos and about thirty baskets of over-salted chips dipped in under-spiced salsa. Time even allows for the sticky, sugary mess of sopapillas, and I tell Bennett to do it all as slowly as possible, which he understands completely. We smile at Jubilee every time those boots walk past to seat another late diner.

At 9:20 p.m., twenty minutes after paying the check, we finally decide we've overstayed our welcome and stand to tell Jubilee we'll wait in the truck if she needs us. But Jubilee meets us at the hostess station with her purse on her shoulder and a smile on her face.

"So…I'm getting out a little early. My dad was about to go wake up my brother to get me, but I told him I have a ride. Would you still be willing…?" She asks politely.

"Yes!" Bennett of few verbal filters is the first to run out the door and jump into the truck. Jubilee watches him in confused admiration.

"Can't even tell, can you?" I ask as Jubilee walks through the restaurant door I open. Bennett is already closing the truck door behind him. "He's always walked with prosthetics. Not even his class at school knows he don't have legs."

"How did you know what I was thinking?" Jubilee asks, crossing her arms with a smile.

"I 'inferred.' " I shrug the flirtation. "It amazes me all the time. I was thinking it too. Um, will Daddy be mad that I'm taking you home?"

"Yes, but only because he hasn't met you so he doesn't know that he can trust you."

"But *you* know that you can trust me?"

"You have never led me to believe otherwise."

"And I don't plan to."

Then there is a silence. Not quite long enough to be awkward, but certainly long enough that neither of us is expecting to open the truck door just yet. There is something about the night air that begs us to stay in it just one breath longer.

"So did you know I worked here, or…?" She asks. "I know I didn't *tell* you, but it's a small town, and—"

"No!" I realize my excessive volume. "I mean, had I known, would I have brought Bennett here to see you at work? Sure. But no, I was just as surprised as you. That's twice today, and not even at the gas station this time."

"Yeah. Weird coincidence, huh?" She replies.

Another silence like the first.

"A weirder coincidence is that this is Ben's favorite place to eat, and I've never even seen you before that day at the gas station. You've worked here how long?"

"Two years or so." She shrugs.

"See? Weird, right?"

"Very. I was thinking earlier if I've seen you before, but I would have remembered you two."

"And I'd have remembered *you*." We both know what I'm saying. But we give each other the grace of not making me admit it yet.

Jubilee looks down and bites a lip. My boldness wins out.

"Honestly, I don't believe in coincidences. I believe the Lord ordains and orchestrates every second of our lives in ways that will ultimately lead to His glory."

"Me too," she says timidly with a deep sigh. Then she whispers barely loud enough that I know it's for me to hear, " 'Thou hast beset me behind and before, and laid thine hand upon me.' "

Which my heart can barely handle. I have to fight for the breath before saying, "Sounds like Psalm 139. Me and Ben memorized that one a couple years back. Is that King James?"

"Yes. What do you read?"

"*New* King James. I think it says 'hedged' instead of 'beset.' Same guy, different hat. And I was just thinking about verse sixteen, believe it or not: 'Your eyes saw my substance, being yet unformed. And in Your book they all were written, The days fashioned for me, When as yet there were none of them.' That's why I don't believe in coincidence. God already knows it like He wrote it Himself, because He did."

"Exactly. I think coincidence is a silly way to explain away God's power, which cannot be explained away. We have free will, and we can certainly choose to disobey Him. But He sees that coming too. Ultimately, He creates and orchestrates everything." She adjusts her purse on her shoulder.

I've never been so attracted to someone like I am when Jubilee talks Bible to me. So now is a good time to dive into the waters without another test.

"So why do I keep seeing you, Miz Jubilee? I'm starting to suspect that God is orchestrating." I hip my hands, then courage leaps in with the boldness. "That's a lie, actually. I started suspecting God was orchestrating the first day you talked to Bennett and God told me to pay attention."

She laughs once, not looking up at me, but looking like that beautiful, mysterious entity I'm growing fonder of every second.

"You guys made my day that first day. You were both just so friendly, and you and I didn't even speak. But it made my day."

"How good are you with blatant honesty?" Is my response.

"I suppose I prefer it in most cases." Jubilee crosses her arms, protecting herself.

"Okay, well...To be honest...You're beautiful. I couldn't stop looking at you, and I haven't stopped thinking about you since that day."

I give her space to react, and she stays her eyes on the ground. There is a beat of silence, then, "When you dropped me off yesterday and you met my brother Hakim? He already knew who you were because I've mentioned you."

"Uh oh. What did you say about me?"

"Just that I kept running into you, and I can't get you two off my mind." She looks up into my eyes for a timid glance then looks back to the ground. "I can't believe I just told you that, but I feel like...like I can. Which makes no sense. I just feel safe talking to you."

I pocket my hands with a little laugh. "Which means I'm safe to tell you my worst fear."

"Uh oh," she challenges, but she's intrigued.

"I'm scared these not-so-coincidental meetings will stop and that I'll never see you again. And that might kill me, because I have really enjoyed the little bit of time I've spent with you." She doesn't look uncomfortable, but I begin talking myself out of a pit anyway. I've never been so forward and open with a woman. "But I also gather from your age and the likely reaction of your father when you get home tonight that you're not the sort of woman I can just ask for a phone number so we can arrange a coffee date."

"Yeah, that would be wildly inappropriate." She laughs because she seems to know it's absurd. But I know she's also serious.

"I figured. But I do want you to know that I'll be asking God what His intentions are since He's got my attention. And I plan to obey whatever it is He's asking me to do," I say it all with suave I didn't have until the Spirit provided it just now, and finally those big, accidentally seductive eyes meet mine.

"He has my attention as well. This is all very strange for me, Elijah. But know that I have already been in prayer about it," Jubilee admits, searching my eyes like she might do while stargazing, seeking out Orion's belt. Smiling with satisfaction, ever so slightly, like she's found it. Then, like she's not allowed the discovery, she breaks the gaze again for the ground. "Thank you. For the ride. Again."

"Anytime, Miz Jubilee." I open the passenger door.

Bennett speaks through the dark once everyone is in the truck and the dome lights fade. "Dad, I think taco *is* a Mexican word. But it's English, too. I think it's both."

My laughter resonates inside the cab of the truck, and even Jubilee giggles a bit.

"Yeah, we use it in both languages, son."

Nine

Jubilee

"Was that the same black man from yesterday?" My father is apparently still up and sitting in the living room with his Bible open

"Yes, sir. His name is Elijah." My whole body tenses, knowing I'll need to defend myself, and maybe someone else too.

"So, you accepted yet another ride from him when I asked you not to do that very thing?" His Honor Judge Adam Monroe closes his Bible and removes his reading glasses, looking up at his defenseless daughter.

In the concealed hiccup before I speak, I pray it: *"God, I feel so trapped. Please help me do Your will and honor my father at the same time."*

"I did," I begin. "It was an odd set of circumstances and I felt it was the right thing to do. There was no need to wake up Hakim when Elijah was already there and insisting that he give me a ride. Our house is on the way to his."

"Well, of *course* he insisted." Dad sighs. "Come sit down a moment, Jubilee."

I am exhausted and long for the soft embrace of my bedding upstairs. But I obey and take a seat near my father.

"Elijah, you said?" he asks.

"Yes, sir." I nod.

"And he has a son?"

"Yes, sir." I nod again, smiling this time for remembering tacos in two languages.

"A wife?"

"No. Elijah's son told me that his mother is deceased. It's just the two of them."

"And this man is how old?"

"Late twenties. His son is eight."

"Jubilee, I need you to be honest with me. Is this man pursuing you romantically?"

The question takes me by surprise, and I don't have an immediate answer. But he only asked for honesty. "I'm not sure. He did mention that he enjoys talking with me and plans to pray about why he keeps seeing me unexpectedly."

"Alright, this is important. Has he told you anything about your physical appearance? That would be a red flag for romantic intentions."

You're beautiful. I couldn't stop looking at you, and I haven't stopped thinking about you...

It will take a lifetime for me to forget those words and the crescendo my heart took when they reached my ears like a song. But were they meant for my father to hear? It didn't feel like a red flag. It felt like a white one. Elijah was making a confession to a trusted confidant, however recent our acquaintance. Are some things between two people meant to be private? Is it a sin if I don't tell my father? I know Dad, seasoned with lawyers and witnesses, will detect the reason. Still, I know I need to evade the question with an explanation.

"Dad, Elijah is a gentleman and has never said or done anything that made me feel uncomfortable, or that I would deem inappropriate."

"Jubilee, I need you to understand something. Eve was deceived by cunning. She likely felt plenty 'comfortable.' That was the enemy's intent. He made her feel like it was appropriate. That's why it is a father's duty to oversee the way that any man makes his daughter feel. I don't know this man, and it was inappropriate for you to have such a private conversation and for you to take a ride with him. I have already lost a measure of respect for him because he has taken such liberties with you."

"Dad..." I start, offended. He puts up a hand to silence me. My eyes are burning and struggling to focus through the exhaustion. I allow the interruption.

"Men like Elijah are dangerous. If he mentioned that he is physically attracted to you, then you are being pursued physically. Period. He knows you are much younger than he is and that you are naive and easily taken advantage of. Given that he is a father, it is possible he has done this before.

It may seem innocent now, but a man like that will talk a young woman into his bed and destroy her innocence, then walk away and never speak to her again. It could happen easily, should you continue to act in violation of my wishes." He booms, likely so that anyone still awake might hear. "Already, it's clear the man is stalking you. How could you have never met him until recently, then see him so often in such a short period?"

"He didn't know where I worked until tonight. They came in for dinner—"

"Jubilee, you're being lied to. Men like him are ill-willed and dangerous. Should you run into him again, do not speak to him. And pray he does not run into *me*."

My heart wrenches for both the possibility that I am being lied to and for my father's likely false accusations of the same. Instead of responding to the claim, something cries out from inside me. I ask respectfully, like I might do when learning anything from my father.

"Dad, what do you mean by 'men like him'? I honestly do not see him as a threat, and I have often been a good judge of character. You've told me as much. So, I think I'd benefit from your wisdom on the subject. For the future."

"That should go without saying, Jubilee." He mumbles. In that mumble, I see a crack. I see a weakness, a tiny lack of confidence. What am I seeing? My father is suddenly leaking humanity.

"Perhaps it should, but...I'd like for you to tell me. Please." I must know. I must look inside this crack. More than logic compels me.

"There are some cultural differences that might be difficult to reconcile," he says with eloquence.

My heart wrenches yet again. "You mean I shouldn't speak to him because he's..."

"A person of color. Yes." He clears his throat for a lecture. I am glad he sees the dire need for clarification and hope he delivers. "I have worked in the court system for decades. I have often been praised for my impartiality and being able to see past differences. Understand that I will never judge a man based solely on the color of his skin. I have, in fact, known a good number of black men and women worthy of honor. However, having approached every situation in a courtroom with impartiality, I have come through many of them with the same conclusion.

"This is not a skin color issue. It is rather a cultural issue. It is statistical fact, Jubilee, that most black families are without a father figure. Time and time again, I have been in family court when these men have relinquished their parental rights, simply by having such indifference for their own offspring that they do not even appear before the court. The prisons are filled with them. For generations. Theft. Drugs. Rape. Assault. Murder. Always having some excuse to remain perpetually between jobs.

"It's a travesty, really. Black men bear no less intelligence nor any notable physical or moral weakness. One's skin color should not suggest a greater propensity for sexual immorality or violence. However, since those worthy of honor are in the minority, it is often safe to assume that a man of Elijah's age is more interested in physical gratification than in a lasting, godly relationship. In court, I do not make such a judgment in advance. For the continued purity and honor of my daughter, I will do it every time."

I whisper what I think will be my only response. "I understand." But the mind God gave me for reason, encouraged by an excellent upbringing by this very man, beg me to speak otherwise. "May I speak freely?"

"Please do."

"You are judging him before you have met him. By definition, that is prejudice."

"As I explained—"

I don't often interrupt him, but see no other avenue in this case.

"Instead of showing indifference, Elijah is a loving, dedicated father, despite lacking a partner to assist him."

"I don't see—"

"He is also a valued employee in a career that he enjoys, and that glorifies God through love and service to others."

"What is the significance of that, Jubilee?"

"On two points at least, he has proven to have beaten the odds you set forth with the statistics. And since those statistics are your justification for showing racial prejudice, I am also inclined to disbelieve that Elijah is exhibiting any of the other behaviors and characteristics of which you have accused him based solely on skin color."

"There still remain the cultural differences, Jubilee," he evades.

I cannot help but heat up my speech. "Dad, I am *also* a person of color. I have never met another person from India. Should I associate with *no one*?

And am I to also accuse my own brother of being some kind of animal because he's from Africa and has dark skin?"

"Mind your tongue, Jubilee," Dad threatens. "Your country of origin and spiritual upbringing are vastly different. Just as that *James* has no significant cultural differences from Hannah's, you should only allow romantic pursuit, and only through me, if a man is similar to you in culture, age, and theology."

"Dad, every time I speak with Elijah, he is talking about the Bible. He has only ever shown himself to be a godly man who also teaches his child to love and rely upon the Word of God."

"Then he should have no issue respecting that he needs to stay away from you. Never speak to him again, Jubilee. I don't trust him."

Dad heads to his room after my reluctant, "yes, sir." I climb the stairs and find Hakim sitting in the hall, leaning against the wall across from my room. He nods to my doorway. We are not permitted in each other's bedrooms, so the two of us will often converse this way. I slide into my usual spot, my doorframe at my back, my skirt draped over bent knees. When we hear the expected door close in our parents' downstairs bedroom, Hakim whispers.

"He's wrong. You know that."

"Is he?" I whisper back. "There are reasons he likes to oversee these things."

"Yeah, but..." Hakim sighs. "In the thirty seconds I got to see Elijah...Dad's wrong, Jubilee. If I didn't trust this guy with you, I would have jumped out of bed and sped into town to get you from work."

"I didn't tell Dad it was Elijah giving me a ride."

"But I knew." Hakim shrugs. "You say he keeps showing up, and I don't even care if it's on purpose. You didn't want an arranged, acceptable marriage. You want to be pursued and make the choice yourself. I like him."

"You don't even know him." I laugh, pulling my braid aside.

"Well *you* like him, and that's enough for me." A wild grin spreads across his face. "You didn't tell Dad that, but obviously you like him, right?"

"Of course. He's a likeable guy. I'm sure most people who know him like him." But Hakim is still grinning, and I move to clarify with, "Wait, like him in what way?"

Hakim just laughs, having received his answer. "We didn't get to ride tonight. I've been dying to hear what's happening with this guy."

"Hakim, Elijah's son said something about him being twenty-eight and he has a birthday still this year. He's a whole decade older than me. Is that too old for me?"

"For you, no. You avoided Dad's question. Please tell me the guy told you you're beautiful."

"He did." I sigh at Hakim's sudden excitement. "But you heard Dad. I'm not allowed to talk to him anymore."

"If you're mature enough to attract a twenty-eight-year-old, you're mature enough to decide who you talk to." He smiles. "Tell me more."

I stay home Tuesday since I don't work and don't have a car yet, and I spend a relaxing morning in my room studying the Scriptures after doing my horse chores. A guide my father gave me for my birthday suggests that I should read in Judges today. I prefer the Epistles but know that there is just as much value in the Old Testament. So, I read about Gideon, yawning at an old familiar story. Then my study takes me into Isaiah, which is depressing at times, and then into James—one of my favorites. James seems a lot like my brother-in-law James. He's straightforward, unyielding in truth, but loving and filled with grace.

I begin to close my Bible and conclude my study for the day. Then:

"Jubilee Monroe. My precious, faithful child."

The statement seems to come from within me and all around me, though not quite tangible in the flesh. Much like the call to listen while I was stranded two days ago. That would be cause for a psychiatrist, right? But even more than I am compelled to take my next breath, I am compelled to answer the known Giver of the call.

"Here I am, Lord," My heart declares.

The answer is unexpected, but just as clear.

"Read about My servant Gideon again."

Before I can manifest the urge to laugh it off, I realize that the clear command will swell and rot inside me all day long if I allow my Bible to remain closed. The call is now a disease. But the command is so simple. Even though my tummy is grumbling for lunch, I sigh, choosing obedience, and open again to the book of Judges.

I read of Gideon's cowardice and how he was hiding from his enemies at the threshing floor.

68

" 'And the Angel of the LORD appeared unto him, and said unto him, The LORD is with thee, thou mighty man of valour,' " I read aloud in a whisper. "But Gideon was hiding…"

I see that Gideon was not a mighty man and had little valor. He even waited until night to obey the Lord and tear down his father's idols because he feared the men around him more than he trusted the Lord. And the Lord Himself had appeared to Gideon. Not a still, small voice, but the Angel of the Lord. How lucky he was to have his purpose told him and his steps directed by the very presence of God.

"Am I not also with you now?"

I'd nearly heard it, once again. But I nod. Of course. God's presence is *within* me, as I am a vessel for the Holy Spirit of that same Angel.

"The Lord is with thee, mighty woman of valor."

But perhaps I said that to myself. Because isn't it blasphemy for a woman of God to be mighty or brave? Still, I cannot take chances. I heard what I heard.

"This is crazy," I whisper. "God…what is it You want me to do? I am not a mighty woman of valor, I'm a nineteen-year-old girl. Gideon conquered the Midianites with just a few men and some trumpets and torches. He turned out to actually *be* a mighty man of valor. I'm not him. And my father does not worship idols."

"The Lord is with thee. Do not hide. Cast down the altar. I have chosen YOU."

"I don't even know what that means." I close my Bible and head downstairs for lunch.

I help out around the house all afternoon, eager to ride with Hakim when he arrives home. We are barely finished with dinner before I beg him. Reluctantly, exhausted, he goes with me.

"I assume you need to talk about something," Hakim infers.

"Why do you assume that?"

Hakim laughs. I sigh.

"I think God spoke to me. Like *spoke* to me. And that I'm supposed to do something, but I don't know what." I wince at the vagueness.

"That explains everything," Hakim teases.

"Like…like Gideon."

"Gideon the proud, faithless swine?"

"Hakim! He did great things for God."

"Yeah, after he required God to do the lamb's wool thing. You know, provide proof of being God? Twice! Then after that he had some stupid number of wives and ended up rebuilding the idols he tore down. Gideon is a bad example," Hakim teaches.

"Well, what if I feel *called* like Gideon, but choose not to behave as Gideon?"

"Then you should definitely listen." Hakim smiles. "What is God calling you to do?"

"Like I said, I don't know." I shrug. "I'll let you know."

On Wednesday morning, I awaken with something on my heart that terrifies me.

"Trust Me."

"Yes, Lord," I promise.

"I have set the path before you. Trust Me to guide you."

"Of course," I whisper into the morning.

"Jubilee, do not fear My servant Elijah. Trust that I have placed him on your path."

I laugh bitterly, though I am thankful that God has warned me of a trial to come. I clarify in a mumble, "A handsome stumbling block?"

"No, Jubilee."

"But Dad wants me to avoid Elijah."

"I want you to submit to Elijah."

I sit up in a start. The call is clear. There is only one God-honoring way for a woman to submit herself to a man, and my heart immediately takes to fear. I just met Elijah. Why would God ask me to do such a thing? But that is not the most terrifying command. In nearly as many words, I was just told to trust God, knowing that perhaps my father's wishes will not align. Yet I know that His overriding command is that I must honor my father. That means God is placing that dichotomy on my path to be navigated...

"With Me. Trust Me to guide you," He repeats into my frantic thoughts.

Just before rising and facing the day, I whisper, "I trust You, Father."

I hitch a ride into town with Hakim, and en route, he notes my silence.

"You figured it out, didn't you?"

"I'd rather not share just yet," I mumble. Hating that he's right.

"Okay, Gideon."

I sit at James's shop for a couple of hours until my car is ready and I can take it to work. All the while I'm wishing I was running into Elijah and Bennett at the gas station. They are probably there, gassing up to go fishing, maybe even looking for me. Still, it's ludicrous to think I'd run into them again. But perhaps that will be my lamb's wool if I do. I realize over the next few days that my life, in which I am content, is suddenly mundane. I feel like I'm missing out on something monumental. But to me, it's a sin to even think it. Maybe this nagging surety is wrong. But how could it be?

My Guide is beckoning me to walk with Him. And if we walk with Him, we can never wander from the path set before us.

Ten

Elijah

We don't like to use words like *slow* and *quiet* in my profession, because God has a way of laughing at that with sudden, boisterous haste. But this Thursday, it's both. The residents are quiet, Bennett had a good morning, and all is well. But I want something wild to happen, otherwise I am going to start thinking about Jubilee. I have to break this habit. It's unhealthy. She's a teenager.

"When did I say you could not think about her?"

The Holy Spirit weighs in. I listen, manning the desk for now. It's so dreadfully quiet and I'm alone. I'm thankful He's talking.

"I don't want to be lustful. You've condemned that plenty of times. I slipped up that one time."

"You were washed."

"Okay, well, I don't want her to become an idol. I want to worship You, not her."

"Will you love and worship Me if I do not give you Jubilee?"

"Without question. You alone are God. Nothing and no one comes before You. I have said the same thing about Bennett. Thank You for Bennett, God."

"Worship Me. And love my servant Jubilee."

"Lord, if You want me to love her, you're going to have to make a way. You're asking the impossible."

"Love her. Trust Me. Nothing is impossible with God."

The quick, impossible conversation ends abruptly when the front door opens and I hear footsteps around the corner from the desk. The footsteps turn out to be a lanky young man with curls and skin somewhere between the hue of mine and Bennett's.

"Hello sir, how can I—"

My heart practically vomits out of my chest. On a second glance, I recognize him. My mind quickly skims over the faces, and eventually places him somewhere horrifying.

"I know you." I stand, shaking his hand. "You're one of Jubilee's brothers. Hakim, right?"

"Good memory. You were kind of easy to find, Elijah. If you're going to be the criminal my dad thinks you are, you aren't laying low enough. I did an internet search for your name and there you were on the website for this place like you have a respectable career or something."

Dry sarcasm. I like it. And I'm scared.

"Well, even if he digs up my entire past, he'll be bored to tears if he's looking for a criminal. What brings you here today, Hakim?"

"First of all, I was never here. She would kill me. But I had to look into the eyes of the man who is actively trying to woo my best friend. That's fair, right?"

"Um…" If black men could blush.

He laughs aloud. "I only have a few minutes, but I wanted to coach you. I really don't think it's fair what you are probably about to be thrown into, so God led me to help you out a little."

"Uh, okay?"

"First thing is, she isn't going to sleep with you. I have to tell you that. It's not just a scary big brother warning thing. She won't. It's like ingrained in her."

"What, like, never?" I smirk, letting myself awaken to the challenge.

"Also ingrained in her is the idea that she needs to always be available to submit to her husband's desires, no matter how much of a pig he is. So no, not never. But just…you'd have to wait."

"So would she." I shrug. I suddenly remember that I have several years of experience on this kid and decide I can use it to my advantage. "Has she also been taught that part of a husband loving his wife like Christ loves the church is not making unreasonable, piggish requests?"

"No." Hakim tilts his head to the left, calculating like he's never heard that himself. He smiles and continues with, "But if you get the chance, definitely teach her that."

"Will do."

"Good. Marriage is like a huge thing for her and it's always going to be the goal. So if you're not in it to win it, just quit while you're behind. And babies. She'll want lots of babies. That's how things are. So, seriously, like. . .take it or leave it."

I analyze, then quickly turn it around on him. "So what you're saying is I shouldn't waste my time if I want to sleep with her, so I should only pursue this if I want to sleep with her?"

We are in a standoff for a moment while he processes. The processing ends with a wide grin. "Exactly." He qualifies, "But if you try anything stupid, I will be the least of your worries."

"Got it." I decide to drop the charade. "Well, whose side are *you* on, Hakim?"

"Um, Jubilee's. And God's. I'm not worried about Dad. But, like…you should be. Sort of."

"Sort of?"

"Well, he told Jubilee she can't speak to you ever again. She is programmed to obey him, so she's having trouble right now."

"So should I honor this programming, or…"

"No. Please. I want you to help her dismantle it like you've been doing."

"Uh…" I wince. "What have I been doing?"

"Bruh…" Hakim laughs, pocketing his hands and starting to look more comfortable. "I *know* you knew not to give her a ride again."

I smirk, still quite satisfied with myself. "She needed a ride."

"Exactly. So don't like make her sin or something. But keep helping her break Dad's insane rules, because it's good for her. And keep telling her she's beautiful, because it's *really* working for *you*."

"So, I'm right thinking no one tells her that?" I sigh.

"Unfortunately. Our sisters don't say it because they are jealous. Her brothers don't say it because she's our sister, and Dad doesn't say it because he thinks he can somehow ward off men that way. Mom says it. And I remind Dad sometimes, but I don't tell her directly." He shrugs. "But…she's Jubilee. This girl isn't some oblivious little flower. She *knows* she's beautiful, and she knows she has a lot more going for her than that too. She's probably a few of your compliments from *acting* like she knows. So keep at it. I want to see what she does."

"But if I'm not supposed to see her, how can I do that?"

"She'll be at the farmers' market Saturday. All day."

I laugh. "So will I. My son has been talking about it. You don't need to help God orchestrate, Hakim."

"I figured, but...just don't be scared of Dad if he's there, which he might be. And you want him to be, because she will want to have his blessing."

"Blessing for what?"

"Well, you are going to need to ask Dad if you can court her. Actually, you'll probably have to ask for a meeting to even be able to talk to him about courtship so that he can prepare his answer. Try to talk to him with grandkids and my mom around. He's nicer then."

"And do you think he'll even set a meeting with me?"

"Probably. Just be respectful when you ask him. And at the meeting, be ready for weird rules and invasive questions. But don't back down, okay? Jubilee is his favorite child. She will get what she wants." He looks at his watch and begins backing away. "I gotta go. Don't disappoint me, Elijah. I'm rooting for you."

"Why are you helping me?" I laugh, bewildered by the whole exchange.

"Like I said, I'm on Jubilee's side. This isn't about you." He walks toward the exit back around the corner. "I was never here."

Eleven

Jubilee

Saturday morning, I am helping my mother pack up the knitted winter caps that she'll be selling alongside Hannah's jewelry at the market. It'll be a hot day and she likely won't sell winter caps, but she tries to contribute where she can.

"Have you decided if you're coming, Adam?" Mom asks of her husband, who is sitting reading his Scriptures. He's waiting to help load the car since Hakim is still asleep and Judah is at work already.

"That *James* won't be there to look out for Hannah. I suppose I should probably go," Dad says.

That James. His kindhearted, hard-working son-in-law and the father of two, well technically three, of his grandchildren. The other spouses, Maren, Elliot, Penny, and Katie, all get addressed or referred to by their first names only. Dad had practically chosen them all himself. Some of them far more than practically. But "that James" was all passion and honor. One of which, Dad admires in the man. The other is what melted Hannah's heart and earned him a "that".

"Oh, Adam, you know James makes good money on Saturdays, especially during the market. There is another baby coming. He's only being responsible." Mom, the only person who has ever spoken reason to Adam Monroe. He signifies his halfhearted defeat with a grunt.

"Jonathan and Bethany will be there too." I shrug, thinking of my nephew and niece, knowing that just as having children turns boys into men, grandchildren seem to reverse the damage. I love to watch my father turn to useless mush as he interacts with his grandchildren.

"I suppose I could do with some good fresh apples," Dad says, lifting a tub of knitted hats and heading out the door.

After getting all set up and then watching the first people arrive on Main Street and ogle over Hannah's lovely creations, I hear something familiar, though bone chilling in present company. To me, it is as Gideon's first sign—lamb's wool, soaking wet with dew. And dry earth all around.

"Hey, Miss Jubilee!" It's Bennett, running to the table on legs that few people know aren't his.

"Hey, Bennett! How are you today?" I greet the heartwarming presence like an old friend.

"I'm alright. And yourself?" He voices the reflection of his respectful upbringing.

"Blessed, now that I've seen you." This, to Bennett's delight.

"You know this child, Jubilee?" Dad is calculating.

"Yes, sir. This is Bennett. Bennett, this is my mom and dad and sister Hannah. Hannah's kids Jonathan and Bethany are playing over at the playground." I introduce, and friendly Bennett's eyes light up when I mention the other children.

"It's nice to meet y'all." Bennett is polite, charming my mother and sister into a smile. "Jubilee, your family don't look like you."

"Not everyone looks like their parents Bennett," I explain again in a laugh, then realize the void. Parents. "Where is your dad? Does he know where you are?"

"He was..." Then Bennett turns back to the crowd of people on the blocked off road and looks around a bit. "Oh, man..."

I speak gently. "Bennett, he's probably looking for you everywhere! You should always stay with him, especially in a crowd."

"I'm sorry," he says, looking like he's going to cry.

"It's okay. We just need to find him." I look back at my family. Mom is already springing into action.

"Do you know Bennett's father, Jubilee? You could go find him while I take Bennett to the playground with the others."

"Yes, I'll look for him." I rise. "Does that sound okay, Bennett?"

"Yes, Miss Jubilee," he says as Mom ushers him away.

"They go to the church? I don't recognize him." Dad is unsettled by being left out of the loop as I slip my sandals on.

"Uh, no," I answer quickly and bolt off through the crowd until I hear a faint,

"Bennett? Ben, where did you go, buddy?"

Elijah's eyes, unveiling his frantic fear, pass over me in the melee when he comes near. I have to reach out and touch Elijah's arm to get his attention. And to my horror, one finger slips inside his short sleeve, and I immediately draw back my hand. But not before I feel it as dry lamb's wool, when the whole earth is covered in dew. Gideon's second sign. My heart leaps when Elijah's eyes find mine.

"Lord, let Your will be done." And it is the easiest challenge I've ever accepted.

"Miz Jubilee!" He says with even more enthusiasm than I'd hoped. We move aside, so as not to get bumped by the moving crowd. "I had a feeling and good information that you'd be here. You seen my son by any chance? I'm about to find a police officer to help me."

"Well, that won't be necessary. I came to find you because Bennett found *me* at my sister's booth, and we realized you weren't with him. He's just over here playing on the playground with my mom and niece and nephew. I hope that…I didn't even think if he could do that with his legs and all. I'm so sorry."

"My son knows his way around a playground, don't concern yourself with that." Elijah smiles. "I'm glad he found you. He always loses me at these things. I didn't even want to come, but Mrs. Parker, his home day care lady, kept putting bugs in these kids' ears about it. And then I found out you'd be here and knew I had to come. What is your sister peddling?"

Everyone in my life uses the same words and terms and speaks the same tired dialect in the same cadence, sometimes with unnecessary complexity and sincerity. But Elijah is so different. It is like a new language that I understand best with my soul but can still interact with using the only language I know. We converse from two worlds as we slowly make our way back to the booth through the crowd.

"She makes jewelry. And my mom knits. They've been selling their things here since before my sister graduated from school."

"I'm gonna take a wild guess and say y'all are homeschooled," Elijah says.

"Yes, we've all graduated now. But why do you say that?" I ask. And he just laughs. I don't know whether to be offended or amused.

I lead Elijah past the booth to the playground, where he spots the waving Bennett atop a platform about to go down a slide. I look on from a distance as Elijah meets him at the bottom of the slide for a brief and gentle reprimand that results first in Bennett's remorseful face, then a warm hug before Elijah sends Bennett off to play again. He expects much and loves much more. Such a wise father.

During the exchange, Mom approaches me.

"He's mighty handsome," she suggests. "Same young man Dad was going on about the other night?"

"Yes ma'am." I mask my pounding heart.

"Oh heavens."

"Exactly." I sigh. She must know the predicament I'm in.

"You sure about this?" she whispers. "Because you need to be *sure*, Jubilee. I want to stress that."

Ah, now I understand. I smile. "You've been talking to Hakim."

"No, my love." Mom clasps my hand in hers. "I heard you *defending* him. There is one man I would defend with such conviction."

"Dad?"

Her nod confirms it, and she releases my hand as Elijah returns.

"Who is *this* beauty, Jubilee?" He offers his hand for Mom.

"This is my mother Leah Monroe. Mom, this is Elijah Bering. Bennett's father."

Mom shakes Elijah's hand with a coy smile. Then, after a glance back at Bennett, Elijah has my eyes arrested in his gaze.

"Thank y'all. It about kills me when he runs off like that."

"No, thank *God*," I correct. "I'm glad he wandered to *us*."

Mom nods, then narrows her eyes at Elijah. Next, she smiles, "You think he'd like some funnel cake?"

"Oh, that's not necessary." Elijah laughs, something about the offer confusing him.

"Well, it's just that Jonathan was asking about it earlier, and I'm sure I could send my husband for some. He's about to wrench his neck over there, trying to see the man with whom we are conversing. A five-minute errand for some funnel cake might do everyone some good." She isn't wrong. Dad is close enough to recognize that Mom and I are talking to someone, but since he missed us walk past the booth, he can't see who we're talking to.

"Mom…" I move my braid aside, embarrassed. What has gotten into her today?

"When Dad comes back to the booth, you head over there. Don't let him worry. Five minutes." Mom smiles, then heads back to the booth. I watch as Dad rises, then walks out of sight.

My heart hiccups, and I feel like I need to apologize.

"She's being odd today. I'm sorry."

"It's fine, Jubilee. She seems like a lovely woman. If you'd met my mother…well, just be thankful for yours."

"Oh, I am!" I impress. "Believe me. One of my first memories is her singing to me about Jesus and braiding my hair on a plane. I'm very blessed by my parents, even in their strangest moods."

He nods. Convinced of something. With little time to make his point, he begins, "I had an unexpected visitor at work the other day who didn't want you to know he stopped by."

"Who visited…?" But after a half beat, I'm annoyed. "Hakim."

"Don't be too hard on him. We had a nice conversation. I learned that the only way I'm allowed to speak with you is if I talk to Dad first."

"You're talking to me now."

"Well, you're a grown woman. You're not a tool I'm hoping to borrow from your daddy's garage. I'll jump through all your father's flaming hoops he supposedly has lined up for someone like me. But I wanted to talk to *you* first."

"What about?"

"About pursuing this thing that God has put in our path. So, you should tell me how it is a man can pursue a romantic relationship with you."

I guffaw. I had barely been half listening, dividing my attention between the children on the playground and the booth, awaiting Dad's return. But my eyes dart to Elijah's to share in the joke. Except he isn't joking. I don't even know what to say except the truth.

"Well," I finally manage, then shrug, looking to the ground, "We don't just pursue romance in our family. We pursue commitment, so…"

"Even better. Is that what courtship is?"

"Yes." Not having expected him to know the term, I meet his eyes again. "Dad has to approve it. That's the first step in courtship. And the last step is almost always, you know, marriage. So, courtship is a serious commitment."

"Hakim explained that, and that's all perfectly ideal for me. But your father doesn't like me, so getting his approval won't be easy," he reasons, unfazed.

"Correct."

"Right. So, I'm coming to you first."

"I value my father's opinion and I honor his rules." I stand my ground.

"Which is one of the many reasons I like you." He chuckles. "I'm not asking you to go against his rules. I just need to make sure this is worth the battle. God has been quite adamant that I need to pursue this. But I need to know where you are with it before I go assuming—"

"God told me not to be scared of you," I blurt. "He wants me to trust you. So if you go to battle with my dad, I'll be on *your* side with pitchers and trumpets, because that's where God wants me to be. No promises, but…"

"Wow." He grumbles, tossing his head back with a wild, triumphant smile. He removes his hat, smooths the sweat from his short black hair, then replaces the hat. He laughs, seemingly involuntarily with a little squeak. He's squirming and barely in control of himself, and I don't know why.

"Did I offend you, or…?" I worry.

"You just told me you were going to defend me to your father so that we can pursue a romantic relationship."

"Courtship, yes." I'm confused. Isn't that what he was after?

"But you told me that by using the book of Judges." He laughs again.

"The Bible is what I know, and I live my life for God, so I tend to interact with everyday life through the lens of—" I start to defend. But he lights up my heart with his next words.

"Gideon, though? You went for a *Gideon* reference when I mentioned a battle? Not David or Joshua or even Moses?"

"God spoke to me about this through the account of Gideon, who was weak in His faith, but God did a mighty work through him with—"

"Pitchers and torches and trumpets and three-hundred men. It just seems like you have more faith than Gideon, Jubilee."

"Well, whatever the state of my faith, God has been faithful to provide metaphorical lamb's wool because of my hesitation, so Gideon fits." I shrug, feeling vulnerable. "I mean, how does God speak to *you*?"

"His Word, just like you. And He talks through other people sometimes, like when Hakim visited me. And other times just...I don't know, He just talks to me. We talk. The Holy Spirit is my dearest friend and God's Word is written on my heart." Elijah chuckles. And I think I might be falling in love with his relationship with God, if that's possible. But his affections are elsewhere. "We speak the same language, you and me."

I smile. And he understands the dialect.

He sighs, and his eyes tear up and his voice shakes a little. I pay close attention. "Jubilee, I was raised by a single mother. I had heartbreak after heartbreak my whole childhood as father figures would come in and let us love them, and then they'd leave us. I promised myself and God that I'd never let Bennett go through that. So I have exactly one chance at this, and I have to get it right. I'm risking two hearts here."

"Three." I cut off the outpouring and sigh, glancing at the playground. "I *love* Bennett, and even the thought of hurting him breaks my heart too. And I know it isn't quite the same thing, but I do understand. You are *not* my father's ideal. And I'm scared. God told me not to be scared of *you*, but I'm scared of *everything* else. If I take this chance and it doesn't work—"

"It'll work," he promises. Those eyes welling, then smiling, "We got God's will and pitchers and trumpets. It'll work."

I'm laughing a quiet laugh when Mom walks past us to the playground with funnel cake. We see that Dad has returned to the booth and is calling me back.

"One thing I need to know before we get there. Favorite color?" he asks as we walk back, eyes ahead, pretending not to be conversing.

"Red," I confess, then elaborate, "Dark red. Not maroon like your truck, but like, deep, blood-red with black in it, not purple. No one knows that but you. My parents wouldn't approve."

He chuckles.

"What?"

"That's Ben's favorite color too."

We arrive at the front of the booth, where Elijah ducks under the canopy.

"Elijah, this is my father Adam Monroe, and my sister Hannah Martin. Dad, Hannah, this is Elijah Bering, Bennett's father." I breathe heavily, trying not to reveal nerves. Hannah smiles, well versed in the signs—and consequences—of handsome men. Dad frowns.

"Red pickup truck." This is said in place of Dad shaking Elijah's outstretched hand.

"Yes, sir. Well, maroon, really. Maroon has purple in it. But I'm guessing that's not the point," Elijah says, likely offended at being left hanging as he pockets his hands.

"Jubilee, go on and take a seat. You've completed your errand," Dad begins, and I obey, reclaiming the chair next to Hannah behind the table. Dad begins the interrogation. "How old are you, Elijah?"

"Twenty-eight, sir. Pretty close to twenty-nine, which is…close to thirty, I guess." Elijah answers. "You?"

"That is completely irrelevant."

He laughs once, annoyed and confused at the conversation. "Okay."

"Now, why would a twenty-eight-year-old man give a nineteen-year-old girl a ride home, repeatedly, even after she was warned against taking them?" Dad confronts immediately, but cordially. Hannah tucks her lips, quieting for the reprimand.

"Well, it seems Jubilee's had bad luck in the transportation department as of late. But I do apologize if my actions were misconstrued as anything but chivalrous." Elijah tilts his head with a smile.

"Chivalry, huh? While I do appreciate chivalry, Jubilee is well taken care of and was not in need of yours," Dad asserts.

"Forgive me if I disagree." Elijah smirks. "The world can always use more chivalry and women always deserve it."

"Forgive me, Elijah, if I disagree that it was your only reason for repeatedly finding yourself in my daughter's presence; in ways that are not entirely appropriate." Dad rises now. Elijah is a lean, but not scrawny, six feet. Dad is the same height, but heavier now. It's intimidating for my brothers and brothers-in-law. But Elijah, merely an acquaintance with every chance to run, or even take a step back, stands his ground.

"Adam…can I call you Adam? Mr. Monroe? Your Honor? What should I call you?"

"Again, irrelevant. We won't be conversing much."

"Fair enough," Elijah says, "But can I finish *this* conversation, though? I know you claim authority over Jubilee's mouth, but since we've established that I'm a grown man, I still have freedom to speak, so…" Dad crosses his arms in disbelief at Elijah's gall. Elijah begins looking at the jewelry on the table and speaks before Dad can untie his tongue, "These are some lovely things, Hannah."

"Thank you," Hannah says politely. Elijah glances at her obviously pregnant belly.

As he's looking again at jewelry, "So Adam, how does one go about speaking to one of your daughters the 'appropriate' way? I can see someone has succeeded at this."

"That would depend on the nature of 'speaking,' " Dad fumes.

"Well, I'm sure it's the worst you could imagine. I'd like to, uh, court Jubilee. If that's even how I ask."

"Then this is a futile conversation, Elijah," Dad says. "Jubilee is not the kind of woman you hope she is."

"Mr. Monroe." Elijah fumes. "I'm certain you know next to nothing about what I hope. So, humor me. Tell me how this works."

Dad starts rattling off the history. "Elliot asked me if he could court Priscilla before she even knew he was interested. I preferred it that way. James and Hannah grew up together. Can't help that. He asked to court her when he already had a ring bought. Not preferred, I'll admit. But James is a good man from a good family. Jubilee has proven more difficult for a man to confess that sort of interest. She has already turned down a handsome, wealthy young man close to her age."

"A doctor, am I wrong?" Elijah asks me directly, easily shaking off Dad's disdain.

"He'll graduate med school soon. How did you know?" I'm impressed.

"The other day, you said 'a doctor would have said he's a doctor.' Seemed to have roots someplace." He shrugs, then turns back to Dad, who is annoyed at his direct dialogue with me.

"Jubilee, I asked you not to speak to him," Dad reminds me. "You reconnected him with his son. You needn't speak again."

"Now *that* would be a problem for me. Silent women aren't really my thing."

"No, you like teenagers."

"Just the one," Elijah dares. I can't help but smile at Dad's carefully concealed shock, which Elijah sees when he looks at me. He winks and then looks at the table, smiling when he sees a certain pair of earrings. I pretend not to have had my eye on the same genuine turquoise beads and dyed blood-red dove feathers all morning, hoping no one buys that pair. He points at them, then speaks to me again. "This the color?"

I give him a subtle nod. He checks the price on the back, pulls out his wallet, pays Hannah, then hands me the earrings after Hannah puts them in a box.

Dad laughs his offense, "You are not permitted to buy *gifts* for my daughter, whom you hardly know."

"I figured as much. Or give her rides home when she's baking in the sun or working late into the evening. Tell her she's beautiful without your consent. Though relatively blameless in the eyes of Christ, I've likely committed a hundred sins against *you*. I understand that." Elijah winces. "Still, I'd like to know when you and I can talk about the, uh…courtship. Thing. With Jubilee."

Dad begins, "No. Absolutely not. This is completely ludicrous, and my daughter is—"

But my mouth starts moving before I even realize it, having remembered the call to not be afraid. "Dad, if Elijah wants to talk to you about courting me, I think you should hear him out."

"Jubilee, this is not your concern."

I laugh, shocked. "Dad, with all due respect, this conversation *directly* concerns me. Elijah and his son have never been anything but kind and appropriate. He's at least earned the respect of a *conversation* with you. It's true, I don't know them that well. But isn't that the *point* of what he's trying to ask you? To have a chance to get to know me?"

Which seems to pleasantly catch Elijah off guard. All of them, really. My tone is almost professional, but the words are new. Not provocative. But loving. Encouraging. Just like my mother. So, it is my mother that speaks up next.

"You can't deny the attraction there, Adam." Mom's sweet voice seems to come from nowhere as she arrives, three children in tow.

Elijah clears his throat and then smiles. "Attraction." He examines the word with scrunched lips, focusing his eyes on mine. "Interesting word choice."

"And why's that? Not denying it are you?" Dad asserts.

"No, sir. But I guess you could say *we* are attracted. Like magnets." Elijah laughs. "The past few weeks, every time I turn around, she's there. Am I right, Miz Jubilee?"

I nod. "It seems that way."

"Now, today doesn't count. I had a tip she'd be here, so any prior intentions for the day have been compromised. But every other time I've seen Jubilee it's been orchestrated by God. She and I had a—probably off-limits— conversation about that earlier in the week. Then I gave her a ride home, scared I'd never get to talk to her again. Everything in me wanted to ask her for her number, but like I told her, I knew I probably needed to talk to you about that." Elijah sighs, then asks it with kindness and respect, "So, tell me *when*, not *if*, you and I can have a conversation about me seeing her again."

I can't look up. I know what Dad would say if Hakim were so bold. My heart is sick over what might happen to Elijah. There is a tense twenty seconds or so, and I am praying hard. Mom eases in like it's nothing.

"Tomorrow evening at five would be fine, I think. I'm making pot pie. My other children normally come over for the afternoon, but Noah and Isaac took their families on a trip this weekend. We'd love to have you and Bennett over. Hannah, you and James can come, too. Bennett and Jonathan seem to have connected."

"That's Jonathan, Dad," Bennett says, his face covered in powdered sugar. He doesn't quite understand what is occurring.

"Lovely children," Elijah tells Hannah.

"Thank you," Hannah says again, a woman of few words.

"Tomorrow at five. I'll be there. With Bennett, of course. Thank you, Mrs. Monroe."

"Leah," Mom corrects. "Have you had a chance to look around the market yet, Jubilee?"

"Not yet. I didn't really look when I went to get Elijah." I finally look up at Mom's face, wondering why she's asking.

"Well, I have some yarn for Bennett and Jonathan to sort if you'd like to take a look with your friend here," Mom says, probably having heard every word of the previous tussle.

"Leah, that is completely—" Dad starts. Mom puts up a hand.

"Go on, Jubilee."

Elijah takes the chance. "I did see some beautiful handmade skirts on that end before Bennett ran off. I've seen you wear something similar and, uh…thought of you."

I look between Elijah and my mother, Hannah, and my fuming father, then put the earring box in my purse and pocket a twenty-dollar bill in case I see something I like. All in a few seconds of course, so as not to keep Elijah waiting.

We walk side by side, my arms crossed, Elijah's hands in his pockets. Neither of us is looking at the market booths at all.

"You think I stand a chance?" Elijah starts.

"Yes. A very good one," I answer with a nod.

"Really? Didn't seem that way."

"Well," I explain, "I know it seemed like my father doesn't value my opinion in this process. But he does. He will ask me, likely this evening, my thoughts about courting you."

Elijah winces. "And you'll tell him…"

"Pitchers and trumpets, Elijah. Don't worry."

Twelve

Elijah

"I have to have her," says the all-consuming fog in my mind. My prayers don't cease all night long. "God, I don't know what I'll do if You don't give me this. Yes, I will love You. But I will be a useless heap of nothing."

If I hadn't decided it the morning we spoke while her car was being prepared to tow, or the other night when I'd taken her home from work and she'd giggled at Bennett's antics, I certainly decided it yesterday at the farmers' market when she touched my arm to get my attention after Bennett ran off. She'd been embarrassed when someone had bumped me and just one finger of hers made it to my upper bicep.

But when I looked and saw it was Jubilee, that gentle touch became everything. That's when it flooded in before me as clear as memories behind. A white dress and a first dance. Making love and making her coffee and watching her braid her hair. I longed with that one touch for all her touches. I'd seen her sitting beside me on the couch with a baby in her belly and theology on her tongue or sitting in front of a Christmas tree in a nightgown with Bennett by her side. I ache for those things as if I lost them.

"God, if I am lusting. . .I don't know what to do this time. If You want me to run toward this, how can I flee?"

When Jubilee introduced me to Adam Monroe, I knew exactly what it would take to get Jubilee. I am going to have to pry her out of his hands with every tool and every prayer in my heart. I'm respectful. My mother taught me that. But I'm also disrespectful when my worth is challenged. I learned that from five different stepfather-like figures. I learned to fight and defend and stand my ground. So now I'm foolish enough to be taking an invitation to defend my new and powerful feelings for Jubilee the way she defended me in front of a father who had already told her to be quiet. I'm asking permission to court her. I'm not sure what that means, but if it'll put Jubilee and me in the same sentence, I'll take it.

"God, I love her. I love her. I love her. I'll do it forever and for Your glory. Just let me do it completely."

"Why do you need to talk to her daddy to ask if you can be her boyfriend? Did you even ask Miss Jubilee?" Bennett asks as I casually mention the serious situation, which is how I often approach things with Bennett. Right now, I am shining one boot, Bennett the other, and we are discussing an important aspect of the future two hours before the dinner at the Monroe house.

"Well, Miss Jubilee is alright with it, but she's young and her daddy wants to make sure your daddy is an alright guy. Just like when you find a girl and marry her one day, I'll want to meet her first. And daddies are even more protective of their little girls," I explain, then pause my brush strokes when I realize what I just said.

"So…are you gonna marry her, Dad? For real?" Bennett asks, both wary and excited.

"Bennett, you should never date or 'court' a woman that you couldn't see yourself married to. And I'd never marry someone you wouldn't want as a stepmom. So, if you have any feelings about her, now is a good time to let me know."

"Miss Jubilee is soooo nice, Dad."

"She is. But she'd be a parent to you. You'd have to mind her like you do me. Even if she isn't nice sometimes. And it'd be forever. If I get to marry her, there's no going back to how it is now."

"Do you love her?" Bennett asks.

I hesitate to let him know what God does. But I do not withhold honesty. "Very, very much, Bennett. She's…yeah. I love her."

"And you'll like kiss her and do that other stuff you told me married people do?" He scrunches his nose in disgust.

"That's just part of it, Bennett. But that would be between her and me. You don't need to worry about all that." I beg my heart to beat a little softer so my son doesn't hear, and wonder how often I'll be called on to hide such big things from him. He and I don't have secrets. I'm glad God is allowing me a taste.

"But would she live here and take care of us like ladies do?" Bennett removes the wariness this time.

"Let's not get ahead of ourselves, Bennett. For now, we're just getting to know more about her."

It's as if God has already spoken it. A promise as true as a rainbow for Noah. A nation for Abraham. And all I want is Jubilee. Now the world knows I'm attracted to her. If only they knew it was soul deep. After waiting so long for the call, I know this is it. *"Lord, let her come take care of us like ladies do."*

I enter the Monroe house and my heart stops, and my mind empties for a moment when I see black hair flowing over Jubilee's shoulders and back and even past the tail of her blouse. Then the three brothers present look either nervous or murderous when my hat drops from my hand at the sight of all that hair and her bright amber eyes and those red feather earrings I bought her. They can see that I see the family secret. That Jubilee is beautiful. Hakim was right. She knows, and she's using it like an electromagnet, and I'm just a paperclip. She's evil, and genius, and she knows she's killing me and claiming all my "yes, dears" forever. I am madly in love with this woman.

Bennett steals the show over pot pie. James, Hannah's husband, and Judah, the youngest Monroe brother, talk cars over dessert. Then the women and children find some convoluted excuse to go outside when the table is clear.

"Can I go play outside too, Dad?" Bennett asks.

"Of course, Ben. I'll be in here talking to Mr. Monroe, alright?"

Jubilee smiles, putting a hand at Bennett's back, "I'll look after him."

In the course of thanking her, watching Bennett and Jubilee bounce outside together, and hoping that Jubilee's offer is permanent, I look around at the men still planted in the room, and learn that this talk happens with brothers present too.

"What do you do for a living, Elijah?" Adam starts.

"I'm a Registered Nurse. I work with geriatric patients at a nursing home in town." I nod. Here it comes.

"A nurse?" Adam clarifies with caution.

"Yes, sir. I wanted to help people heal. I looked into becoming a doctor, but they don't have near as much patient interaction. It's more about the

science than the healing. Which is all well and good for somebody, I'm sure."
I share my heart, "But I wouldn't rather do anything but this."

"Is it true you're twenty-eight?" Judah asks.

"Yes, sir." I sigh. "I understand the hesitation. In your place, I'd be a little concerned."

"Do I have a reason to be concerned?" Adam asks it.

"No, sir," I contend. "A reason to be proud, I'd say. Your Jubilee is an old soul." I sniffle, trying not to think too deeply about her in present company.

"She's a teenager." Judah is brazen.

"No, *you* are a teenager. Jubilee is a 'lady,' as my son so wisely puts it." A combined insult and admission that makes every man in the room stir, except for Hakim, who hasn't stopped smiling.

"Do you know what courtship is?" Adam destroys the merriment. Ah, so that's why Jubilee never really laughs when she wants to

"Jubilee clued me in a little bit." I recall the information from an hour-long stroll while my son sorted yarn yesterday. "I have a question about the chaperoning, though."

"Of course you do," the pompous little Judah slithers off his tongue.

"I don't bend on that one, Elijah," Adam warns.

"No, sir. In fact, I like the idea, provided my son courts as a chaperone." I lean my arms on the table. Ready to negotiate.

"Oh, he has terms. Dad, how do you not love this guy for her?" Hakim laughs. James smiles a little. Adam ignores them.

"And how old is Bennett?" Adam asks.

"Just turned eight."

Adam ponders a moment. I tremble. What am I doing here? There's no way Adam will agree to this. Why does my spirit long for Jubilee's?

James clears his throat respectfully. Adam looks at him like he's committed a crime. "Um, sir, Hannah and I took Jubilee with us sometimes when we courted. And sometimes my little brother would chaperone. Honestly, it's more motivation to do the right thing when you have a kid with you that looks up to you. They were our best chaperones."

Adam nods. "I can accept that Bennett would be a suitable chaperone per your request provided I can be assured that he'd indeed be present at all times." Adam speaks slowly and with that pompous authority. I see where Judah gets it.

"I can assure you, sir. It is honestly a relief not to have the pressure of pawning him off on someone so I can 'date.' Other than my time at work, I have no reason or desire to be apart from my son," I promise. "Jubilee knows he's part of the deal, however far she and I take this relationship."

"You do understand that a courtship should only occur if marriage is the end goal? It's a serious commitment. From what I understand, you hardly know my daughter," Adam says.

I say a quick but desperate prayer for God to give me the words. I can feel that Adam is at a breaking point. After a breath, the words arrive.

"The night Bennett was born, I didn't know a thing about him. He was a brand-new person. But from that night, I was committed to raising him like I'm committed to breathing the air. Parenting is like that. You get tossed in. The kid doesn't even know himself, and you have to help him figure out everything. But you commit to it because you love the kid more than any of the things you sacrifice for them. I know you're with me on this, Adam. There is evil in this world and there are things to fear. I never understood why commitment would be one of those things." I sigh through my nose to ease my nerves.

The other men shift in their seats. Smiling. Adam speaks. "Pardon Judah and Hakim, but I have to speak on a sensitive subject."

They both agree in the awkward robotic fake speech this family somehow thrives on. He hadn't mentioned James, meaning he only pardoned the unmarried. I know what is coming. He is turning the dad thing around on me.

"My primary concern with you, an experienced *father*, courting my daughter is the fact that once a man has been with a woman, there is no way to return to an attitude of purity as long as he is in a woman's romantic company. I worry that you'd be far more susceptible to temptation than a man who has never been with a woman. Once you drink of the well, so to speak, there is no going back to thirst. I don't know the situation with your son and his mother, but no matter what, this is new territory in this family. Unprecedented, you understand? And I have a right to be concerned for my daughter's honor." Adam is being overly civil, meaning he isn't being civil at all.

"You do have that right, Adam. Every man is susceptible to temptation, regardless of his background." I see that all the men are eager to hear my answer. "But Jesus Christ is the Lord of my life, sir. When we are tempted,

He allows a way of escape, and I constantly ask Him to show me what that is."

"I understand that Bennett's mother is deceased?" Adam continues.

"Yes, sir," I nod, trying to keep the grief from returning again.

Adam tilts his head sideways. "I've met widowers. You don't seem like a widower. You haven't said anything about his mother, fond or otherwise."

"Um, okay…her name was Patrice, and much of who I am is because of her. She was a troubled but wonderful woman. I miss her every day." I stir, mourning welling a little too much. "I see where this is going, and the circumstances of Bennett's origins are a private matter that require a far greater degree of trust and acquaintance than I have obtained here thus far. I guess, just like how Jubilee told me physical contact requires further commitment. Same deal. I will say that it is not what you think, and be careful not to judge," I say with respect.

"Were you even married to her?" Adam starts his rejection of my silence on the matter. But God gives me a stay.

Jubilee crosses the threshold of the front door with caution and wild beauty.

"Sorry to interrupt. Um…Bennett was asking if he could ride a horse? I usually ride about now anyway, and I'd love to teach him. But it's obviously up to you, Elijah." She uses just two fingers to move the hair out of her face and place grenades in my soul.

"I think he'd like that. Could you sit with him, or does he have to be alone? I'm not sure what would happen if his shoe got caught or something." I rise to meet her.

"I'll sit with him to make sure he's stable. I've ridden with my nieces and nephews before, so I also have a helmet that would fit him," Jubilee assures in her sweet but confident voice.

I nod. "I trust you." I'm not sure why or how I feel like I can so soon, but the statement is nothing but truth, and not just when it comes to riding with Bennett.

Jubilee smiles coyly, then looks to her father, her voice becoming more timid. "Um…Dad? Is it okay if I change? I've never ridden in a skirt, but I wasn't sure with our guest if…"

Adam sighs, narrowing his eyes at his daughter in thought.

"Change into…" I inquire of the brothers quietly while trying to pretend I am not examining the flawless caramel skin on Jubilee's lower legs.

"Jeans," Judah mumbles with an eye roll. Hakim speaks up.

"If I were a girl, I'd end up severely injuring myself if I had to have a skirt on while riding a horse. It's not safe since she's never done it and she'll have another person on the horse with her," Hakim says to both Judah and the man who raised him. Then an aside. "Let her put pants on…as if it's another person's choice what my adult sister wears."

"Enough, Hakim." Adam says, then nods solemnly at Jubilee. "Go on and put your jeans on, Jubilee."

"I'll be right down." She heads up the stairs, which are against the wall just inside the front door.

I voice a consideration. "I can't say I've ever seen her in jeans."

Hakim laughs once and pats my back. "There's a very good reason for that. Dad, you realize that when he sees her ride…"

"I said enough, Hakim," Adam says.

"Can we continue this outside? It'll be his first ride. I'd like to see it." I grab my hat from the rack by the door and set it atop my black curls.

"So, you're from Texas and your kid has never ridden a horse?" Judah asks when the men arrive at the fence around the barnyard.

"There's a very good reason for that," I quote Hakim, who is heading to the barn and then leading the horses out with a hat and boots on. I lean clasped hands on a horizontal rung of the fence, hooking a boot heel on another.

But I quoted him incorrectly. Because it's nothing for me when I watch her walk to the barn in funny slippers. It's even a little awkward that she's wearing pants from that distance. But then she comes out of the barn with a riding helmet in her hand, laughing at how excited Bennett is, I cite this as the moment my entire body, mind, and soul fall in love with every part of Jubilee Monroe's. She becomes a piece of me, and I don't know how to extract her if Adam Monroe banishes me from her.

"Lord in Heaven," I think I might have said out loud, then in my heart, *"What are You trying to do to me?"*

She walks out in boots with confidence, swaying all that hair back to put a straw hat on. Then she's almost free as she steps up, swinging those jeans apart across that leather saddle, oblivious to the witchcraft she's working. She's seeing how far back she can sit so that my son can fit on the saddle with her. Then she walks the gelding around the yard to get him used to the feeling. She seems carefree and even ignorant to her unbridled, graceful variety of gorgeous. I feel like I'm seeing all of her.

Leah has put some oats in Bennett's hand, and he is getting acquainted with the horse across the way when Adam, James, and Judah begin to laugh louder than I thought they knew how in the suppressed and subdued family.

I come to and realize they're laughing at me. They've been watching me watch her.

"I apologize, Elijah. We prefer our girls wear skirts, but there's really no way to ride but in jeans," Adam says. "I won't count this one against you."

"It ain't the jeans." I look back over at Jubilee and speak. "It's her soul that's being immodest at the moment."

"I'm sure it feels that way," Adam mocks. "Even so, we encourage the girls to dress modestly."

And I feel like now that I'm eternally Jubilee's, whether or not anyone else knows, I'll speak my mind.

"With all due respect, Adam, it's a man's responsibility to rule over his spirit, not a woman's to do it for him. It's between him and God if he chooses to lust after a woman in his heart. God will judge him. None of that blame should be on a woman simply because she's beautiful. I do agree that a woman should cover whatever she wants left to the imagination. But after that, it is not her responsibility what a man imagines about what he can't see and ain't his." And when I conclude, James is smiling over at his lovely expecting wife, who is singing to their unborn baby as she walks with her mother from the porch. And Judah is thinking. Not being pompous for once. Adam doesn't speak for a moment. Not until he can best me, I gather.

"So, what is it that you're imagining about my daughter right now?" Adam asks, and Judah and James snicker.

"Well, that's between me and the Lord, like I said. But I won't say I don't wonder how her soul will look in a white dress." And at that truth, they are all silent. Anything else would require confrontation. And then Bennett is walking over, and Jubilee is following with the horse.

"Wanna lift him up?" She asks with a smile I haven't seen before. Something about that horse brings her alive. Even her family seems to know that, because they were hesitant to let me see it.

I lift my son onto a horse with Jubilee, who sits back, merely steadying him and teaching him as he takes the reins. Hakim does the same with Jonathan, Hannah's oldest. Hannah and Leah join us at the fence.

I have probably never been as content as I am watching them on that horse. Like she's Bennett's mother, even though she's only known him a few weeks. I watch Bennett's wonder as Jubilee teaches him to control the horse and praises him ecstatically when he gets something right. She is patient and kind and so, so beautiful. I'm in my paradise right now, despite whatever her family thinks of me.

We watch in silence a time, and then Judah finally asks it. "So is Jubilee courting a twenty-eight-year-old black man with a son?"

Adam clears his throat. "Her curfew is ten on weekdays and eleven on weekends, and I want to know the whereabouts and time frame of each chaperoned outing. She needs to check in in the middle of each outing if your chaperone is Bennett. Obviously, excessive physical displays of affection are unnecessary at this point, and telephone communication, which I will personally monitor, should remain at a minimum. Let's be clear that I do not trust you, Elijah. You have too many secrets. But I trust her, and she seems to have her heart set on this. Don't make me regret this. I'm taking a big chance on you."

"Why would you take a chance like that on something as precious as your daughter?" I shrug, both offended and trying to return from cloud nine.

"Because your son is a good boy. That doesn't happen on its own. For that, and your obvious love for the Lord, I'll allow you to court her." We shake hands, which Jubilee sees from a distance, tilting her head.

Hannah and Leah try not to look too excited. But it's far too easy. So, I stir the pot. "Hannah, do you make rings?"

"What, like engagement rings?" she asks, surprised. "I can't tell if you're joking."

Adams chuckles. "Obviously, we should touch base again if things do move in that direction."

I sigh disbelief. "You mean even though courtship generally leads to marriage, and you've given me permission to court her, I'd still need to…"

"Ask for her hand, yes," Adam clarifies. "At this point, you've only asked to spend time with her. If you wanted to get married, I'd essentially be handing her over into your care for the rest of her life. There's quite a difference. There are things I'd like to discuss before then."

"I don't disagree with that time-honored tradition, Adam. I'm just not sure what else we'd need to discuss when that time comes that we didn't today." I backpedal, "Not so. There is one more thing I'd want to say to you."

"And what's that?" Adam asks.

"Um…thank you. Where I come from, fathers would never think to protect their little girls the way you do. So, thank you for protecting her."

He is flattered, but doesn't let on except with silence.

"But honestly, I think it makes much more sense to ask for a woman's hand in marriage than to ask to spend time with her."

"It's just the way we do things." Adam defines exactly his philosophy on all things liberty.

"Understood." With a satisfied smirk, I end the discussion, though Adam thinks he's won.

Jonathan and Hakim dismount and lead Lightning over to the fence. Then Jubilee and Bennett ride over right as Hakim sees his sister and mother's smiles.

He gasps. "You said yes? I thought you were gonna give him the boot!"

"Dad?" Jubilee asks, in just as much disbelief as Adam heads to the porch.

"You ask that Elijah." He yells from halfway to the house. James chuckles bitterly until one look from Hannah halts him.

Jubilee watches me as I walk into the enclosure to help Bennett down.

"Did he…I mean, you're still here, so that's a good sign," Jubilee asks.

I chuckle after Bennett runs from the enclosure with Jonathan. "Said he trusted your opinion, like you said. So you must have a favorable one."

She laughs once. Tosses her hair. Then nods. Clears her throat.

"Do you ride, Elijah?" She finally asks from the horse. Her way of easing me into whatever the title of my new role in her life is.

"Of course. My mother had a boyfriend who trained horses," I reply. "Bit out of practice, but I could give it a shot."

"Dad, do Thunder and Lightning count as chaperones?" It takes me a second to realize Jubilee means the horses when she yells to her father.

"I think so!" Hannah smiles a little smile, answering for her father. "I'll look after Bennett."

"As long as you don't dismount." Adam probably feels like he's losing something as he follows the rest of the family inside the house for the last hour of daylight.

Hakim hands me a carrot for Lightning with a word of warning. "She's stubborn and not as tame as she acts most of the time. But if you give her enough time to warm up to you, she'll trust you forever and most likely won't run off. Oh, and this carrot is for my mare." He winks as I laugh. "Congrats."

I spend a moment introducing myself to Lightning. Then I mount her with ease, having spent many years riding daily until Terry decided to kick me and Mom out. But I cast away that painful thought. And Jubilee looks at me like the first time a child sees a butterfly. Her smile makes me a little uncomfortable, so I use Lightning to make a full circle around Thunder and Jubilee.

"Let me show you the trail. Lightning knows it, so just trust her," she tells me as I circle.

"Lead the way."

I watch Jubilee's hair flow gently against her back for a time when we are riding the horses single file. Then Lightning takes me up alongside Jubilee when the trodden path widens. I see Jubilee's form against dusk and let out a high-pitched sigh.

"What?" She giggles.

"You are the most beautiful thing I've ever seen," I confess.

"You're a subtle one," she jokes. "But...besides Bennett, right? He's beautiful."

"Woman. The most beautiful woman," I correct. "And subtle takes too long. I'd be proposing marriage right now if your daddy didn't say I couldn't."

Then she laughs out loud accidentally just before she tucks her lips. The horse. It just frees her. "So, was Bennett's mother, rest her soul, a whirlwind romance? I assume she was quite beautiful as well."

She's guarding her heart. It's fair. There are details she deserves to know before agreeing to further commitments. But is it too soon to tell her?

She winces. "I didn't mean any judgment, Elijah. It doesn't change my mind about anything, whatever you tell me. I'm just curious. But you're certainly entitled to your secrets."

Her gentleness makes me open up. I do so cryptically. "I didn't acquire Bennett through conventional means. I didn't know about him until the night he was born."

"Oh," Jubilee processes. First assumes, then smiles. "Are you saying he isn't your son?"

"Course, he is. In every way possible except biologically."

"Impossible," Jubilee says matter-of-factly. "Bennett has your eyes."

"He has his mother's eyes," I correct with sadness.

Jubilee giggles. "I've never seen a blonde with eyes like yours. His mother was blonde."

"What makes you—"

"He has blond in his hair. He didn't get it from your side."

"Bennett's mother was black, and he has her eyes."

"That's—"

"I *also* have his mother's eyes." My voice is shaking as I share.

"Oh. So he's...I mean, biologically...your brother? Half, I assume?"

"You're clever. That's sexy."

"Excuse me?" Jubilee guffaws. "Please tell me you don't actually find that appropriate."

"Oh...um..." I seek a correction. "I like it that you're intelligent."

"Thank you." Jubilee giggles.

"I find it sexy." I laugh and she gasps.

She laughs aloud, shocked and amused, then clears her throat. "The second time you gave me a ride, my father told me you were just trying to talk me into your bed. You're not doing a good job proving him wrong."

I snicker. "Every man is constantly trying to talk his woman into his bed. That's the way we are. I just prefer it also be *her* bed, and that some of that talking is wedding vows. With where I came from, it's obvious to me that God intended sex for marriage. Didn't even need to test that theory."

"Good." She nods. Pleased. Then she narrows her eyes and considers the facts in a stayed gaze. "So, you adopted your baby brother...a disabled child...when you were twenty-one and single?"

"Well, you can't legally adopt a child, in Texas at least, until he's two," I confirm. "But he's been in my care since he came home from the NICU."

"What would possess you to do that?" She's in disbelief.

"He's my family and he needed me. Or...I think maybe I needed him."

"Wow," she says. "That's really…"

"Sexy?" I chuckle.

A sensual little glint creeps into her eyes with the smile. "Something like that."

The horses come to a stop.

"Why did they stop? Is the Angel of the Lord in the trail?"

"Hakim and I always stop here before we give them the cue to gallop."

"Thought you'd never ask." Since Thunder is apparently faster than Lightning, I get to watch that black hair straight back in the wind. Back in the barn when we unsaddle the horses, I hear a clear call from the Spirit when she takes off her hat and rustles her hair. I'm glad for God's well-timed indication that she's already mine forever. Otherwise, I'd be taking her into my arms to savor the moment instead.

"Great ride, Elijah. We'll have to do it again sometime." She smiles, removing boots and replacing them with those ugly slippers.

"Are you allowed to ask me out like that? Seems provocative for our first non-chance meeting," I flirt.

But she giggles as we leave the barn. "Technically, no. But we're courting. It doesn't really matter who asks who, right?"

"What did you say to him?" I wonder, apparently out loud. "Your father doesn't like me and doesn't seem to be easily convinced. But he said he trusts you and your heart was set on this. Thank you for keeping your promise with the pitchers and everything. But what did you say? Or was it just God working?"

"It was God working, but…it was also definitely what I told him."

"Alright, let me have it."

"I…" Jubilee bites her lip. Caught. Then she examines my waiting eyes and sees that I'll likely take wiles in place of the response she doesn't want to give. "I think maybe someday I might tell you that."

Thirteen

Jubilee

"When can I see you?" He asks me on the phone Monday morning. I'm still recovering from yesterday when he told me I am the most beautiful woman he's ever seen.

Woman. That alone shook me. And it had come from him, handsome and full of life and pain and experience I only hope I can someday read all of. When I watched him mount my brother's horse and then ride a circle around me like he wasn't at all as rusty as he claimed to be, that's probably when I fell completely in love. Which I can't even explain or fully justify. I've known the man a month. We met accidentally over gasoline and smiles. How could I be in love?

After he and Bennett left last night and Hannah and James headed home, too, Dad told me he's still a little "iffy" about the age gap and experience, but he likes Elijah's faith and thinks we could have a "smart" union. Hakim and Judah told me that Elijah really enjoys *looking* at me. I'm not sure how I feel about that. Elijah is also in clear violation of the telephone conversation rules laid down last night after our ride. Dad explained, as he watched us exchange phone numbers, that he reads every text, and every phone conversation is to be as public as an in-person conversation. I am in my bedroom, groggy from sleep, and Elijah called early enough to know it. But I don't correct him. Because all I know is that when his voice is the first in my ear on Monday morning, I feel like I could stand starting my morning this way every day for the rest of my life. Preferably with those sad onyx eyes beside me.

"You can see me whenever you want," I reply in a low tone amid the tingle of deviance and the ache of love.

"I prefer today. And tomorrow and the next day and so on and so forth until one of us dies." I can hear the smile in his voice. "But let's start with today."

"Okay." I smile too. "Um…I work from two until eight on Mondays."

"Seven to seven for me now. They just moved the shift back to what it was, thank God. I just dropped off Bennett and I'm headed over to work now. We could try this evening. Are you allowed to come to my house?" he asks.

My heart seizes. "I don't know how Dad would take that, and that's pretty close to my curfew."

"Understood. Well, where will you be at one? That's usually when I can take a lunch. I have to stay close to work."

"Where do you work?" I wince. He's technically my boyfriend and practically a stranger.

"Sunny Rest Nursing Home. I figured Hakim told you, sorry. It's about three blocks from where you work, so I thought it might be convenient for you. We can even sit on a bench outside and eat together. Bennett won't be around, but there are usually a lot of my nosey coworkers walking around, and at least one of the residents is like family. So we wouldn't be alone or in public with oblivious strangers," he suggests.

I know it'll take some convincing with my father, but I'm already counting the minutes until I can see him. "That's borderline with the chaperones, but it's probably my only chance to see you, so I'll meet you there. Text it to me like you didn't just call, okay?"

"Oh, are we sneaking around now?" he flirts.

"I'm just not sure what could happen over the phone. I never understood this rule. You can call me whenever you like, Elijah."

"At the altar?" He asks after swallowing a bite of the sandwich I brought him. "First kiss in front of everyone? At the *altar*."

"I don't understand how that's weird." I giggle at his disbelieving tone.

"I didn't expect that one is all. I have a friend. She's actually my pastor's kid. And she's engaged. But she and her fiancé kiss all the time. She's a good Christian girl and they've never crossed the line. I guess I never considered it to be sin." Elijah shrugs.

"Well, it's not a sin, but it can lead to temptation, I'm told. My dad's courting rules are designed to keep us from temptation." I take a tiny bite of my sandwich, timid with him still.

"Which I respect. Boundaries are good. It just seems like strict and specific rules imposed by someone not in the relationship can put limits on the liberty of the cross," he points out. "In Christ, we're free to do anything that isn't sin. Sometimes we *need* to take liberties to serve Him better."

"Kissing is not a necessary liberty," I implore.

"I'm not just talking about kissing. I'm just a tad concerned that you follow Daddy's rules and don't always know *why*. Shouldn't you allow God to guide you according to His liberty in your life? Like with the phone."

"Liberty is a slippery slope. Dad says it's best to just stick close to the heart of God."

" 'Dad says', huh? What if the heart of God *is* liberty? And at what point is *your* liberty going to be according to your own conscience, not your father's? As in First Corinthians ten, 'For why is my liberty judged by another man's conscience?' " he challenges.

"What if I *agree* with my father? Also in First Corinthians ten we learn that all things are lawful, but not all things are helpful or beneficial. We have to be careful not to be a stumbling block for those who are weak. We have to look out for the well-being of others per God's commands, not just what feels right to us," I argue.

"Agreed. But is it helpful for those who are weak if you live self-righteously? Who benefits, Jubilee, when you hold the whole world to a standard that is not the heart of God, but the fruit of one man's conscience? The Holy Spirit convicts us as *individuals* for a reason."

"But if we are convicted by the Holy Spirit, it should show in righteous actions."

"Absolutely. But the Garden of Eden had countless trees for Adam to tend. Only one of them was sinful to eat from. It's like your daddy chose his favorite sinless tree and expected everyone to *only* eat from that."

"But this isn't *Eden*, Elijah," I practically interrupt him with passion. "This is the world after the fall, where sin is no longer contained in one tree. It's everywhere. It's in all of us and in every molecule of this world." I look to the nearby building. "There are wise elders in nursing homes whose families have forgotten them. We live in a world where perfect little boys are born without legs, Elijah. There is sickness and malice and famine and war. And *death*. So yes, if there's a tree even close to the tree of life, I'm eating from *that* one."

"Understood and appreciated, Jubilee," Elijah retorts. "But…"

"But what?"

"Well, in order to obey our call to Christ, which includes preaching the gospel to the hurting and forgotten, and feeding the orphans…we have to be willing to approach their tree. Even if you're scared it might be near the forbidden one."

"So are you saying the Lord would have us sin to serve Him?"

"Never, Jubilee. God always gives us a way of escape," Elijah practically whispers, "But just as there were many trees in Eden, some of them more exotic than others, there are ways God has us serve Him that may not fall within one man's rules. Pretty soon, that man will start to worship that one 'safe' tree, and his own attempt at righteousness can become an idol. In reality, none of us is righteous without Christ."

And I have to think on it. Suddenly, I'm not intimidated by his age, but rather comforted by his wisdom, even if he needed nine-and-a-half years more to attain it. Then the Spirit reminds me, and I laugh.

"Tear down the idols."

"What's so funny?" he asks.

"That makes sense." I nod. "I guess I never thought of self-righteousness as an idol."

"Anything can be an idol so long as we put the focus on that and not on the Lord." Elijah shrugs. "It is all for Him. If at some point it ain't, you got yourself an idol."

"Wow. How can a man teach my Spirit more during one lunch hour than my father did in nineteen years?" That's what I'm thinking. Aloud, I only tuck a hair behind my ear and smile.

"That's an interesting look." Elijah smirks. He'd enjoyed it, apparently.

"Sorry, I just. You're very wise. And I'm…very young." I sigh. "I feel like an apprentice or something."

" 'Let no one despise your youth, but be an example to the believers in word, in conduct, in love, in spirit, in faith, in purity.' " Elijah quotes First Timothy. "You're that example to me, Jubilee. I've never met a woman like you, nineteen or ninety years old. You can learn from me, and I've already learned things from you. It goes both ways. I don't want us talking about our age gap again."

I nod compliance, deeply thrilled by his view of me. "What have you learned from *me*?"

"Reverence, for one. I've never seen someone honor their father like you do. You're teaching me. I'm slow. But I'm learning." He captures my eyes. "But I have a favor to ask…if we're to the point of asking favors."

"Sure. Anything, Elijah." I ready myself for service.

"From now on, I want *you* to decide how far you take the liberty of Christ. I'd never want you to sin or feel like you're teetering on it or make decisions based on the desires of your flesh. But don't use your father's convictions to decide your own. Search your spirit. Search the Word. Pray like crazy. Be your own godly woman." Elijah is asking more than he knows. "Because what if you haven't even found your fruit tree yet?"

"But I still have to honor my father," I remind him. "I do live in his house and I have to abide by his rules."

"If you live according to God's call for your life, then your father will be honored, Jubilee." Elijah smirks, then ventures the bold. "But hopefully someday, you'll live in *my* house, and we'll have to lay down our own rules together. I'd like you to have the foundation of knowing God's purpose for you. So seek Him, okay?"

"Elijah. Oh, Elijah. Marry me today." The heart song. The words? "I'll do my best."

Fourteen

Elijah

"Okay, so what is courting?" Jessie asks, swimming her decorated hand playfully through Garrett's after service while Bennett plays on the nearby playground. Four hands are clasped in front of Jessie's abdomen, and Garrett is cozied up behind her, arms wrapped around, his head rested on her shoulder.

"It's where her father would kill me if I touched her like that."

"Like what? Like, at all?"

"Basically." I shrug. "I'm thinking I need to marry her sooner than I originally thought, just to get away from his rules."

"*That* isn't a good reason to get married," Garrett teases.

"We're already headed for the altar. Just…probably sooner."

"Because 'rules'?" Jessie winks.

"She got caught making plans with me behind her dad's back and he revoked her phone privileges for two days. She's a grown woman. The sooner I can break her out of that madhouse, the better."

"But you've known her how long?"

"A month. We've been courting a week. It's long enough."

"'Lijah, that is not even a whole menstrual cycle for some people. You have *not* known her long enough. Sorry," Jessie reasons.

"I agree." Lucinda comes from behind me with the opinion. I know Jordan is with her when Jessie and Garrett take to social distancing like it's 2020.

"Why's that? You on the PMS train too?" I laugh at the parted young people as I ask for clarification.

"We haven't met her or even seen a picture of her." Cindy hips her hands. "How can you marry a girl we haven't met?"

"More importantly, have you worshipped with her?" my pastor implores.

"No, I haven't had the privilege. She goes to a little Baptist outfit a few blocks from here. She isn't permitted to worship here, and I am not exactly welcome to worship there, even if I wanted to."

"IFB or SBC?" Jordan asks.

"Uh, the fundamental one."

"Ah, I see."

"But we agree on most points of theology, don't worry. That's most of what we talk about."

"Not on the phone, though." Jessie rolls her eyes.

"No. But I'm late to go have lunch with her family and get a reprimand for the phone." I check the time on my phone, then yell at the playground. "Ben, let's go see Miss Jubilee."

In the two-second distraction, Jessie rips my phone out of my hand like an annoying kid sister. But I allow it. I know what she's looking for. They all gasp when I presume Jessie arrives at a photograph of my love laughing at something Bennett said off camera. There is a sunset in that one, so I used the opportunity to pretend to take a picture of it, and instead captured Jubilee.

"You can*not* be serious. Is this her?" Jessie frets, turning around the exact picture I thought, then flipping it back so all Durants and Garrett can admire Jubilee's beauty.

"Yes. You happy now? You've seen a picture."

"India, right? Do people from India always look so young?" Lucinda muses. "How old did you say she was?"

"I probably didn't say. Love y'all. I'll see you next week. Let's go, Ben."

I see Jubilee daily, usually with Bennett around, unless she joins me for lunch at work. We usually convene at the Monroe home for dinner on Sundays and Bennett rides Thunder with Jubilee. We also try to catch a ride together after most of the family leaves.

The third Sunday after our ride, I keep her in the barn a couple minutes longer. I know immediately I'm asking for temptation. We're in complete privacy when I step in front of her to block her exit from the barn. Save the one touch at the market, and a handshake when we met, it's the closest we've ever been. I hate that.

So, I reach out and allow the back of my hand to graze her satin-smooth upper arm. Just once. And she closes her eyes in contentment, then opens them and looks to the ground in shame.

"Elijah..."

"Sorry." I cross my arms, trying not to smile. "I just wanted to tell you something."

"What do you want to tell me?" She crosses her own arms and stays her eyes on the ground.

"I'm in love with you," I confess.

She looks up at me with an adorably scrunched nose. "I sorta figured that."

"Yeah, but you deserve to hear it from me."

"Well, since you certainly deserve the same," she starts, then gives me a nervous sigh before, "I am also in love with you."

"Jubilee, you don't need to say that just because I did. It's just that when we came over here a couple weeks ago to ask about courting you, I told *Bennett* I was in love with you, and I didn't want you hearing that from him."

"That's really soon after knowing me." The words sound like a warning, but the tone is pure flirtation. I stay tuned for the next thought. "But a couple of weeks ago when we came home from the market, dad sat me down and told me he'd really rather not allow you to court me."

"Yeah, but he said you—"

She interjects: "told him he *had* to let me court you. Because I'm in love with you and God told me to submit to you. That's the only reason he even spoke with you."

"Is that true or is that just what you told him?" I don't know how my knees aren't giving out right now.

"I'm not foolish enough to lie to my father, Elijah." She smiles. "He's a judge. Half his job is spotting a lie." She shifts her weight to the other hip. "But did you lie to Bennett?"

"No, I don't do that. I like to flood his world with the truth so that spotting a lie is easy. Sometimes I tell him *too* much. That day, I even slipped and told him I hope to *marry* you. I told your dad the same thing. I'm having trouble not shouting that one from the mountaintops."

"Good." She nods, reminding me of that market again. "One chance, right?"

I smile, then apologize, gesturing to the soft skin I'd just enjoyed. "Still, I really shouldn't have touched you without asking. I'm sorry."

But she surprises me. "I've been searching the Bible for God's heart on things and liberty, and it doesn't say anywhere that you can't touch me."

"Your dad says it will invite undue temptation." It appears I am switching sides.

"But...?" She knows I'm not done.

"But the other night when that waiter thought you were my daughter, it could have been avoided if I was allowed to display my romantic affection somehow. We're in love, right? Sometimes I want a tiny reassurance of that. It's not tempting, especially in public or around Bennett."

"And your assurance matters to me more than what Dad will say. I think if we set some reasonable boundaries, I don't mind some innocent affection."

By late July, I start holding her hand when she gives me permission, even though most of her siblings waited for engagement for that. I begin putting an arm around her at restaurant booths across from Bennett. Grazing her back or waist to guide her and claim her when we are in public together. It's no more than the way I might touch Bennett, and that is our agreed boundary. Sure, between us it's romance. But I love that Bennett disturbs nothing when he divides our hands during walks in the park, holding one of each. I've always prayed for a woman to hold his other hand.

As we grow closer, which happens in just weeks, Jubilee talks about Gideon. She tells me she now has a nagging urgency like she is to defeat the Midian army all alone and tear down idols in a night. She isn't quite aware what that means and asks for my wisdom. I tell her to seek God and ask Him to reveal it to her in His time. But I know I need to buy a ring.

After a month of courting, I am at work, counting the seconds until lunchtime when Jubilee will arrive. Our plan is to walk to a place for takeout and eat in the courtyard as usual. She ordinarily brings food with her, but I am too chivalrous to allow that to continue.

It's a slow day again. No one is too sick, no one is dying. I am spending this morning yawning through passing out medication until I hear a familiar, welcome sound I've grown to love over the past few years.

"You're a stubborn old bat, *Bisabuela*! Just use the walker. No one will fault you for being ninety years old and needing it."

Jessalyn Durant is a schoolteacher, but I always wish she'd volunteer at this nursing home more often. She's a stern but kind presence. I look down the hall to see that Lucinda is at old Milagra's other arm. Millie was born in Mexico and married the missionary who led her to Christ. They moved back to the States early in their marriage. The culture, the language, and the rich sienna skin have faded in generations of women who have consistently married blonds. So it's a lovely spectrum of a sight when three generations, one missing due to an untimely demise, walk down the hall in tandem to take an old woman for a walk. No walker required.

"Well hello, ladies!" I greet them, "Miss Millie giving you trouble again?"

"Well if I don't give them hell, they will never get it otherwise!" Millie, frail in body, but sharp in mind.

"True, I certainly don't think heaven will be the same if any of you choose not to dwell there," I follow their slow steps, then grab a cane from a closet and hand it to Millie, "Compromise?"

"Anything for you, Mr. Elijah," Millie winks, then outs me as she takes to a just-as-slow hobble down the long corridor, "Has he told you ladies about the hot dates with his gorgeous little lady?"

"Uh, no." Jessie looks at me, fire in her eyes. "You can't be talking about Jubilee."

"Yes, that's it. She's here twice a week eating lunch with him out in the courtyard. They seem smitten," Millie tattles. "I make sure to watch in case he tries anything too fresh."

"I welcome your eyes, Miss Millie. Jubilee and I are courting. We aren't permitted to be together alone."

"Last we heard, he had just started courting her but was talking about marrying her." Cindy sighs. "Apparently she can't be bothered to come to church with him, so we haven't met. I've seen one picture."

"Oh, she's beautiful, Cindy," Millie rasps. "I'm sure Elijah hasn't looked far enough past that to see if she's a God-fearing woman."

I try not to take offense. "She attends church with her family. We don't worship together yet, but we certainly do so apart. She is possibly the godliest woman I know."

All three women are offended and tell me so in a noisy clamor, some of it in Spanish. I merely smirk, not correcting myself in the presence of three godly women. A missionary's widow, a pastor's wife, and the fiancée of an aspiring pastor. They are silenced, and suddenly impressed.

"Okay, now I insist on meeting this woman," Cindy says first.

"Does she happen to be meeting you for lunch *today*?" Jessie takes it further.

"In about an hour, yes." The confession comes reluctantly.

"Take a long lunch. We'll go somewhere and sit down. You don't have a family to vet this young woman, so I'm taking the initiative," Cindy, Jessie's older version, enforces her law, intentionally loudly enough that the nurse at the desk hears.

"Fine by me." The nurse took the cue. "It's a Q-word day, and someone needs to solve the mystery of that girl he's always eating with."

"Janet, you're no help." I laugh. "I need to run it by Jubilee to be sure she's ready for that kind of—"

"Don't you dare. I won't have you warning her. I want to meet her as she is, not as you've groomed her for us," Cindy decides. "Now if you'll excuse me, I'm taking a very slow, long walk with my *abuela* and daughter." They breach the exit doors into the sunshine.

When Jubilee arrives, stopping at the front desk, as usual, I am already approaching her.

"Hey!" She turns to me, dressed in the same dress she'd been wearing the day I gave her a ride into town. Packaged perfectly for any surprise, as always.

"Hey, uh…is it alright if we change our lunch plans a little?"

"Oh, are you busy? I don't mind a rain check."

"No, I'd just like for us to go out. Sit down."

"Bennett's at daycare. We…I'd love to Elijah, but without a chaperone—"

On cue, Jessie and Cindy arrive at the desk from Millie's room, ready for lunch. When I gesture to them to begin the introduction, Jubilee speaks instead.

"Lucinda. And Jessie," Jubilee shakes their hands in introduction, but knows them like family.

"You're earning points already." Jessie giggles.

"He speaks very fondly of you, and often," Jubilee says.

"Not as fondly and often as he speaks of *you*," Jessie notes under her breath.

"Ladies, this is Jubilee. My…" I laugh at nerves and uncertainty. "Girlfriend? That one always seems weird to me. What does your father prefer?"

Jubilee is the steady reassurer in this case, "He referred to you as my 'suitor' the other day. I don't think his terms would make sense to most, Elijah. 'Girlfriend' is accurate."

Lucinda looks her over after the introductions, and I place a reassuring, loving hand on Jubilee's back. I see Cindy notice the modest length of the dress, the poise and grace of the young woman. But mostly, the beauty on par with her hopes for me. She has feather earrings and a practical handbag and bright eyes full of youth and wit.

"I think you'll do nicely," Cindy says aloud.

Jubilee laughs once, not allowing her nerves to take root, "Will Bennett be joining us?"

"Uh, no. This is an adults only meet-and-greet," Jessie jokes, "Bennett will totally defend you no matter what. He's an unfair advantage. We already know how *he* feels about you."

When we are seated at the quiet restaurant, the women don't hesitate to start in.

"Jubilee, you are astoundingly gorgeous," Lucinda says. "But you know he doesn't have money, right?"

"I'm not destitute, Ms. Cindy. And I'm sorry I haven't been able to get us all together until now. I'll still work on getting Garrett and Jordan into the mix. But you've been busy with your wedding, Jessie, and I've been…"

"Spending every spare second with a woman who is supposedly 'not a prospect because you met once or twice at a gas station.' " Jessie giggles.

"You watch it. I had no idea what God was doing." I laugh.

"Congratulations, by the way. Elijah and Bennett are both excited for you." Jubilee addresses Jessie, "When is the big day?"

"Two-and-a-half weeks away. And thank you." Jessie simmers, sobering at Jubilee's sincerity. "I hope you know we're just teasing, Jubilee. We've been praying for this old guy to find someone for as long as I can remember, and we're honestly very happy for him."

"No harm done, Jessie." Jubilee smiles warmly. "I wouldn't mind you bringing up any concerns, though. I want Elijah to be sure about this, and I don't know if he should do that without your approval. Your family is important to him."

"Jubilee, I love these two, but God approves. Why do I need their opinion?" I try to keep the mood light. Worried they'll ridicule Jubilee's traditional tone and expectations.

"You wanted my father's." Jubilee shrugs.

"Correction, I *required* your father's."

"And I require theirs." Jubilee settles the matter, looking back to Lucinda and Jessie with a smile as I nod, sitting back and watching whatever may unfold.

"Oh, you have *my* approval," Jessie allows immediately. "Mom?"

Lucinda has been looking over the young stranger who captured her dear friend's heart. It seems she is unable to find a single physical flaw, until she considers why. "There is the one thing Elijah didn't mention. If...I may."

"Mom!" Jessie whisper-yells. "Do we have to do this?"

"Jubilee invited me. Her father did this with Elijah. Dad did this with Garrett. I want to do it with her."

"You may, Mrs. Durant."

"Cindy, please," Lucinda allows.

"It's alright, Ms. Cindy. Jubilee and I try to ride above reproach if we can, so I'm not sure what could be bothering you," I admit. "But know that if you ask her anything I don't like, I'll defend her."

"I expect you will." Cindy chuckles. "It's just that Bennett said something, but I wasn't sure what he meant. And I saw the one picture, but I thought I was seeing things. Now it makes sense why you'd care so much about what your family thinks." Cindy hesitates no more. "From what Elijah's said, you seem a bit older, so maybe I'm mistaken. But you *look* about Jessie's age."

Jessie looks offended. "Are you saying I'm immature?"

Cindy takes to tact. "I'm saying Elijah is several years older than you and has more life experience, and in a wife, he'd require someone closer to his age. He has always told me you are far too young for him, Jessie."

Jubilee sighs. Embarrassed. She bites a lip and looks at me.

"You can answer yourself, can't you, Jubilee?" Cindy insists.

Jubilee nods. "Of course. It's just that Elijah made an ultimatum about this a few weeks ago, and I don't want to disrespect him by mentioning something he asked that we not discuss."

"You wouldn't be disrespecting me by answering a direct question, Jubilee. We have nothing to hide. But let me field this one, if that's okay, Cindy."

"Oh, a sensitive subject." Cindy winces. "Go on, Elijah."

"Well, Jubilee's a *little* younger than me." I wince. Jubilee snorts laughter. Looks dotingly into my eyes and I inquire in a whisper. "What, is that not true?"

"You said we have nothing to hide," Jubilee reminds me.

Jessie giggles, hand to mouth. "They are so precious. And Jubilee, you're like my favorite person right now."

"Okay, so Jubilee is a little bit younger..." I say again. Jubilee tilts her head. I sigh. "Than...Jessie."

Lucinda gasps. "So when Bennett said nineteen, he really meant *nineteen*?"

"Yes," Jubilee answers, "My birthday is very close to Bennett's. Age was one of the first things we discussed when we met."

"Oh, so you *just* turned nineteen." Jessie is wide-eyed.

"You'll be twenty-nine soon. That's nearly a decade, Elijah." Lucinda warns.

"It's a number," I defend. "I love this woman. Her age is irrelevant to me."

"My father didn't like it either." Jubilee softly comes to my rescue. "He is especially unhappy with Elijah having enough life experience that he is a father."

"Well, but..." Jessie begins, then backtracks, not knowing what Jubilee knows.

"Bennett is his biological *brother*, I know," Jubilee continues, "But Elijah won't let me tell my father that."

"I only tell that to people I trust." I wink at Jubilee.

"I respect that, but it makes my father assume that you..." There, Jubilee's confidence halts, and she silences. Perceptive Cindy perks up at the sudden silence. I unleash a satisfied smile.

After a time of calculating, Cindy whispers. "No wonder, Elijah. Forgive me for doubting your choice."

"I'm lost." Jessie laughs.

"Um…me too," Jubilee admits.

"I'm willing to bet this gentleman has never even kissed you." Cindy keeps her voice low and discreet.

"No, ma'am."

"And obviously…nothing else…" Cindy confirms.

"Lord, no, Cindy. Her father'd have buried me by now." I am embarrassed, pretending to cover Jubilee's ears.

"Oh…" Jessie suspects where her mother is going.

"Things like that are for marriage. I've never even had a girlfriend until Jubilee. I've had Bennett."

"No *wonder*," Cindy repeats her own conviction.

"No wonder what?" I worry.

"Women your age, Elijah…I suppose it's not unheard of, but generally…Why did I never consider that when I was trying to set you up with single moms?"

"'Lijah wanted a virgin," Jessie says teasingly, thoroughly rattling Jubilee, though it only shows in a slight blush to her cheeks.

I frantically try to simmer the young Jessie. "That's not exactly mealtime conversation where Jubilee comes from, Jessie."

"Sorry," Jessie whispers.

"It's okay." Jubilee clears her throat. "I understood your meaning."

"And you're not wrong. It was always a dream of mine to find someone…"

"Undefiled?" Cindy suggests.

"I'd have taken whoever it is God had for me, of course. And God can forgive and redeem any person or situation. There's just certain things that I hoped to have in common with the woman God made for me, and I am very thankful that He answered that prayer how He did. All this time, I thought I was just waiting. But God was just preparing *her*."

"Yeah, but why didn't God make it so you two were closer in age? You could have adopted Bennett *together*, right?" Jessie surmises.

"Well…" Jubilee interjects something that I'm not sure I can handle. "Yes. I do wish I could have been around, and the proper age, when Elijah was frantically searching for help with Bennett. But the truth is, as the youngest girl of eight children, I am accustomed to spending time with people much older than me."

Jessie gasps. "You like older men."

"Well…" Jubilee tries to stave off embarrassment. "I like *Elijah*. But though it makes my father uneasy, I do find Elijah's age to be an advantage. I get to learn from his experience and biblical knowledge. I have the privilege of seeing him with his child. But, to my delight, he is *not* experienced in some areas that might make me uneasy. Elijah is the best of all worlds."

Jessie's arms flail in excitement. She is bubbling with questions. "Are you from one of those families where they don't believe in birth control and there are like tons of kids?"

I laugh embarrassment, despite wondering Jubilee's stance. "Jessie, that is a wildly inappropriate thing to ask, even *not* at the table."

"Okay, that's probably true." Jessie winces. "But I hope an invitation to my wedding isn't too inappropriate? You are exactly the "plus one" this guy needs. I'd love for you to come, Jubilee."

"Thank you for the invitation, Jessie. I do love weddings."

"Go ahead and put down that plus one for your head count, Jessie. But I'll still need to get her daddy's approval," I answer. "All of our outings have to be approved. I even had to text him about the change today, though he did like the chaperone situation better. A wedding might be different. But for you, Jessie, I'll try."

Fifteen

Elijah

One Wednesday in August, my maroon pickup takes Bennett and Jubilee to a quiet little lake an hour from home. I set up three fishing poles and Bennett sits twenty feet away. It's enough space for an adult conversation.

"I'm amazed Daddy dearest let you come. Lots of 'evil could befall you' at this completely deserted lake with me and my son." I know from her giggle that she's coming my way on things.

"You know, he's not so bad, Elijah. Believe it or not, he's a lot softer than he used to be," she muses, braiding her hair to keep it from blowing with the wind. A worthy reason for restraint.

"Lordy. How did he used to be?"

"Well, for example, he—" Then Jubilee silently scolds herself. Swiftly shaking her head.

"Jubilee, I'm a safe confidant. If you need to tell me something…"

"Well I *don't* need to. We don't talk about it," Jubilee answers, frustrated. Then her heart changes before my eyes. "I love my father. But I hated him for this."

"Tell me," I encourage.

Jubilee sighs. Bites a lip, and nods.

"That bad, huh?" I can see it's prominent in her heart.

"I feel like I'm gossiping just saying it." Jubilee winces.

"You're not gossiping, you're confiding," I remind her.

"Okay… just…it's a big deal. Don't tell a soul."

"Of course."

"Well, all my siblings who are married got married for love. For the most part. Noah and Penny are so cute, as you know. And Aaron and Katie met when they were camp counselors together at our church camp. James and Hannah have been in love since they were six. Maren and Priscilla have been best friends since they were babies, so Maren was always around, and she and Isaac eventually fell for each other. So, I don't want you to think it's the norm in my family…" Jubilee sighs.

"Priscilla." I note the void.

"She hated Elliot," Jubilee supplies. "She has Obsessive Compulsive Disorder. It's relatively controlled most of the time, but I remember her coming home from church one time and washing her hands for twenty minutes because Elliot held her hand during a prayer. He was the guy who wouldn't shower and his clothes were always disheveled."

"I don't like where this is going."

She continues, not missing a beat. "When they were barely eighteen, Elliot came to Dad. He lied and said they'd been growing fond of one another and he'd like to court Priscilla. Elliot is from a wealthy family. He's still an excellent provider. Their home is massive. And Priscilla likes nice things. Dad didn't consult Priscilla, but he thought it made sense. So, he agreed to let Elliot court her."

"But she still hated him," I assume.

"Yeah. But Dad still forced her to court him because he'd made an agreement, despite it being based on a lie. She begged him and cried her eyes out. I'd never seen her do that. Isaac and Maren, who were newlyweds at the time, also begged Dad to listen to her. But he made her."

"Your father said courting is as good as marriage in your family."

"It is. And Priscilla's a martyr. She hated courting him, but eventually agreed to marry him of her own volition. God knows why. Probably to allow Dad to save face. I remember she almost called off the wedding the night before, but went through with it after all. Now they've been married a decade and have children together and everything. They get along okay, I guess."

"Jubilee, this is serious. Are you telling me your sister is married to and has children with a man that everyone knows disgusts her because her father thought he was a good match? That's arranged marriage. *Forced* marriage, even. This is the twenty-first century in America. A *free* country. You can't be serious. There have to be laws against that."

"Elijah, if I've ever hated him, it was for that," Jubilee impresses. Then nods. "But then Dad made sure Noah and Aaron didn't do what Elliot did.

Their wives adore them. And he gave James a really hard time when he wanted to court Hannah, even though it was clear those two were in love. Then I had the freedom to turn down Peter because Dad asked me how I felt. With you, he's been difficult. But only because he can't allow himself to make the same mistake again. I don't always understand him. But I don't hate him. He does grow from his mistakes."

"But only after it costs his daughter the happy life she *could* have had."

"Priscilla is fine, Elijah. She is perfectly happy raising children and living a life of luxury and security. Elliot isn't an extremely attractive man, but he loves and spoils Priscilla and the children. Also, the next time we saw them, Elliot was suddenly the cleanest, best groomed, best dressed guy his age. He didn't even resemble the guy that asked for Priscilla's hand."

"Well, that's at least some encouragement." I nod and take the chance to switch gears. "I always thought it was an honorable tradition; a man going to a woman's father and asking for her hand."

"I agree."

"But what if...what if a woman is already drowning in tradition? What if it would mean more for a woman's future if a man *didn't* ask her father?"

"I think if a man respects a woman at all, he should seek the approval of her father."

"I agree. But what if he already has that and even gets permission every time he sees her? What if a guy already jumps through lots of hoops for the woman he loves? Should that guy still ask for her hand?"

Jubilee scrunches her eyebrows at me. I continue.

"I think there are certain redundancies that perpetuate unnecessary tradition." I smile out at the lake. "And I think that if we really went after the Holy Spirit's call for our lives and understood the need for liberty, we'd do away with crazy redundancies."

Jubilee nods. "The problem is honor. Because if a woman loves a man who wants to break tradition, she could be dishonoring her father in the process. Or maybe the man would just be doing it to get out of having to talk to her father again."

I drop the charade all at once. "Jubilee, I talk to your dad every day. I texted him a few minutes ago to let him know we were around the halfway mark of this outing. He asked me to do that, so it would be disrespectful if I didn't. It's completely crazy, but there's no discomfort or humiliation I wouldn't endure for you, Miz Jubilee. You really think I'd have a problem talking to your dad?"

She bats her pretty eyes. "We were working from a hypothetical."

"Well, *not* hypothetically, I need to ask you this. And you can be honest, and you can make me do whatever you want. But who, exactly, would benefit and be edified if I *did* go talk to your dad again before asking you to marry me?"

Instead of an answer, or even an acknowledgment of the question, we sit in silence, looking out at the water. She distracts herself by turning her legs aside, trying to keep her pole in the water and her skirt modest. A difficult feat that could have been avoided with jeans. Finally, Bennett sighs, impatient.

"When are we gonna have enough for a fish fry?" he calls out.

"Soon, Ben. I bet we'll catch some today. Wind is dying down."

"Mrs. Parker says we do it wrong. She says Mr. Parker uses lures and the bait at the store in the jar." Bennett whines. "Mr. Parker says a hook and a worm is old-fashioned and silly."

Jubilee smiles and waits for my answer. "Bennett, how many times I gotta tell you we ain't using a hook and a worm?"

"But that's what catches 'em, Daddy." Bennett says, rolling his eyes. "Even if you don't have all the fancy stuff, they still come for the worm and the hook gets 'em. It's not how you say. Ask Miss Jubilee."

"It *is* how I say," I correct. "They don't come to the worm, son. That's just a good meal we provide to thank them for their part in our fish fry."

"What do they come to?" Jubilee wonders. Because her old-fashioned dad has probably always talked about hooks and worms.

I smile at Bennett, who rolls his eyes and stops complaining. Finally, I lower my voice and answer. "They come to the quiet."

"I think that's silly," Bennett says, and I shush him.

But when we allow the birds to chatter and the water to gently lap at the shore amid this quiet, that's when Jubilee looks at me.

In the quiet, when all was peace and we were going about our lives as content and surefooted as woodland creatures, that's when we found one another. We hadn't let chaos enter. Neither of us desperately needed a romantic partner. We were obeying God. So when He uttered a "Look" to me, and she tells me, a "Listen" for her, we could respond with ease, sure that this was His will.

She reaches over and grabs hold of my free hand. All worm-gutted and dirty, but it doesn't matter at all. Not with the deep, contented quiet that lured us in.

She whispers, "I think it would be more of a benefit and edification if you kept it between us."

"He'd be angry," I whisper back.

She bites a lip, daring my eyes. "But I love him. And I think he has a chance to learn something from you that no one else is willing to teach him."

I take the dare. "And what's that?"

"That you're a good, godly man who lives his life to serve the Lord, even though you aren't…him."

I take it with silent flattery, then test waters. "Does it make you nervous when we talk about getting married this soon after meeting?"

Jubilee shakes her head. "God told me to submit to you, then gave me a sense of urgency that hasn't gone away."

"Yeah, you've told me that."

"Right. And I think marrying you would be the greatest blessing He's ever given me. It would be silly for me to put my own timeline on that."

"But if you *could* put your own timeline on it…"

"It would scare you away." She laughs.

"No, try me. What's your ideal?"

"Um, okay." She winces the fear, completely underestimating the urgency of my love for her. But she begins to answer. "And I can pick any day?"

"Yeah, just be honest, though. Don't exaggerate."

"Hmm…" she considers, but there is a wild spark in her eye as she dreams out across the lake, so I sense hyperbole coming. "Sometimes I think that if we'd gotten married the day of the farmers' market, it would have saved us some heartache. Dad keeps disrespecting you. You keep wondering if I'm sure about this. Bennett keeps telling me he's praying I'll come home with you two and stay there forever. And he's worried you'll get annoyed with my Dad and give up on this. But a wedding is final. There's so many questions we wouldn't be asking if we had just obeyed God that day and gotten married."

"Well…" I sigh, seeing things her way. "I think we all needed the challenge involved in what has happened since then. I needed to jump through hoops. You needed to know I would. Your dad needed to see me do it. And Ben needed to know what it takes to honor a woman."

"You're probably right." Jubilee finally looks at me. Then she shrugs and turns her face out to the lake again, closing her eyes against the breeze. "But now that we've learned the lessons from it, I'm with Bennett. It will never be too soon for you to ask me to come home with you forever."

I use the laugh to try to cover the flutter of my heart over the pines. That's exactly what I wanted to hear. "So, I've been talking to Hannah. I hope you don't mind."

"My *sister* Hannah? Why?"

"Yeah." I start in on what I disguise as an anecdote. "The day we started courting, I asked Hannah if she makes rings. Like engagement rings. She got to thinking. Then she bought some special equipment and started doing some experimenting. Then she called me up and asked if I wanted her to make a ring for you. For when we were ready. No pressure, of course."

"Really?" Jubilee giggles, her eyes and black hair bright and playful like her mood against the summer sun. "Are you going to let her? Gosh, I'd *love* to see what she came up with for a ring. She's so creative."

"Bennett's been begging me to show you." I laugh, then reach into my pocket and set a ring box on the rocks between us, opening it for her to see.

For a full eight seconds, Jubilee emotes admiration for Hannah's work. White gold inlaid with various squares and rectangles of turquoise all around, and a round diamond set flush in the center. Amateur craftswoman. But superior craftsmanship. I wait, relishing Jubilee's joy and ignorance.

But she's too quick-witted to keep at it that long. Mid-word, she silences, and her eyes widen as her gaze snaps to mine. She covers her mouth with stunned fingertips as she realizes I'm wiping away a nervous tear.

I, of course, take to full laughter, but delay no further. "Will you marry me?"

Mouth still covered, eyes still wide, she nods enthusiastically.

"Yeah?" I confirm, joy bubbling into laughter as Jubilee's hands touch the ring.

"Of course!" She giggles. "I didn't think you'd ask so soon. You caught me off guard."

"See, this is why I told you not to exaggerate."

"I didn't," she admits. "I would *love* to be a part of your family. I thought you'd make me and Bennet wait. I'm *so* glad you didn't."

"God wants this, and He wants it now. I've never been more sure of anything." As I'm speaking, we are transferring the ring to her finger, marveling at how well it fits.

"Me too." She shakes her head in bewilderment. "Oh my gosh… I was helping Hannah at the market and she…she tricked me. We went and looked at rings at this lady's booth. She seemed really interested in my ring size. I can't believe I didn't catch that…"

"It's always the quiet ones, huh?" I laugh and pull Jubilee into a hug on the jagged pebbles of a mountain lakeshore.

It's like we've been married a hundred years and everything but this isn't right. It sneaks in like quiet, with a still small voice. Still, inside we're both exploding with joy. And since we are both pretending we aren't, we end up releasing it all in laughter when Bennett, at this very moment,
catches the "biggest fish ever" in the quiet.

Sixteen

Jubilee

Elijah's fishing spot is over an hour away from home, so I have plenty of time to consider what I just did. I just agreed to love and serve this man for the rest of my life, but that much was easy. The consequence for how we made the agreement comes to me halfway through the drive.

"You're quiet." Elijah ejects me from my frantic thoughts when he sees that the chatty Bennett is now asleep in the backseat.

It comes out in one terrified wave.

"I don't know what he is going to do when I tell him we're engaged. He can be very strict and harsh when he is deliberately disobeyed."

"Your dad?" he confirms, then worries. "Abusive?"

"No. But..." I clarify with an anecdote. "We have a curfew. We are not even to leave the house after a certain time unless we are coming straight from work. One time Hakim went out with some coworkers to a bar and didn't get home until midnight. He didn't drink. In fact, he made sure they all got home safe."

"Okay, what did Dad do?" Elijah worries.

"He had a police officer run their names and one of them had a DUI on his record. Dad made Hakim quit his job and find another one because he said those coworkers were a bad influence. Hakim still hasn't fully forgiven him." I sigh. "And then there was the thing with Priscilla, and she didn't even do anything wrong. But when he decides something, it is decided. I am terrified for what he will decide."

"Do you regret..."

"Elijah, I am *glad* you didn't ask him first. I regret nothing."

"Then let me talk to him."

"No. The whole point was for me to break traditions that he considers to be hard, fast rules. To tear down idols, remember? I need to face him without you and take the consequences." Hot tears beg for escape, but I rebuke them silently.

"Okay, worst-case scenario, what will he do?"

"Break off our engagement. Well, try to. But..."

"But?"

"But I'm marrying you," I mumble.

"What was that?" He's coaching me.

I laugh. Taking the coaching. "I'm *marrying* you, Elijah. I don't care what he says."

"Whew..." Elijah dramatically pretends to fan himself. He growls flirtatiously, "You better."

"But I don't know what to do. I can't just not accept a consequence."

"Well what are the consequences if you don't marry me?" He asks.

My heart stops beating, and I feel physically faint for a moment. I correct it with an emotional sigh. "I can't let that happen."

"Exactly." Elijah gives me the scariest advice I've ever heard. "Jubilee, if he tries to break off our engagement, I want you to go to your room and pack a bag and call me. I will come get you. I'll find somewhere you can stay until we can get a wedding planned. Maybe by then Dad can cool off and still walk you down the aisle. Worst-case, he doesn't."

"Elijah, that would break his heart. He *still* talks about the joy of walking my sisters down the aisle."

"I know. He's a good man, which means the worst-case likely isn't what we'll see. Just don't be scared to put up a fight for what God is calling you to do."

"Pitchers and trumpets," I whisper and bite a lip.

He smiles appreciation, then sees a pull off, and takes it. He checks his cell signal, then smiles, initiating a video call.

"What are you doing?" I ask, glancing at Bennett as he stirs in the backseat.

"Before you get a ridiculous reaction, I want you to get the one you deserve." He shrugs.

"Hey, 'Lijah!" I hear, and then see Jessie, walking as she talks. "I just walked in the door to church to get ready for service tonight. What's up?"

"Your mom and dad there?" Elijah asks.

"Yeah, they're right here. And Garrett's with me. Why?"

Elijah moves his phone so that I'm in the frame, and I see that Jessie is joined by her parents and Garrett.

"Hello, Jubilee!" Lucinda exclaims.

We both see Bennett appear behind us on the screen before we knew he was there in the truck.

"Hey, Ben! You guys catch anything today?" Jordan asks. They must all know his schedule, and it warms my heart.

"Yeah, we got a big one! The biggest ever!" Bennett exclaims.

They all encourage him, then Elijah takes the opportunity. "I'm calling because *I* caught something too."

He looks at me, then nods to my left hand. He wants me to bring it into the frame as well.

When my hand comes into focus, there is a collective gasp, then an ear-piercing, phone-glitching shriek. We must watch in slow, pixelated motion as the phone apparently transfers to Garrett's hand so that Jessie and Lucinda can hug and cry and jump up and down. The way they congratulate us, repeatedly, wholeheartedly, brings a tear to the corner of my eye that I have to wipe discreetly. They tell me how thankful they are for me and my love for this man and his boy. After the short but potent phone call, I sit stunned.

"Thank you." I barely manage it, feeling another tear coming. "I really needed that."

Elijah claims that tear with his thumb as it drops to my cheek. He whispers, "I know."

Front hugs are for marriage. But I receive a deep one, right outside the truck and in view of my parents and two youngest brothers when Elijah drops me off. But the hug is really a prayer for my wisdom and courage. When we break apart, I wave to Bennett in the back seat and then head up the steps to the porch as Elijah starts to back away.

I breach the front door, and Mom flees to her bedroom behind the kitchen, which means she is scared to see her child's demise. And that is just over what probably looked like a long front hug. Dad doesn't even know the worst. I let the reprimand begin. Undue temptation. Commitment before consummation. Judah stands nearby with his arms crossed, looking smug. Hakim stands at the window pretending to look out at the horses, but he's really there to defend me. He glances at me twice. On the second glance, he catches the blue-green against the sparkle on the hand that smooths back my hair during the reprimand.

First, Hakim's face is pure terror, but Dad doesn't see it. Then he emotes silent pride and satisfaction before looking back out the window, lips bitten between what is normally a toothy grin.

"Jubilee, are you listening?" Dad booms when he sees me glancing at Hakim. The lecture has reached a peak of anger and self-righteousness. There is no better time than now to secure my gravesite. So, I don't answer his question.

"Dad, Elijah asked me to marry him today, and I agreed." I show him the ring. "We're engaged."

By the end of the conversation, Dad has done worse than our planned worst-case scenario. He threatened a restraining order and sending back the ring in the mail. But it turned out to all be noise in the end. All I did was listen to Elijah. I went up to my room, announcing my exact intentions. I was packing a suitcase.

I had sent a text to my fiancé, knowing Dad gets all my texts. *"Come get me?"*

"You serious?"

"Yes, I'm packing my bag."

"I'll be there soon."

But I don't even make it to the front door. Dad is standing at the bottom of the stairs.

"You can't be serious," Dad is bitter.

"He'll be here soon. You saw the text."

"To take you home? In his bed at last, I see."

"There is a room in his church. I am not going to bed with a man who is not my husband," I howl. "We do not avoid temptation for *you*. We do it because God commands it. I do…" I hiccup at anger and tears. "I do what *God* commands." I wipe at my tears and conclude. "If I cannot do that with your blessing, that is *not* my fault."

My suitcase gets caught on the banister in my haste to make it to the door. As I fight to pull it free, Hakim takes Judah out of the room. Finally free, I turn to head out the door. Instead of arriving at the door, however, I arrive in the same strong arms that rescued me from hunger and heat. Again, he is my jubilee, and I am his. It is a warm, mighty front hug, and becomes the place my father prays over me. For peace, of course. He wants me to be levelheaded and calm again. But that is not the only purpose. The realization hits him around "in Jesus' name."

"When Elijah brought you home…"

"He prayed over me. Over this."

I pull back from the embrace and look out the front window. Well before the agreed-upon ten-minute mark, the truck is again kicking up dust. Dad sees too, and mumbles,

"He really came."

"Of course, he did," I mumble too. "He's a man of his word."

Dad shakes his head, smiling with bitterness. "Go out there and tell him everything is fine and he can go. Then unpack your bag. You will not be staying in any room at his church. You live *here*. We will discuss the terms of this engagement in a moment."

"Without Elijah?"

"Elijah's terms are unchanged since he didn't come and ask for new ones. You and I have things to discuss."

"It was the only way to compromise, Elijah. I apologize. I know you want me to be my own woman and stand up for myself, but almost running away from home was emotionally draining. I had to give somewhere." I fret on the bench we've shared for several weeks.

"I'm surprised he agreed at all, Jubilee. Your church is fine. I'll marry you anywhere."

"It's not the place that bothers me. You wanted Pastor Jordan to marry us. You were just saying that the other day when we went over there for dinner."

"It's alright. They'll be happy with an invitation. I assume going to Jessie's wedding is off the table, though? I know your dad's spent two weeks deciding."

"Um, no, actually. He's allowing me to go," I declare. "I made sure to ask him while negotiating terms."

"Really? You're alright with it being at another church? Your daddy know that?"

"It's a wedding. People get married at lots of places. It's not as though I'm going to a service." Which offends Elijah, I see, but he doesn't speak it.

"Alright. It's a date then. Dress beautifully and I'll pick you up at seven forty-five on Saturday."

Dress beautifully. What does a man mean when he says that? I've been up since five. Hair curled and elegantly twisted back at the sides. Subtle makeup highlighting my lips and eyes. Now I'm standing here in my dressy boots and a slip at 7:30 a.m., trying not to bite the freshly clear-coat polished nails as I stare at five different dresses on my bed. Where are my sisters when I need them? Oh, that's right. Married to men who at one point asked them to "dress beautifully" and it caused them this much agony. I remember helping make these choices. But now I'm on the other end of it and all alone.

Maybe not boots. Maybe that's too country, though Jessie seems like a boots sort of girl. But what if this is an elegant, classy sort of family? Lucinda seems classy. A pastor's daughter. No, certainly not boots. The blue satin dress for sure. There is a knock at my bedroom door. Mom comes in and sits on Hannah's old bed.

"Elijah is here. He knows he's far too early, though." I love my mother. So caring. So intuitive.

"I'm not even dressed." I sigh, hipping hands against modest satin and staring at the bed of dresses. "My wedding will be casual, so no one has to make this decision."

"Well, Elijah looks dashing." Mom smiles. Knows I need more. "He's wearing a tie and a light blue shirt that looks wonderful with his skin tone and jeans and his boots."

"Blue, huh?" I bite my lip after the heart flutter. I can't wait to see him in it.

"Are you sure you want to marry this man?" Mom asks with terrible timing.

"I don't understand how that is relevant. I need to choose a dress…and shoes."

"Summer," My mother says with a smile, removing the wool and black options from my bed. "Morning." She takes away the dark blue and long sundress. Leaving only the cotton dress with the ruffles and satin ribbon. I hate that one. It makes me look like I have no shape at all. The dark blue falls over my curves with gentle ease before it stops below my knees. Also, it goes with my boots. So I defy my mother with a smile and put it on. Mom sighs and helps me zip it.

"So stubborn, you are," she whispers, standing behind me as I look in the mirror. Continuing the previous interrogation. "Jubilee, I only ask because your sisters couldn't wait to start dress shopping and wedding planning. Even Priscilla. He seems like a good man, but a very determined one. I want you to be sure you have not merely bent to his determination."

"That's a valid concern, Mom." I turn, looking at all angles of myself. "But that's not the case. You and Dad think it is too soon. So, I was giving *you* time to accept it."

"Well, I don't suppose it was too soon for Eve when she met Adam in the Garden of Eden," Mom replies.

"They were the only two people alive." I smile with a speck of sarcasm. "That was the first marriage ever to occur. The timing of it was irrelevant. God literally made them for one another."

"God never changes, my Jubilee. The only difference is Eve didn't have any dresses to choose from." Mom smiles with a speck more of mischief. My face reddens, just as my mother had hoped. Mom leans in and whispers, "And you'd be surprised how much your father has accepted."

"Well, aren't you the overachiever?" Elijah says as I reach the bottom stair, after Hakim whistles jokingly from the couch.

"What do you mean?" I ask, enthralled by the dashing man and his casually dressed boy.

"I told you to dress beautifully. You really took that to heart." He laughs. I smile. Mom winks. Dad clears his throat. Elijah is annoyed. "Right...let's go get something to eat. I wouldn't let Ben put on his tux yet on account of pancakes. Morning weddings are tough that way."

"In this case, it's a blessing. I have to work tonight." I wince.

"What time?"

"Six."

"I'll have you home by five." He nods.

"You can just take her straight to work if you'd like, Elijah. I don't want Bennett to have to cut short his wedding party obligation." Which everyone has to look twice to be sure actually came from Adam Monroe.

"I won't have a way to get home from work," I reason. Hating that it is the case.

"I'll go back into town and get you. Just call me when you're almost ready." Elijah nearly laughs at what is obvious to him. I wouldn't recognize his condition if I hadn't seen my brothers fall victim. He's lovesick. The terminal kind where he'll serve a woman until his very demise. And since I'm the woman in this scenario, that makes Dad have to leave the room…because it's hitting him. For the first time in his life, the man who fights and wins every battle is suddenly conceding to a neutral peace treaty instead.

The ceremony is beautiful, and the guests are many. Jessie is wearing a big puffy cupcake dress and a simple beaded headband on her short hair. Garrett is grinning like he's won the lottery. But at the reception, in a large rec room in another part of the church, something happens that shocks me. I am witness to something that when I'd see it on an approved movie as a child, my parents would pause it and explain how very wrong it was that it was occurring. But these people. These reasonable, wonderful people, are doing it without the disclaimer and with great joy.

Dancing. They are dancing. The youngest to the oldest of them. I'm worried that they might be provoked to sensuality as I've been taught, but it never happens. In fact, I don't hear one foul lyric or see one gyration of the hips that isn't met with laughter of ridicule. Jessie and Garrett dance first, front to front, more concerned with holding in tears and smiles than anything else, even though anything further might be sanctified for them. Then they all dance. I can't decide whether I should flee it or love it. But I suppose all sin starts that way.

While Elijah is off helping Bennett change, I have a pleasant conversation with Cindy, and then Jessie comes and sits at the table like she isn't a princess today. Jessie jokes and tells me that she'd love it if I wore a traditional Indian gown in deep red. And while I certainly wouldn't trade being a Monroe, I wish I lived in a world where I could choose the color of my gown.

After the wedding, Elijah grabs a pizza, since it is nearing suppertime, and we share it on a park picnic table with Bennett. Elijah chuckles when I take a timid bite after we pray.

"What?" I ask after chewing.

"I suppose that's a step up from what I expected." He teases, then takes a large bite of pizza.

131

"What did you expect?"

"Fork and knife, honestly." Elijah snickers. "My prim and proper Jubilee."

"Can we have tacos when you guys have a wedding?" Bennett asks after we clear the picnic table. "I like pizza, but Jessie said she didn't have pizza because it isn't fancy enough for a wedding. Are tacos fancy?"

Elijah winces, embarrassed. "Bennett, why don't you go play for a minute or two?"

I make conversation as we watch Bennett run to the playground. "It was nice to see your um…"

"Family. Church family." Elijah shrugs. Nods. "They've been a Godsend every second we've been here."

"Pretty wedding," I comment further. "Big. Complicated and elaborate. But beautiful. Jessie was gorgeous."

Elijah laughs. "Oh, you are a woman after my own heart, Jubilee Monroe."

"How so?"

"Because you seem opposed to big and elaborate. Means I could expect small and simple for our wedding."

"Probably. I'm pretty easy. My Dad's always told me that. My sisters wore cupcake dresses like Jessie. I'd have to have something to go with my boots. And we can't go too fancy, because we have to have tacos."

Elijah sighs. Winces. "How long does it take to plan a wedding?"

"Usually a couple months for us, but up to a couple years for some people. Why?" I wonder at the random question.

"Because we keep talking about our wedding, but we haven't even set a date. I feel like maybe it was all too soon and you're not really sure," Elijah opens up.

"My mother said something similar this morning." My lip quivers. "I'm *sure*, Elijah. I could plan it in a week if you asked. But…"

"There's a but." Elijah's looks devastated.

"When my siblings got engaged, everyone was so excited." I emote. "And here I am, filled with joy and right in the center of God's will, and I got home and my father threatened a restraining order against the man God made for me. We almost had to elope! I love my father. My family is such a huge part of who I am. But no one is excited for me. I'm just 'allowed' to marry you. I don't know how to reconcile the joy inside me with their disappointment. We plan weddings *together*. My Mom and sisters and me. I've dreamed of doing that for years. Now I can. But I can't."

"If they aren't excited, you'll have to be even more excited to compensate. But we need to set a date so that it makes this real for them."

"Well, when do *you* want to get married, Elijah?" I finally inquire.

"We have some time before you have to be at work." A spark alights in his eyes that I love and make a point to find again.

"I owe my parents a wedding, Elijah. It's too late to elope." I bite my lip.

"Alright, I'll be good. But soon. As soon as you're comfortable with. At the soonest, I'd need a couple of weeks so that I can get some time off for you if you want more than a weekend. Then, probably before the year is out would be my ideal on the 'at the latest' end. We're still on the same page with the urgency thing, right?"

"Yes, absolutely. Especially after going to a wedding today."

"Alright, so just set a date and let me know. It's completely up to you. That way no one accuses me of pressuring you. Don't ask for anyone's opinion. Consider this in your heart with God and get back to me. Okay?"

"Okay."

"And be joyful. Joy inspires joy. Plan our wedding. Marry me. If they love you, and they *do*, they'll come around to joy," Elijah promises.

This Sunday in late August when I look in my full-length mirror in my bedroom after church, I feel like I'm looking at someone else. What if this skirt, though modest and lovely, isn't my style? What if I want to always have the freedom I have when riding a horse? What if I don't want to change this evening if I ride with Elijah? He's seen even my best dresses and skirts already. But he likes me in jeans because they suit me.

But would it be a choice of the flesh to wear jeans? An abuse of liberty? I think it's practical, and goes well with my favorite riding top and boots and feather earrings and freedom.

Jeans reflect the kind of woman that came home with an engagement ring, my father having known nothing about it. Unacceptable in the eyes of some. But so are the legs of my favorite child, and the change needn't occur in him for acceptance. So today I descend the stairs to greet a family dinner wearing jeans. An engagement ring. And a little more independence as my husband-to-be pulls into the driveway.

When Judah lets Elijah in, my first utterance is exactly what I know he wants to hear.

"The first Sunday in October. In the afternoon, after church. I spoke with the pastor this morning and his assistant put it on the calendar." I cross my arms. "I'll start planning this week."

"Alright. I'll put in for vacation. I might have to do some doubles or trade shifts to make it work. But I will make it work." Elijah practically stumbles. I set a date, and I can see what it's doing to him.

"That's in six weeks, Jubilee," Mom whispers. "What's the rush? Wait until after the new year."

"No, we want to keep it small and simple. So there won't be much planning needed. The short notice will keep crowds from coming, but it should be enough notice for Aaron and Priscilla to make it, I hope."

"You've known him three months," Judah scoffs.

"Yes. And in thirty years, I'll have known him thirty years and three months. At which point, no one here will remember or care how many of those years and months we were married. Hopefully."

"October. I wonder if the leaves will be changing by then." Elijah smiles, getting even more used to the idea.

"Oh!" I remember, sure my father hears this piece of business. "My pastor did say that it was short notice for premarital counseling with him. But guess who his first recommendation was to fill the gap?"

"Who?" Elijah suspects it.

"Pastor Jordan Durant. They live on the same street, and their children grew up together. Reverend Sweet thinks Jordan is a wise man of God whose house is well in order." I give Elijah a little smile that makes him chuckle.

Dad advises, "Well be sure to call that pastor this week, Jubilee. There's no guarantee he can fit you in either. But if Reverend Sweet trusts him, I do too."

"I bet he'll find a way to squeeze us in," Elijah nods, taking out his phone. "I'll text him right now."

"Text him? Is that appropriate?" Dad wonders. "Do you have the man's number?"

I explain as Elijah texts. "Pastor Jordan is Elijah's pastor, Dad. Ben was the ring bearer at his daughter's wedding yesterday. They are close."

After sending the text, Elijah looks me over and Dad looks horrified. So, to secure the tension, Elijah winks at me and mumbles, "Have I told you I love you in jeans?"

I'd expected blatant reprimand for those jeans and all my fire. But other than Hakim's wink, I receive little better than *nothing*. Nothing happens. Perhaps they shouldn't be so used to my Spirit-driven antics at this point. None of us know exactly what is coming, but today I am quietly breaking their hearts, though they dare not say it.

Seventeen

Jubilee

"Have you chosen a wedding party?" My mother asks.

"We're just going to have Bennett stand with us, since we're all becoming a family. And he'll take care of the rings, too. That way none of the children feel left out. We'll just keep it simple. I already told Elijah he can wear boots and jeans. I'd like to find a tea length dress to go with my boots as well. Possibly in ivory." I plan with a smile, sitting around a table with Mom and Hannah mid-day.

"Short?" Mom sits back at Hannah's dining room table. "You want a short dress that isn't white?"

I nod. "Mid-calf or ankle. It's an informal ceremony, Mom. We only want to invite family and some people from church. Elijah's church family pretty much *is* his family. So I'll have a few dozen people there, and poor Elijah has four. He may invite some of his colleagues, though."

There is a knock at Hannah's door and she sighs, practically in tears. The poor thing can barely see her feet to walk these days. She's due any second.

"I'll get it, Hannah. You stay there."

I realize as I pass Hannah's clock that the door is probably a visitor for me anyway.

I open the door to my favorite silhouette. Elijah Bering in scrubs and cowboy hat.

"I was on my lunch, and you said you'd be here today. Mind if I come visit?"

"Not at all." I let him in. "I was just talking about you."

"Really?" Then he walks into Hannah's dining room. "Howdy, ladies. How's the planning going?"

"Were hoping to get a dress ordered today." Mom smiles, "Have you eaten, Elijah?"

"I'm fine, Mrs. Monroe."

"Nonsense." Then Mom rises and walks around the corner into Hannah's kitchen, restarting a recently cooled griddle for grilled cheese.

Elijah thanks her, then looks to Hannah. "You look pretty ripe there, Hannah. How much longer you in for?"

"I will likely have a newborn at your wedding, Elijah. The midwife says another week or two," she shares.

Elijah chit chats and eats for a half hour, then thanks Mom and Hannah generously, before apologizing.

"Unfortunately, I have to get back. Sorry to eat and run."

Mom smiles. "It was a pleasure to see you as always, Elijah."

I walk Elijah out, having noticed that he left a little more time than he needs to get back to work. We stand by his truck in the heat.

"I wanted to secure a date with you for this evening, if I could. I'd like to take you out to dinner to finally celebrate our engagement. You and Bennett, of course," Elijah rattles off.

"Alright. Maybe I can stay here until you get off at seven? I know Hannah needs the extra set of hands. I can leave my car here for Judah and you could take me home after."

"Oh, in that case, would you mind...no, nevermind. Forget I started asking that." Elijah sighs, frustrated.

"Elijah, I highly doubt that I'll mind doing whatever you were about to ask me to do. Just ask."

"No, it was just a transient thought. But Ben's school is..." Elijah points to Hannah's house, because the school is a block behind it. "And Mrs. Parker's house is beyond that. He has to walk there after school. I just thought for a second that maybe he'd like spending the afternoon with you. Especially on his first day. But I know that's an awful lot to ask. You're my fiancée, not a babysitter. I realized after I thought of it that it might seem like I'm using you. I don't want you to think that. Which seems like I'm manipulating you, and I don't want to do that either." He laughs at his awkwardness.

I smile and take to lighthearted sarcasm. "Hmmm, walk a block in this beautiful weather to rescue my wonderful soon-to-be stepson from the awful pea-soup-cooking Mrs. Parker and bring him here to play with his friend while we wait for you to treat us to dinner? You might have to twist my arm, Elijah." Elijah chuckles and I continue. "Honestly, I'd be more upset if you *hadn't* asked and I found out later he'd spent his afternoon two blocks away when he could have been here with me. If I didn't have a job, I'd take care of him *every* day. You know that."

"Wouldn't *that* be nice? I pay Mrs. Parker a pretty penny for after-school care. He'd much rather be with you." Elijah is probably joking, but I jump at the chance to serve him.

"I'll put in my two weeks' notice," I promise. "You'd probably be saving at least as much as they pay me at work, anyway. My time would be better spent looking after Bennett."

"I wasn't serious, Jubilee." Elijah chuckles.

"I was." I shrug. "How can I call myself his stepmom in a few weeks if I can't do basic things like picking him up from school and watching him while you work?"

"Miz Jubilee, there is no way I can ask you to do that. And there's no way your daddy would *agree* to that. You'd probably have to be at my house after school, and he has never even allowed you to come there. So I can't ask that." Elijah looks like he's humbled.

"You're not asking. I'm offering. I'll make that clear when I talk to Dad. Just call the school so they don't think I'm kidnapping him, and Mrs. Parker so she doesn't wonder where he is. I'll put in my notice tomorrow. You act as if I *like* my job."

"But don't you need the money?" Elijah worries.

"Not really. I pay for my own gas and phone and car insurance, but only voluntarily because I didn't want to be a financial burden on my parents."

"Well, let me cover everything from now on. Then I'll feel better about you losing money to watch him. It's high time we discussed all this, anyway," He reasons. "We'll have to sit down and figure out how to get everything combined. I suppose we could keep a second account, but marriages work better if *everything* is married."

My mother has never paid a bill. She is given a weekly budget for groceries and personal use, and my father takes care of the finances. It is the way things are done in the family. Finances, beyond how to be a thrifty homemaker, are not for a woman to concern herself with. Not that women don't have access to the money, it just isn't their jurisdiction in the family.

Elijah, whom I have known three months, wants to open it all up for me to see. But it makes more sense. He and I want to be a team.

"I agree. One account. What bank do you use?"

"I'm a member at the credit union in town." Elijah again points, this time in the general direction of the bank.

I snicker. "Me too. Isaac manages that bank, so we'll just go in and—"

Elijah is chuckling, and likely addresses himself when he says, "Why does that not surprise me?" Then he sighs and takes my hand, running his thumb along my engagement ring and says, "You're like a dream, you know that? I don't deserve you." He gives me a quick hug, then starts walking around the front of his truck.

I giggle. "Bennett gets out at three, right?"

"Yep. If you're driving, get there twenty minutes early because the pickup situation is chaos."

I have seen the cars blocking traffic and lining up around the corner from here, always glad I was homeschooled when I see the chaos. "I'll walk."

I go to the front office at three, homeschooled Jonathan in tow, to be sure and catch Bennett at his classroom before he walks to Mrs. Parker's house. Bennett is the last one out, with no reason to hurry to a place he hates. His look of despair before he sees me, and the change to sheer joy and excitement and the hug around my legs when he sees me are the reason I know I am plenty ready to be his mom full time.

I breach the front door of Hannah's house with the rambunctiously excited boys to a photo on a modest fashion website that would have my mother and sister practically squealing, if they engaged in such nonsense.

All lace, tea length, sheer sleeves and ivory, not white. When I say the word "perfect", Mom already has the measuring tape around my waist so we can make the ordering deadline.

But when an ad in the corner of the page catches my eye, I gasp and lean closer to the laptop screen, "What is *that*?"

Hannah comments, having just swallowed a bit of an apple. "We were just talking about that. Very elegant. Were you thinking for centerpieces? Seems a bit bulky, and it wouldn't even hold water if you wanted flowers."

"No, not for centerpieces…" I laugh once at the ad before clicking on the minimally decorated table. In the center is a simple terracotta-look pitcher with holes throughout it that allow a candle inside to illuminate the entire scene. I've never seen anything like it, and suddenly I have to have it. But since Hannah has never deserved anything by my grace, I explain. "I know it's not traditional, but pitchers with fire inside are sort of a thing with us. If I walked down the aisle carrying this, Elijah would *love* it."

"In that case, consider it a gift," Hannah says, then places the reasonably priced item in the cart of the other website before switching back to the window with my wedding gown. Mom continues to measure me.

This is happening. This is really happening.

All at once, and for a much greater purpose than any of us can conceptualize.

Eighteen

Elijah

"You want me to come to your house?" Jubilee finally answers after a silence over the phone in September.

"It'll be yours soon, Jubilee. Strange you know what the mortgage and utilities cost, but you've never set foot in the house. I want you to start to feel at home here, especially when you start bringing Ben here after school next week. Actually having been here would be a good start."

"You're right. It's just that Dad needed the two weeks' notice more than *Los Arboles*," she confesses. "He already told me he doesn't like that I'll be there in the evenings because there is access to a bedroom and it would be too easy for us to get away from our chaperone."

"I understand. But will you ask him? For me?" I insist. "If he gives you a hard time, I'll call him."

A typical exhausting telephone conversation with Adam against my weariness from a week of work ends with, "Well, the plan is to wait until Bennett isn't looking so we can crawl into bed together."

"That doesn't amuse me, Elijah. Temptation creeps in quietly."

"If you trust me with her honor, trust me with her honor."

"You talked to her on the phone a moment ago when she was alone in her room. One more instance and I take her phone, yet again. Perhaps earn trust in the little things first." That would be the fifth time he's taken her phone for two days each time. That's half our engagement without phone communication.

"Just let her come to my house, Adam. She'll *live* here next month." I sigh. "Please don't keep making me regret not eloping with her."

And that one works.

After a quick conversation with Jubilee asking her to bring over anything she has packed, my heart is moving in shockwaves and earthquakes when her car pulls into the driveway. I'm glad Bennett speaks.

"Dad, should I put my legs on?" He usually rests them on Saturday unless we go somewhere with Jubilee.

"No. She won't mind, son."

I show Jubilee around the humble little two-bedroom, two bath home, and she's beaming by the end of the five-minute tour. A home to make and keep. Something she's wanted her whole life, I bet, and this one is in dire need of a woman's touch.

"You don't have anything on the walls…" She comments, seeing only an old portrait of me and a toddler resembling Bennett above the fireplace.

I call to mind all the pictures of flowers in Jubilee's current home. Barely pink walls and other old-fashioned decor. I love Jubilee enough to allow my home to transform into the same, if need be. But that would be the only reason I'd allow it.

"Well, soon-to-be woman of the house, what do you suggest we put on the walls?"

She bites a lip as her eyes light up. The first timid word surprises me. "Color."

"Alright…" I ask for more.

"Nice, rich colors. And horses. Tack. Old wood and antiques. Things that remind me of the barn and riding. I've always wanted to decorate a house that way. I feel like myself when I'm in my barn."

I sigh in relief. "Let's go shopping."

We shop for three hours for decorations, and Jubilee buys about half, feeling bad for spending so much on antiques and horse pictures and such. Bennett, now a horse enthusiast himself, is loving it. It works out, because when we are in town I get a notification that our new phones are ready to pick up at the cell phone store. When we moved Jubilee's line from her parents' plan to mine, we both got free phones.

Then we return home after eating lunch and spend the afternoon painting the wall behind the fireplace, then hanging things and setting things here and there. I love her creativity and the way the space feels warm when she's done with it.

We have dinner, which Jubilee conjures from the scraps in my kitchen, and we turn on one of Bennett's kid movies while we set up our new phones. Then I start talking crazy when I see Bennett is asleep, head on Jubilee's lap.

"Will you stay if I put him to bed?"

"I shouldn't. He's our chaperone." Exactly what I thought she'd say.

"Jubilee, in October there will be conversations he can't hear and times he can't join us. We can't have him thinking we never need to be alone. This is a short engagement. There are things we should talk about." I prepare for a ring to be thrown at my feet and for her to storm out until I remember she's still hiding behind herself and wouldn't do it even if she had the inkling.

"We've talked about money and wedding plans and controversial interpretations of Scripture in front of him. What else do we need to discuss?" She asks.

"Um, okay," I laugh and glance at Ben to see if he's faking sleep before making my case, "This altar kiss nonsense? Parenting roles? Babies? Sex?"

She alights with laughter, instinctively covering Ben's ears on her lap. She whispers, "First, we will be discussing much of that in our premarital counseling with Pastor Jordan, he said. Second, don't you think it's risky to put our chaperone to bed so that we can talk about intimacy?"

"So do something risky with me for once. You have permission to be here and your curfew ain't for two hours. You are not in violation. Be your own woman," I prod and persuade. Seduce, even. I can see Jubilee hates that she's falling for it.

She sighs, getting lost in my eyes. I love that I can make her feel things, and resolve to be careful not to abuse the ability. Except I'm probably abusing it now. "I would like an opportunity to seek God about that."

Nevermind. I think it's her doing the seducing.

"As long as you promise not to say that on our wedding night."

A remark that loosens her up a little. She tucks her lips. Nods her agreement.

"At least help me put him to bed?"

"I would be honored."

I remove Bennett's legs and help him groggily change into a t-shirt and shorts. Jubilee comes in his room with me, and he can't stop smiling when two more held hands and closed eyes say his prayers with him. I kiss Ben's forehead and he insists on a kiss from her too.

The little rascal gets one.

She's the last thing he sees before we shut off the light and bid him goodnight. The kid wouldn't be happier on Christmas Eve.

She gathers up her things and I head to my kitchen to pour myself some whiskey. Jubilee startles when she sees what I'm doing.

"What?" I challenge her.

"Is that alcohol?" She seems deeply disturbed.

"Is that horror?" I ask of the look on her face.

"Um...I don't know. That's something else I need to seek God about, I think. I didn't know you drank alcohol."

Suddenly the horror is mine. "Jubilee, if it will change things between us, I do *not* drink alcohol. This will go down the drain right now. I don't want you calling off the wedding or something."

"No! Goodness no. I'm marrying you exactly as you are, Elijah. I just didn't know...*that*...about you."

"You're disappointed," I surmise.

"No. I mean, I don't...let me seek God. Is that fair? You always ask that, and you've given me a lot of opportunity for that tonight." She clears her throat. "Do you smoke, or...?"

"No. Cigarettes are cancer sticks. This is a sleep and relaxation aid."

She nods, eyes to the ground, but says nothing.

"It bothers you."

"Yes." She hates that she's saying it.

"Thank you for being honest with me."

"I should go," she says, backing toward the door. Then a nightly routine scoots into the room with a request.

"Jubilee, will you rub my legs? They hurt." Why Bennett asks her, I don't know.

"Um..." She sits, looking to her whiskey re-cabineting fiancé for what exactly Bennett means.

"The prosthetics aren't always that kind to him. We have a balm that we put on his legs that helps." I explain with damaged pride. "But I'll do it. You can go if you need to."

She marvels at the way Bennett swings himself up onto the couch. I grab the balm from the coffee table, and pull back Ben's shorts to begin rubbing his "feet." I see that Jubilee does her level best not to be alarmed by the way his legs were formed. It can be gruesome if one is not ready for it, no matter how deep Bennett has dug his way into their heart. But she smiles, watching me rub the balm into his sores on his right leg, soothing his reddened and ailing skin.

After a moment, only long enough for her to observe my technique, Jubilee sits on the floor next to the couch and starts on his left leg, unaffectedly rubbing something freakish and fearful to most. It soothes him that we are both rubbing. When we are finished, I carry sleepy Bennett to bed so the carpet doesn't claim the balm.

I exit my son's room and close the door, thinking Jubilee is gone since she isn't on the couch. But then I look straight ahead and she startles me. She's grabbing her purse from the chair by the front entry. Leaving, indeed. But first she's approaching me to say goodbye.

But I have to speak first. "That was by far the kindest thing I've ever seen anyone do. There's no way I'm the first man to fall in love with you."

She smiles at my flirtation. "It's not kindness. It's love. He's an absolutely perfect little boy and I adore him."

My heart soars. "I'm glad I found the other person in the world who sees that. It almost makes me less jealous that he got a kiss from you when I get hand holding and side hugs." Then gravity takes hold and I recall the point of contention, "Jubilee…"

"It's okay. I love you. You're perfect to me too. I should accept…"

"You should accept exactly nothing that makes you even a little uncomfortable. Not with me. You talk to God and tell me where you two land with this."

"Thank you." Jubilee nods. "I wish I could stay, but I really should go. I've been with you over twelve hours. I don't want Dad to worry." She's sincere. Then she nods. "But…" And then she stands on her toes and plants a kiss on my cheek. I probably look like a goo-goo-eyed school boy when she backs away because my heart is sure goo now.

She giggles, confirming the woozy sort of look in my eyes. "I love you both too much to have you be jealous of Bennett."

"I love you too." I walk her to the door and entice her. "Hey, call me on that fancy new phone when you get in your room. I narrowed down the belt buckles for the wedding for me and Ben and I've been meaning to ask your opinion."

"Elijah, he's already given me a phone warning today. I'm not supposed to—" But she looks up and sees something in my eyes that makes her sigh and say, "We'll have to whisper. They will hear me on the phone, especially if I have to have you on speaker because I'm looking at belt buckles."

"So we whisper." I shrug. She agrees, not knowing my ulterior motive. I wait for her call, fiddling with some settings on my new phone. I smile when I see her face appear on the screen.

Three minutes into the conversation, I get exactly what I was hoping for. I hear a knock at her bedroom door and Adam Monroe's voice.

"Hand it over, but don't hang up. I'd like to speak with him."

I hear Jubilee sigh, then I say, "Hey, Adam. I'm on speaker, I can hear you."

"You know the rules, Elijah."

"Yeah, she went home early since Bennett was in bed. We're still within curfew, though. That's the rule I'm following." I bite my lip. Morbidly excited.

"You know she is in her bedroom alone. Conversations are to be public. I told you that this morning."

"We were just talking about my attire for the wedding."

"The consequences stand, Elijah. I'm taking her phone for two days. You can contact me if you need to get in touch with her."

"Actually, you can't do that."

"Can't I?" His pompous air is still clear through the phone.

"Yeah. You signed that form this week to allow Jubilee to move her number over to my plan, remember? So that new phone in your hand legally belongs to *me*. The primary user is Jubilee, so she has authorization to do with it as she pleases. You do not. Taking it would be theft, Your Honor."

"Jubilee is my daughter and she lives in my home, and she will obey my rules."

"Yes sir. And for that reason, she is obeying the curfew you gave her, and that'll go for talking on the phone too. But you will not be taking this woman's phone away again as if she is some disobedient child. It remains with her. Do we understand?"

"That was a cunning trap, Elijah," Adam grumbles. "And that isn't a compliment."

"Well, thank you anyway." I take it further. "You have your phone with you? While we're here, I'd like for you to delete the parental control tracking app from Jubilee's phone and from yours. It automatically downloaded and requires a password to remove."

"Then how will I see your texts and monitor your phone conversations, Elijah?" He asks.

"You won't." I sigh. "Can you take me off speaker and step out of her room? Jubilee doesn't need to hear this part."

I hear the sound change. He must be eager to hear me explain that one.

"I'm listening."

"Well, Adam, sometimes a man needs to talk to another man, just the two of them. Right? Like you and me right now."

"Correct."

"Well, me and Jubilee are the same. And while our relationship is by no means *sexually* intimate, it is still going to become increasingly *intimate* until we are married. I would like to be able to converse freely with the woman I love."

"I think you know why I can't allow that, Elijah."

"What, you think I'll seduce her over the phone?"

"You're certainly capable, Elijah. You have her heart, and you have convinced her to do things I never would have imagined Jubilee would do."

"Adam, she has *my* heart. I'm going to honor her, and I'm going to help her honor *you*. But you need to leave me room to *romance* her too."

"When you're her husband—"

"Also, by removing all that stuff from her phone *now*, we are avoiding an awkward conversation later when I'm her husband and you have even less business knowing what I'm saying to her." That, I conclude with laughter.

He sighs. I won. "Let me hang up the phone and remove the controls. She can call you back when I am finished."

"Thank you, Adam," I tell him with warmth.

"Don't thank me yet. I absolutely detest this idea, and I know I'll be proven right. You've simply left me no choice but to comply. The phone is yours."

"Well, we'll see. But that's not what I was thanking you for."

"Oh?"

"Yeah. You and I didn't talk before I popped the question, and I know you're still not happy with me about that. But I told you before that I wanted to thank you for protecting her. Thank you for holding on so tight, even if it makes me crazy sometimes." I make a confession. "I didn't have a father to set a standard for how to love a woman. Thanks for filling the gap."

He heard me clear and true, but I know the sigh is all I'll get. "If I remove these controls, please do not violate any other rules. Do we have a deal?"

"I'll do my darndest."

Jubilee calls back ten minutes later and says, "That was really gutsy." She laughs. "How did you know it would work?"

"I didn't. Otherwise it ain't really gutsy is it?" I chuckle.

"He removed the parental controls and repealed all phone rules. He said, 'He'll probably talk you into his bed. Don't say I didn't warn you.' " Jubilee is whisper-giggling.

"Oh, he's probably not wrong, but I'm playing the long game there. For now, belt buckles. What do you think of the one with the turquoise? Bennett likes that one best. Matches your ring."

"Yeah. I think that one is my favorite."

Nineteen

Jubilee

"What's that heavenly smell?" Elijah asks as he walks in the door from work on Monday evening, four weeks before the wedding.

"Fajitas," I answer, licking a finger of the signature lime cilantro sauce my family adores.

"You're telling me this childcare deal includes *supper*?" Elijah nearly melts.

"She let me taste it, Dad! Miss Jubilee cooks soooo good," Bennett proclaims from his stool at the kitchen island.

" 'Childcare deal'?" I smile. "That's not what this deal is. You worked all day. Why would I then make you cook? I'm glad I can do this more consistently now that I'm not working. Also, I stayed under budget stocking your kitchen with the essentials before I picked up Bennett. Homework is done. Ben's room is picked up. And I threw in a load of his laundry. You have about fifteen minutes to get settled before it's time to eat." Being a homemaker comes naturally. As does the rush of blood and emotion when Elijah responds with one of his recently allowed deeply rooted embraces. For a moment, I struggle to understand which natural occurrence is also righteous.

"So, I can go take a shower?" The single father asks with soulful relief as he releases me.

"If you can be back in fifteen." I smirk. Pleased to have pleased him so well.

"This is life-giving, Jubilee. You just don't know how much of a blessing you are," he emotes.

"It's just the beginning, Elijah. This is what I've been wanting to do for you since we met."

"You're telling me I can hope for this type of over-the-top spoiling all the time when I'm your husband?" Elijah asks, backing toward his room after kissing Bennett's head.

"Cooking and cleaning and helping with spelling words doesn't seem over-the-top to me." I laugh. "But you can hope for and expect it. And if you have your list, I can stay until curfew tonight."

Elijah sighs, advancing again and planting a kiss on my cheek. "I adore you." He retreats to the master bedroom he occupies alone.

The first concern Elijah mentioned in a meeting with Pastor Jordan was not having an opportunity to speak with me privately because I feel awkward discussing certain things over the phone. Pastor Jordan suggested that Elijah make a list of things he'd like to discuss. That way if I stayed beyond the time Bennett went to bed, our time would be structured so that temptation would not be as much of a concern. I took time to pray about that, and finally concede tonight.

After Bennett is in bed the second time, Elijah plops on the couch, dutifully placing his list on the coffee table. I giggle and sit next to him, pulling my own list from my pocket.

"Four weeks," he says. "You sure you're ready for all this?"

"You mean the wedding? We don't have that much left to do." I ponder, unfolding the notebook paper and smoothing it out over my skirt.

"I mean being a part of all this." He gestures around his house, but chuckles when he sees all my newly placed decorations, "Which I guess you already are."

"And in four weeks I won't have to leave in the evening or explain myself to my father all the time."

"Yeah, I'd much rather talk like this all cuddled up in pajamas with no other worries in the world."

"Me too," I whisper, closing my eyes and considering future firelight and hot cocoa.

"Which reminds me: Cindy found out we were planning to do a staycation after the wedding and she told Jessie, who insisted on watching Ben for a few days. So I booked us a modest little honeymoon sort of deal. We're staying within a hundred miles, don't worry." Elijah smiles.

"Oh." I move my hair aside, respecting and submitting. "That might be fun."

Elijah chuckles. "I'm going for peaceful and romantic, not 'fun.' If I wanted 'fun,' we'd take Bennett, and it wouldn't be to the place we're going."

"I guess that's what I meant," I offer.

Elijah sighs. "You scared of being alone with me for a few days?"

"I'm alone with you now." I roll my eyes and cross my arms. "Which breaks all the rules and makes me feel guilty. If Dad finds out, we'll be in for it."

"I don't answer to your dad anymore. You said we could do this," Elijah says, almost flirtatiously. "What's liberty for if not evenings like this?"

"I agree. But until Dad walks me down the aisle and gives me away, you do still answer to him at least a little," I remind him. "So where are we going for our 'modest little honeymoon sort of deal'?"

"Sorry, what was that? I don't answer to you yet." Elijah winks, awaiting my reaction.

I playfully hit Elijah with the accent pillow I bought the first day I visited. Elijah takes the chance and reaches in to tickle me, which he's never done, so he's never heard me giggle quite like I do. The playful quarrel ends with Elijah balanced in his hands on either side of my hips on the couch and his eyes smiling into mine.

I'm taken by the smell of his skin and some spell he cast. Our smiles deepen and relax. And as if I'm not a Christian or the daughter of Adam Monroe at all, I nearly entertain Elijah's next wild words.

"When will you let me kiss you?"

"Four weeks, Elijah," I whisper. "We can kiss in four weeks."

He shakes his head and returns to the other cushion with a frustrated grunt, swiping his list up along the way, "And that's the first thing on my list."

"What is?"

"Well, I want to know why I have to share our first kiss with everybody."

"Tradition." I shrug, "We have the rest of our lives, Elijah. We don't have any reason to ignite any passions this close to the wedding. We can share a million kisses nobody knows about starting in a few weeks."

Elijah never quits that easy. "Believe me, I'm looking forward to that. But I feel like our first kiss will belong to everyone else, and I didn't save my first kiss until I was twenty-nine to share it with anyone but you."

I try to meet him halfway. "Well, maybe we just won't kiss at the altar. Aaron and Katie did it that way. They wanted it to be private, probably because Elliot and Priscilla's kiss was so awkward. So, they went into the pastor's office after the ceremony. We could do that, Elijah."

"I *do* want to kiss you at the altar, for the sake of tradition. Just not the first kiss. *I* want that one."

"It isn't fair for you to ask for me to make that decision right now. I can see you've been considering this, but for me it would be a heat of the moment decision."

"Oh! No. Not..." He nervously readjusts the accent pillow beside him. "Not now. You're right, that's not fair. Just think about it, okay? Weigh the options in your heart with Jesus and let me know. I'll love you and happily marry you either way."

I nod understanding. But he isn't content yet.

"So they. . .they kiss for the first time at the altar and then. . ." He clears his throat like he does when he's searching for tact. "I mean, I assume they have a regular, you know, wedding night?"

I avert my eyes and cross my arms across my chest. "I assume you mean with intimacy?"

"Yeah."

"I don't know for sure, Elijah. Obviously this hasn't been reported to me." I try not to panic. "Why are you asking me that?"

"Well, there's just a lot between a sweet little altar kiss and sex, Jubilee. If they are capable of doing that all at once, that's an accomplishment, wouldn't you say? I've always wondered how people manage it." He laughs, nervous over the subject matter. And it's like a genius telling a joke about astrophysics to an infant. I have little clue what he's saying right now. I spot my ignorance, yet don't even know how to respond but with silence.

The silence grows. And swells. Then Elijah clears his throat again, and it turns into the dry cough he sometimes has. Finally, he speaks.

"Jubilee...I'm stuck here. I don't want to destroy your innocence, because I love your innocence. You know that. I also don't want to have an awkward situation on our wedding night. So we can save the list for later, because. . .you need to tell me what you know and don't know."

"How can I tell you what I don't know?" I laugh and look up at him.

"I mean did anyone teach you…"

I bite my lip and sigh, then make my confession. "My parents tell us that intimacy is how babies are made, and that occurs between a man and a woman in private. I'm not oblivious. But most of the families in my church feel it is too much of a temptation to teach us beyond that. I know that my brothers have sometimes been permitted to research it when they were engaged. And I know that Hakim looked it up when he was about thirteen just out of curiosity. But—"

"You cannot be serious…" Elijah's hands go to his head in disbelief.

I explain faster. "We have this tradition where Mom and any married sisters and sisters-in-law have a talk with the bride-to-be while they do nails and things the night before the wedding. During this, they explain the exact mechanics and progression of intimacy. Dad does the same with my brothers, even if they've done research. I've never actually been in the room for it; I'm usually watching the children. So, you're telling me there's a lot between a kiss and intimacy, and I do know that and I believe you, but I don't actually know what or how much."

"The night before the wedding." He stares holes into my eyes. "Jubilee, my eight-year-old knows the mechanics of sex."

I gasp. "Why does he need to know that?"

"Because it's a natural part of human reproduction, Jubilee. And because it's a fallen world and far too many kids are abused and don't know it because their parents didn't teach them about all those processes and mechanics and desires." He laughs, unable to believe this travesty that I didn't know was a travesty. "You recently told me that your sister who suffers from OCD almost called off her wedding the night before? Was this before or after this talk?"

"Um, during, actually," I recall, confused about why that matters. "It was just with Mom and Maren in Mom's bedroom. No one had any children yet, though Maren was expecting Lawrence, and I was just a kid. But Priscilla got *very* upset. She was even vomiting, which she reserves for especially horrific things like when she accidentally touched horse mess once."

"Well, I don't blame her. How can a woman be expected to consent to a marriage without knowing everything she's consenting to?" That wounded him deeply.

"God told me to marry you, and I trust Him. And I trust you. We can't possibly know all the details of what our life will entail, right? I may not have a chance to consent to every trial. How is this different?"

"Sex isn't meant to be a *trial*, Jubilee. It's designed to be a beautiful thing that lovers share to gain a deeper connection." His laugh is bitter. "So your dad warns you about me wanting to take you to bed with me, and you don't actually know what *happens* there? No wonder he's so worried about boundaries and you being here. You're probably not even a hundred percent sure that we've never done anything intimate."

"I have a good idea of what it is and isn't just from reading the Bible, Elijah. And I also had some courses about reproduction with animals when I went to school, but I honestly don't know how much translates. Hakim started to tell me once when I was studying, but I knew my parents didn't want me to know, so…

"So, your parents let you read God's Word but they won't explain those things to you until you're hours from experiencing it?" It seems like an interrogation now.

"It's a temptation. And we're actually. . .we have to be eighteen before we read Song of Solomon. So I just read it last year and didn't understand it in the least," I admit.

"This is wrong, Jubilee. I love you and I have promised God that I'm going to care for you and protect you. I want you to know what you're getting into."

"I will, Elijah. The night before the wedding. Hannah was just saying last week that she's looking forward to being on the other end of the talk."

He sighs. Laughs bitterly. Then sighs again with resolve as he stands and goes to his bookshelf and pulls out a thick book. He is almost in a daze as he brings it back to the couch. "Okay, well…this isn't something I thought I'd be doing, and I can't guarantee it won't be awkward or a temptation or something, but I don't care. I'm using my liberty on informed consent for the woman I'm about to marry."

It's an anatomy textbook, I see when he sits again.

"I don't get to pray about this?" I laugh.

"Not this time. I'm teaching you how I taught Bennett. Medical terminology and diagrams and everything. I like this book because there aren't any photos and there are minimal external drawings that would make it a temptation." He clears his throat. "But you won't even be able to tell your dad if I teach you. Or whoever teaches you the night before the wedding. There's no way they'd take that well. Can you live with that?"

I think back to the first time Elijah told me I'm beautiful and I didn't tell my father. Some things are private. I know that. This is likely the *most* private thing, and I am only meant to experience it with one person. So though the wedding is weeks away, I know the right answer.

"This is your area, Elijah. Not theirs," I concede. If I'm being honest, I've always wanted to know. And my insatiable need to learn things has almost taken me to researching everything about sex. But my parents wouldn't have approved, and I assumed God felt the same.

"Darn tootin'." He chuckles, then begins to open the book, which has some dusty sticky notes marking certain pages. Then he closes it. "Just promise you'll still marry me?"

I roll my eyes. "Yes. I'll still marry you. I'm not Priscilla, and I don't know *nothing*."

He nods and opens that book and I realize that I didn't know nothing. Just *next* to nothing. Through his precise descriptions and colorful explanations of black and white sketches, he keeps laughing at my gasps and snorts and giggles. And as I learn hopefully as much as the eight-year-old in the other room, my childlike reactions relay to me that Elijah is right. This is meant to be explained to a child, not a woman wearing an engagement ring.

Some explanations get awkward in present company, and he asks if I need him to stop or save it for another day. But I'm in too deep now, and to be honest, it is fascinating. He explains the progression of things—the hormones and cognitive and physical processes necessary for this act. Some of those I understand. But there are just a few words and connotations that are completely new to me, and I have never heard intimacy described this way by a Jesus-chasing Christian.

Pleasure. Passion. Fun. Beauty. A sense of peace and a greater bond when it's over. It's chemicals and hormones, the book says. But Eljiah says it's obviously deeper than that, otherwise why would sinners obsess so much? Why would Christians protect it so much?

We protect it. That is for certain. This knowledge was so protected and scoured clean and sanitized from the Christian world that I am nineteen years old and I didn't even know what to expect as someone's wife. There are times during our conversation that I wonder if my wise, learned, authentic Elijah is lying to me.

"Are you sure?" I ask.

"Jubilee, yes."

"And this is all normal?"

"Well that isn't fair. I'm only 99 percent sure that it's normal. It's only not a hundred because I lack experience." He laughs. "We'll talk again in a few weeks, and I'll let you know."

Finally, he goes into what I'm more familiar with. Pregnancy. When he gets past conception and fertilization, which has also been partially veiled from me, I know the rest. And everything connects and makes sense.

"Hmm," I finally say, cradling my trembling being. I'm feeling a thousand things and trying not to think about some of them in the context of the man sharing the couch with me.

"You okay?" He asks.

"Yeah, I'm just processing," I admit. "Thank you for…"

"Warning you?" He laughs himself to that dry cough again. "We're still getting hitched, right?"

And I laugh just once. Because I think I might understand a new connotation of just about everything.

He laughs so loud I worry Bennett will wake. "I've corrupted you."

"Well then you better marry me, right? Make me an honest woman?" I sigh, trying to make jokes to cover the nerves.

But he gets serious and scoots close to me, moving hairs from my face and causing my heart and mind to do things that I wish I still didn't understand. He sighs and speaks low, reassuring me. "I don't want you to be scared, okay? God designed this, and we'll celebrate His design. And then when we're ready, we'll let that translate into babies."

"When *we* are ready?"

"Yeah. We should get acquainted first, though. Figure out all this new stuff we have to learn together before bringing babies into the mix."

"You want children, right? I mean *more* children. Obviously, we're starting with one."

"Of course. I told you that in counseling."

"Yeah, but when I told you I wanted ten, you thought I was joking."

Which he answers with silence, wide eyes, and a hard swallow.

Thankfully, in the quiet, my phone rings and both hearts emerge from chests in the startle.

It's Hannah. The baby is coming. When I hang up the phone with Hannah, I stand.

"Speaking of babies..."

Elijah's eyes light up. "Really? That's great! You headed to the hospital, or..."

"Her house. Almost everyone in my family does home births. With a good midwife, of course," I explain.

"Oh...how does that work?" Elijah is intrigued.

"It's actually pretty amazing to witness. She gets to be comfortable and have lots of time with the new baby. I've never even been to a hospital birth, but I guess it's...different?" I'm smiling. Ecstatic over getting to meet a brand-new person today.

"Well I don't know. I've never attended a *home* birth." Elijah chuckles. "There's stuff I don't know too."

"If Bennett were awake, I'd ask you to come. Hannah and James accept visitors twenty-four-seven when their babies are born," I offer.

"Well call me when the baby gets here. Maybe we'll come then." Elijah nods, standing with me. "Give Hannah and James my best."

I kiss the goodbye on Elijah's cheek, which makes him smile.

"About the kissing thing, which took a weird turn. Jubilee, I want you to be able to live with whatever you decide. That's more important to me than having your first kiss to myself. Obviously there is a lot that you plan on giving to me, so I'm willing to give up some things. I wanted to say that." Elijah concludes a previous conversation with grave sincerity. "So, if you don't want to..."

"Elijah." I laugh a little. " 'Want to' is never lacking with you."

Twenty

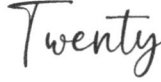

Jubilee

My heart is pounding as I'm driving into town, trying not to tremble from all that transpired. I forget the internal battle, or try to, when I see that the family vehicle is pulling out of Monroe Drive just ahead of me. I suddenly feel like I have something to hide.

We all arrive at the Martin home at the same time as the midwife, who enters at a sprint.

We enter and hear Hannah moaning in her bedroom, and the midwife speaks. "Wash up ladies, this won't take long."

My mother and I obey, and Hakim, Judah, and Dad all wait out in the living room while we join Hannah and James in their bedroom. James is holding Hannah's hand, crouching at the side of the bed at a calm that defies Hannah's panic.

The thing I love most about childbirth is that finally, everyone *says* something, as Hakim or Elijah may analyze. From what I gather, a woman is called to her limit, unable to live behind all her social graces. She is removed from modesty and submission. Perhaps everything that makes her a lady at all is not present during childbirth. Therefore, that is when a woman's true heart is revealed.

Growing up with Hannah was growing up with a polite and demure young woman. She followed all the rules and never talked back. Her smile is infectious and her love for Christ perpetuates it. When she married James, many were confused. James is known for his mild rebellion. His passion. His drive to succeed. Frankly, the union didn't make much sense, and many wondered that the infatuation they had for one another since age six would dwindle. Even I had my doubts. But when Hannah brought their first child,

Jonathan, into the world when I was just thirteen and scared to be in my first delivery room, that's when I really met my sister.

As illustrated tonight: "J…James! Why does it hurt so bad already?"

The midwife, "Don't think of it as pain, sweetie. Just listen to your body."

"I *am* listening!" Hannah screams. "It *hurts*! And I was addressing my husband."

The midwife checks the clock to time the powerful contraction, apparently trained not to let the outbursts get to her. Mom shushes Hannah. And James smiles like he's madly in love. He always looks at her that way, but new education is leading to new observations. "Do you feel any pressure yet, baby?"

Hannah breathes. Calms. Bursts into tears. "I'm sorry for yelling. Why do you put up with me, James? I'm so fat and ugly and I can't even control my own words."

James laughs once and smooths Hannah's sweaty hair from her face, looking with intensity into her eyes. He whispers endearingly in that voice I always feel I shouldn't hear, and now I know why. "Baby, you are a *goddess*."

"That is blasphemy." Hannah smiles back at him.

James chuckles, then when the next contraction hits, he breathes with her, like she's forgotten how. Or maybe like them breathing deeply together like that is how every child should come into the world. She is herself right now. Insecure, fiery yet gentle, and deeply in love with James. That's who I know her to be and the reason why I love to attend her births. There is so much of herself she hides. Things that are forgiven today, but that tomorrow they'll all pretend to have forgotten. I hand James a cool cloth for Hannah's forehead, and he winks at me. Because he knows exactly what I'm thinking.

Hannah asks a lot about her other children, asleep in the next room, during contractions. A lot about her baby's well-being. And as we near the end, only a half hour after arriving, I know my favorite part is coming. The part when Hannah overflows with joy. She's told me she doesn't actually see her baby's face until hours later when she can finally keep the tears from clouding her light brown eyes.

Hannah gasps. "I think she's coming next contraction."

"Already?" James asks.

Hannah nods, panicked.

The scorned midwife smiles. "Positions."

Mom and I hold one of each of Hannah's legs and James has a hand and cheers her on triumphantly until Hannah brings his second daughter and third child into the world. Her cries set us all to tears.

"Hello, Mary Jubilee Martin." James says, wiping his own tears just after the cord has been cut and the baby is quiet at Hannah's breast.

I had been only a little jealous when Bethany Priscilla was born. And Leah has been used in various forms. I understand that though I'm part of the family, I came in rather late. I'd been unoffended. But now I'm something else.

"Jubilee?" I ask in a squeak.

"Of course!" James laughs. Whispers to me, "We only did Priscilla first because she would have thrown a fit otherwise. We knew you'd take it with grace, like everything. And since we had another girl, we also knew what to do next."

Mom sniffles as she holds her newest grandchild when Hannah allows, and then I get a chance to look down into another set of deep brown eyes like James's and treasure her, just as I do the other two Martin children.

"Think Mary is ready to go out?" James asks. "I think I heard my parents get here."

The midwife nods. Hannah smiles. Accepts a kiss. James growls, "Goddess." Hannah giggles. And then James takes the little baby out into the living room while us women clean up the room and Hannah prepares to become that woman she isn't once again.

A half hour after texting a picture to Elijah with the baby's name and stats, I hear some familiar chatter from the living room. Something about marriage and babies and soon-to-be mommies named Jubilee. All in Bennett's voice. Hannah smiles wearily.

"You better go out there. You're so lucky to be inheriting an eight-year-old."

I go out to the living room to see that Bennett is holding the new baby with the help of James. Elijah looks up and greets me with a hug.

"He came in the living room and asked where you went. Which is ridiculous. It was eleven o'clock, you wouldn't have been there anyway. I showed him the picture and he wouldn't quiet down about seeing this baby until we got in the truck and came here," Elijah explains. "I hope you don't mind. He loves her name."

After a short conversation and introductions with James and his parents, James returns with baby Mary to Hannah. James's parents leave just as Mom is coming into the living room.

"How late were you at Elijah's house, Jubilee?" My father booms, completely out of place and inappropriately. I often wonder what kind of a man would come from him if men could go through childbirth.

"Uh...I was about to leave when I got the call. Nine-ish?" Which might actually be a lie. I was thinking about having ten babies with a devilishly handsome man who had just explained the facts of life to me. So, I wasn't leaving yet.

"Was Bennett awake?" Judah asks. "Your chaperone. Was he up, or were you alone together?"

Is he kidding? I don't know what to say.

Elijah answers. "A baby was just born. Is this the time or place for this discussion? Can't we be joyful?"

"Jubilee, did you violate my rules? Was Bennett asleep?" Dad asks again. No. Apparently, we can't be joyful.

"Dad, we..."

"Was he asleep?" Dad asks with even more authority.

"Probably." Elijah shrugs. "He likes to eavesdrop, so if he'd been awake, he'd have come out right when Jubilee left all excited about Hannah being in labor."

"Your chaperone, whom I was hesitant to approve, was *asleep*? I knew I could not trust you to go to his house. And you take your things there as if you already live with him. And you're discussing God-knows-what over the phone. How often has this happened? You being alone together?" Dad demands. "Has this happened every time you've gone to Elijah's house?"

"No, just tonight, and it was something suggested in counseling," I confess, glancing at Elijah before setting my eyes to the floor at Dad's feet.

"I know I should not have allowed that liberal pastor to counsel you," Dad says.

"Dad, he's—" But Elijah cuts me off.

"So, what's the punishment for that? Is my fiancée grounded for four weeks until she can come over and stay the whole night? What actually *happens* when your courting and engagement rules get violated?" Elijah hips his hands and shakes his head. Judah and Hakim take a physical step back from the situation and Mom is in silent panic.

"So far, the young men and women courting my children have been respectful enough not to break them," Dad says, then asks, "Elijah, have you been engaging in amorous congress with Jubilee?"

Elijah's eyes narrow, genuinely unsure if the answer is yes or no. He chuckles, and I wonder if he feels something like I did a couple hours ago. Astrophysics to an infant. "Um…what century is this? Sorry Adam, I'm… what exactly is 'amorous congress'? I need to brush up on my Jane Austen."

Hakim sighs, annoyed with his father and in fear for his soon-to-be brother-in-law. "He means sex, Elijah. He wants to know if you two are. . ." To which Mom responds with a slap to Hakim's arm. We don't often say "sex" in a context like this. Or in any context, I suppose. And when we do, half of us don't even know exactly what *that* is.

Elijah loses his standoffishness. His eyes widen and he swallows hard. Then the fire lights inside him and he emits a bitter laugh. "Adam, in what universe would you think it's appropriate to ask me that in mixed company like this?"

"I'll ask whatever I wish in whatever circumstance I wish. The appearances suggest the worst. There's no proof otherwise. Your evasion of my question also suggests guilt."

"*Appearances*, Adam?" Elijah plants his feet, ready to do battle. I pray, readying my trumpet and fire-filled pitcher. "If you recall, the Savior of all humanity was conceived out of wedlock. When Joseph obeyed God and married Mary, he forever allowed it to *appear* as though he himself had fathered Christ, even in historical documentation. There was no proof otherwise, but Mary and Joseph did not sin, and God was their judge. Likewise, when Jesus Christ was passed from authority to authority, beaten and accused and put on trial for crimes He did not commit, it would appear to the passerby as though He were guilty. He was usually silent when He was questioned. That made Him seem guilty. He hung on a cross among thieves, Adam. It would have *appeared* that He was condemned for His own crimes. They mocked him, even though Jesus was innocent before God His Father. Aren't you glad Jesus didn't decide the *appearances* were more important than our salvation?" The family is silent. I am falling in love again. But Dad refuses to be defeated.

"Of course, Elijah, but what could you possibly be doing with Jubilee that you find more important than being above reproach when it comes to my rules for courting her?"

"That isn't your concern, Adam. It is, in fact, *no one's* concern. Thus the objective in being alone. Were we supposed to have *never* been alone together when we get married?" Elijah snickers at the ridiculous prospect.

"Yes," Judah says. Dad smirks. Proud of his son's rudeness. "You're supposed to make a permanent commitment before allowing that temptation."

"Jubilee is wearing an engagement ring. An entire wedding is planned. She's the primary beneficiary on my life insurance. We share a checking account and a cell phone account. We're looking into what it'll take after the wedding for her to adopt Bennett and change the title on my house. We're in this for keeps. I'm not sure what else you're asking me to do," Elijah argues.

"Obviously, I've been too lenient. Jubilee, I don't feel it is your responsibility, but because you made the arrangement to care for Bennett, I'm willing to bend so that he can be settled after school. However, until the wedding, I'd like for you to come home before supper."

"Dad, Elijah doesn't even get home until seven thirty," I negotiate. "I planned out meals to be sure I can cook them dinner. It's already late for Bennett to eat. I'm helping to get him to bed at a decent hour."

"Then I expect you home by eight," Dad commands. "Preparing meals for the family is a *wife's* job. Be thankful that I allow it."

"Dad, I would get to see Elijah for less than a half hour *most* days. I wouldn't even get to help clean up dinner or kiss Bennett goodnight." I push it further.

"Awww," Bennett says to himself, disappointed. My heart wrenches.

"It's alright, Bennett. We've done without Jubilee spoiling us before. It's only for a few weeks." Elijah comforts his son. But he's probably fuming over more rules and boundaries.

"Eight o'clock. I feel that's generous." Dad's ultimatum.

In a beat, my mind goes back to earlier while I cooked dinner. I hear my love's voice, and the pure relief it echoed. *This is life-giving, Jubilee. You just don't know how much of a blessing you are.* God is using me to bless him, and I know the proper response, however uncomfortable.

"*No,* Dad." Which is likely the second time I've said it in the years I've been his daughter. The first was likely when I was still an adjusting adopted toddler.

"Excuse me?" Dad demands, shocked. The others are in just as much disbelief as I crash my pitcher to the rocks, my torch ablaze.

"I won't stop 'spoiling' them. I like being there to put Bennett to bed. Further, I enjoy serving them dinner and spending a little time with Elijah. We had an important conversation this evening because I stayed. I *love* him, Dad. These two are my family. I'm called by God to serve them. I will be home by ten o'clock during the week and eleven o'clock on the weekends per the original agreement you made with Elijah. I will continue to move my things over to his house, because logistically, it makes sense and eases a burden later. We are making a huge transition in our lives, and we are trying to ease into it. I haven't done anything wrong, and with all due respect, I need you to please stop thwarting my efforts to serve my family." I breathe slowly, trying to hide the fact that I'm trembling all over.

"Legally, they are not your family *yet*," Dad reasons pompously.

"And biologically, I'm not *yours*." I bring up the thing I swore I never would, ever since fruitless seeds were planted. There are some quiet gasps amid that trumpet call. Then I take it all back to godliness. "But you are my *father*, Dad. When has a lack of common DNA ever stopped you from loving and protecting me? The wedding might be a month away, but these two are my family *now*. I get the chance to ease the burden of a single father and a child who has never had a mother. Elijah didn't ask or expect me to do this, but God wants me in their life. In their *home* when they need me. So, that's where I will be."

"This is a slippery slope. It is only a matter of time before the temptation and opportunity begin to rule you," Dad warns, rightfully so.

"Yeah, I bet they won't make it more than a month before there's 'amorous congress,' " Hakim mumbles. Elijah winks at him, outside Dad's notice.

"Have you been in his bedroom?" Dad knows he's drowning. Losing.

"Yes," I say with confidence. "We know that it is best for us to have a constructive way to occupy our time since we are spending less time in public. So, we have been doing some decorating. Yesterday when I went over there after church, the three of us spruced up Elijah's bedroom."

"Jubilee has a knack for decorating, and I wanted her to feel like it's her home when she moves in," Elijah adds.

"You *painted* his room?" Dad asks in a skeptical tone.

"Yes," I offer with a shrug.

"What color?" He challenges.

"We were going for warm neutral on the walls, besides in Ben's room. So, a light brown." I nod, not mentioning the deep red bedding Elijah picked out—for raging hormones and passion and pleasure, I now understand.

"More of a café latte, I'd say." Elijah smirks.

"A latte is like coffee. I think it looks like chocolate milk." Bennett, though looking exhausted, reminds us of his presence. Elijah and I laugh a little while he continues. "Mine is blue. Miss Jubilee picked the color. We moved all my furniture around and organized my toys after we painted. Dad had to work all day on Saturday so he can be off for the wedding, so we surprised him with my new room. Then he liked it so much we painted his room and this weekend, we are painting the kitchen. Miss Jubilee will live with us soon. I can't wait!"

By now, the whole room has lightened up at his chattering. Even Dad has softened a bit. Elijah laughs. "Okay, Ben. Thanks."

Then the midwife emerges. "Jubilee, I have another call. Full moons are like this. Hannah is doing well, but if you could stay the night, I'd feel better."

"I'll stay. I've had an overnight bag in my car for a couple weeks in case I needed to."

"Thank you." Then she leaves with all her things in a hurry.

"So, you could have easily stayed at Elijah's house?" Judah asks. My parents scowl, thinking the same. Hakim winces.

Elijah laughs in disbelief. "Really?"

"No! Miss Jubilee is not married to my dad yet! A man and woman can't live at the same house until they get married," Bennett says. "It's not what God likes. My daddy always obeys God."

"The mouth of babes." Elijah clears his throat. "Come on Bennett. Waaaay past bedtime and you have school tomorrow." Then he valiantly leans in and kisses my cheek before putting his hat on and tipping it with a wink. "Miz Jubilee."

I smile coyly at what that action does to my heart ever since we met at that gas station. "Love you."

"Love you too." Elijah exits, and then I am alone with my family.

"He kissed you," Judah says.

"Um. . ." I glance at all the shocked faces. "Yeah, but. . .just my. . ."

"He's *changing* you," my father remarks.

"Helping me grow, Dad."

"He didn't answer my question. Jubilee, sexual immorality is a serious offense against a holy God," Dad asks gently. "Tell me if you think he's been inappropriate."

If I *think*. Because I wouldn't really *know* by his understanding. *How very dangerous*. I suddenly understand his every fear. How much easier would his job as a protector be if he were a better educator?

"Nothing has changed," I promise him, though it likely isn't true, and shouldn't be. "Elijah has never said or done anything that I would deem inappropriate. He likely never will." And that much is true, though I don't know if it tells Dad a thing. He knows that what I deem appropriate has shifted vastly.

I retreat to check on Hannah, and I am glad to be able to stay twenty minutes away from my scowling family for the night, in service of a baby who shares my name.

Twenty-One

Elijah

I like to live in the present, so it doesn't happen every night. Not anymore, at least. But tonight, a baby was born, and that's always been a trigger. The response is sleepless nights or nightmares if I find myself remembering two troubled childhoods—mine, and the one I swore never to give my own children, but almost did.

One phone call made me an orphan and a father in one night.

"Is this Elijah Bering?"

"Yes."

"You're listed as Patrice Bering's next of kin. She's been in an accident. We'll need you to come down to the hospital."

"Is she alright?"

"Son…I'm sorry. Let me clarify. We'll need you to identify her. She passed not long after the cesarean."

"Cesarean? You're mistaken. This must not be the correct Patrice Bering."

"Well, that's what we need you to tell us."

"Doesn't she have a boyfriend that can—"

"They're looking for him. Mostly to arrest him. He left once the baby was born. Poor thing."

"I'll come down there and get this sorted out."

Patrice Bering's face was nearly unrecognizable. Scrapes and burns covered most of it. But I knew it. At just forty-two, it was weathered and gaunt. Years of abusing alcohol and drugs while various boyfriends took turns abusing her showed in every chasm and pit across her face. But it was the same face that kissed me goodnight as a child, and shushed me in fear as we hid from drunk boyfriends who would come home raging. It was the same cocoa butter scented face that raised me the best she knew how, though she admittedly didn't know much of anything. It was with a choked-up whisper that I told that doctor,

"Yeah, that's her. That's my mom. What happened?"

"The driver wrapped the car around a light pole. He's facing a lot of time for a lot of bad deeds. He seemed to know the baby was his. Just didn't seem to care."

"I wasn't aware my mother was expecting. We haven't spoken a lot recently. Don't see eye to eye."

"I understand. She had a baby boy, thirteen weeks premature. He's deformed and detoxing. They don't think he'll live very long. We'll help you decide what to do with his remains if the father doesn't return."

At that, I winced. "His remains." I glanced at my deceased mother. "If this woman gave birth to a son as her last deed on this earth, I have a living brother. Not...remains. Hers are the only remains at this point. Let's not borrow more."

"Of course. How insensitive of me."

"You're forgiven. May I see him?"

"He's...It may be a lot to take in. The father couldn't handle it."

"Again, may I see him?"

It was a lot to take in. Patrice Bering had again done the best she knew how. And again, it wasn't much. I was so sure the call would come that I made sure to take out a life insurance policy for when, not if, I'd be obligated to bury my mother while she was still young. It didn't make it easier seeing her on a cold table. A junkie. A nobody. She could barely afford food, let alone gifts for most of my life. But with her last breaths, she'd left something behind that changed me the moment I saw him. Wrapped in too-big tubes and medical tape, that baby was the frailest thing alive. But he was alive. A lot to take in, indeed. My heart could barely handle it.

"As you can see, he's—"

"Beautiful," I whispered at tears. Grieving my mother but looking into the very last piece of her.

A presence walked up behind us, also peering into the glass. It was the baby's father, the boyfriend, a leathery-skinned blond addict in his midfifties I had only met once when Mom came around asking for money.

"Disgusting, in'he? Luckily, they say he'll give up soon. I won't have to figure out what to do with him. Nobody would want to adopt him, and—"

"I'll take him," I heard myself say.

"More power to ye'. I'll put it in writing. Knock yourself out."

"They're looking to arrest you."

"I know. I just came to say goodbye to Patrice and then they can have me."

He didn't put it in writing. Or turn himself in. He went into a hospital restroom and intentionally overdosed on heroin. Bennett and I were both orphaned that night. Two lost causes found a family.

"You thought of a name?" They asked me after my mother's funeral when I was still dressed in black but visiting Ben.

"My mother's maiden name was Bennett. And I'd rather he keep our last name, not his father's, whatever that is. Bennett Bering."

"That's nice." That nurse was likely thinking about the way it would look on a headstone. "Middle name?"

"Mephibosheth."

"What was that?"

"Mephibosheth. A man with crippled legs who spent much of his life dining at the table of a king."

"That's a lot to live up to."

"I know."

Right now, standing in Bennett's doorway after covering up his incomplete, perfect legs and listening to his deeply trusting breath, I am remembering when the nightmares came every night. Bennett fought for every hour of life, and it was nearly the death of me loving him through it. When he was out of the woods and sleeping in a crib in my room, the nightmares increased. I'd often check to be sure my cold-sweat startles didn't wake him. Right now, I'm remembering all the trailers and apartments we have occupied. The split-level house we rented because I wanted my son to live in a house. But he hated climbing all those stairs.

I'm remembering when everyone we knew in Texas started to persecute us. They'd tell me my son was worthless. The pastor at our church called him an abomination. With the adoption final, I no longer needed assistance from the state of Texas. We packed up everything we could into the bed of my truck and put the rest in storage to be moved later.

We drove north, wondering if maybe it was all true. We were unlovable and unacceptable. Lost causes after all. We ran out of gas in Colorado and barely made it into a church parking lot. I didn't know it could get so cold without snow, but the truck told me it was negative nineteen degrees outside just before the gas ran out. It was a Saturday night, late. I wrapped Ben up in my coat with me in the back seat, but still didn't see any way out of the situation except a tragic headline in the frigid little town's newspaper.

"I love you, Benny." Something I called Bennett until recently when he begged me to stop.

"I love you too, Daddy. I'm cold." Which I was sure would be the last words from his mouth. All his genius that they said would be retardation would be wasted on the Colorado cold in some town not even the surrounding mountains could pity enough to touch.

Three raps at the window cured me of those thoughts.

"There is a room in the church for you," the man said. He was about ninety-five. Gray hair, back hunched over so he waddled like a penguin in place of walking. He unlocked the doors and led us to an attic with a warm apartment room set up for a man and his boy. I never saw that man again. But when I described him to the confused church staff come morning, they didn't question the spine-tingling occurrence. They were thankful.

"You're a nurse?" The pastor's wife asked as she served Bennett some Cheerios from the food pantry.

"Yes ma'am. A male RN. I've heard them all. No need to tease." I'd answered. Smiling at the way the woman's teenage daughter hardly cared that Bennett was without his legs.

"I'm not gonna tease you." The woman in her forties winked. "Where are you headed?"

"Away from Texas," I admitted.

"Well, I'd say you made it." She chuckled. "I saw a post for a nurse position over at Sunny Rest. One of the nursing homes. My grandmother is there, and we try to stop by as often as we can. If this is far enough away from Texas, I bet it'd do *Abuela*'s heart some good to see a man like you walking those halls."

"Mom!" The daughter, a teenager, scolded. "I am so telling Dad."

"Thank you. First step was to find a church, and then a job. Then a place to live. Hadn't anticipated the cold. I'm glad that man let us in." I had said. "Step one accomplished, so long as nobody here calls my son an abomination."

"Born out of wedlock?" The woman asked point blank.

"Yes, ma'am. But he and I are both orphans, so we don't keep track." I'd admitted right then and there, even though I usually keep it a secret much longer.

"Brothers?"

"Legally, Bennett is my son. He needed a father, not a sibling."

"Either way, feel free to stay up here until you two get on your feet. I'll look out for a place for you in the meantime. I'm Lucinda. Pastor Jordan's wife. This is Jessie, our little girl. You're not the first to show up here claiming an old man let you in, so don't worry about that. Let's just get you settled so you can know just how far you are from whatever happened in Texas."

Jubilee, my bride-to-be, thinks I go to my church because I don't know any better. She's right. I don't know better. I've known a lot of worse, though. The Durant family saved my life. They found me a job and our first Colorado apartment, and became family. Gratitude doesn't quite cover it.

But there's a lot Jubilee doesn't know. Even though she's every dream I've ever had regarding women, she has no inkling just how far she is from the worst of my dreams. She's pure. And wild, and not even she knows that. Not yet. I'll marry her soon, and I'm terrified. Does she know how many demons she's marrying?

I'm terrified that all she sees is quiet kindness. Something she sometimes tells me is bone deep, because it isn't a choice to be kind and give all I have. She sees that truth. Admires it. But she doesn't know that as a child I was always someone's burden. Therefore, I must fight everything I've ever known to let the world know that no one is ever a burden. I've seen enough pain never to inflict it.

I return to bed after checking on Bennett. Drinking what I probably need not, and imagining what I ought not, but she is the easiest place to turn my dark thoughts to joy. She doesn't deserve to enter this darkness of mine, but I decide after nightmares triggered by a baby that she needs to know.

Tonight, ten days from our wedding, Jubilee is waiting for me on the couch after I return Bennett to his room with freshly rubbed legs. I'm glad this is one of those nights she's chosen to stick around. She stays until at least Ben's bedtime most nights. She and Bennett even surprised me on my birthday last week with a "big ol' fish fry." But she only sometimes stays after Ben is in bed, even after telling her daddy exactly why she should be here. But I shouldn't complain. I'm glad she's here tonight.

"So, I have an important question." I sigh, starting right in as I sit next to her.

"Okay." Jubilee smiles.

"Are we rushing into this?"

"Yes." She retains her smile with the quick answer. "But only in the same sense that Mary rushed from an empty tomb to tell the disciples. You getting cold feet?"

"No!" I clarify. "Of course not. You kidding? Every time you have to leave at night, I count down how many more times I have to feel like my heart is driving away in that little hatchback."

"So why would you ask?"

"Because we finally got a chance to sit down and talk about some sensitive subjects a couple weeks ago, and—"

"And I was completely ignorant about stuff you have completely figured out, so you had to explain it to me."

"You don't have to put it that way." I chuckle, even while still speaking. "We just ran out of time that night to discuss everything and I feel like we're avoiding bringing everything up again."

"There are a lot of different facets to marriage, Elijah. And while God has been faithful to prepare my heart for each of them, some have been easier than others. So yes, to be honest. I'm avoiding certain conversations from that list."

"Interesting," I mumble, encouraging her to elaborate.

"Well, caring for a child, cooking, cleaning, and making a home are natural to me. They just require adaptation and practice, and I've already started doing a lot of that. It's everything *else* that I'm trying to figure out how to prepare for."

"And considering I'm not hiring a housekeeper or a nanny, you're basically prepared for nothing," I chuckle. "We're doing this in ten days, Jubilee. Is that enough for you?"

"It's the *transition* that's the hardest. Drawing this out wouldn't help."

"What do you mean?"

"For instance with, you know. . .intimacy."

"Yeah?"

"Well, I've just been taught a hundred ways to avoid certain feelings and temptations my whole life, so I've spent a lot of time in prayer trying to understand how to not have those feelings, then suddenly allow them to occur after the wedding." She tilts her head as she reads my eyes. "But you seem to have that transition figured out. Maybe you can give me some wisdom here."

I shrug and confess. "I'm marrying you, Jubilee. Avoiding feelings is going to make me miserable for ten days and then never help me again."

"So you're just *allowing* the feelings?" She's in awe, and trying to learn from the worst source for it right now.

"To an extent," I shrug, "Yes."

"But we're not married. Not for ten days." She's uncomfortable, tucking a long black hair behind her gorgeous ear and combing her fingers all the way through to the end. I told her too much. She doesn't need to know my struggles.

"Jesus died for ten-day gaps like this, Jubilee."

" 'Shall we continue in sin so that grace may abound?' " She quotes Romans directly, and I take on the next words.

" 'Certainly not!' " Then I allow a burdened sigh when her fluttering eyelashes cause my heart to ache. "But I'd argue that grace is designed for things like our inability to navigate this messy transition. I sleep in a bedroom you painted for *us*, Jubilee. I can't tuck my desire for you over in the corner until the wedding like we did with that red bedding set. I need grace."

She nods fervently, not like she's just agreeing with me, but like she's relating. That, and her sigh of relief, catch me off guard. "That's helpful. Thank you." Then she gives me a little smirk that would cause a knee collapse were I not sitting. "And you can put the bedding *on* the bed. I keep telling you that."

"I have that on my list of things to do the morning of the wedding. Those fancy sheets are *not* for a lonely bachelor."

I watch her reaction closely because she's going for subtle tonight. She's not going to get up and storm out. She's not going to gasp or protest or giggle like a schoolgirl as she did the last time. I can see she's doing her best to submit to this conversation. I'm glad I'm watching when she first displays a little smile in response. But then she gets down to the business of continuing our conversation.

"Are you scared at all? Because I'm terrified. I'm ready, but you've had more time to be okay with everything that's going to happen."

"Let's just say that God didn't have to do much to prepare my heart for that part of things. I'm too excited to be scared or even just 'okay.' " I laugh, and it gets her laughing too. But then I say what I know will break her heart. "But...there is stuff I'm scared of that *you're* excited about."

"I know." Jubilee shifts in her spot, sighing and looking heartbroken, as expected. "Are we about to have a conversation about birth control?"

"Can we start *before* that? I need to warn you about something even before we consider all the angles." I tremble at nerves.

"Warn me? What else don't I know?"

"Well, I know your father has talked to you a little about what it will mean marrying an older man. You're untouched by the world, but I'm not, Jubilee. I have baggage." Embarrassingly, the last word trembles out and a tear falls from my eyes.

Jubilee jumps to my aid, handing me a tissue. "Elijah, I love you. I am completely prepared to walk through anything with you."

"Even if I start leaking at random? Forgive me." I sniffle.

"Forgiven," she says, gently smiling a lovesick smile. She doesn't even know.

I just let it out. "Jubilee, I had a rough childhood, and just barely when I got out of college and was about to make something of myself, I inherited a child of my own. But from the get go, he and I had it rough. Things were plumb messy until we rolled into this town. You caught us at our best, and that's not saying much."

"I don't understand..."

"It *stays* with you, Jubilee." I cough dryly, avoiding a tear. "Jesus redeemed me and my conscience is clear, but this world...it's rough. I've seen the roughest of it, and this poor kid did not get the start I wanted him to have."

"But he got you." Jubilee shrugs.

I assume she doesn't understand and keep rambling, "I didn't know the first thing about raising a kid. In between Mom's sugar daddies, I'd go days without eating as a kid, or eating dry ramen Mom stole off the shelf. I was starting from scratch with Ben, and I wasn't ready for him. I just started reading and learning and I didn't have two pennies to rub together most of the time."

"Long term memory starts at two most of time. I'm sure you know that. But we can have fragments of memories starting much earlier, especially if there is trauma."

My heart sinks. Why would she say that? "Jubilee...it's even worse thinking he probably remembers it all."

"I'm not talking about him," she says, eyes glistening. "I was two when my parents finally brought me home from a horrible little orphanage in India. These women were saints and would get what they could from local merchants. Sometimes milk. Sometimes a little bread. But it was never enough. And you...you can never tell my family this. Nobody knows this, Elijah, but...I *remember*."

The room goes quiet as we take in a painful commonality through the gaze into two versions of brown eyes.

"So..." I finally say, gaze still strong, but overflowing from us both. "You understand why I'm a little hesitant. A little...triggered, I guess you can say, by the idea of having another child. At least right now, obviously."

"But what if..." She sniffles, utilizing the tissue I hard her. "What if the exact thing we're scared of is the thing that can heal us?"

I allow a beat, then nod. "I'm certainly on board with that. Bennett was exactly what I didn't know I needed and so were you." I sigh. "But I still think this is something we should be on the same page about before we dive into marriage."

"You're right. We need to have this conversation," she agrees and starts in. "Ever since Jessie mentioned it that time at lunch, I've wondered what she meant by birth control. I looked it up, but had to stop researching because it got into areas I wasn't allowed to. . .Anyway, after you and I talked, I realized we would probably have this conversation eventually, so I researched everything I possibly could. I want you to know that I did my best to be open to your angle. Which is, I assume, using some type of birth control for a time?"

"Uh, yeah. I mean. If it were my choice. But it ain't. How did your research turn out?"

"To be honest..." Jubilee takes my hand, sighing. "It broke my heart, Elijah."

"How so?"

"It's odd, but what hurt me about it was this little warning on nearly every method I researched. About how it could prevent pregnancy but not HIV or other sexually transmitted diseases or infections," she begins. Smirks a little, "And I know what that means now."

"But Jubilee, I explained this. I've never been with anyone, so we won't need to worry about—"

"So much of the culture is backwards, and... and you don't even see it," Jubilee says, then trembles an exhale. "I don't blame you for that, obviously. I...I love you, and I respect your point of view, even to the point of submitting to it if we decide that is best. But in this case, it is *backwards*."

I am floating somewhere between offended and aroused that she'd dare, but still manage to stay calm. "Okay, if I don't see it, help me see it."

"Sex is a culture-wide idol. There are even sacrifices made to it, including our fertility. Sexual intimacy, and often promiscuity, is seen as so important that there are countless methods of preventing pregnancy, which is, apparently, even more important than preventing disease. There seems to be little concern, even among lovers of Christ, that we dare stand before God and say that children, when the same size as bacteria, are on the same level as disease." Jubilee sniffles at a passionate tear.

I smile outside her downcast vision. "Parenting is a difficult undertaking. Just because someone chooses to be on birth control, which is within the liberty of Christ, that doesn't make them promiscuous. For instance, Jessie is on the pill because she and Garrett aren't sure they are ready to have kids. Not everyone can take on an older man and an eight-year-old like you're doing."

"God gave me that honor, and I'm happily obeying," Jubilee reveals. "But all I had when I chose to obey the call was faith. More than I had the tangible assurance that I was 'ready.' I trust God."

"Alright so…that's your analysis of the culture. It's a little flawed, but I can see your side. You haven't told me the basis for what you and your family believe. If the culture is backwards, what is…'forwards'?" I plead, desperate to understand her.

"We…" Jubilee clears her throat for a preface. "Elijah, I don't want you to think I'm naive or brainwashed. I want you to know that I understand how foreign this is to you."

"Jubilee, I know. Just tell me. Explain this to me."

"We believe that sexual intimacy is reserved only for marriage. Marriage is an illustration of Christ's relationship with His bride, the church. So intimacy within marriage is considered to be blameless and righteous, because it is sanctified by God."

"So far, we're on the same page," I encourage.

"I know. We also believe, as the Bible states, that a husband and wife are encouraged to engage in physical intimacy because it helps remove sexual temptation. And you helped me understand that it causes a bond between them, and is a way of showing and sharing their love," Jubilee continues, trembling.

"I like that part," I mumble, and we both chuckle.

"I assumed you would." Jubilee smirks. "But we also understand that after a time of indulging in a private way, God usually blesses a marriage with something everyone can see. As He says in many contexts in Matthew specifically, 'Your Father who sees in secret will reward you openly.' And we know from Psalms 127 that 'the fruit of the womb is a reward.' A *reward*. A *joy*. A *blessing*. Not a disease to be eradicated."

"Of course, but—"

"Entering into marriage but preventing children is like a child waking up on Christmas morning and saying, 'No thank you. I don't want any gifts right now.' "

I only laugh in response, knowing she isn't done.

"Elijah, I love you. And I look forward to every joy that marriage will give us. *Every* joy. I don't want us to prevent one in favor of another. And honestly—" She bites her lip and changes her mind about saying the honest thing, but I'm not having it.

"Uh uh. Don't you dare. Tell me."

"Okay. Your fear of having children is completely valid and speaks a lot to me. It means you know that children are no small commitment. But being scared isn't a reason to delay God's will in our lives. Not that I ever would, but what if I let my fear of being intimate with you keep me from doing it until I felt readier?"

And she looks at the shocked, gaping hole in my mouth for about thirty seconds before she speaks again.

"That wouldn't even compute, would it? And you haven't even experienced intimacy." She hums a laugh, probably making fun of my piggish self. Then she frowns. "What doesn't compute with me is that you *have* experienced the many wonders of fatherhood. You did nothing to earn it, but by God's grace, you got Bennett of all people. I don't believe you'd have made any effort to prevent that if given the chance."

I've lost, but still, I try, "Birth control is rarely 100 percent effective, Jubilee. God isn't going to be stopped by our efforts if He really wants to."

"I believe that it isn't birth control that prevents pregnancy. It is our blatant refusal of God's blessings. When it 'fails' it is by His grace overriding our stubbornness." Jubilee pets her hair some more. "Couples purport to be praying about having children while taking birth control. If they really wanted to surrender to God's will, they would pray those prayers with completely open hands."

I sigh, then stand and walk to my kitchen, to Jubilee's fear.

"I know that's radical to you." Jubilee tries to laugh it off, but has found new resolve in sharing her heart, and is not likely to be moved. "It's just that I have *been* that disease. If I began in a culture like this one, I'd have been extinguished long before I could be left on the doorstep of an orphanage. I was unwanted, and then I was a burden. And I have met too many children to believe that any child is meant to be *prevented*, in whatever way that occurs."

She should have led with that one, but it was an afterthought. I chuckle, remembering just a few months ago when Bennett was singing "I Surrender All" on a stage full of children. God didn't let me see that for no reason. I reach into a cabinet and retrieve a gift bag in turquoise and red, which reminded me of the earrings I bought her the day I met Adam.

"I've been that disease, too. And all I wanted was for Ben to not feel like that." I mumble, returning to the couch with the gift bag, and handing it to my bride-to-be as I ease into my concession. "You make a valid point there, Miz Jubilee."

"What is this?" She takes the bag gingerly.

"This is me proving that I knew exactly how this would go." I shake my head, not merely submitting to her, but allowing God and Jubilee to change my heart. No child is a disease. Every child is a gift that we can never do enough to deserve. I own that now too.

She opens the bag to a pill bottle and a tiny pair of cowboy boots.

She giggles at the boots and looks with confusion at the bottle.

"They're prenatal vitamins. I asked some of the doctors I know, and they say that brand is the best."

"I see." She wonders, squinting her eyes.

"I want you to start taking them," I explain. "They help get your body ready for pregnancy and obviously help a pregnancy be healthy and viable. There are a hundred differences between my mom's pregnancy with me and her pregnancy with Bennett. And he's beautiful, of course. But only one of us got to wear boots as a baby. I just want to give any other little ones the best chance we can."

"So you're saying—" Jubilee sobs laughter, sniffling at tears.

"That despite my fear, I agree with you. Babies are a blessing, no matter when God wills them." I smirk. "So let's not delay *any* joy."

"Elijah, that would mean the world to me." Jubilee's eyes meet mine, and she's wiping tears of relief. Her relief looks like what I felt the day she came downstairs in jeans and told me she was going to marry me in six weeks. How selfish of me to *expect* the thing I'm looking forward to in marriage and ask her to delay *her* joy?

Right now, she's beaming light across the warm neutrals in which she dressed our home. She is about to set the gift bag aside, but I watch her feel its weight. One item had slipped through the tissue paper, and she reaches in to feel for it.

"Oh yeah. Jessie wanted me to give that to you. She knows you may not wear it, but she just thought you might laugh when you saw the name of the color."

Jubilee's whole face reddens when she pulls out the little glass bottle of nail polish. The nail polish is a gorgeous deep red. And the color the company chose to call it is *Indian Wedding.*

Jubilee indeed chuckles. To my surprise, she whispers, so as not to perk her father's ears a mile away. "Did Jessie know this is my favorite color?"

"Not until I told her after she gave this to me."

"Please thank Jessie when you see her. I may not ever be brave enough to wear it, but I do appreciate her thinking of me." She sniffles, probably still thinking of potential babies. "I am so blessed to have you in my life."

I melt at the kiss that lands on my cheek.

Twenty-Two

Elijah

I have to work right up until seven in the morning the day before the wedding. Besides the effort contained in twenty-four straight hours of work, it took truckloads of convincing to get Adam to let Jubilee crash on my couch overnight to look after Bennett. The wedding rehearsal will occur in the afternoon, after just a few hours of sleep. But it's all worth it when I walk in my door like a zombie at seven-thirty and an angel is sleeping on one end of the couch, and my little boy is crashed on the other.

The stinker. Now he spends the night with her before I get to.

I sit on the couch next to Jubilee's stomach and smooth her hair from her face. The only thing remotely as beautiful is the dreamy sigh of the boy on the other end. Tomorrow, this little family will be stitched together forever. Jubilee awakens when I kiss her forehead.

"Hey," she says, sitting up. Fully clothed, as I expected. "Sorry, I meant to be awake when you got home."

"It's okay. You've had a long week," I say just above a whisper, blinking slow.

"You look so tired. Let me freshen up and then I'll take Ben over to my parents' house."

"No, just leave him here."

She rolls her eyes. "I love my sisters, but this week has been trying, to say the least. Bennett keeps me sane when I get to have him with me. You get some rest, and Ben and I will see you later at the church."

"You sure?" A quiet house sounds like a dream.

"Absolutely. Go on to bed. I'll get Bennett dressed."

She grabs her little overnight bag and heads to the bathroom. I turn and gently shake Bennett's shoulder.

"Wake up, Bud."

"I'm awake. I'm pretending." He opens one eye, then the other. "I didn't want to see if you kissed her."

I take the chance for a whispered pow-wow.

"I don't kiss her except how I kiss you. You know that. Not until tomorrow. But I'm finally on vacation! You excited for the wedding?"

"Yeah, but you're taking away Miss Jubilee for three days," Bennett says with sadness, sitting up.

"And you get to go be spoiled by Jessie and Garrett for three days. Come on, man. Give your dad a chance for some romance in his life."

"Ew."

"Not 'ew.' I need to be a good husband. Good husbands take their bride away for a few days. How bout this? There's snow in the forecast tonight. We'll have hot cocoa when we get home from the rehearsal dinner. Just me and you. It'll be our last night like that. Let's enjoy it."

"You don't make hot cocoa as good as Miss Jubilee."

"In that case, thank *God* it's our last night just the two of us. Were you a good boy for her?"

"Yeah. She let me sleep on the couch because she wasn't sure she could carry me to bed after she rubbed my legs. And we were tired because we made stuff for the wedding yesterday. Dad?"

"Yeah?"

He looks toward the bathroom. "When you and Jubilee's brother Hakim are not there, her family says *really* mean things to her. I'm real glad she gets to live here with us. We say nice stuff to her. Well, I try to. I didn't call her ma'am once when the movie was distracting me, but she didn't get mad."

"What do they say to her?" He's only eight, but a kid isn't a bad spy.

"I don't know. They just talk about all the nice stuff she does for us, but they talk like she's bad for it."

"Well we know the truth. You just keep being nice to her, okay? And when you're over there today helping, you be extra good, okay? Extra, extra good."

"Yeah, I will. Miss Cindy told me on Sunday that if I'm bad they will think you and Miss Jubilee is bad. So I'm extra good."

"Thank you, Ben. Miss Cindy is a smart lady."

Jubilee emerges from the bathroom, fresh-faced and lovely, and on a mission.

"Get to bed, Elijah. I can get him ready to go."

I can't sleep past about one in the afternoon, so I decide to head over to the Monroe house to rescue my bride-to-be before the rehearsal. When I pull into the drive, I see Hakim outside with the already saddled horses. It is an odd time for riding, especially with the wind blowing a rip into the air, but I try not to be concerned.

When he sees me, he approaches with haste. "Dude, you are the exact person I wanted to see."

"Why?"

"I'm working on getting Jubilee out here to ride with me. But really, she needs *you*." Hakim sighs.

"Hakim, I've told you I don't like that I just took over that part of your relationship with her. You can ride with her anytime."

"I don't like horses, Elijah. I ride for Jubilee. I'm honored that you took my spot. Really. And today…You wouldn't believe the stupid passive-aggressive stuff they've been saying to her."

"Like what?" I have to know.

"For one, they saw prenatal vitamins in her purse, so they keep saying that she'll conveniently have a premature birth several months after the wedding."

"No, she's not…we haven't…" I hadn't thought of what might happen if someone discovered those.

"Elijah, Jubilee tells me everything. Those vitamins meant something huge for your two, and she tried to explain it, but they didn't get it. And they asked Bennett what he thinks of Jubilee's scrambled eggs since she made him breakfast and it makes them crazy that she slept at your house. And, of course, Ben said he liked them, and they just laughed like children. That one really got to me."

I growl frustration, gritting my teeth. "So, they use my son to be cruel to my fiancée?"

"They think this quick engagement thing is scandalous. But you can't rescue her fast enough, Elijah."

"I just hope *you* can manage without her."

"I'll be fine." He backs toward the house with a smile. "Have *you* had the famous scrambled eggs, though?

"Naw, I came home and crashed this morning."

"They're like magic." He winks. "Stay here, I'll go grab her."

Hakim leads out a young woman who looks like a ball of repressed tension and pain. I could bottle and live on the way she melts when she catches sight of me.

"Hey," is all she says.

"Horses are saddled. Go," Hakim demands. "I'll watch over Bennett."

She manages to hold it all in until we get back into the barn, where she finds my arms and falls apart, weeping for two whole minutes.

"I love them. I just...I have to say that out loud, because I'm having trouble believing it today." She sobs.

"Twenty-four hours, Jubilee, and you can love them from a distance."

"And you up close." She sighs, her head on my chest. It's probably time to get back inside, but as that night at the restaurant, something about Jubilee's demeanor is begging me not to.

"Everything okay?"

"No." She sighs, "I've been trying to find a time all week to give you something that belongs to you, and I will feel much better once I do."

I look to her pockets, confused. What is she giving me that I don't already have?

"All I have is yours. Did you borrow something, or..."

She giggles, shaking her head, as the hand not weaved into mine goes to my cheek. My love gracefully raises up on her toes and allows her lips to fall into mine. The first kiss happens with surprise from both of us. The next occurs slowly, with intention. There is a quick break, not quite long enough for a sensible thought; but long enough for our foreheads to touch and eyes to meet in the cold, smelly barn amid horses and hay, and Jubilee to nod. I then capture her lips with passion, forgetting about everything but the way my soul cries out for her. We are both taken by the ease of our budding love affair. When the first of it ends, I realize we are wrapped up into each other's arms and look down into her eyes with a satisfied grin.

She giggles as I sigh with lovesickness. "Can't say I was expecting that."

"I have compromised and sacrificed so much for this wedding. This was yours. I'm sorry it took so long to give it to you."

"I'm not," I confess with a lover's growl. "Because you need to be my wife the next time that happens."

Twenty-Three

Jubilee

October snow is falling on changing leaves. All my sisters and sisters-in-law have been around all week with my brothers and their families. After the wedding rehearsal, I am at Hannah's house with all of them. All the males are at my parents' house and we have the little girls with us. This night is customary, but the last time it occurred I was young enough to look after my nieces and nephews, and not hear the womanly conversation. I am weary from the week of their "expertise" and mean-spirited but kindly-worded comments. Elijah promised to endure the same for me, since the men look forward to the tradition. But only for a bit, he said. He and Bennett had a hot chocolate stag night of their own planned.

While Priscilla is going on about how "miserable" intimacy is, and Penny is saying that it isn't so bad and I'll get used to it, Hannah rolls her eyes outside their notice, and we share a secret smirk. That is her only given opinion, but I know better. I have heard James call her a goddess and kiss her sweaty brow as his seed was born into the cruel world screaming with joy. Those children were made and delivered with passionate love, not misery. I take her unvoiced input as gospel against ignorance, still feeling an hours-old secret kiss on my lips and spirit. His affection scares me exactly zero now. I could have kissed him all night. Well, it's a theory I hope to test, anyway.

Finally, Hannah brings out her manicure supplies. My sisters file and clip and scrub and begin painting their nails subtle shades of pink and clear as they continue the awkward crash course on the facts of life, which they don't know is just a refresher for me. It's ironic for these women candidly talking about their intimate experiences with men, but they believe anything flashier than light pink is unheard of for modesty's sake. I pretend to examine those half dozen shades of nothing that flatters my skin tone. But I am praying bitterly in my heart that what I don't yet have courage to do will not be done out of spite. They are chit-chatting and enjoying their time together. I am glad to have provided their excuse for fellowship, but I know I am the unimportant, ignored bride-to-be in a room of women who are sure they did better.

"They won't even notice, Jubilee," I tell myself. *"Just do it. This is your wedding, not theirs."*

So, I stand and walk to my purse amid their tittering, and pull out my treasure with a smile. How did Jessie know to find the deepest, loveliest shade of blood-red and buy it for me? We talked once about my unwillingness to marry Elijah in a red gown, and she remembered. Jessie and Lucinda have been left out of this entire week, though they had helped me with many wedding details. I was honored to do this for them. No. Not for them. For me. What is liberty for, if not this gorgeous shade of red?

They don't notice for a moment. I look at my carefully prepped nails, then warm the polish between my hands, letting the glass bottle clink against my engagement ring as I roll it back and forth. I open the bottle, then wipe the brush on the lip before spreading the first taste on my left thumbnail like jam. It's so beautiful against brown skin and the delight of my heart, this first red nail of my entire life. I almost don't notice the heavy silence that spreads across the room like that polish as I finish my left hand and start on my right. When I notice, I ignore it, though they want me to look up and inquire. I fight the urge to look with everything in me.

And I never do. The silence stays, and there is peace for the first time all week. I let them assume and think what they will. I know there are rumors that I've been to bed with Elijah already to enjoy something that would have been explained quite poorly if not for him. And for these red nails and my relative innocence, I choose not to think anything of it. God knows.

We have a simple ceremony in the creaky, musty church where I grew up. As was the plan, only family and a few close friends are present. The ceremony starts with me beaming, quite literally, as I walk up the aisle in an ivory dress and a pitcher clasped in fingers with red nails to a man in jeans and a button-down shirt for the casual wedding. That pitcher of defense and complete trust in God compound Elijah's joy, and he is laughing aloud when I arrive with it. Bennett had been given a secret instruction to take the pitcher and set it at his feet during the ceremony.

The ceremony ends with Elijah barely keeping the smile at bay as he joins his mouth with mine at the start of our new marriage. I was poisoned by the thought of possible misery tonight, but feel my soul emptying into him for the duration of the long kiss. Bennett takes up the pitcher and leads us back down the aisle, as instructed.

Later in the evening, Jessie approaches and taps my arm while Elijah is across the room speaking with my pastor.

"That was an *intense* altar kiss," she whispers, wide-eyed with joy and wonder.

I tensed up earlier at the same subject matter when Priscilla and the rest of my sisters had accused me of having kissed Elijah before today. They said the altar kiss was 'rehearsed' and not awkward enough. But when Jessie mentions the same thing in different words, it is more of a relief. It's like I can remove a mask with Jessie the way I do with Elijah.

"Everyone keeps mentioning that kiss. I guess I don't understand..."

"It was passionate. That isn't a bad thing. It was beautiful." Jessie giggles. "'Lijah's a brother to me, Jubilee. It's weird seeing him kiss a girl at all, let alone like *that*. My mom, on the other hand, has been praying for years to see him kiss someone like that. She about swooned. Sorry, I don't mean to embarrass you."

"It's fine, Jessie." I laugh a little, allowing my innocence to show. Glad to be speaking to the bubbly Jessie.

"Don't tell them I told you, but he and Garrett spoke the other day on Elijah's lunch. He says Elijah seemed really nervous about tonight, which is totally adorable," Jessie shares.

I'm confused. "Why would *he* be nervous?"

Jessie scrunches her nose. "Oh, I don't know, because he loves you and wants it to be amazing."

"From what I hear, 'amazing' isn't possible." I think of my sisters sharing wedding night stories and horrors until I silenced them with red nail polish.

"Okay, so it might be totally awkward and generally uncomfortable. Probably painful. There's no way around that when it's new," Jessie admits. "But for me it was all that...and *amazing*."

I look to Jessie in disbelief, genuinely unaware that an act I'm merely supposed to get used to, and only eventually, could somehow start out "amazing."

Jessie winces. Thinking she's told me the wrong information. "I mean, I've heard it isn't *always* awkward or painful the first time. But even if it is, it only gets better after that, and you'll fall in love with him over and over as time goes on. I'm not trying to scare you, sorry. You don't need to be scared. You can trust Elijah completely."

"You're not scaring me. Quite the opposite, honestly." In fact, Jessie told me exactly what I needed to hear, and then something even more.

"You and I should have coffee and talk about married life sometime," she offers. "After you've experienced it, of course."

"I'd enjoy that very much."

Garrett arrives with Jessie's parents at the unintentional pow-wow.

Cindy chuckles. "That nail color is stunning."

"Thank you. Jessie bought it for me. And thank you. It was perfect."

"Oh, do you like it?" She asks like a young girl, putting hands to her face.

"I love it!" I exclaim, then allow a little gossip. "My sisters think it is 'indecent,' but I'm working to ignore their opinion."

"Indecent? A...nail color?" Garrett doesn't understand. None of them do, because it doesn't make sense.

At this same moment, I wave to Elijah, who seems to be receiving a lecture from a man of God. He gives me a discreet wink, mid-sentence with my ancient pastor with the too-high voice.

"This was a nice wedding," Garrett comments with a smile.

"Thank you. It's really small and simple, I know." I heed present company. "Much different from *your* gorgeous wedding."

"It's *beautiful*, Jubilee. Don't be modest," Jessie compliments. "I *love* the taco bar."

"Bennett's idea," I explain. "He's a part of this too, so he probably had more of a say than Elijah did."

"I'm sure Elijah had very few parameters," Jordan contributes.

"Just the one, actually." I allow the snicker. " 'As soon as possible.' "

Everyone in the conversation laughs aloud and then Jessie emotes. "Yeah, he makes fun of our almost three-month engagement and then he goes and cuts that in half! I bet you were frantic trying to get things planned."

I shrug, "Actually, I chose the date. He was willing to do this as late as the end of the year."

"Oh," Lucinda says, some sensual suggestion in her tone.

"I know, it probably seems like a whirlwind romance."

"Isn't it?" Cindy asks, raising an eyebrow.

"I suppose, but it was more than that. God *insisted* on this timeline. Not that it was difficult to obey."

"Bennett absolutely loves this too!" Jessie says, swiping at a tear.

"Thank you, by the way, for taking him for the next few days. You didn't have to, but—"

"Don't mention it, Jubilee. You two deserve some alone time after the courting thing." Garrett smiles.

"Garrett!" Jessie whisper-yells.

"That route was taken for the glory of God, son. We have no right or reason to judge," Pastor Jordan says to his son-in-law. I can't imagine ever hearing my dad call Elijah "son."

"You're right, Dad. Sorry." Garrett immediately recants, "What I meant was…"

"I know what you meant, Garrett. No harm done. And Pastor Jordan, we are so grateful that you were willing to do our premarital counseling on this timeline."

"Jubilee, I always support it when someone forsakes everything to obey God's call. Especially when two people have the *same* call. It's clear to me this was the Holy Spirit."

Just at the perfect moment, Bennett runs by with Jonathan, both boys with a cupcake, barely avoiding collisions with a few different groups of people. It's Elijah's chance to break away from the lecture about not attending church with me. He passes me and the Durants while yelling after Bennett. But he slows for just a second, kissing my cheek on his way.

"You're a lucky girl, Jubilee. I hope you know that," Cindy says.

"Blessed, Cindy. And yes, I know."

"So…remind me who your immediate family is. There are so many people I don't really know," Lucinda requests.

"Well…" I look to a wall, where my sisters are in a group, glancing my way and whispering…which is what everyone seems to be doing today. "Anyone with red hair is my sibling or one of their children. Those women over there are my sisters. Two by birth…well…*their* birth, and the rest by marriage. But they've all been married since I was a child, so it sort of melds together who actually originated in my family."

"Other than the 'indecent' hair," Jessie clarifies. I love the way they listen and respond. So engaged and intrigued.

"Right." I snicker, then go through the list of siblings, ending with: "Hakim is my one non-red-haired brother."

"I liked Hakim. He sat with us on the groom's side," Garrett says. "Funny guy."

"Hakim is one of my dearest friends. I'm glad God made us siblings."

"And the tall blond that keeps staring at you?" Cindy mumbles.

"That would be Peter Samson." I wince. "My family calls him 'the one that got away.' He's a newlywed. The wedding was the same day as yours, Jessie. And I found out today his wife is expecting. He's grateful I didn't marry him, which he told me earlier. He's just in a bit of shock, like the rest of them, that I just married a single father ten years my senior who happens to be black."

"You are such a blessing to them, Jubilee," Cindy encourages. "You know this is what God wanted for you."

"I know, it is just quite a liberty I'm taking. No one has done what I did." I shrug. "But what's liberty for, if not this?"

Twenty-Four

Jubilee

"Jessie will take good care of him, Elijah." I offer in a soothing tone. He is visibly fretting over his son after having interrogated Jessie again about his care. His eyes are on the slightly snow-packed road ahead.

Elijah chuckles. "I know. But the last time I left him with someone overnight was when he was a baby and I was working nights. I never liked that idea."

"I had him overnight when you covered that night shift," I remind him.

"That's *you*, Jubilee. I don't bat an eye putting his life in your hands. And I love Jessie, but...I'm his dad. I worry."

Beyond flattered, I smile. "We could have stayed back home with him."

"I considered it," Elijah admits. "But I wanted to give us some time alone, and I figured this was a good way to teach him...well, how much I value you. He needs to know I married a wife for me, not just a mom for him."

A twinge of fear enters, even though I'm usually quite comfortable with him. "So...where are you taking your new wife that required three days of groceries? We going camping? It's a bit cold. I mean, if we are, I'm okay with that."

Elijah smirks, probably at my constant submission. But I'm only obeying God, and he can't fault me for that. "You remember the lake where Bennett and I go fishing?"

"How could I forget?" I smooth my hair aside, remembering following the quiet to Elijah.

"Well, there's those cabins on the other side. Bennett and me wanted to go camping one time and I checked them out. Found out they aren't really camping cabins. More like rustic on the outside, fancy hotel suite on the inside. Like where a couple might spend a quiet honeymoon." Elijah clears his throat nervously. "There's a kitchen. I didn't like the idea of you having to cook when it's supposed to be a vacation. That's why we got things *I* would cook if you want a break."

"I love cooking, Elijah. It's one of my hobbies, not a chore." I smile. "It would be like asking an artist if they want to paint while visiting Paris."

"Alright. Well, you said you'd rather just have a quiet week at home than be touristy. I split the difference. Half the week alone an hour away from home to get acquainted with my wife. Half at home to get settled as a family."

"Sounds wonderful." Then I worry we'll ride in silence against my fear of getting "acquainted".

But Elijah whispers, "Wife."

"I suppose that's odd to say." I try to comfort him.

"No," he declares. "The word just finally makes sense. It's like yesterday it was just a word. Now it's a full-blown proper noun. Like you have a new name."

"Actually, I do."

"Yeah. Wow. Jubilee Bering." Elijah hums once at the name. Whispers again. "My Wife. I might just call you that for a while. Wife."

I giggle.

"Sorry." Elijah chuckles, coming out of the deeply sentimental. "That's probably offensive. Sorry."

"Don't be." I take a chance to flirt. "Husband."

I look out the window at the October snow softly colliding with the windows of the truck. I remember the way I looked out at the bright glint of the summer off the dry terrain the day Elijah broke all the rules by delivering me and some popsicles to my family's home. I started to open up that day. He began to break me free like Bennett's tooth a few weeks ago. The first wiggle. Today's contrast is illustrated well in the bitter cold outside the truck. I'm all his, and he knows he can do as he pleases. But I feel closed off today. I'm terrified.

Suddenly, Elijah hums a snicker at first, amused at something. I look to him, wondering what he finds so funny about the dangerous snow-packed road ahead. He sees me wondering.

He clears his throat. "The last time it was spring, I didn't even know you."

I hum. I had just been thinking about summer. We are on the same wavelength, as always. But as I look back out at the snow, he probably thinks I'm indifferent.

" 'Rise up, my love, my fair one, And come away. For lo, the winter is past, The rain is over and gone. The flowers appear on the earth; The time of singing has come.' " He recites, regaining my full attention, a bitten lip and a stir in my heart.

"Song of Solomon," I reply, then move to interpretation. "That's a very poetic book..." Because I know he'll relish it, "...a very *provocative* book."

Elijah laughs aloud. "Provocative? What sort of man do you think I am?"

"Pretty sure you're my husband," I flirt right back, snickering.

"Do you understand that passage, Jubilee? You told me before that you didn't understand the poetry," he mumbles.

"I think so." I sigh. "I think it means we don't have to wait anymore."

"Yeah. We can celebrate the beauty of spring together." He sounds impressed. "The time of singing. I like that part."

"Me too."

He appreciates that, and takes the in. "So...I've spoken to a few different guys the past few days. They all had different versions of how this night was supposed to go."

"Yeah, Jessie mentioned you talked to Garrett." I'm intrigued. There is so much pressure and confusion and fuss. All of it unspoken between us. I think Elijah is going to speak. Men don't tell women about what men talk about. But Elijah is a different sort of man.

"I did. And James on a different occasion, and then your brothers sort of bombarded me last night like you promised they would."

"My sisters did the same." I smile sheepishly. "Then Jessie talked to me at the wedding."

"I heard. Everyone seems to have an opinion." He seems frustrated. "And they all have a different way of looking at tonight; fulfilling a duty, receiving and giving a gift, and half a dozen others."

"Misery." I add with a sigh. "That was what Priscilla said."

"Oh, how encouraging." He laughs with bitter humor.

"They mean well," I note.

"I know they do, but...like with everything else, we will probably stray off their path a little. Hopefully more than a little in Priscilla's case."

"Of course." I stir. Where is he going with this?

"So can we talk about how *I* hope this night will go?" he requests.

"Okay…" Sometimes men change. I've heard that. They are one way before the wedding and then they become monsters. Is that Elijah? It couldn't be.

"Because I have some very specific demands, and I expect you to do your best to meet them, even if you might be slightly morally opposed," he says gruffly. Out of character in every way.

"Of…of course, Elijah. It will all be very new to me, but I'll do my best."

"Good. So, the second thing I'd like you to do when we arrive and get everything unloaded is to get in your most comfortable pajamas while I make hot cocoa, even though Bennett says you do it better. Then we'll sit by the fire drinking our hot cocoa while I pull all fifty thousand of those flowers out of your hair," Elijah "demands" with warmth.

I sigh relief at his lightheartedness. "That sounds wonderful. My sisters insisted on the flowers since I didn't have a veil, and my mother grew them in her garden. I think I'd like to keep some of them for her." I nod sincerity. "But you said that's the second thing, though. I expect the first is more, um…traditional."

"Extremely. And I'm honestly still in shock that I went through my whole wedding without having received the rite of passage I'm asking you for tonight." Elijah glances at me, then smirks. "Tradition, in my book, involves me dancing with my bride."

"You want me to…"

"Dance with me. Yes."

"And then drink hot cocoa in pajamas."

"By the fire. Yes. I made sure there'd be a fire."

"On our…wedding night."

"Those are my demands," Elijah concludes.

"But…"

"But what?"

"But the winter is past," I manage in metaphor, looking out at the snow, then back at my love.

"Jubilee, we're in love, and we're *ready* for love. But spring doesn't come because you go around forcing the flowers out of the ground and beg the earth to tilt so that it's warmer. Spring comes because it is a natural inevitability after you've lived through months of cold and snow and…hot cocoa. Then 'the flowers appear on the earth.' Because they must. We've never done spring, so let's just enjoy some winter…in the fall. Everything else will happen when it happens. Sound fair?"

"Not remotely." I fall madly in love once again. "But it does sound very much like…you."

Elijah

After the requested first dance in full wedding garb, we get into pajamas and talk for hours about the day and Bennett and about nothing and everything. We laugh together until our throats hurt. Side by side on a loveseat by the fire, we are increasingly more relaxed and comforted without expectation, while I gently pull tiny white flowers from thick, exotic hair.

The conversation picks up over and over and there is never a lack of outpouring important enough to convince us to quiet. When the soul-deep spiritual connection bends its way into wee hours stomach grumbling, we continue bonding over a snack as if sleep or any other motive is some distant, ridiculous prospect. Then at the first silence. The first lull. I sigh with devastating honesty.

"You are the most beautiful thing I've ever seen."

"Oh?" Her voice sounds like she's in some dream state.

"I've been wondering all day and all evening if you'll suddenly vanish, Wife."

"It's snowing out. I better not, Husband." I think she senses the shift in motives, but ain't sure to what. "You tired?"

I reach out and take her hand, daring her eyes. I shake my head slowly. "You?"

"No," she dares in a whisper.

I smile at the glint in her eye. It's like a green little tulip bud after a late blizzard. Suddenly, when we were spending an evening like a couple of best friends, I lean in and contact my forehead with hers and it's like a robin's song. It's new and foreign to us. But suddenly it's spring and we don't know how to look out at the snow anymore.

I plant a little peck of a kiss on her lips, and she giggles.

"Can I kiss you? I didn't even ask." I wince at the whisper.

"You don't need to." She shrugs. Consent probably doesn't exist in her world, but I'm glad to have it. She warms up her speech to a simmer and sneaks it into a whisper. "I *love* to kiss you."

I kiss the woman I love as I had at a stuffy old altar. But like the conversation of the preceding hours, the kisses continue and swell and grow. Our souls already open, our love easily begins to transform. I'm twenty-nine, so what restraint I had left got spent on the past four months of knowing Jubilee. Now a married man, my spirit forgets to screen the whisper when I finally find a break in the kisses.

"You want to come to bed with me?"

Her giggle is barely a whisper, but her smile is bright and welcoming. I watch myself weave my hands through hers before I realize why she's laughing.

I laugh too. "Finally, huh? I guess His Honor Adam Monroe was right about me." And it about kills the mood, realizing what a pig I am—a dirty sinner who in no way should be in this cabin thinking of taking pleasure in this young woman.

"On many points, yes. He's a wise man, Elijah. But he does have his blind spots." She shrugs and suddenly stands up, smirking. I think for a split second that she's finally made her choice between me and her father, and I'm the fool.

"Blind spots?" I humor her, crossing my arms. Nerves and anticipation about to kill me.

"Well, he foresaw quite a lot." She shrugs, then gets a wild little half smile on her face like a blanket of snow melting to reveal fields of yellow flowers. "But you're the wiser one in this equation. There's a variable here that only *you* considered."

"Really?" I flirt.

"He didn't think that maybe *I'd* be the problem." She bites her lip, and I almost die.

I'm completely unprepared when that flannel nightgown turns into a staticky mess that nearly gets caught up in her hair before it falls into an inside-out heap near the couch. It takes more focus than I'm capable of, but I manage a few words as she's backing up across the room to the bed, and

I'm apparently standing and following her, and apparently my shirt is meeting carpet.

"You're right. I knew you'd be a problem." I laugh.

I've pondered, more than I'll admit, what it might be like to take her wild beauty into my arms. And she's right. I've always seen it. But no one would believe all the wild I find in her tonight. I want it to leak into all she is so that she can set the whole world free. But not tonight. I'm not sharing this with anyone.

Jubilee

Having quickly found my way around the cabin's little kitchen, I crack eggs into a bowl. I light the stove and scrape a wooden spoon against an old stainless pan as the eggs turn solid. The coffee is already brewing, and the store-bought pastries already plated, sweet sticky fingers licked. I was crafted for this. Not poured through a pigeonhole or locked behind its bars. I love it.

The tingle of rebellion teases the corners of my mouth as I use a wet paper towel to rub some stray egg from my nightgown. I've never cooked breakfast in a nightgown. Not at a home where modesty and service-readiness are stressed. I don't own loungewear, and rarely has anyone not sharing my bedroom seen me in a nightgown at all. I suppose that's still the truth.

His voice startles me from behind. "Every time I wake up in the morning, I think to myself, 'Maybe *today* will be the day there's a beautiful woman in the kitchen cooking breakfast.' I always thought I was dreaming a little too big."

Two mahogany hands meet in front of my stomach, squeezing tight. Gentle lips meet the side of my neck after hair is moved aside. The intimate embrace only lasts a few seconds, about a millennium short of what I wish it would. Elijah takes a seat at the breakfast bar. He leaves a rush of blood and hormones behind that isn't fair.

As he pops a grape into his mouth with an evil smile, he sees he got to me. "I'm sorry, did I throw off your rhythm?"

"Completely!" I comment on the big picture. "I think next time you should dream bigger, and you'd get to eat before 10:30 in the morning. I don't know what happened. I never sleep this late."

"We were up until four." Elijah pardons his bride. "You're due a little rest, Lover."

"You're calling me 'Lover' now? I was barely accustomed to 'Wife.' " I serve my husband breakfast and coffee.

"Well now you're both," he reiterates, then takes my hand as he bows his head for grace.

After the prayer, Elijah takes an unsuspecting bite of my scrambled eggs, and his eyes widen.

"What in the—" Elijah finishes chewing. "Jubilee…what did you do to these eggs? They're incredible."

"So I'm told." I smile.

"Is this the eggs Hakim was rambling about?"

"Yeah." I nod, flattered. "I have a couple secret ingredients. It's fun to watch my mother try to figure it out."

"Well you needn't tell me. Just keep fixin' 'em." He chuckles. "Wow."

"I will." I nod. As we eat in silence for ten minutes, I hope the intimacy hasn't reverted back to awkward culinary analysis and hollow compliments. Elijah secures my hopes, as always.

"So, you ready for babies?"

"It's snowing. I don't think the stork will arrive today." I flirt back. "And it's a good thing, because I'm enjoying our time together."

He laughs nervously, not having realized how easily I can dislodge his swagger. "I thought you wanted to get to changing diapers ASAP."

"I do. As soon as possible. 'Possible' isn't for the better part of a year, at *least*, as God designed it. This is our honeymoon. Diapers hadn't crossed my mind." I wink. "Your plans for last night were wonderful, Husband. What do you have planned for today?"

"Your turn." He smiles, lifting the fork to his mouth again.

I bite my lip. "That snow out there does look like good snowman snow."

"I was thinking the same thing."

"You were not."

"I've been a dad far longer than I've been a husband," Elijah encourages. Giving me time and space to think and grow. "I try not to waste good snow. Especially if it leads to an excuse to get cozy by the fire again."

"And maybe dancing?" I request, swaying a little.

This one surprises him, who knows I am not one for innuendo. I mean dancing. I bet he wonders if he's speaking to a different woman than the one in lace and white flowers yesterday.

"What will your father think?" he teases.

"Fortunately, you don't answer to him anymore," I whisper, and he lights right up.

He slides his empty plate aside and doesn't even wait for me to finish chewing my last bite before his lips are at my neck again.

"So, the snowman and dancing is a little later, right?" he whispers, enticing me.

I giggle, "If that's what you want, Husband."

But he backs up and gives me a stern look, despite his obvious desires.

"What's wrong?" I flirt.

He keeps his voice low and intimate. "I know you've been taught to give yourself to me whenever I ask. But—"

"Elijah." I smile, trying to keep things from getting so serious that they can't get passionate. Not a chance.

"Let me finish, Jubilee. This is important to me."

"Okay," I allow in a sincere whisper, trying not to beg him to keep kissing my neck.

"This 'lover' thing is for both of us, and it *takes* both of us. I will not have a predator and victim situation in our home. I want your heart, or I don't want your body. Do you understand?"

"You *always* have my heart." I try to laugh again and lighten the mood. Why is he making this difficult for me?

He laughs, but bitterly. "So, I'm just supposed to take advantage of you because you love me?"

"You're supposed to take the gift I'm giving you."

"But what if it's too much for me to ask? I never want to ask anything unreasonable."

I sigh, reaching up and running a thumb across a cheek that I've never seen with the bits of stubble that have merged. And I pray, trying to convey to him what God needs him to hear.

And it occurs to me, "Have I never told you how attractive you are to me? Quite a temptation until recent changes."

He rolls his eyes, hiding his smile. "Jubilee."

"I'm serious, Husband. In your effort to be 'reasonable,' you are being a tad sexist."

"How so? I'm trying to be sensitive to—"

I rise from my barstool and step between his knees. His hands meet my waist, and he seems to expect me to say everything but the thing I say. "Can we make love? But only if you want to," I whisper into his ear with all the wiles I can summon. "I want your heart, or I don't want your body."

The exact expected result occurs, which is a more complete grip on my waist and his whole being becoming molten goo.

"Girl, you know you have both all the time," he growls.

I back up and hip my hands, getting animated. "Are you sure? Because I never want to ask anything unreasonable. I'm just trying to be sensitive."

He laughs appreciatively and reaches out for my waist. I step back, beginning a chase that ends in an understanding.

I never leave dishes on a counter, or my heart dangling for the capture, or caution out on an October flurry.

But the winter is past. I'm his. He's mine. And that much is always reasonable.

Twenty-Five

Elijah

In Jessie and Garrett's front entry, Bennett runs and buries his head in Jubilee's stomach before acknowledging his own father.

"Um...chopped liver?" I laugh.

"Sorry. Hey, Dad!"

Garrett and Jessie laugh. Jubilee smiles slightly, beginning to remove her coat.

"No, don't take your coat off, Miss Jubilee! Come see the snow fort I made with Garrett." Then Bennett pulls Jubilee out into the melting snow to sit inside a cozy snow fort.

"You know, Dad and I built this enormous snowman the other day..." she says as the door closes.

I finally beat him to something. But that's a silly contest now.

"Isn't she cold wearing a skirt? It was pretty cold the past few days." Jessie asks, shivering.

"Naw. She wears like eight layers of clothes all the time, I swear," I share lovingly. "She's probably *warmer* in the skirt than the rest of us in our jeans."

"Well...she's not in eight layers *all* the time, right?" Jessie bites her lip. Garrett shoots his wife a look.

I chuckle deeply. "Enough of the time that I can only publicly speak to my wife being prim and proper. Any other talk would be indecent."

Jessie snorts laughter. "You're 'prim and proper' too, 'Lijah."

I lower my voice. "You were at our wedding. I am not *that* kind of prim and proper. I didn't even get to dance with my bride until later when her parents weren't around."

"How sweet!" Jessie puts a hand over her heart. "You *danced* with her? All alone? I *hope* she found that as romantic as I do."

"She did." I glance out at a snow princess to be sure she isn't listening. "You know the nightgowns that you see on dolls and in old movies at Christmas? The red plaid ones? She literally owns one. She's unshakably old-fashioned, and I love every second of it."

"He says in his wranglers and boots," Garrett comments.

"Mmmhmm, after taking off his hat in our house." Jessie continues the banter.

"Yeah, after opening every single door for every woman ever."

Garrett and Jessie then take to teasing laughter.

"You two can't exactly talk." I chuckle. "Most folks think abstinence and big fancy weddings in your daddy's church are pretty old-fashioned."

Jessie giggles. Rolls her eyes. "We were not as abstinent as *you*. You didn't kiss her til the altar."

"I did, actually. I wanted the first one to be private, and she indulged me the day before the wedding," I reveal.

Jessie gasps. "You gonna tell her dad?"

"Well, ain't nothing he can do about it now." I wink at her, unable to conceal my smile lately.

"Wow, looks like someone lost his scowl, as my mother says."

"Jess, leave the guy alone," her husband scolds with a laugh.

But she doesn't listen. She instead glances outside then says, "Is it true you had to teach her about. . .you know?"

I roll my eyes and look to Garrett, who would be the only possible source of such information.

I sigh. "In hindsight, she probably knew *enough*. I just didn't like the idea of her going into a marriage without *all* the information. At least the book knowledge."

"I'm glad you did. She told me at the wedding that they thought you two had been sleeping together because she painted her nails in that red I gave her. How do those things even connect?" Jessie giggles and squinches her face, shrugging her hands.

"Yeah, I haven't figured out that one yet. I'm a man. This morning, three days after our wedding, she's making breakfast and I'm like, 'Hey, is that the color Jessie got you? Matches your nightgown, I like it.' " We all laugh at my ignorance.

"You didn't even notice?" Jessie cackles.

"Seriously, Elijah. I mean, even I know that Jessie…" Garrett humorously moves to and examines a recently placed wedding portrait on a nearby wall, "…She had those white tips on her nails at our wedding. Everybody knows that. Obviously, all I was looking at was her *hands*."

We are all laughing aloud together, then Jessie says, "Speaking of hands, I loved the *pitcher*. I assume with you two, it had some biblical significance?"

"Yeah, I was thinking like, 'keep your lamp lit?' " Garrett asks.

"Well, in the original reference, there were also trumpets in this case." I shrug.

"Gideon?" Garrett chuckles.

"Yeah, that's the least romantic thing ever," Jessie decides.

"Says you. You have your romance, and we have ours." I shrug, changing the subject. "Was Bennett good for you?"

"He's an angel, Elijah," Jessie responds. "No trouble at all. He and I didn't even have school because of the snowstorm so we got to hang out with him all week." Garrett works from home. I wonder if he got anything done with Ben bugging him all day, but I don't ask.

"That's good to hear. We missed him quite a lot. We'd never been without him before, so there was a void."

"Please tell me you relaxed and enjoyed each other without thinking about him at least *some* of the time." Jessie seems disappointed.

Just for the rise of it, "Wait…we were supposed to *relax*? We only got the memo about enjoying each other."

Garrett laughs and Jessie gives a muffled squeal into her hands, then whispers, "I'm so happy for you."

I wink just as Bennett and Jubilee burst back through the door.

"Can we go home?" Bennett says with excitement.

"Yeah, get your stuff," I tell him, and the boy runs off into a bedroom.

"Just to warn you, we may be building another snowman today before the snow melts," Jubilee says. The presence of the child seeming to have brightened and opened up her entire countenance.

"I expected it'd happen with the way we jabbered about him the whole time we were building our snowman." I grab Jubilee's hands and startle before enveloping them with mine and breathing on them. "But I assume you'll wear *gloves* during this adventure? Over these nails that have been red *all* week without me noticing."

"Yes. I left them in the truck." She is visibly warmed more deeply than just her hands. She teases me since Jessie is giggling. "By the way, my nails were the *first* thing Bennett noticed at the wedding."

Jessie smiles. "Jubilee, all Bennett has been talking about is you going home with them and *staying* there. He kept saying, '*Overnight. Forever.*' That kid really loves you. Not that you doubted."

"But that's good to hear. Thank you, Jessie. Garrett. For looking after him." Jubilee responds with a smile.

Jessie concludes, "Prim and proper. You are the sweetest thing ever, Jubilee. I'm glad this geezer found you."

"Me too," Jubilee says, smiling into my eyes. Which warms me to the toes.

After hot cocoa as the snow boots dry by the fire, the hour grows late, and Bennett's next school day inches closer.

"Okay, Bennett. Legs off. We'll rub 'em before you go in your room. Me and Jubilee will be in our room in a little while and what did I tell you about that?" I quiz.

"Your room is off limits now that Jubilee lives here because she's a girl," Bennett says groggily. "But you'll be here tomorrow, right Miss Jubilee?"

"Yep. I'll still be here."

After we rub Bennett's legs and put him to bed, I look to my gorgeous wife in the silence of the living room with a wide grin.

"You're staying."

" 'Overnight, forever.' "

"We're home. As a family."

Jubilee smiles, standing and returning the cocoa mugs to the kitchen. "Before the wedding, I was starting to feel like I was *leaving* home when I'd leave you guys at night. I feel like we've been a family for weeks now," Jubilee confesses, loading the dishwasher.

"That's good. I was worried you'd get homesick."

"My parents are a mile away. I miss my horse, yes, but I can go ride him anytime. The only thing I *really* miss is the car. Things will be tricky without a second car," Jubilee shares. Remembering the heart-wrenching experience that was handing over all her keys to Judah. Then realizes her offense. "Not that what we have isn't perfectly sufficient, Husband."

"I know it's not ideal, but we'll make it work for now." I stand and join her in the kitchen. "So, what do you think Daddy dearest would say if he knew about my nightly two fingers?" I reach up into a cabinet that contains my whiskey.

Jubilee shrugs. "You've never had a drop when I've been here, Elijah. Technically I have no proof that you do any more than pour it. You didn't have it the past few days either."

"Removes inhibitions. Not a lot. But enough. Wouldn't have been wise with a beautiful woman I was expected to keep pure. But now that I don't have that burden anymore, I figured it'd be fine." I retrieve a glass from another cabinet, as Jubilee has seen before.

Almost without a thought, she puts out a hand and gently touches the bottle as I'm about to tilt it to pour into the glass.

"Why do you drink it?" she asks for the first time ever.

I'm not annoyed, just a little confused, thinking I've explained it before. "It helps me sleep. I have some memories that come out in nightmares if I'm not careful. The past couple nights I've been okay, though. Nothing but sweet dreams with you around."

"What um…what memories? I mean, maybe if you need a substance to suppress them, you shouldn't be suppressing them," she suggests, hoping she's not overstepping any bounds. "I mean, if you don't mind me commenting. I obviously don't want to bring up those memories if they are that awful."

"You're my wife. You can comment at any time, Jubilee." I recap the bottle, setting it aside. "But I feel like this is a discussion about alcohol, not memories. You never did tell me how you feel."

"I'm undecided," Jubilee says like a question.

"Okay?" I encourage her to elaborate.

"Well…I was raised to believe that alcohol is sinful..."

"So, you think I'm sinning," I interject.

"No. I think you're taking more liberty than I'm used to."

"I generally do." I chuckle. That's the story of our life together.

"Yes, but…" Then Jubilee bites her lips, knowing she's about to cross boundaries.

I'm amused. More than amused. Invigorated. I can sense that Jubilee is about to *say* something. Some opinion that's all her own and not in line with mine. She isn't undecided. She's just scared to be the independent woman she doesn't know she is.

"But...?" I prod, smiling.

"Well...'All things are lawful for me, but not all things are helpful; All things are lawful for me, but not all things edify.' That's from First Corinthians ten, which has been my guide for liberty since the day you told me to seek God. So far, I've run all the choices you've made by that standard, and they are all edifying. Even the choice to propose to me without asking my father or to kiss me before the wedding. That all had a purpose. It all helped because it grew our relationship for God's glory. But so far, I see that drinking causes you to sleep and suppress memories. But what if that doesn't actually help?" Jubilee winces.

"How do you mean?"

"I mean..." Jubilee sighs nervously. "You have some secrets. And that's okay. But normally, you're the sort of man who is honest about his feelings and doesn't hold them back. I find that attractive. So why would you use a somewhat controversial liberty for a purpose that is both out of character and possibly not as edifying as it could be?"

"It just helps me sleep, Jubilee." I'm amused again. "The amount I drink doesn't have the side effects that sleep aids do. It's a safe, effective alternative. And I'm not dependent on it."

"Yes, you mentioned the past couple nights you haven't needed it, which would suggest a lack of dependence. It also suggests that you don't need help sleeping," she argues. Is she arguing with me? And why do I enjoy it?

"Well, Sunday night we didn't sleep a whole lot, and then the past two nights...Apparently I sleep well with you next to me."

"I'm sleeping next to you *tonight*, Husband. Perhaps my presence is an even *safer* alternative. And you *can* be dependent on me." Her eyes narrow. Hurt. Confused.

I see. Not just the devastating look on her face, but also her point. The choices before me are clear. Each choice is sacrificial. Jubilee's way or the bottle of whiskey. It isn't a *fair* choice. But it isn't really a choice at all. Because if I'm hurting the woman I love or causing her to stumble, I'm not using liberty to edify at all.

To demonstrate the choice, I place the bottle in the cabinet where I found it and return to Jubilee across the kitchen.

"I'm not suggesting this has to be a permanent solution. But I'm grateful that you're willing to compromise for me," Jubilee says, almost professionally.

I dip my head in complete laughter.

"What?" She smiles.

"Prim and proper Jubilee." I shake my head, adoring her. "We'll unbridle you yet."

"I'm just who I am, Husband." Jubilee looks like she's terrified she isn't who I really want.

"You, Mrs. Bering, are an imprisoned soul tapping the bars with a tin cup, waiting for the guard to walk by too close with the keys."

Jubilee giggles at the analogy.

I take my wife's hand. "You're laughing, but I'm the guard now. And I want you free."

"What am I in for in the first place?" Jubilee perpetuates.

As I pull her by the hand into our bedroom: "Impossibly, illegally good scrambled eggs."

After a time of sharing red bedding and our favorite secret, I can see we are settling in to something beautiful. She sighs, draping an arm over my bare chest, completely tranquil and at ease with me.

"You alright? You warm enough? I can turn up the heat. I know women tend to be cold, and—"

"I'm fine, Husband. Quite wonderful, to be more accurate." She shares, sighing again at that dose of pleasant chemicals and hormones that books didn't quite do justice.

"I second that." I smile, turning to her. I sigh, my soul completely open. "I feel like how I feel at an altar call during a worship service when sinners are getting saved and your spirit just wakes up and wants to sing."

"Worship? Elijah, if you're saying you're worshipping me, that's a problem." Jubilee objects, even though it's through giggles.

"Only Jesus, Lover." I pull her body right up against me, burying my face in her shoulder. "But the time of singing has come. And you're the song."

If she is Gideon. If she is taking up pitchers and horns against the countless ranks of the Midianites, maybe conquering an army isn't so hard or painful. Thus far, becoming a wife and mother has been nothing but a pleasure for her—I've made sure. Oh Jubilee, *you're the song.*

But I can't help but wonder if God has barely positioned her for battle.

Twenty-Six

Elijah

I begin fighting a cold almost immediately after our honeymoon. My usual dry cough turns into a more irritating one that starts to bark at my chest. I'm a little tired too, but I'm a fighter. I'm good at telling colds they can't have me.

But our first big argument occurs at 7:00 a.m. on our one-week anniversary. We are lying in bed and my beautiful wife is trying to make me go crazy on a Sunday morning.

"I just want you to try it, Wife," I try, my voice weak from coughing.

"I want to worship God. I don't want to go to a concert," she whines. "It is so easy for you to drop me off at my church and then go to yours. So easy. It's on the way."

"That's not the point, Jubilee! We agreed that enjoying *everything* together was included in this marriage. I want to take my family to church to worship God *together*. It's not a concert." I keep my tone level. Respectful. She grunts and throws herself out of bed, pacing the bedroom in that flannel nightgown. Ignoring the distraction, I continue. "You listen to the songs on the radio all the time and sing along with them. Why is it impossible for you to do the same thing in church? You went to Jessie's wedding with me! And we've met with Jordan there several times. He's an excellent Bible teacher."

"A wedding and meetings are not the same as attending a service! Why can't you and Bennett try *my* church, Husband? I grew up there," she argues.

"We got married there!" I raise my voice.

"Not the same thing. I just said that," she sasses.

"I can't uproot Bennett. You have absolutely no concept of how many times I've been forced to do that. The Durants are family to me. At our

210

church, they teach the truth, they play good music, and they know about Bennett's legs and love him *more* because of it. You are my wife. I am the spiritual leader. Come to my church. Please. You'll love it." I stand as well, wanting to rip out my hair or beg her on my knees. Or something.

"Elijah, if I don't go to my church, my parents will think—"

I cut her off with a tooth-grinding growl. "I went through a lot, Mrs. Jubilee Chandra *Bering*, to make you my wife. Now that you are, you need to figure out whose opinion matters to you more. If you want to go to that church because you truly believe it is the best place for you to worship God and don't care to respect your husband's leadership, I will drop you off there. But if it is for your parents, I'm asking you to please let me take you somewhere more suitable for us as a family. Your parents' church is *asleep*. I think you know that. I promised God and myself that I'd help you come *alive* for Him. Do you trust me enough to let me do that?"

She smirks, despite my heated words concluding six inches from her face. It's likely the meanest I've ever been to her and the worst I have in me. This tone would terrify Bennett. But Jubilee only sees it for what it is. Fear and love desperate enough to *beg* her to do the best thing. She has every right to argue back, and I'll ultimately respect her choice. But what happens is something else completely. Her eyes seem to ignite with that little smirk.

"What?" I ask in the same "mean" tone, then step back, softening. I'm learning to understand that look in her eyes. Before I let her answer, I explain further. "I don't ask a lot, Wife. I don't expect a thing from you. But just try this okay? And since I know you want to honor your parents as well, we will have dinner at their house, as planned, and your father can breathe down my neck all evening. If he asks anything about church, you let *me* explain it to him."

Her eyes soften, but they are still aflame. She clears her throat. "*If* I go with you...when do we have to be there?"

"Service is at nine." I'm still gruff, trying to keep the upper hand. So I hardly see it coming after I watch Jubilee do a few calculations in her head before she asks.

"Is Ben still asleep, you think?" She whispers, then bites her lip.

"Yeah, why?"

She reaches out and grabs my hand and I decide I like the way fights end. This one ends with the thing that we can't seem to get enough of. When you've never made love, you think it'll be more like the removal of an appendix, and less like caloric intake. But it isn't a onetime operation. However satisfying a meal, you'll still need to eat again. You'll starve if you only eat the once. And she's running on the same crazy fast metabolism as me, and so that's all we've done if we can catch a moment. It's like it can't wait more than a few minutes when we waited four months and decades each before that. I'm a glutton and so is she. They say this phase ends and things level out, but since we still manage to do the rest of life with joy, I don't see why we can't keep up this pace.

After indulging yet again, I'm the first to apologize for the fight.

"I'm sorry," I whisper, my pillow a raven's wings that I can't stop running my fingers through.

"Why are *you* sorry? I was disrespectful to you." She winces.

"You were asserting your father's—I mean your opinion." I forgive her, kissing her shoulder.

"And that's why I'm sorry." She sniffles. Her emotions wild, breaking free. "I'm sorry. There's just a lot of change all at once." And then, because she's a flaming temptress, and yet still a sweet, godly girl…she cries.

I love that I'm finally starting to see greater depths of that storm behind her eyes. And I love the way her sobs ease the minute I pull her back against me, brown and black skin all wrapped up together in our chocolate-milk-colored bedroom on a Sunday morning.

"What do I wear to your church?" She muffles into my shoulder.

"Can I pick it out?"

"Absolutely not." She laughs, probably half right in thinking I prefer she always wear her current attire.

"Don't worry, I'm not sharing this with anyone. Let me choose your clothes."

I take a quick duck bath, then get dressed while Jubilee is still in there shampooing all eight miles of her hair. I go to her side of the closet, which has always been emptied for a woman, just in case. But now it's full and smells like her. And I pick out my favorite pair of her jeans and a button-down flannel in shades of purple. I almost love this top. Around the time I hear the water shut off, I take out my single dad sewing kit and use the tiny scissors to snip the thread at the back of the top button. Now. Now I love it. I watched her put on a similar top a few days ago, and loved the way it flattered her until she closed everything up with a top button it looks like her mother installed to keep tempted eyes away. I hide the evidence of the deed, then lay out her clothes.

"Your outfit's on the bed." I call into the bathroom, "I'mma get Ben moving."

Ten minutes after getting Ben into his bathroom, the exact accusingly raised eyebrow and hand on a hip I was seeking appear in our bedroom doorway. She's wearing a lovely outfit for church. There is zero cleavage—that would be out of character for her—and she looks comfortable and classy.

I give her an appreciative whistle.

"Mr. Bering, I just don't know what to do with you sometimes." She sighs.

"Do you like it?" I ask.

"Honestly, yes. I was more worried about the jeans," she admits, starting a pot of coffee with a free collarbone and red feather earrings under all her hair.

"That's what we wear. You'll see."

"Jubilee!" Cindy finds us after we drop Bennett in his Sunday School class and gives my new bride a great big hug. "Oh, if you knew how long I've wanted to see this man bring his beautiful *wife* here on a Sunday morning. How is it being the lady of the Bering house?"

"I'm not sure she'd have an accurate answer to that after a week, Ms. Cindy," I mumble, trying to protect Jubilee from answering. I know she'd rather not be here fulfilling my pastor's wife's dreams for me. She has dreams of her own.

"Oh stop, Elijah," Ms. Cindy scolds. "Let your bride speak for herself."

Jubilee smiles, and gently says, "It's been a dream come true, Ms. Cindy."

"So?" I ask when we pile back into the truck and head to the Monroe homestead after church.

She's beaming. A hundred things going on in her spirit right now. The one she verbalizes? "They lift their hands."

It's true. At a church Jubilee recognized for their blatant allowance of liberty, and expected for any sin to be celebrated, the wildest use of liberty was not wild at all. The truth was spoken, even where uncomfortable for sinners. We spent time laughing with the Durants and Gordons after service. God was glorified. And we lifted our hands during worship.

"So, next week?" I smile in hope.

"We'll go back. We need to be together as a family. I'm sorry I doubted you."

I kiss her cheek and we pull out of the parking lot.

For some reason, Bennett is extremely quiet at the Monroe house, not even wanting to ride horses with Jubilee on the warm day, and content to sit on the porch alone. Adam also gives me suspect looks every time I go anywhere near Jubilee. So naturally, I try to be as affectionate as possible. That makes Adam smoke at the ears, to my morbid delight.

But just before Jubilee gets into her riding boots, Adam calls across a yard full of people to say, "Leah, get a safety pin, will you? Jubilee seems to be missing an important button."

"It's fine, Dad. I'm putting my jacket on." With her eyes, Jubilee begs me not to say anything as she zips up her jacket high on a day not quite cool enough for a jacket. But I smolder down deep. How dare he?

James shakes my hand when us men lean against the fence. It's the first moment I've had to greet him with the chaos of getting the family served. Meeting at the fence is customary ever since the day I asked to court Jubilee. Jubilee rides with little Bethany today, since Bennett is out of sorts. Hakim dismounts after just a short ride with Jonathan, eager to converse, it seems.

"I trust by now you've gotten addicted to Jubilee's scrambled eggs," Hakim inquires.

I grunt appreciatively, to Hakim's laughter. "Hakim, if I'd known about them things, I'd have taken that woman off y'all's hands months ago. What does she put in them? I made the mistake of asking her and now she won't even let me in the kitchen when she's cooking them."

"She won't tell us either. Mom has been attempting to replicate them all week and hasn't gotten it right," Judah shares.

I appreciate my wife along with them. "I thought I'd become a decent cook trying to raise a healthy son and all. But when Jubilee came along, she proved me wrong right away. She plumb spoils us."

Adam starts in. "She did that before the wedding, didn't she? Cooked for you every day? Stayed at your home until far too late. Sometimes overnight."

"All that turned out to be a good way to ease the transition for Bennett. Wasn't such a shock when she moved in. There's still some adjusting, but I'm glad for the way we did things," I defend, begging myself not to cuss him out.

And then Adam opines. "I understand the marriage is new and you need time to get settled. But I expect Jubilee will make it to church *next* week? Many of the elders that watched her grow up were hoping to see her there today."

"We attended a wonderful worship service this morning, Adam." I tell him with confidence. "As a new family."

Adam laughs bitterly. "You took her to *your* church, didn't you? Elijah, Jubilee's church home is an important part of her. As I mentioned, she grew up in ours. I'm sure you'll reconsider next week."

"I'm sure I *won't*," I venture, winking at Jubilee on the horse. She smiles back.

Adam huffs, and he's probably thinking out the next way he can accost and accuse me.

But I just can't help myself. I speak first. "So, here's my rules."

"Rules?" He answers with pomp and shame.

"Well, yes. You had rules for me *before* the wedding. I followed them, with very few, well-considered and prayed-over exceptions. So now that we are post wedding, I have some boundaries I'd like to go over."

Adam chuckles, "Elijah, it doesn't work like—"

"It's just that you seem to be unaware that there was a recent role shift. Much like the courting thing where you protected your daughter, I have boundaries that I believe will protect my wife."

"I don't follow."

"That's clear," I say. "The first one is the church thing. I worship with my family at a solid, Bible-teaching church we agreed to attend together and you don't give me grief about it."

"Elijah—"

"The second one is a little more personal and feels odd to have to say it to her father. Nevertheless, I ask that you do not comment on my wife's body or clothing."

"She was missing a button. I was—"

"She is wearing the top the way it was designed. It's flattering. She's allowed to look and feel beautiful in what she wears without you saying she's doing it wrong or sinning or something."

"It's immodest. Did she also wear the jeans to church?"

"I'm trying to understand how that is any of your—"

Hakim clears his throat. He's right. I'm taking it too far in that direction. So, I come in from another angle. I look to the Bible.

"What I mean, Adam, is that the lovely woman on the horse right there is flesh of *my* flesh. That means you are no longer scrutinizing your child's modesty. You are looking to see if any of *my* nakedness is showing. So, you can see why this might get awkward if it continues."

"Don't be dramatic, Elijah."

"I'm laying down a boundary. A clear, fair one. Don't overstep it," I insist.

"Elijah, it is unbecoming of a young woman—"

"Adam, that woman was born without the capability of 'unbecoming' and we both know it. You keep your house in order, I'll keep mine in order. My wife's wardrobe choices are not up for discussion, though since you're her daddy, I can permit you telling her she looks pretty. And we will be attending our family church. Period." I give the ultimatum. "If any additional boundaries need to be set as we settle in, I'll let you know."

Jubilee has dismounted and is leading the horse into the barn. I walk across the barnyard and meet her inside the barn. The dust makes me cough when I arrive, and she startles.

"You think you'll be alright going to work tomorrow, Husband? I think that cold is about to catch you," she frets.

"I've never taken a sick day, Wife. Not for me, at least. I only take them for Bennett."

"Speaking of whom…" Jubilee winces. "Is he okay? He's never refused to ride with me."

"I've been wondering the same thing," I concur with another cough.

"Maybe I should get *both* of you home." Jubilee is glad for the excuse she'd been searching for.

Bennett insists on showering himself and rubbing his own legs. So, Jubilee curls up against me on the couch instead of that ritual.

"I really thought he and I were getting along. Suddenly he won't even look at me. He was fine this morning," she whispers. "Lucky me, tomorrow is my first day alone with him as his actual evil stepmother."

"He's probably just adjusting. And if not, he'll come talk to me when he's ready. That's how he's always been. Too honest and open to keep it to himself. But you can't force it or he won't say a word. Has to be his choice." I note, distant. Still thinking of Adam fuming today.

"I had a dream last night. I don't usually have dreams, but I had an apple right before bed because we had some of those lovely McIntosh Judah gave us for our wedding, and I don't usually do that either. I didn't remember the dream until I was riding," Jubilee casually inserts.

I'm alarmed by the subject change, but indulge her. "An odd wedding gift, I thought."

"Agreed, but he's just a kid, and I am honored to have received anything at all from him. Anyway, in the dream, I was in the garden."

"We don't have a garden. You mean your mom's?"

"No, sorry. Eden. The Garden of Eden. Do you remember when we talked about Eden and how there were lots of fruit trees to choose from?" Jubilee clarifies.

"Ah, yes. I remember." I sit up. I sense this is a theological discussion.

"I was walking around the garden craving apples because of Judah's. So, I was looking for an apple tree. But my dad was there, following me around with an apple. But I realized that I didn't actually want an apple. I wanted an orange. My dad hates oranges and started yelling at me. Then I heard you calling me. And then I turned around and there you were. And you handed me an orange slice from an orange you were eating. You had the exact thing I didn't know I wanted."

"I do what I can." I chuckle. "Was that the whole dream?"

She smirks. "No, first I ate the orange, and my craving went away. Then I saw Bennett, who was eating a tomato, and I was scolding him, because a tomato is only *technically* a fruit. I thought he could do better." Jubilee sighs. Frowns. "I woke up terrified that I'll be an awful mother, and not allow him to seek God's purpose for him."

I'm enchanted. "You're not your dad."

"I know. But there's obviously a part of me that's scared I am," Jubilee frets, pulling her hair aside. "Not that he's a bad father. It's hard to learn from his godly influence and simultaneously reject pieces of it as a mom. But I'm trying," Jubilee says with a mysterious little smile that weakens my knees. Then weaves her hand into mine to stand all my back hair on end.

"Be anxious for nothing. Come here," I rumble.

It used to just be thoughts. Thoughts difficult to deal with, but something that time and sleep could pass. But when she's here, willing, within arm's reach, I realize how much of my self-control was Spirit led until this week, when the Lord released the bonds. Before my brain has time to send the signals, my arms and lips comply. I only realize we've been kissing when she giggles.

"Is this okay?" I pretend to have been mentally present.

"Always," she whispers. "It's always okay."

My need for constant consent annoys her. Her telling me that consent is "implied," and she is always ready to submit to me annoys *me*. We're working on the balance. I sigh appreciation for her answer, but before the kisses continue, our hearts jump when we hear:

"Um...Dad?" Bennett scoots in warily. "Sorry..."

I first wink at Jubilee, showing her the ways of Bennett. "What is it, son?"

Bennett pulls himself onto the chair, then glances at Jubilee a few times, crossing his arms.

Jubilee, a keen and perceptive servant, stands to exit.

"Where you goin?" I ask.

"Bennett wants to talk to his Dad." Jubilee nods. "It's okay. I'll just—"

I sigh sharply. "Ben...Jubilee is my wife now. And your stepmom. You can talk to her about anything, just like you do with me. We're a family. We don't exclude family members. You understand?"

Bennett nods, remorsefully. Sadly. "Sorry, Miss Jubilee."

I pat the spot on the couch next to me, and Jubilee takes a seat again. "What's on your mind, Ben?"

"After y'all got married, I was excited. So, I told everybody at school that Miss Jubilee was staying and I was maybe gonna have a baby brother." Bennett lights up. "And then this fifth grader told me if I'm really your brother then *your* baby won't be my brother. Is that true?"

I clear my throat. "Bennett, I've told you a hundred times that I'm your dad. It doesn't matter how you were born."

"But if you have a baby from…" Bennett smiles a blushed snicker. "The thing you told me where babies are from, then it'll be your baby. Like with DNA. But I'm not."

I say a quick prayer in my heart, then speak first.

"Well, with DNA, you'd still be related to our baby, but—" Then my articulate ways fail me.

Immediately, Jubilee morphs from young wife and stepmother into half of a parental unit.

"But DNA isn't everything. You and your dad have the same eyes from DNA. But most of who you are is not from DNA at all," Jubilee explains. "I'm adopted. Not by a family member, either. My DNA is from some anonymous pair of people in India. But my parents are my parents. And my siblings are my siblings. The only difference is they *chose* to love me the way they do. It was hard for me during a couple seasons in my life, but I came to realize that it's the same with God. None of us are in His family the way that the Israelites are. But because of Jesus, we're adopted in. And we're all brothers and sisters in Christ."

"Miss Jubilee is exactly right." I breathe relief at Jubilee's assistance. "Is that what's been bothering you today, son?"

"I guess. I knew Aiden was wrong." Bennett sighs. Looks to the ground. Starts his exit. "I…thanks for talking to me. I love you. Night."

As he scoots away, I bid him goodnight and hold a hand up to silence Jubilee until Bennett is gone.

"He's still upset," Jubilee whispers. "Shouldn't we…?"

"He'll talk to us again if he needs to," I whisper.

"That's amazing. Dad would just bombard me, and only if he decided I was sinning," she whispers.

"Even if you just wanted an orange?"

"Yeah. So we just wait? I worry that isn't the best way to—"

I interrupt with a chuckle of pure joy.

"What?" my wife inquires.

"*We.* 'We' is new."

She panics. "Elijah, if you'd rather I take a step back, I will. I wouldn't dare step on your toes when you've parented him so well thus far."

But I shake my head then lean forward and kiss my bride. " 'We' automatically means Bennett is better off than he's ever been. And so am I."

Twenty-Seven

Jubilee

The night and day change happens overnight. Bennett scoots out of his room at 10:00 a.m. on a Monday he doesn't have school. He got to sleep in, and I still made him breakfast, even though Elijah ate his eggs and left for work hours ago.

"Hey, Ben!" My first words to him.

"Hi." The only begrudging word Bennett utters until after breakfast *and* lunch, when I try again.

"Hey, your dad took the truck today, but I was thinking tomorrow after school we could go shopping and get something for Dad. I like to Christmas shop early and I could use your help shopping for him. What do you think about that?" A worthy attempt, I think.

"Whatever." And then he goes back in his room and shuts the door. Elijah calls at about three after I read a book and stare at horse decorations periodically.

"How's your day going, Lover? I miss you. Finally got a chance to take lunch so I thought I'd call," he says, muffled from chewing.

"It's going okay." Then I lower my voice to a whisper. "He's never going to speak to me again. Something is wrong."

"He's not back to normal yet?" Elijah says with a sniffle.

"No. And it won't be soon. You getting sick, Husband? I thought you beat that cold already."

"It caught up, unfortunately. Take care of our boy, okay? He'll come around."

I take heart when Bennett comes out of his room with his legs on and starts setting the table without being asked. As he's placing forks and I am stirring spaghetti sauce, I decide to take another chance.

"Hey, Bennett?" I barely glance at him.

"Yes, Miss Jubilee?" He says, only respect propelling him. I suppose that's enough.

"Wanna hear a secret?"

"Sure." He's annoyed with the mere sound of my voice, I can tell.

"I love you."

"You love my *dad*." Which is said bitterly.

"I do. Very much so. But the secret is, I loved *you* first."

"Did *not*," he groans, trying not to smile.

"Come on, Bennett," I reason. "You know I'd have never spoken to your dad if it wasn't for you. You should know by now that I wanted to be your mom just as much as I wanted to be his wife. So, any reason you ever wished you had a mom? I want to be that for you."

I expect the silence, so I don't let it offend me. My mom always said the lessons we learned the deepest didn't even seem like they registered at first. They showed later when she was glad to have taught them anyway.

Elijah comes home with a full-blown cold. He's up all night blowing his nose if he isn't tossing and turning. He barely makes it to work Tuesday, and only because I drive him before taking Bennett to school. I spend the morning holding little Mary to help keep Hannah sane, then take Elijah some lunch.

He pulls his coat around him as he takes a seat on our usual bench, sniffling against the chill of the air and his head cold.

"You sure you should be here, husband? Is it good to expose the residents to this?"

"I'm fine. I've been masked and gloved all day until now. Don't worry."

I unwrap his lunch—deli sandwiches wrapped in paper from his favorite sandwich shop—and keep my eyes on him as he shivers.

I comment, "And I suppose we may need to find a new lunch spot. The weather will likely turn on us soon."

"Things you don't consider when you meet and get married in practically the same season." He chuckles, winks, then coughs.

"Promise you'll tell me if I need to come get you?" I request, worried for my love. "There is no shame in taking the occasional sick day."

"I will."

"Promise."

"I promise. I'll call if I need to go home."

After I pick up Bennett, he and I end up in a sporting goods store for fishing tackle and a box. Bennett tells me that Elijah accidentally left his by the lake over the summer and it was gone when they came back.

"It doesn't seem like him to forget something like that," I remark to Bennett as he's looking for the best tackle box, sitting on the ground since they are lining the bottom shelf. He's scooting along, which any eight-year-old would do. But no one else in this store knows that's how he gets around naturally. The prosthetics are probably an annoyance.

"It was the day you came with us and he asked if you'd marry him," he reveals. "He acted funny after that until the wedding."

"Sorry." I wince. I both love and hate how much I rattled Elijah's world.

"He's happy now." Bennett sighs. "You make him real happy."

"Buddy, you can tell me if something is wrong," I attempt.

"I know," he says, sadly. He picks up a box in forest green, which I know to be Elijah's favorite color.

"Is this about the thing we talked about the other day?"

Bennett nods.

"Oh, I thought we clarified—"

"You said you love me and you want to be my mom."

"I do. That was the truth," I promise.

"So if you have a baby with Dad, you won't like him better than you do me? Because my brother will have legs, I bet. And will you decide not to love me because—?"

I fight tears at the outflow of remorse over the child's concerns.

"No, Bennett!" I practically scream. "I told your dad not too long ago how perfect you are."

"But I'm just your stepson and Dad's brother. This kid Aiden at school says—"

"Aiden has no idea what he's saying. I loved you *first*, remember? Nobody else who comes along will get to say he introduced me and Dad."

"But you'll love my little brother when he comes along?"

"Of course. Better than my own soul, I expect. But I wouldn't *dare* have a baby without you as his big brother."

Then my phone rings. Bennett smiles when he sees my smile at who is calling. I answer.

"Hey, Husband."

"Hey, Wife." A groan. His voice has dropped an octave since lunch. "They told me I'm too sick to stay."

I am putting my new husband to bed for the afternoon after he expended the remainder of his energy encouraging Bennett on the ride home. As I watch Elijah's eyes droop, I'm thinking of just the kind of man it takes to adopt a brother as his own child. A choice which forced him to wait until he was twenty-nine to get married. My heart sinks. I suppose I must seem like a child to him sometimes with all his wisdom. As he's falling asleep under my fingers stroking his hair, I whisper in my spirit with passion.

"Lord, make me the woman he deserves."

Twenty-Eight

Elijah

I am up half the night coughing. I slept all day and now at night when my wife and son are trying to sleep, I'm coughing. It isn't even productive. Just coughing. And I'm out of commission otherwise too. Jubilee kept bringing me soup and crackers and tea, and I barely noticed when she came to bed. I can't remember the last time I had a cold this bad.

I'm pacing the living room now, miserable. Everything hurts, and my unrelenting cough is beating against a sore throat. And to my horror, now I've woken up Jubilee. She comes out at 2:00 a.m. yawning, headed to the kitchen.

"Aw, Wife," I say with a growl and stuffiness. "I didn't mean to wake you. I was trying to stop coughing."

"Don't worry about me," she says, rummaging around the kitchen. Then she curls a finger for me to go to her, so I do. I can't see exactly what she's doing because my eyes are watering, but she says, "Open."

Then suddenly there is a big spoon of pure honey in my mouth. Way too sweet, with that unmistakable bee vomit essence. Jubilee bought me some at the farmers' market over the summer, so it has been sitting in the pantry, untouched.

"I thought 'swallow' was implied." She giggles.

I comply with a smile, then blink and see her smiling at me in the silence. The *silence*.

"I'm not coughing."

"Nope." She goes to the cabinet and takes something out, washing it in the sink.

"How long does this last?"

"Long enough for you to go to sleep." She shrugs. "I'm giving you something else for *that*."

I wipe my eyes to see that she's washing a dusty old shot glass with my alma mater's name. Not that I was ever much for shots. I was my roommate's wingman at a party once. It was the night I realized my love for whiskey and its effect on my sleep cycles.

Jubilee dries the glass carefully and I watch her retrieve my whiskey from the cabinet and pour some into the shot glass like a professional bartender. I smile, appreciating it.

"Have you ever done shots before?" she asks. "I guess it doesn't really feel that great going down, so that's why I wanted to coat your throat with the honey first. I guess you just drink it all—"

By this time, I am setting down my glass and giving Jubilee a motion to fill it again.

"At once." She finishes her sentence, tilting her head. Then tilting the bottle. "So 'yes' on the having done shots?"

"Where'd you learn about shots?" I ask through the rasp of my illness and the whiskey.

"Online, five minutes ago," Jubilee confesses as I take the second shot.

"How many...?" she asks, filling the glass again.

"Uh..." I tilt my head, which isn't quite swimmy. "One more. Been a few years since college. My limit was five then."

I take the third, Jubilee blurring and my body relaxing. I hold onto the counter for dear life.

"Oh good. The idea was for it to work quickly." Jubilee smirks.

"Can we talk about why you're encouraging me to drink alcohol?" I ask sleepily. "I thought you hated that I drank."

"I hated that you were drinking instead of seeking God for why you couldn't sleep. It wasn't beneficial," Jubilee explains, washing the glass again. "Tonight it is. You need to rest or you'll never get better. I'm glad we had this in the house."

"Me too." I step up behind Jubilee and pull her against me, burying my nose in her hair. "You smell *so* nice."

She giggles, pulling away as I fiddle with the hem of her night gown. "You can stop right there, Husband. You're not doing anything but resting tonight."

She pulls me by the hand, and I'm relaxed and dragging my feet back to our room as she speaks. "I'll go into town tomorrow with Bennett and get some other stuff that'll help you feel better." She kisses me once on the mouth, fearless of what she'll catch from me. "Love you. Go to sleep."

Morning signals the downslope of my cold, with a little more energy and a productive cough. I'm glad to be fit and healthy enough to heal. I start to get ready for work.

Jubilee enters the bathroom as I'm about to spray shaving cream into my hand.

She laughs once, taking the can from my hand. "Not even." And she hands me my phone. "You work with elderly people. You are not better yet, and they get sick easily. Don't try to be tough. Call in."

"You just want my hotness home with you." My voice is still not right, but it's strong enough to try seduction.

Jubilee smiles and tosses that gorgeous mop of hers aside, shrugging flirtatiously. "That too." Then doesn't give me a thing. Tease. I re-fall in love with the new Jubilee I knew was rattling around inside.

"Is it alright if I take your truck into town for a while? I'd have to go by my mom's first. I need to check on Thunder, and I have to have Mom remind me what she puts in the oil she makes for colds. Then I need to get stuff for it after I drop Bennett at school," Jubilee requests over breakfast.

"*Our* truck?" I rasp, correcting my wife, whose mother obviously has jelly for a backbone and shackles for independence. "I'm sick. Why would I need the truck?"

"You have a right to know where I'm going and what I'm doing," she reminds me. "I want you to know I'm not just running around town. I have errands…"

"You can run around town if you want to run around town. You have a cell phone if I need you, Wife," I remind her, disconcerted that she still has growing to do. "Ben, get ready. Time for school."

"Can't I stay? I want to finish my book," Bennett asks, having been scolded twice for trying to read at the table.

Jubilee giggles and kisses his head, "You can finish it when you get home, Buddy. Let's get going. I have to stop at Grandma Leah's."

I miss her when she goes. It's silly; she's only gone two hours. She's back after I take a nap, and then she putters around in the kitchen a while before she picks up Bennett. After dinner and a movie and putting Bennett to bed, we sit on the couch together like we have the extent of our marriage."

"Can I work tomorrow?" I whine.

"We'll see how you feel in the morning," Jubilee responds.

" 'We'll see' is parent spy code for 'No,' " I remind her.

She smiles at the memory, but still says, "You should go to bed now. Go on and just get a little whiskey so you aren't too groggy. Then I have something that will clear up your chest a little more."

I'm lying on my stomach, reading the news on my phone and Jubilee is in the bathroom. She started the day handing me my phone, and now I hear the bathroom door open, and she takes my phone, setting it on my nightstand. She sets some little decanter next to it with floating things in some oil.

"Take off your shirt," she whispers. And at such a request from my Jubilee, I've nothing to do but obey. She pulls the covers back to my knees. "Lay your head down and relax."

Which seems reasonable too. She sits on her knees beside me on the bed, clouding my mind and clearing my sinuses by rubbing a fragrant oil on my back with her gentle touch.

"Wow. What's in that?" I ask.

"Family secret," she says, yawning. I am bewitched by the massage and thinking of ways to ask her to heal me further when she speaks. "Turn over. Let me get your chest too."

God and tradition and everything tells me I'm supposed to be honeymooning this woman every chance I get, and that's certainly the preference. Instead, I turn over and fall asleep to the healing touch of my bride. Maybe that's the same thing. Maybe not. All I know is it's this. Liberty is for this.

Jubilee

I emerge from my room the same time Bennett comes out of his, and the two of us startle one another in the little hall. Bennett wiggles his nose.

"Is that the stuff you made in the kitchen today?" he asks.

"Yep. It's helping Dad breathe. So hopefully he can get better. Why are you up?"

"My legs hurt. Will that work on my legs?"

"Probably not." I smile. "But I can rub them with the other stuff if you want."

"I hate that stuff." Bennett rolls his eyes. "But Dad pays lots of money for it, so we can use it."

"I'm sure I can come up with something else for you, but for tonight let's use the stuff the doctor recommended, okay?" I lead the scooting child over to the couch and begin the routine I've grown to love. I'm glad he's allowing it again.

"You don't push as hard as Daddy. I like that," Bennett says.

"Well, moms get to be a little gentler if we want."

"So, if you're my stepmom, what is Miss Hannah and Mister James?" Bennett ruminates.

"Your aunt and uncle. All of my siblings are your aunts and uncles, and their children are your cousins."

"Jonathan is my cousin?! That's so cool!" He alights.

"I heard he was excited about that too."

"Not all of the other kids like me. Even if they are my cousins."

"Well, they are silly, then. Because you are my favorite kid ever," I confess. "You have one of the best hearts, just like your daddy."

"I want to be just like him, Miss Jubilee. But can I still be like him even if he isn't my real dad?"

"Sure you can." I shrug, finishing rubbing my boy's legs. "But if not, being *you* will be just as wonderful."

Twenty-Nine

Jubilee

I have loved Bennett from the moment he hung out the truck window with a "Hey!". But here on Christmas morning, for the first time I feel like I'm his mom. Sure, we only have an eleven-year age gap. And some, when they find out the age gap between me and my husband is nearly the same, say I should be a child in his eyes. Well, if I was a child before, I'm not now. Once one begins to appreciate childhood, one is no longer a child. And today, watching Bennett's face as he opens toys and a new homemade balm for his legs, I love my perspective as a parent.

And then I look to Elijah, wondering who has looked at him the way we are looking at Bennett. I've never known someone to be so open and honest, and yet so full of secrets. That is one of those things I attribute to his age. Still, my hope is to chip away at the secrets he says give him nightmares. So, when we are in our room dressing before heading to my childhood home to continue Christmas, I begin, gently and respectfully as always.

"What was Christmas like when you were a child? With your mother." I'm sitting on our bed, gathering my hair into a loose braid over my shoulder.

"My father died before I was born. He was the only man she ever really loved, considering that's the only man's name she ever took. She never got back into the spirit of holidays and things with him gone. Sometimes we had a tree. Sometimes we didn't. She couldn't afford presents. That's why Bennett and I go big on Christmas." He pulls the sweater over his chest and smooths his hair. Just a beautiful, beautiful man.

"I think it's wonderful."

Elijah smiles with some pain behind his eyes. "You ready? I don't want to be late."

"Yeah." I tie off my braid and stand, smoothing my skirt and sweater and checking all angles of myself in the mirror on the wall. Elijah is watching intently.

"Any weird Christmas rules I need to know?" He asks. "Anything special we need to say or do or avoid saying or doing?"

"I like you a lot better than I like my parents' weird rules." A kiss in passing. "Be you."

I give Priscilla a big hug, glad she made the trek with her family again. Aaron and Katie couldn't come back again, but I'm glad they chose to come to the wedding. We all open gifts, and the children play with their new toys. I have tea with my sisters and sisters-in-law in the dining room and the men are in the sunroom out back.

"So…any baby news yet? Are you expecting?" Priscilla asks in a low voice. Maren and Penny smile. Hannah bites a lip.

"We've been married less than three months." My coy answer.

"That's plenty of time," Penny says. "You're not on birth control, are you?"

"Penny!" I protest in a whisper under their giggles.

"I'm just asking." Penny beams. They all stare. They actually want to know.

"No on both counts. I'm not on birth control. We opted for prenatal vitamins. And I'm not expecting," I grant them, and they are all slightly disappointed.

"Priscilla thought you were on them because you were already expecting at the wedding," Maren finally says what was already a rumor.

"A baby was only possible *after* the wedding," I finally allow.

"Well, God's time. I wouldn't worry," Priscilla encourages in her way.

"You know we already have a child, right?"

They all look at one another. Priscilla leans in. "I heard he's deformed. Is that true?"

"Wha…Who did you hear that from?" I'm startled, having thought we'd kept Bennett's legs a secret.

"The grapevine," Maren says haughtily with a shrug. "Mom and one of Hannah's children saw one day when you two were out riding. He fell and she was checking to see if he skinned his knees. But from what I understand he doesn't really *have* knees."

I think only of perfect Christmas morning smiles. "He's a wonderful little boy. It's obviously not easy, which is why I was taking prenatals even before the wedding. We wanted to be sure I did what I could to ensure proper development. But God made Ben just the way He wanted him to be."

"But isn't that a curse? Doesn't it mean that God is showing you a piece of your sin if your child is deformed?" Penny, who has likely never opened more than a Bible study of someone else's opinion, is clueless. Noah likes her that way. It makes his meager wisdom law.

"I read in Leviticus that if a Levite had a deformity, they were not to enter the tent of meeting because they were unclean." Maren clarifies with evidence, a 'subordinate' to a much wiser man.

"Interesting. I read in John where Jesus Himself declared that a certain man's blindness wasn't due to *anyone's* sin," I rebut with a shrug and some fire.

"It could still be that he was a result of sin, Jubilee. You can't discount that. I hope it doesn't leak into you." Priscilla, my haughty sister.

"'Leak into me?'" I laugh aloud. "Sin doesn't work like that."

"Well, I understand Elijah was never married before you, and yet he has a son." Priscilla. So wrong and she doesn't even know.

"Despite his not having come from my body, Ben is *my* son too. We're hoping to start the adoption process as soon as my age allows. I don't talk about your children this way, do I? Despite Elliot the Third having his father's prominent nose." I'm losing the will to fight for Bennett without fire. Just like a mother.

Priscilla gasps. But when said child, and one of Isaac's little redheads run through the room together and then exit, we all take to snorting laughter. Even Priscilla, who certainly didn't marry Elliot for his looks, smirks.

"He's beautiful, Priscilla. You know I'm only joking," I say with a tone that makes them all apologize profusely for having spoken ill of Bennett. Fake, of course. I'm starting to see that now.

The back sliding door opens, and Elijah seamlessly joins the female conversation. He's a nurse, it's comfortable for him, though odd for my family. But I see that since he comes in, Hakim and Dad both feel safe to join us.

"I hope we have one that looks like Jubilee." He winks at me.

"Not that he or she wouldn't be a win-win for either of your genetics," Hakim ventures. No one ever denied that I got a looker. It just took our brother to admit it. Then, having missed the rest, his eyes widen. "Wait, are you pregnant?"

Elijah and I laugh. He answers, "Not yet, Hakim. Let's not start that rumor again."

"But I assume it is more plausible this time." That one is from Dad.

Elijah reads the situation, mainly in Dad's eyes as he leans against the wall opposite him in the cramped dining area.

Hakim speaks up. "Dad, why are you asking him that? In mixed company. Again."

"I didn't ask him anything." Dad yawns and shrugs. "Though I do wonder why you are so protective of that kind of information, and so bothered by pregnancy rumors."

"Probably past trauma," Priscilla allows with an eye roll that Dad smirks over.

"Past...?" Elijah begins and then understanding washes over his face as he nods. "Ah. You mean Bennett."

"No, you don't under—" I start. But from Elijah's wink I know he wants to have the pleasure.

"The doctors weren't sure if she *ever* knew she was pregnant. It's possible she was too high most of the time to notice something like that. I know when I was a kid that was the case sometimes. She was too high to remember to buy groceries or keep a job. But she was really good at getting men to take care of her, so I honestly didn't go hungry too often. I was fortunate. Trauma, sure. But none of it from Bennett." Elijah is amused at their confusion.

"Your brother, correct? Patrice was your mother." Dad is completely unfazed. "I looked at court records shortly after you began courting Jubilee."

"You never mentioned anything." Elijah is intrigued.

"Neither did you." Dad looks like maybe he's impressed.

"I'm lost." Hannah laughs.

"I adopted Bennett when he was two," Elijah says, his eyes stayed on Dad's.

"Only because you couldn't before then." I roll my eyes at the humble man. "He was his legal guardian from the time they released him from the NICU. He's the only father Bennett has ever had."

232

"Do you share a natural father?" Maren wonders. Not even I know where Bennett came from really. I doubt Elijah will give a straight answer.

"No, my father died before I was born. Our mother died just after Bennett was born, and Bennett's father died shortly after that. Which only makes *me* an orphan. Bennett has two parents who love him because God recently saw fit for him to have a mama." Elijah smiles, then turns to me and straightens the red feather of my earring with loving fluidity.

"You knew all along, Dad?" I finally ask.

"Your husband seems to have an aversion to vindicating himself."

"It's not that I don't want to be in everyone's good graces. But it reminds me of that blind man in John 9 Jubilee just mentioned before we came in. There was all kinds of speculation about him and that Man that healed him. And he says look, I don't know the details. I just know I was blind and now I see. In my case, the details don't matter." Elijah smiles. "Because I am justified by the blood of Christ and nothing else."

"And your righteous actions, obviously." Dad is probably half complimenting, but Elijah takes offense. Not for him, but for God.

"No, sir. I live righteously only as a result of God's grace and the way He works within me. He justifies and sanctifies. I just love Him and obey Him. But even that was only possible because He loved me first."

"Interesting thought." Dad doesn't agree.

"Yeah, I bet." Elijah chuckles.

Suddenly, Bennett runs into the room and buries a red, pained, sobbing face in my chest, and I wrap my arms around him.

"Buddy, what's wrong? What happened?" I gasp.

"Jonathan saw my legs when we came here last and said they were cool. So he told the other kids and I showed them and they said it was gross and they…" He sniffles. "They laughed and called me ugly and said God doesn't love me…" And he sobs, which calls his father to drop to a kneel at his side.

Elijah sighs, then pulls back Bennett's head and demands his wet eyes. "Say it."

"No! It's not true. I'm a freak. I'm a mistake. My father didn't want me because I'm so ugly." Which he's been holding in for quite some time, it seems.

"Say it," Elijah says with the firmness of a father.

"I am fearfully and wonderfully made." It is just a defeated whimper of a statement.

"And what?" Elijah whispers.

" 'The Spirit Himself bears witness…' " Then Bennett sobs.

"Don't stop, Buddy." I lean in, stroking his arm.

" 'The Spirit Himself bears witness with our spirit that we are children of God, and if children, then heirs—heirs of God and joint heirs with Christ, that we may also be glorified together. For I consider that the sufferings of this present time are not worthy to be compared with the glory which shall be revealed in us.' Romans eight, sixteen through eighteen." He rattles off in deep breaths and sobs.

I kiss my stepson's beautiful forehead in the sight of all. I look him in the eye and make a promise I'll keep for life:

"I love you."

"I love you too, Miss Jubilee." He inhales quickly, the tears stopping. I shake my head.

"Mom," I say it fiercely. "No more Miss Jubilee. You call me *Mom*. You have a mom and a dad who would be lost without you, Ben. And a God who made you just perfect."

Bennett smiles big and hugs me deep. "I love you, Mama."

"You realize you weren't even able to bear children when that boy was born?" Priscilla, of course.

"Neither was Sarah when God gave her Isaac." I conclude, then stand and meet the admiring eyes and affectionate kiss of my husband.

Dad clears his throat to stop the kissing.

"She is so provocative!" Maren whispers to Penny.

Then Elijah smiles and turns to them, his eyes looking directly into Dad's. "I tell her that all the time."

I giggle and push his chest flirtatiously. "Let's go home, boys."

"It breaks my heart that they didn't even do anything when their little spawns made fun of our Bennett." I whisper to Elijah after a much better Christmas evening spent at home. He's smoothing my hair out against the pillow, listening to me rant.

"I always forget Hannah and James are so different from the rest of them. Poor Jonathan probably thinks it was his fault," Elijah concurs. Then he allows some silence before turning to me with a smile. "What do you think of the name Benjamin?"

"It's a nice name." His expectant eyes tell me the question isn't random. "For Bennett's brother, whom we haven't even conceived yet?"

"Yeah. Benjamin."

But I don't answer right away. I take a detour in the conversation. "Three months isn't a long time for us to not be pregnant yet, right?"

He recognizes that I'm asking the RN. "No, Jubilee. Fertility doctors don't even bat an eye until it's been a year. And your cycle is longer than some women. That means as much effort as we give it, we haven't had a ton of actual chances to get pregnant in two-and-a-half months."

"Okay," I whisper, still astounded that I married a man who freely discusses my cycle.

"Honestly, I'm glad it hasn't happened yet."

My heart breaks and I barely say, "Why? I thought…"

"They thought the quick engagement was a cover-up. But now we've been married almost as long as we courted and no pregnancy. They probably feel silly now, knowing you honored God."

"We." I correct with a sigh of lament over a patient womb. "They know we *both* honored Him."

"Don't worry." His tone is soft, and he taps my nose with affection. "It'll happen when God wants it to happen."

"But what if God doesn't want it to happen? Should we really be talking about baby names?" I fret.

"It's one of those things we never got around to discussing before we ran down the aisle together. So yes. We should lay here in bed and dream together. It's what lovers do."

I nod at his wisdom, however whimsical. And I concede. "The problem with Benjamin is that we have a Ben already. That would get confusing. And I love the name Bennett because it isn't traditional. Benjamin is."

"So, we have a philosophy about this?" He chuckles.

"Yeah. All of my siblings and nieces and nephews have names that sound like the people at your nursing home. I like my name because it's a little different. So, as much as I'd like a little Elijah running around…I'd prefer something that stands out a little for our babies. But something that goes with Bennett for sure. Did you name him?"

"I did. Bennett was my mother's maiden name. Then I added Mephibosheth. And then Bering because I honestly didn't even know his father's last name," Elijah explains.

"Well, I like it. The whole thing." We shut off the lights and settle in for sleep. The silence overtakes the room after Elijah "spoons" me from behind. I startle when he speaks.

"What about Bartholomew?"

"No!" *Is he serious?* No, he's snickering.

"You wanted it to go with Bennett. That's the first 'B' name I could think of." He justifies. Though there's no modern justification for such a name.

"Actually, I like the two T's. Jessie's husband Garrett? I love his name. Maybe we could steal it since Jessie isn't having children." I yawn.

"Oh, so not Belthasar, then?" he teases. "Sorta goes with Mephibosheth."

"Maybe as a middle name, then," I joke.

We laugh hysterically about baby names far too late into the night, choosing to be better lovers than we are respecters of tomorrow's responsibilities.

Thirty

Jubilee

Elijah's body is finally taking a chance to rest after living twenty-nine years without a fit caregiver. He gets sick again in January, and in February it turns into pneumonia. He's always been good about saving money, and was planning to buy me a car soon, but we've dipped into our savings a couple times because he's missed so much work, and a second car is the least of our worries.

Elijah's cough is going far beyond the remedies I grew up with. He coughs all night, even with his preferred sleep aid in his blood. I don't mind that it keeps me awake at night, but it is becoming increasingly difficult to pretend it doesn't, and I don't want him to feel bad about something he can't control. Elijah keeps losing his voice from the force of his cough. Even Bennett is worried, but I try to keep him focused on school.

The doorbell rings on a Saturday morning in late February when Elijah is still asleep. I look to Bennett, who shrugs. Then I open the door.

"That husband of yours still sick? We haven't seen you in a month of Sundays!" Lucinda Durant, of course—the pastor's wife with her married adult daughter in tow.

"Hi, Cindy. Jessie. Um…come on in. I'm folding laundry. Sorry." I move the pile from the couch into a nearby basket.

"Wow. I wish I could look that good folding laundry on a Saturday morning." Jessie says of my neatly braided hair, "eight layers" of clothing, and fresh, clean face.

I was taught to always get dressed in the morning. It was best for modesty and readied me for service right away. Elijah was the first to call me odd for it once we began living together.

"Um...thank you?" I shake my head. "Elijah's still pretty sick. He's asleep right now..." I say, then hear the shower running and roll my eyes. "Actually, he's probably stubborn enough to be up now. He'll never get better at this rate."

"I told him he should listen to you, Mama. But he doesn't," Bennett says. Jessie and Lucinda melt.

"Mama?" Jessie asks. "That is so sweet."

"Oh, I've prayed for a woman to come into these boys' lives for five years. Where were you all this time?" Lucinda asks.

I laugh once, leading everyone to sit. "Well, five years ago, it wouldn't have been appropriate for me to be acquainted with Elijah in the capacity which I am now."

Both women squint their brown eyes just the same.

I'm being too prim and proper. "I was fourteen five years ago. Elijah was twenty-four. That's...illegal."

The master bedroom door opens as the women are laughing aloud the way they do. Elijah appears, freshly and quickly showered. He probably heard them and wanted to rescue me.

He sets to hugging them immediately. "Y'all quit harassing my wife," he rasps.

"We brought soup," Jessie says, handing Elijah a little container.

"Well, thank you!" And he puts it in the fridge, returning to put an arm around me on the couch.

Jessie looks around the room. "Garrett and I were saying the other day how you guys have a decade between family members. It's like this perfect stair-step family across generations."

Cindy takes it a step further. "Which means since Bennett is almost nine, you're about due for another family member."

"Mom," Jessie scolds in a whisper. Hating the pressure on her to have children, and not wishing it on others. "That's totally not what I meant, guys."

Elijah coughs, then chuckles. "It's actually alright if you meant that. Either of you. Jubilee and I are open to having a child whenever God allows."

"Ah, so now we know where Jubilee stands on the family planning thing." Jessie is pleased. "It looks like you caved about trying to have a baby right away."

"It wasn't like that, Jessie. Jubilee helped me to see some things that I didn't see before we met, and now I wish everyone could hear it. Sorry to put you on the spot, Wife, but you should tell them about it."

I can see Elijah wants me to be bold and share my heart. To opine, even in present company. I sigh.

"We're not 'trying,' technically. Because there's no difference in what we do whether we prefer or don't prefer to create a child. I just…I don't believe that we have control over that or that we should try to. I've always thought it was God's choice." I quickly backpedal. "But that's not to say God doesn't *allow* family planning. We have the liberty to do that. But in my family, we've never done it that way. Not that I have to do what my family says. I just honestly don't feel that's God's purpose…for me. You know, for us." I sigh, trembling. Expecting Jessie to storm out of the house.

Instead, she squeals, unoffended. "So you two are gonna have like *twenty* kids?"

Elijah guffaws. Jokes. "Well, if we want to keep the customary ten years between them, I'd be pretty old by the time number twenty came around."

Lucinda snickers. "Well, I'll keep my ears open for a pregnancy announcement. I guess we're just waiting on that."

"And on God's will." I look to my husband who gives me those enraptured eyes I fall for every time.

"Oh, heavens." Cindy relishes the obvious romance. "Anytime now, I bet."

Elijah first laughs, then lets out one little closed-mouth cough like everyone does sometimes. But that restraint is short-lived as always, because then he's coughing. Coughing. Coughing.

"Husband!" I rub his back as his body convulses each time he forces that air onto his forearm. I hand him a tissue from the table and nearly yell in his ear to be heard over the coughing. "Do you want to try the honey?"

He shakes his head, putting up a finger as he stands and goes back into our bedroom.

"We thought we were on the downslope of this one…" I hear him try to get the fit under control in our room.

"Well…that's sort of why we came, Jubilee," Lucinda says. Uh oh. She always means well. But I know a lecture is coming, and wait for it in silence. Jessie starts.

"Mom and I visit my great-grandma Millie at his nursing home, and the last few times we've gone, he hasn't been there. Some of his coworkers told us he's used more sick days this year than in any other year combined. And it's February. The are all worried and they say it's not like him at all," Jessie says.

"I know. He's a hard worker. At first I thought he'd just been stubborn not using sick days, because the first few times I had to fight with him to keep him home. But sometimes now..." I sigh. "Sometimes I can't even get him out of bed. And *I* have to call him in. It doesn't seem like him, but I thought maybe since I just haven't known him that long..."

"Oh no, sweetheart. You know him well. He's strong as an ox and never takes a minute to relax. Other than that constant allergy cough of his the past year or so, I'd never seen him sick. Last summer just before he met you, I was flat out begging him to go on a date with someone. But he refused to sacrifice a minute of work or a second with Bennett to do it," Lucinda assures me.

I laugh. "Well, he didn't. Not even for me until our 'mini-moon.' And we still spent a lot of that with Ben."

"Which is another atrocity. But for now, I'll leave that alone. Jubilee, sweetheart. I'm concerned for Elijah. Has he been to a doctor?"

"He had one of the doctors on staff at work look him over once. The doctor suspected pneumonia and gave him antibiotics." I nod. "Worked for about a minute. He's just so sick. I'm trying to think of a way to help him get better, I just..." I wipe a tear and glance at Bennett, who I'm glad isn't listening. "Oh goodness. Pardon me."

"For being upset that the man you love is suffering?" Jessie asks. Rolls her eyes. "You're pardoned."

"How can we help? He's family to us. That means you are too. Let us help." Cindy reaches out and grabs my hands.

I can think of a hundred things I need help with around the house and in my life and with Bennett. But never would I ask for any of them, except the one.

"I know that God is able to restore his health completely without our aid. But prayers help."

In March, someone at school finds out about Bennett's legs, and then everyone knows. So we have to go in and explain his condition during a special show and tell time. Elijah isn't terribly sick for it, but like clockwork, mid-month he starts the cough again, pneumonia again. And this time the antibiotics don't touch it. He has to ride it out. Early April, I approach Elijah after Bennett is in bed.

"I've been seeking God. And I think you need to take leave and get better." I wrap my hand into his. "Every time you get back to work for a week you get sicker than the last time. You're out of sick days, but not out of sickness."

"I have to work. Life takes money, Jubilee. I have three lives to support. I can't just not work," he reasons.

"One of those lives is *yours*, Husband. You have to get some rest and maybe you'll get better for good." I try to bring up my offer slowly. "I have everything I need to be a veterinary technician. A new office just opened up, and I heard they are having trouble finding people to—"

"No way." Which is what I figured he'd say. "I'm not letting you work just because I have a cough."

"I can work. I'm very good at it, actually. I'm home all day by myself when Bennett has school. I can get a job to fill that time instead so you can rest."

"Jubilee, I know you can. That doesn't mean you want to," he says.

"I *want* to keep this family functioning. I'll do whatever it takes to make that happen."

"If you become the breadwinner, your father will never forgive me. I'm a man. I need to provide for my family." He coughs a deep, chesty cough.

"Husband, whose convictions are those? Yours or my father's?" I accuse with his own words.

He laughs a little. "Jubilee, read the Bible. God *made* men to provide. It's not just a duty, it's what we often desire to do. And given the choice, you *quit* your job to take care of our Bennett and started managing things here at home before we got married, because it is what you felt called to do." He coughs. "You and I have structured our family according to God's call for *our* lives. I'm not being sexist here."

"I understand that it isn't our ideal. But sometimes a man gets sick, and a woman caring for her family takes on a new meaning for a while. We need money and you are sick. There is no shame or sin in me working, especially if you're unable. What is liberty for, if not a time like this?"

"I want you to do what you want to do. I want you to be happy," he pleads.

"I love animals. That's why I have the degree. I just couldn't find a job in that field at the time. It'll be great."

But isn't great at all. Elijah gets an extended unpaid medical leave approved, and I get a job with the new veterinarian in town. But they know I'm not even twenty years old, and I'm an underling making half of what Elijah did as an RN. Our little family is barely scraping by, and not saving a penny. I get bit and scratched and peed on and I hate every minute of work. All I do is the dirty jobs analyzing stool samples, cleaning up messes in the waiting room, and mucking horse stalls. But the hours line up with Bennett's school, with just an hour where he walks over to Hannah's afterward.

I know Elijah has a good day when I get home and the house is clean, and dinner is made, and he can't keep his hands off me. But those days become rarer and rarer, and usually my work isn't done until my head hits the pillow at night next to a sleeping, ailing man.

Then in May, Elijah has a coughing fit after dinner, and I watch his face go white when he coughs up a disconcerting amount of blood and something pink and foamy looking. We go to the emergency room, which runs some tests and schedules Elijah for a follow-up with our primary care doctor.

The three days before that appointment are agonizing, and not just because we know the diagnosis is bad. I begin awakening in the morning with the same headache as him, experiencing the same loss of appetite, and even begin throwing up at random times. I begin to worry that we both have some disease I brought home from work, though the timing doesn't line up. I worry for Bennett's health and care and for what we'll do about money should we both be too sick to work.

My dream life is in danger—the Midianites encamping around us.

Elijah's follow-up happens on one of his good days, and one of my bad ones. I am vomiting, about to call the doctor for my own appointment, and Elijah must drive into town to take Bennett to school and go to his appointment alone, when I had taken a personal day to go with him, not to be sick at home.

I flop into bed after what I hope is the day's last bout of vomiting. I'm whimpering and trying to bring the room into focus. I look up at a good focal point on my dresser—a pitcher containing a candle we have sometimes lit for romantic lighting. A layer of gray dust has covered it, a consequence of an exhausted lady of the house. Next to the pitcher is a tiny pair of cowboy boots, also forgotten about with how chaotic life has become. And just after I bring those into focus, I burst into wild laughter amid my sickness, wishing Elijah were around to hear it.

Nearly forgetting the nausea, I leap out of bed and back into the bathroom, unable to contain my smile as I count back days and weeks and realize the reason for my extra-long cycle was probably not the stress, as sometimes occurs.

I read directions on the little box of pregnancy tests I keep around, almost feeling deviant for finding myself in need of one. When I am staring at the result, Elijah breaches the front door, making his way to me while calling my name.

"You still sick, Wife?" Elijah asks in his normal raspy voice, with some added sadness as he knocks on the bathroom door.

"No..." I stash the test behind the toothbrush container, realizing adrenaline has probably offered me a temporary cure. "Come on in."

He opens the door and I turn and lean against the counter. Elijah sighs and closes the door behind him, leaning against it. There is a dark gloom in his eyes.

"Husband." I gasp. "What...what's wrong? Is everything okay?"

Elijah pinches the bridge of his nose. Clears his throat. Sniffles. And then begins sobbing.

"Hus—. . .Elijah. Oh my goodness." I become the embrace he was seeking. The soaked shoulder. The refuge.

He cried at our wedding. Some called him less of a man for that. But that's not what he is to me now. I adore him, knowing that he's completely open to me, and waited until the second he saw me to fall apart. I am his soft place to land. My dream life is intact and strong. In the next instant, I realize it also means that something is horribly, unprecedentedly amiss.

In just a moment, my husband composes himself. He steps back and waves me off with an embarrassed smile and leans against the door again.

"Sorry. I'm such a tough guy, huh?"

"It's alright, I'm just concerned. Tell me what's wrong, Husband." I hand him a tissue from the counter.

"I was raised by a few different father figures. Mom married some. Some she didn't." Since that doesn't make sense yet, I wait for more. "I can almost identify them by the drug my mother used with them. She was a mess, Jubilee. She had a part of her, though. A big part of her. That just didn't live in that same world. That part of her dreamed of sitting on a porch holding hands with an old man that had loved her for half a century. She never could make it past a couple years with anyone. As I grew and came to know the Lord, He made sure He burned that into my heart, even though my Mom didn't always teach me what is right. When I married you, that's what I saw. Not just a flaming honeymoon phase. I saw my porch out there. And you. In fifty years."

"Me too." I nod to encourage him.

Elijah sniffles again. "Thing is. . .my mother, rest her soul, both planted and destroyed that dream for us. Because there's a chance I won't even get to celebrate *one* anniversary with you. All those chemicals and all the smoke since I was a kid. . .I got lung cancer, Jubilee."

I try to keep my head and hide my trembling while that all seeps inside my pores. More secrets from his past. A heart-wrenching present. And maybe no future at all. I try to be strong. But more and more, I'm beginning to lose that battle between the appearances and the truth. I sob.

"I'm sorry." His face distorts. He whispers, "I'm so sorry, Jubilee."

But I can't respond to that. "I wasn't even there for you when you found out. How bad is it?"

"Pretty bad. I have a chance. Not a great one, but we're starting chemo and radiation this coming week in some pretty high doses. I'm gonna fight this to the death for you and Bennett, but I also need to make sure you know that I might be leaving you for heaven." Elijah sniffles. "I don't know how to tell my son that."

"We'll have to pray about that." I wipe a tear. "Don't worry about that right now."

"You're right." Elijah renews his faith. "Doctor thinks this has been brewing a while, and I know God led us to get married at the right time. That sense of urgency we had wasn't about avoiding temptation. It was about *survival*. I don't know where Ben and I would be without you right now. God brought you to us at the perfect time. I'm *so* thankful."

"Me too." I nod. "Even with our trials this year, you and Ben are the only thing I've ever wanted."

"There's...something worse." Elijah sobs once more, then clears his throat. "If I survive this, I'll have gone through high doses of chemo and radiation. The..." He sighs, not able to bear saying it without crying. "The doctor said it's likely I'd be sterile. Definitely short-term. Possibly forever. We have Bennett. I'm thankful for him. But I'll probably never give you other children of your own, Jubilee. Of *our* own." He breaks down in tears again.

I begin sobbing as well. I can't speak. But Elijah suddenly realizes that my tears are not of grief or sorrow. Not even joy. They are tears of worship. I pull Elijah close as those tears persist.

"Jubilee, what's..." He wonders, pushing my shoulders away to search my eyes.

"God is so good." I manage a squeak and sobs and then begin praying, "Thank you, Lord Jesus. You are so gracious. You are Lord over all, and I will worship You no matter what trials come, Father. I don't deserve Your goodness and overwhelming grace. I don't deserve this..."

"Wait, what don't you deserve?" Elijah asks, smiling over my outpouring.

"We are so abundantly blessed, Lover." I laugh, then turn around and grab the test off the counter, handing it to the unsuspecting Elijah.

He laughs robustly to a cough. "You're pregnant."

"I'm pregnant," I confirm. "*We* are pregnant."

"I..." He laughs again. A cancer diagnosis no damper for this level of joy. "So, all you have is morning sickness? That's a relief. But the 'lover' thing has been so sporadic. This wasn't even a thought in my mind. When did this happen?"

I shrug. "I hadn't been paying attention. If I hadn't been so sick, I wouldn't have even checked. The boots on the dresser reminded me that it was possible. I felt so silly."

Elijah chuckles. "Some nurse I am. I can't believe I didn't consider pregnancy."

"I know quite a bit about pregnancy too. I should have certainly known there is a tiny *person* in my body. I've just been so worried about *you*..." My sigh is weighty. "Rightfully so, I suppose. *Cancer*..."

Elijah shakes his head and reaches across the bathroom, pulling me close to him again. "Satan doesn't get this one. We're not talking about cancer for the rest of the day. I was concerned all the way home that I wouldn't get to have a baby with you. Don't you love the sound of God laughing?"

Thirty-One

Jubilee

"The Lord is with thee, mighty woman of valor." I awaken with the words all around me and respond.

"How did I forget You, God? I know You're with me, even now. Why am I relying on my own two hands?"

I pray, driving between Bennett's school and work the morning after our first announcement. Baby first. Joy first, we'd decided. To which Bennett had responded by smiling and cheering and even tearing up a little before going to his room and setting aside all the toys his little brother might like.

"Lord, please don't let this be a girl."

But now I'm ashamed before God for working so hard, all for naught, it seems. I've kept us afloat with this job, but never considered that it wasn't me at all. And as I'm waiting in the parking lot, fifteen minutes before I'm to commence getting peed and spat upon, I hear a Voice inside me, trying to remind myself that God can gather wisdom that way into a spirit. Just like with the stir about a man and his young son at a gas station. And with the smile over such things, God speaks clearly.

"Rejoice."

Perplexing. I'm feeling nauseous, and I'm headed into a job I hate to support a sick husband and disabled child that I didn't even know a year ago. *"Where is there joy in that?"*

But I hear Bennett's voice in my head.

" 'The Spirit Himself bears witness with our spirit that we are children of God, and if children, then heirs—heirs of God and joint heirs with Christ, that we may also be glorified together. For I consider that the sufferings of this present time are not worthy to be compared with the glory which shall be revealed in us.' Romans eight, sixteen through eighteen."

Of course. But does God want me to take joy, even in suffering?

"Rejoice in the Lord always. And again I will say, Rejoice!"

I suppose that if joy is to occur despite circumstance, it is a good time to test that theory.

Today, I choose to wear a smile of gratitude as I'm peed on, picking up poop and vomiting for the sake of my unborn child. If I share in Christ's suffering, then there is no greater joy. Then something happens. Suddenly I'm not an underling. In fact, today the veterinarian meets me outside the restroom with concern over my illness. When he learns of my pregnancy and other circumstances, he takes me off all dirty jobs to protect my child against things that can harm him. He puts me at the front desk, where I make appointments and deal with records and such, and he gives me a little raise.

All for the sake of joy. And all for Christ. What else is liberty for but joy?

I arrive home with the news and the makings for Bennett's favorite meal on his last day of school. Over dinner, we tell him something that almost makes my joy falter.

"But you *die* from cancer," Bennett says.

"Sometimes," Elijah answers. Then coughs a little inside his mouth.

"Dad wants to stay with us as much as we want him to, Bennett. So, we'll do whatever we can to fight this. And you and I will have to do as much as we can to help him get better," I reason.

"But you're sick too, Mama." Bennett uses the name that both he and his dad have been calling me for days.

"I'm expecting, I'm not sick. And God is taking care of all of us. Don't you worry."

But Bennett worries. All the time. Every day. And doesn't say a word about it. Which is what worries us the most.

Not having done more than speak on the phone with my parents in a few months, they invite us to dinner, unexpectedly nice enough to include Bennett in the season's joint birthday party. Luckily, Elijah hasn't started his cancer treatments yet, so we might both be strong enough to tell them what's going on. But before that, I need some spirit cleansing.

"Wanna ride?" I text Hakim one night after dinner when Bennett is reading and Elijah is well enough to watch him.

"You don't even need to ask," he responds.

"Be there in five."

I realize in a few moments that the jostling of the horse doesn't feel like something a tiny unborn human should endure. Everything I've read says it is okay, but it seems too risky if this is our one shot at pregnancy. When the path widens, I ask Hakim to stop, and we tie up the horses.

"I thought we were riding," he says, joining me in the dust.

"I thought I could. But now I think I better not."

He lights up all at once. "You're knocked up, aren't you?"

I wince. "Something like that."

"Gees. About time. I was starting to think you were holding out on that man of yours," he teases.

I sigh. "Maybe I should have."

"Why? You've always wanted to be a mom, Jubilee. Even more than Priscilla and Hannah," Hakim reminds me.

"I know. God made me a mom even before He made me a wife. So it's good I wanted to be one already." I nod. It all makes so much sense from His perspective. "But Elijah's sick, Hakim. And I'm trusting God. I know He orchestrated the timing of our marriage and everything so that I'd be there to take care of him and Bennett. But I'm pretty scared."

"Scared, why?" Hakim asks. "And…sick how? Just the pneumonia, or…"

"He has cancer," I say it almost like a question. "All the pneumonia is because of that. That's why he's so sick all the time. Lung cancer."

"I didn't realize he'd ever smoked." Hakim is taken aback.

"He hasn't." My voice trembles. "Never once in his life. But his mother did, and she also made drugs in the house. They think that contributed."

"So much for not being responsible for the sins of our fathers." Hakim mumbles.

"The other night he thought maybe it was his punishment for being slow to forgive her a long time ago." I laugh bitterly. "But he says a lot of things. And he trusts God's will, whatever that is. I think he's just scared. But don't tell him I told you that, okay? I don't think he wants me to know."

"Lung cancer is a good reason to be scared. Is it bad?" Hakim asks.

"I think it is, but Elijah won't tell me how bad. He's probably trying to protect me."

"I can't say I'd do anything different. You've got a lot going on. Sometimes God gives us the diagnosis but not the prognosis so that we trust Him. Elijah's doing the same thing," Hakim explains right into my spirit. "I say trust your man. He's not a bad one."

"You're right about that. It's like…" I clear my throat, crying a little. "It's like a cruel experiment. Not that God is cruel or would do such a thing, and I trust Him. But Elijah needed a warrior, and God sent *me*. Elijah deserves so much better than this." Better than Gideon.

"Come on, Jubilee." Hakim scoffs. "You don't even see it, do you?"

"See what?" I remove my hat and run my fingers through my hair in frustration.

"You're a woman of virtue, just like every woman in this family. But *your* virtue comes with *fire*."

"Elijah tells me about that 'fire' all the time. Like I'm some wild animal or something and don't know it."

"You're not like a wild animal. You're like a horse. The rest of them are like sheep. You're a horse."

"I'm a horse." I laugh. "Thanks for that."

"You stay the course. Follow your Master, even if He wanted to lead you to your death. But once the path is good for galloping—or even if there isn't a path there yet—He gives the cue, and you go for it. You scatter the sheep and leave the rest of us in your dust." Hakim smiles. "And sometimes you're unpredictable. But when you married Elijah, it surprised everyone but me. Because I've ridden horses with you for a decade. I think Dad is terrified you'll be," Hakim whispers for drama, "an inspiration."

I giggle, because he's probably right. "Unfortunately, being an inspirational horse doesn't equip me to handle all this."

"But *God* will. You just have to make sure He's your Master." Hakim punches my arm. "It's getting dark. We should get back now since you're knocked up and have to *walk* the horse." He stands, helping me to my feet.

"Knocked up?" I finally call out. "That's so vulgar. Where did you learn that? I am trying to teach Bennett 'expecting,' just like we learned."

"Yes, you're 'expecting' due to 'amorous congress.' You could be talking about anything." He laughs, "I assume the 'trying to teach' is because Elijah says stuff like 'sex' and 'pregnant.' How vulgar."

"We use euphemisms, Hakim. Just not ones that suggest promiscuity."

"Or being born in the year 1600." Hakim shakes his head, handing me Thunder's reins to lead him. "When in doubt, say what Elijah says. Not what our parents say."

"They weren't *all* wrong. You and I know the Lord because of them."

"Do we?" Hakim asks. "I mean, sure, we learned about God's rules and sin and how to avoid it. Which is great, don't get me wrong. But I'm betting grace and liberty are relatively new to you, even though Christ died specifically so that we could experience them."

"We can't use grace as an excuse to sin," I rebut.

"Didn't say that. But we can't use sin as an excuse to hate, either." Hakim shrugs.

I nod, recently understanding exactly what he means, but feeling dizzy and stopping a moment.

"There goes that expectingness again." Hakim snickers. "Are you telling the family at the birthday dinner?"

"That's the plan. We aren't sure whether to start with the baby news or the cancer news. And the fact that he doesn't work right now…Hakim, it's so against what they believe, but we didn't choose this." I begin fretting and share my heart. "I'm terrified that Dad is going to say something disrespectful to my husband when we tell them he has cancer. I won't know how to be respectful to Dad if he disrespects my husband."

"Jubilee, I have your back," he promises. "Tell me the last time I hesitated to stand up to Dad. Elijah has to maintain a certain level of reverence because it'll always be true that he married Dad's youngest daughter and rescued you from our stuffy childhood church and there's even a rumor that he *dances* with you sometimes…"

"Who told you that?" I bite my lip.

"Your son." Which makes joy wash over and through me. Hakim smiles. "And keep doing it. It'll teach Bennett how to be like his dad. Not *ours*."

I smile and mumble. "Once Dad finds out I'm expecting, I think dancing will be the least of his objections."

"You're married, Jubilee. Babies come from healthy marriages. Even Dad knows that." Hakim shrugs.

"Yeah, and our *marriage* is healthy. But Elijah isn't. Mom taught all of us girls that there are certain unwritten rules for things in marriage. One of them is that if my husband is so sick that I have to wait on him hand and foot *and* hold a job, it is completely uncouth for him to also expect—"

"Amorous congress." Hakim winces.

"Yes. So by their calculations, cancer and pregnancy cannot coexist. They are going to think horrible things about him."

"Should they? I mean, is he asking too much?"

"Hakim!"

"As much as I love Elijah, I wouldn't be your brother if I didn't ask."

"No! We just see things much differently than they do. It's very wrong to view sex as a chore or part of a punishment and reward system. *That* is cancer. And we're both legitimately pass-out tired quite a lot, so it's not very often right now. But why in the world would we stop doing something that brings us together when everything in our life is trying to rip us apart?"

"Wow." Hakim laughs. "See? Fire. I really wish you'd show that to Dad more often. But if you don't on Sunday, I will. I'm always ready to ride with you, okay? I'm on your side."

"Thanks, Hakim."

Elijah

After dinner on Sunday, when dessert is cleared and the children are all playing on the swing set out back, I clear my throat to draw both attention and a full breath.

"We…" Then I cough, though I have all of their attention.

Jubilee smiles a little, rubbing my back as she speaks. "We have a couple of announcements to make."

"First she gets a job because you have a cough, now she speaks for you too, Elijah?" Which Isaac thinks is funny and Noah chuckles along with him.

"Shut your trap, Isaac. Jubilee has something to tell us." Hakim, of course.

"Go ahead, Jubilee." Leah says, beaming. Leah has heard the same announcement before and sees it coming. Her carefully concealed joy sets my Jubilee to comfort.

She laughs once. Smiles. "Well, first of all, we're expecting."

The little gasp and then the coos and subdued shouts of joy and light clapping overtake the room.

Adam merely smirks, then his eyes narrow. "Usually that's a plenty big announcement in itself."

Jubilee nods. I look to her with remorse, and find my voice, albeit raspy. "The same day we found out about the baby, I found out that I have lung cancer." I smirk, then give gentle rebuke. "Isaac, that's the medical term that explains my 'cough.' "

Isaac deflates. Then all hell breaks loose. Quietly, of course.

"Have you been using the oil?" Leah asks.

"It's cancer, Mom. Not a chest cold." Jubilee smiles. I cough and wheeze a little, stemming from a little laugh over that oil I've always enjoyed the application of.

"Do it anyway. He'll breathe easier. I'll make you some more that is more concentrated."

"Yes, ma'am. And thank you. It does help him sleep."

Jubilee feels the tears coming for all that is overwhelming her, and the accusations in the form of encouragements, and she excuses herself from the table. She walks out the front door in the silence. When the wooden screen door clatters shut, I sigh.

"Y'all…" I clear my throat. "I know I'm not the favorite around here, but I need to know that if I don't make it out of this alive, that Jubilee and Bennett and this baby will still have support from her family."

"Do you have life insurance?" Adam asks coldly.

"I do. I also had the foresight to make sure Jubilee was the primary beneficiary even before the wedding. Considering all that Jubilee is having to do to keep us afloat financially, I'm worth more dead than alive right now. I'm sure that's plenty satisfying for you, Adam. But however strong Jubilee is, she will have two children to raise on her own if I leave her on this earth. And she'd be a widow at such a young age, and I *do* give her emotional and spiritual support that she'd suddenly lose. I just need to know…" I cough uncontrollably for a moment.

Leah captures my eyes. "We'll take care of her, Elijah. Her and the children."

"Children," Isaac grumbles. "So, forcing her to work wasn't enough for you?"

"You are not seriously going there right now." Hakim scolds his brother, even though I'm oblivious.

"Okay, I didn't force her to do anything. I'm a little lost." I admit, remaining cordial.

"Exactly." Hakim seems to be agreeing with me, and I let him defend what I don't understand. "Everything in their life is trying to tear them apart, and you are grumbling about the blessing that is coming because they stuck together?"

"A single man doesn't get a say in a matter like this." Adam, of course, is siding with Isaac.

"Well, a married woman does. And what I just said is basically from the horse's mouth," Hakim says, then smirks to himself like there's an inside joke.

"We'll see how she feels when she's a twenty-year-old widow with two children she shouldn't have had to raise because of one selfish man." Noah's comment about makes my blood simmer and sputter.

"Caring for her includes caring for her heart. I hear you say anything like that after I'm dead and I will come up out of my grave and—"

"But you're alive, Elijah," Hakim points out, settling my blood again. "What about *now*? Jubilee needs help and encouragement *now*. She rode with me the other day, and she can barely take a few steps without getting dizzy and she works full time and runs the household and cooks and cleans and takes care of you and Bennett...how is she dealing with all that?"

My silence as I fight tears speaks for me. I nod. "If Jubilee or I ever doubted the power of God's presence...we aren't doubting it now. We know He's with us. And that's how we're dealing with it."

"But—" Hakim attempts to continue the rant.

"Enough, Hakim. It's time we pray," Adam interrupts.

After an emotionless, solemn prayer, Hakim rises from the table, red in the face.

"You know, there are families that all they ever do is pray when there are starving children in developing countries with no hope but Jesus, who they don't even know. Sometimes all you can do is pray. But I'm living proof that this isn't one of those families. When did we stop being the kind of family that *serves* others? Jubilee needs us. Why are we not jumping up to help her, when you *know* she'd do it, and *has* done it for you?" Hakim heads to the stairs.

"Get back here. Where are you going?" Adam accosts.

We can't see him, but Hakim answers in a quote from James two when he is likely halfway up the stairs, " 'Show me your faith without your works, and I will show you my faith *by* my works.' "

"And how exactly are you doing that?" Adam looks like maybe he's convicted, but his tone, louder from yelling it so Hakim can hear, doesn't let on.

"I'm *packing*, Dad." Hakim descends enough so we can all see him again, then looks around at his confused family. "Question is, what are the rest of *you* doing?"

Jubilee

I stand at the edge of the horse yard, looking longingly at Thunder's beauty.

"Don't worry," I tell my unborn child, gently grazing my stomach with fingertips too tired for nails of any color to describe. "You're worth all of this. We are so thankful God sent you."

Liberty, I decide, is more than being allowed to have two fingers of whiskey before bed or kiss before a wedding. It is the ability to pave deeper paths for Christ. If every role was set and every path paved by convention and tradition and law, there would be no room to care for a cancer patient or adopt an unwanted child. I see, more clearly than ever, that I must not let strict guidelines judge a life God Himself gave me. Maybe someone's sin somewhere down the line caused all this. Certainly in Eden. But now, blameless in the aftermath, I must navigate it all with liberty, not condemnation.

What is liberty for, if not this?

I roll my eyes when Hannah, Maren, and Penny come out of the house to interrupt my thoughts after a time. I know they mean well, whatever their errand, so I accept them cordially.

"Are you allowed to ride him?" Hannah asks. "Because of the pregnancy, I mean."

"I am, technically." I nod. "But I don't plan on it. I tried the other day, and it didn't feel right. Too risky."

Penny wonders, "How many weeks are you?"

"Um…" I tilt my head side to side. "We aren't sure. I have an appointment this week, and then I'll have a due date, I hope. Elijah was concerned that I would neglect my prenatal care to take care of him, so he got me set up with an OBGYN with a practice at the hospital where he's having his treatments. That way it's really convenient for me to—"

"OBGYN?" Hannah asks it. Then immediately regrets it. The others stare at me like I grew a second head.

"Um…yeah." I wince, wondering if I should tell them the horror stories of attempted home births that Elijah told me from the perspective of a nurse. "It's what my husband prefers."

"Your husband isn't the one who is expecting." Maren quite nearly becomes a misandrist when it comes to her body while she is pregnant, as if once Isaac does the work of impregnating her, she holds over his head that her body is more sacred and capable than his. Twice, she has not allowed him in the room when his children were born, citing ancient biblical practices as her reasoning. Priscilla is similar, but mostly because Elliot isn't much help in a delivery room, and usually leaves of his own accord when Priscilla loses her composure for the pain. He likes Priscilla composed. Both James and Noah are intricately involved in the gestation, birth, and the rest of their children's lives, as is Aaron. To me, that says a lot about their marriages. But Maren is appalled that I would bend so easily to a plea of my husband, when Maren herself barely has a say in anything *except* this area.

"I disagree. Elijah and I are in this together. I always thought I'd have a home birth, but my husband feels strongly for the alternative, especially since he is sick and won't be able to help me prepare as he'd like."

Hannah clears her throat amid the awkward silent protest of the sisters. "Elijah has a long journey ahead of him, and I know you have to work, so I'll take care of your baby when he or she comes, Jubilee. For as long as you need me to. And I'll watch Bennett all summer too. I know he hates that daycare, and there's no need to pay for one if I'm at home with Bennett's best friend all day."

"Thank you, Hannah. That's extremely helpful. That really lifts a burden." I sigh. "Now if only I can figure out a way to be at chemo and work and driving Ben to school once it starts all at once. That will be a feat. I could use another body and set of hands sometimes. I'm just so tired."

They aren't used to hearing much pain and emotion in this family. So at first they are silent. Then Penny decides to be compassionate. She's inspired to share some minuscule piece of her heart. "I think we can all relate to that."

And even Maren nods.

We all turn when the front door opens and Hakim walks out, heading to the garage with a couple of suitcases. Then Judah holds open the door, and Isaac and Noah are carrying large pieces of wood out and putting them into the back of Elijah's truck.

"What's going on?" I ask. I don't let them answer before I go to the garage to talk with Hakim. "What are you doing?" I ask him.

"Packing my car. I won't bring too much. I know you don't have a lot of room to spare. And I'll buy a trunk so it is all consolidated." He says, leaving his door open and heading back inside. I pass the truck as I follow him and see that what they are loading is a disassembled bunk bed.

"Whose bed is that?" I ask Hakim.

"That was Noah and Aaron's. It's just been sitting in the basement. It was already broken down, so it eliminates a step." Which still doesn't answer the question.

I enter the bustling house. My mother is in the kitchen with casserole dishes out, giving fetching and cooking orders to her grandchildren.

"Mom, what's going on?" I'm getting confused. This is not a normal Sunday meal.

"Just making you a few meals to freeze and use. I'll try to bring over a couple every week," she says. "I haven't even…been to your house…" she trails off.

"Mom." I say with gratitude. "That's really sweet of you. And I know you're busy, and I'm busy. It's okay if you haven't been over."

"No it's not. It's not okay," she says, then barks more orders at the children.

I walk away and see that my father is nowhere in sight, and my husband is out on the back porch alone. I put arms around him from behind. He still carries so much of my strength, and I am only strong when I hold him close.

"What's going on?" I'm hoping someone will finally answer.

He doesn't answer right away. I first feel the chuckle in his belly. "I really love your brother Hakim. He's a good man. I knew that the first time I met him."

"He says the same thing about you. But what makes you say that?"

"Hakim decided to move in with us. He thinks you could use a hand, but as long as he's here, you'd never ask him to help you. So, he wants to be in the thick of everything so that you don't have to worry about asking. The rest of the family seems to be following suit." Elijah clears his throat. Moved beyond tears.

"I was outside for ten minutes and Hakim decided to live with us?" I'm floored by the family that often forgets how faith takes action. Today they remembered.

"Says he'd been thinking about it a few days. He even wants to help with bills, but I told him we'd have to see about that. I agreed to him coming because you could use the help, Wife. God knows *I'm* useless. Heck, I'm part of the problem. Worse than useless," Elijah laments.

"Stop that. You're plenty good enough for me." I move to Elijah's front and embrace him.

"Hakim does demand that we pay him," Elijah adds. "In scrambled eggs."

Thirty-Two

Elijah

Before I could build good muscle, I worked. Nursing was a surprising profession to my mother, who ridiculed it. But I'd spent an entire youth doing manual labor. I raised horses with one stepdad. I spent a summer framing houses with one of Mom's live-ins. With yet another, I restored a '67 Mustang before watching her drive away after that father figure left us too.

So, the fact that I can't even walk halls and pass out meds and care for old people is demeaning at best. And getting winded tightening the bolts on an old wooden bunk bed is unheard of. But I see in Hakim's face when the coughing turns to blood in the sink that maybe someone sees I'm not making this up. I'd do anything for my son and die for my wife. But last week I passed out from lack of oxygen while trying to make them dinner.

"This is really bad," I hear Hakim whisper to Jubilee in the other room.

"Yeah," she whispers back. "Thanks for coming to help. We'll need it."

Jubilee is the kind of woman that someone told she had to be strong. But in my opinion, all women are strong already. See, men carry all their strength on the outside. In their muscles and bones and hard heads. Women carry it on the inside. Just by living to a certain age, they have a week every month where a man in her position would check himself into a hospital. But a woman will push through it. And now that Jubilee is expecting, I see that she's just going to press on through that too.

"Slow down, Mama. Think about that baby," I'll tell her in the evenings when she feels like she needs to conquer the world.

"I'll slow down when I'm dead," she'll say.

I think that anytime a woman bawls her eyes out for no apparent reason or gets moody or fiery, she has a right. Because her spirit was built to be strong. But God put it in a form with very little upper body strength and hormones aplenty. The same form makes all that physical strength of a man just crumble at her touch. But the form is so soft and gentle and fragile that the world mistakes it all for weakness. That has to be frustrating.

So, Jubilee keeps it all in. Fights against her form, because someone told her that even a leak of emotion is a sign of not trusting in God. She'll apologize if she gets too happy about something. Excuse herself from others' presence if she sheds one tear. But I've seen her wilds enough to know that she's hiding more strength that she knows. And if she lets it flow into that fragile form, she might just find it makes her stronger.

She wants to cry right now, watching me wheeze my way to calm over a sink. Scared for me. Carrying my baby and all my strength inside her. But she's not showing any of it.

Hakim clears his throat. "Um…what do you usually do to get Bennett to bed? I'll do that and you take care of 'Husband.' "

"He needs to take a shower and rub some oil on his legs." I say, though raspy and wheezy. "And say his prayers."

We say goodnight to Bennett, and Hakim supervises our bedtime routine from a distance. Then I lie on my stomach as my wife sits beside me and massages fragrant oil into my back. Then my chest, when I see the dark circles under her eyes.

"You need to rest, Jubilee. The baby."

"I just have a few more things to pack for your hospital stay." She yawns.

Tired as can be, I stand up and literally dress her in her summer nightgown and tuck her into bed next to me and watch her eyes droop.

I whisper, "You are testing God. You cannot do this if you refuse to sleep."

She sighs, her spirit in pain. I clear my throat and think it is a good time to discuss some things.

"I had a lawyer draw up a will while you were working this week. The main thing was Bennett. Something happens, I don't want anyone trying to question if he's your son." I smooth her hair.

She sniffles. "Stop it. Don't even talk about that stuff." And before she finishes speaking, she's in full tears and sobs, willing to be soft for me, all her strength bared and beautiful.

"Jubilee, it's practical," I tell her, demanding her overflowing eyes with mine.

"I've never...loved *anything*...the way that I love you. Don't you understand that? If you die, I'll die too. So, don't you dare..." She sobs.

"I'll do my best to live, Wife." And I'm weak. But I hold her until she falls asleep in tears.

"So, they are putting a port in first?" Hakim asks in the quiet of the morning before we've woken Jubilee and Bennett.

"Yes. Normally they'd want to wait a while to do the chemo after that, but this cancer...it's aggressive, so they have to be aggressive," I nearly whisper.

"She's smart, you know. She knows it's worse than you're saying," Hakim shares.

"As far as lung cancer goes, it isn't as bad as it could be. But this might still kill me." I'm blunt with Hakim in a way I'd never be with Jubilee.

We hear the thudding of feet and some distant vomiting. I smile. "Jubilee's up."

Hakim laughs. "It doesn't bother you that you knocked up a teenager?"

"Hey, she's twenty now, so she's not a teenager anymore. She was when *that* happened, but who's counting?" I correct with some more laughter and a cough. "So, what about you? Got any young women in mind?"

"Oh gee, how do I pick from the pool of super fun, bright, opinionated girls at my family's church?" Hakim chuckles the sarcasm.

"First, come to *our* church," I suggest. "Second, you gotta see past how they have been taught to act, Hakim. Like with Jubilee..."

Hakim interrupts with a guffaw, "Jubilee was never like the rest of them. She was like a sore thumb or maybe even a zebra, and everyone knew it. I am *so* glad she didn't marry Peter. You were the absolute best thing for her, bruh. You taught her to be who she already was. It's hard to explain because you didn't know her before. I swear she came to life the day she met you guys."

"That was the Lord. I'm just here making her life complicated and exhausting."

"Maybe that's what joy takes." Hakim shrugs. "Can you even appreciate something if it comes easy?"

Jubilee drags herself out of the bedroom in the next moment. Hair in a braid. Dressed in jeans while she still can. She waves to us, then knocks on Bennett's door and opens it.

"Time to get up, Buddy. Dad starts his treatment today." Her voice is so tired.

"It's still dark out," we hear in a mumble.

"Yeah, they do surgeries super early like this," Jubilee explains. Yawns. "That way it's easier to fast. But after we drop off Dad, I'll take you to breakfast. How does that sound?"

"You have to go to work," Bennett reasons, scooting out of his room.

"I'm only going the second half of the day today."

We listen to her talk Bennett through the getting ready process. I say to Hakim, "I don't know what I'd do without her right now. What Bennett would do. I started getting sick the week after we got married. Everyone thought it was quick, but we just kept feeling a push to start our life together. Turns out that if we had waited even a week…"

"Well, God is on your side, no matter what my dad says. He wasn't about to let you be without her."

After a procedure in twilight anesthesia, I awaken and Bennett and Jubilee say hello before I get wheeled to radiation. Then after radiation, Chemo. After that, Jubilee is there again with Bennett, and kisses me, running her hand across my hair, knowing it'll probably be gone by the end of the week. I barely recognize that I'm being spoken to and try to focus on her voice.

"Hakim wants to know if you'd rather he stay here or at home with us," I finally make out.

"Hakim," I say, the world foggy except for the beautiful woman I'm having trouble believing is actually my bride. I'm wondering who Hakim is.

Jubilee giggles. "We'll all come see you in the morning. Love you."

"Bye, Dad," says Bennett.

My son. Oh God, let me live to watch him grow.

"Bye. Love you," I say aloud. Then I put my head on the pillow and open my eyes and Jubilee is wearing different clothes and sitting at my bedside holding my hand.

"Hey," I say. "How you doing?"

I smile, not having missed a moment. Or maybe a lot of them.

"You…" I look around and try to orient himself. I sigh, realizing I missed a lot. "Did Bennett sleep okay?"

"Yeah. He's right over there." She points to the corner.

"Help me sit up?"

And she does. Hakim is in the room, too.

"Hey, Ben. Hey, Hakim. How are you?"

"Good," they say in unison.

"Hey," I scold. "Quit treating me like a sick person. My patients over at the home absolutely hate it when I treat them that way, and now I know why."

"Sorry." Bennett laughs. "You still have hair."

"For now. What time is it?" Two thoughts that don't connect except in the foggy brain.

"You have about twenty minutes before chemo," Jubilee whispers through remorse.

I groan. Exhausted. Nauseous. Why didn't I just let the cancer kill me?

One week of treatments, followed by three weeks of "rest." Times five. But I only have to spend the first cycle in the hospital. Then I'm sick at home, no energy, hair slowly thinning, and can't really touch anyone for a week. And then I start to regain energy. Contribute to the family and try to be a husband. And then I go in for another cycle. Without Hakim, I don't know how my beautifully growing wife would manage it all. It isn't even his hands that help. He reminds her of her joy in Christ, and I think that's what she needed.

Jubilee

"How is he?" Jessie murmurs sadly into my living room one Saturday morning. She comes alone, which is odd. The entire Durant family usually brings a big meal every Saturday that takes us two days to eat, and they always gift us with something else Cindy "couldn't resist" from the baby aisle. These mornings, they usually minister to Elijah's spirit. Make him laugh if he's strong enough. But today, Jessie brought the meal alone. Other than Elijah, who is sleeping in the next room, the house is empty. Hakim always takes Bennett for "adventures" on Saturdays to give them both a respite.

"Oh, you know him. That stubborn man is fighting this tooth and nail." I smile. "Even if he doesn't win, Elijah is at peace with God using this for whatever purpose He has."

"But are *you* at peace with that?" Jessie wonders.

"That doesn't really matter, Jessie. I obviously want him to stick around. I feel like the world would be much darker without him in it, and I'd like him to help me raise these two kids. But I know that God is with me no matter what. He'll never leave me or forsake me. I trust Him." I rub at my belly this day in August when the window air conditioning unit is working overtime.

"I…" Jessie sighs. "I admire your faith, Jubilee. I'm sure you've noticed that our church is filled with all kinds of people. Some of them are wonderful, godly people. But so many of them, including a lot of my friends, are only Christians when they are in the church. You and Elijah surpass them all in faith. So even though you're going through quite a lot right now…I could use some encouragement from someone like you."

"Your parents and your husband are faithful as well," I encourage.

"Yeah, they are." Jessie's voice cracks. "So much so that my dad feels called to plant churches in Mexico. And Garrett feels called to go *with* him. He says he finally knows what God wants him to do."

"I assume this isn't a short-term mission?"

"Well, Garrett and Dad are going down there in a few months to check things out. Then after my great-grandma passes, which they think will be within the year, Mom and I will be joining them…permanently. That's the plan, at least." I'm confused. Jessie is so solemn—in so much distress as she says it.

"What a wonderful opportunity for Garrett! Elijah and I are both impressed at how he's grown."

Jessie laughs bitterly. "We were settled here! We own a house. I got a teaching job. I lead the children's ministry at church. We were considering having children. He never once mentioned to me that he wanted to be a *missionary*. I'm *not* moving to Mexico."

"But Jessie, your husband feels called by God to go there. He has a purpose for him. And you can have children. Plenty of missionaries have children. Children are not required to be reared in the United States."

"I'm not having children in *Mexico*." Jessie scoffs. "And he may feel called, but *I* don't feel called. Am I just supposed to tag along and pretend to love it? Leave my whole life here and just…just *go*?" Jessie sighs. Sniffles at tears.

My world is upside down already. And Jessie just found a way to twist all I know yet again. I swallow hard, in disbelief that this reasonable, vibrant young—older-than-me—woman could let something as wonderful as an opportunity to serve God bring anything but joy to her heart. I want to reprimand her and tell her that she's wrong and sinful. But then I remember liberty, and remove my father's words from my tongue to encourage a friend.

"Lord, give me the words."

"Honesty." I sigh and obey.

"Pardon the phrasing, but…what if this isn't about you?" I say with caution, then quickly clarify, "Or your dad or Garrett or anyone? What if all of it is for God's glory and we just need to accept it?"

"I understand what you're saying, but I can't just…" Jessie sniffles her freckled little nose to a scrunch, and I interrupt her.

"Jessie, my husband is fighting cancer. If he doesn't make it, I'll be a single mother. If he makes it, I'll likely never get another chance to be pregnant. I wanted a *big* family. I wanted to be a stay-at-home mother. Instead, I'm a sole provider. I am so grateful to my parents, and always wanted to please them. But the works God had for me will *never* please them. My life, as *I* planned it, is a wreck."

"I…I'm sorry, Jubilee. Maybe I shouldn't have burdened you with—" Jessie begins her remorse.

"But my life as *God* planned it is so much more meaningful and beautiful than I ever would have planned," I share, teary-eyed. "Worst-case scenario? Elijah doesn't make it. But if Elijah dies, I got to *know* him. And Bennett will not be put into the system. I'll have Elijah's child, and his spectacular DNA will live on. I am nothing but abundantly blessed, Jessie. Your chance to serve God in ways you didn't expect is a blessing. Don't overthink it like Jonah and end up in the belly of a whale. Just go to Mexico."

"Well, I'm not going quietly."

"Submit to your husband and go with *joy*. There is only reward in that. I'll pray that your heart is softened."

"Thank you, Jubilee." The embrace comes with tears, Jessie appreciating even harsh advice. Faithful are the wounds of a friend.

At this moment, Hakim enters the house, and Jessie sees it is her queue to leave. Hakim watches her walk out and waits for her to drive away and Bennett to retreat to his room before inquiring.

"Jessie, right? Pastor's kid?" He wonders with a smirk.

I'm wondering if Hakim is finally tapping into his ability to be attracted to a woman. "Hakim! Jessie is married! She's not a prospect."

"Whoa!" Hakim laughs. "She's pretty, don't get me wrong. But that's not why I was asking. You're confusing me for Noah, who would have married a monkey if she'd been around at the time."

"Hakim!" I try not to, but the giggle comes. Noah got married on his eighteenth birthday. He had always struggled with angst and temptation. Frankly, God was faithful to have delivered the then-seventeen-year-old Penny, who turned out to be a good match for him. She's an adorable picture of submission and domestication.

"Sorry…" He snorts the joke away. "Um…it just seemed like you'd made some kind of impact…"

"She needed some advice." I shrug.

"So you give advice to your pastor's daughter that makes her cry and hug you?" Hakim smirks.

"I was just the vessel."

"Your man tells you how amazing you are, doesn't he?" Hakim worries.

"Pretty much every time we speak."

"Good." Hakim winks. "You checked on him recently?"

"It's been an hour, I should—" I begin to rise.

"Sit. You should sit there and grow that kid. And *I* should check on him." Hakim the encourager disappears into the master bedroom.

Thirty-Three

Elijah

Since it gives us an excuse to be alone together on our anniversary, we make the follow-up appointment after the last round of chemo on that day. We wind up celebrating one year of marriage on that porch, holding hands. But they tell me it'll be the last.

We sit in silence there in the frigid, snowless air, both of us remembering the appointment.

"It hasn't metastasized, so there's hope. You have a good 30 percent. We won't have to give up hope. We can do another round of—"

"No," I'd said.

"Husband, you're not thinking straight." She probably thought that I didn't want to fight anymore; that I was just giving up. But that wasn't it exactly.

"Jubilee, if I'm going to die of cancer, I want to die of *cancer,* not chemo. I want to die with hair and maybe an appetite and some sliver of dignity." I coughed. "I want to regain enough strength to dance with you and fish with Bennett and hold my baby."

"You'll drown in your own lungs, Elijah." The doctor warned. "It will be agony."

"*This* is agony," I pleaded. "If I do nothing, how long do I have?"

"You're stage four. Six months would be a stretch. And sure, if you have a chance to heal from the chemo, you could have some months that seem pretty decent. We did kill *some* of the cancer. But without treatment, you will eventually decline. You will die a painful, terrifying death." The doctor knew he was being too real, and corrected it with, "I'm sorry."

"My baby will be born in three months." I smiled. "I won't make it to fishing season, but—"

"I'll take them fishing, Elijah," Jubilee promised, tears collecting in her gorgeous eyes. "I'll teach the baby that the fish come to the quiet. But we have the holidays coming up. We'll carve pumpkins, even though I was never allowed as a kid. And we'll eat turkey and have a Christmas tree just like last year. Let's do that, okay? Don't worry about what you'll miss. You won't even care when you're in glory."

I nodded to my bride, "Let's go home and sit on the porch and celebrate our anniversary."

So he sent us home. Scans are to occur every six weeks. And when the pain becomes too intense to bear, I am to call for pain meds. For now, I want to feel everything. Today, it's Jubilee's hand in mine, and the cold, and the fear, and the quiet.

Jubilee

"Excuse me? I've been thinking of getting a puppy, and I need to know which breed would be best." That is an odd reason to interrupt a receptionist's phone call, so I look up immediately. Jessie and Lucinda are there at the desk, their mouths smiling just the same, but their eyes dimmer than Bennett's last night when we told him his dad might get to meet Jesus.

I finish my phone call after holding up a finger to them, then lift myself from my chair with much effort to walk around the desk and hug them. "You won't want to take a puppy to Mexico."

"Yeah, we don't want a puppy. Or to talk about Mexico." Jessie rolls her eyes then continues, "Do you have two minutes? We wanted to talk to you."

I get a tech to cover the desk, then walk around a corner to have a private conversation. To my comfort, Lucinda spends the entire conversation with a hand that wanders about my expansive belly. I have previously given her permission to touch her basically-a-grandchild through my belly as much as she wants.

"We did a whole bunch a of research, and we got you something that we think might help Elijah. It might make him feel better for longer, and it might even fight the cancer. But you'll hate it." Jessie bites at her lip, and Lucinda takes over.

"It's perfectly legal. In this state."

I've done my own research and sigh. "I hope you're not talking about cannabis. I'm not giving my husband drugs so that he can live longer. He's at peace with this."

Lucinda puts on the pressure. "Let him hold his baby, Jubilee. Let him take Bennett fishing. He was saying that he won't make it to summer, and—"

"I was raised by a judge. He's seen drugs destroy people's brains and lives and families."

"The same is true of alcohol, Jubilee. And he told me it helps him sleep and that *you* give it to him," Jessie pleads. "And he wouldn't be rolling joints, okay? It's oil. You dilute it and then rub it on his skin. That's all."

"I already have an oil for that that helps his lungs feel clearer." I stand my ground. "I'm not giving him drugs."

"You could extend his life. You could *save* his life, Jubilee."

"'Could'? Jessie, if he's going to take dangerous drugs, it needs to be surer than that."

"Dangerous drugs?!" Lucinda guffaws, nearly alerting the waiting room with her volume. "The man is bedridden right now because he's recovering. And not from cancer. From cancer 'treatments.' Don't tell me you aren't willing to give him dangerous drugs. We are not asking you to sin here. We are giving you a medicine that has been used for thousands of years."

"And what is liberty *for*?" Jessie brings it to a climax with words those dearest to us know that we often exchange. "If not doing what you can to save someone's life? Even if it doesn't touch the cancer, it will help his pain, Jubilee."

"My parents will—" I begin.

"Not need to know. Heck, *Elijah* doesn't need to know. He's told Garrett that you rub his chest with that oil every night. Add this." Jessie finally presents it.

It's in a small clear glass bottle with a black rubber top attached to a glass dropper. Some of my mom's ingredients come in similar containers. It doesn't look like sin. It looks like a golden elixir that maybe could heal him. Maybe another day. Maybe less pain. Maybe. Their bedside manner wounds me. But like mine for Jessie just weeks ago, it is faithful. And *maybe* is better than the doctor's prognosis.

"This is the potent stuff, so don't use too much. Just add like a dropperful to your mom's oil," Jessie instructs. "You could probably even add some to Ben's leg stuff that you make."

"That is *not* happening." I laugh.

Lucinda also produces some medical gloves from her bag. "I know he likes it when you rub him, because we proved after all that he's a man." Here, we all giggle. "But this oil isn't good for baby."

"How much did this cost? Because when I was researching it seemed pretty pricey, and right now. . ." I try, but Cindy rebukes me.

"Don't you dare. I'll buy every bottle he needs."

"Thank you." Then I nod, banishing the tears. And then hormones refuse to allow those tears to be banished, and my dear friends hold me as I cry for a few minutes.

Bennett is in bed, chatting with his uncle before they retire, and Elijah is calling me wearily from our bedroom.

"I'll be there in a minute!"

I'm in the kitchen, a decanter on my left, a little bottle on my right. And I'm actually considering dosing the oil. I open the decanter and unscrew the cap of the oil.

No. I wouldn't dare. I replace the glass stopper.

This is drugs. It is bad. How dare I? What if he gets addicted or something?

But what is liberty for? And what if it works? Is it bad if it does only good?

"Father, does this give You glory? Tell me what to do."

I sigh. And Elijah has a coughing fit that leads him to spit blood into his trash can. They happen often at night, which is why I give him a sleep aid that dulls the pain ever so slightly. He moans. It hurts all the time. How can I let him hurt?

"He is still rejoicing."

"I know, Father." He's right. Elijah doesn't need painlessness or health for me to love him, and he's at peace, rejoicing and worshipping Christ every moment. He doesn't need drugs.

"Rejoice, Jubilee."

"I'm rejoicing. You are God, and I am at peace. I don't need this to be any easier to rejoice."

I put the oil in the cabinet with the whiskey and rush into the hall with the usual decanter. Before I turn from Ben's door to mine,

"Stop."

So I stop outside Bennett's door and hear a devastating whimper. Then I hear my brother's "Shhh" from Ben's room.

"Let's pray, okay?" Hakim offers, ever-so-gently.

"Okay." Bennett is in full tears. Elijah's coughing fits are far too loud to be a secret, so I know the reason. "Dear God…"

"Keep going," Hakim encourages.

"Dear God, if You need to take him, I won't get mad. I know You know better. But please, God, don't make him hurt so bad while he's here…"

Before I even realize I've done it, the dropper is emptying a second time into the decanter, and I am heading back into my bedroom to dose my husband. We're all at peace. We're all rejoicing. We rejoice every moment, and we trust God for everything. But for maybe. And for Bennett. I'm using liberty for this.

"No whiskey tonight?" He's barely awake as I make my way to his bedside, minus one nightly routine.

"No, I'd rather not mix that with this. And I have to wear gloves for this. Sorry." I pull the ivory gloves over my hands, carefully snapping the left one past my handmade ring. I swirl the decanter around, then drizzle oil on his chest and begin massaging it in.

"Mmmm…" Elijah offers, his breaths calming as they do when I rub the oil in. "Tingles. Is this the stuff Miss Cindy told me she gave you?"

"Yeah. I can't believe I'm doing this." I sigh, the latex an odd, slippery, rubbery addition to the ritual. "I put in twice as much as Jessie told me to."

"The worst that happens is it kills me." He opens one eye to catch my reaction to his joke.

I sigh, not quite to the stage of grief that allows humor. "Shut your eyes, Elijah. Go to sleep."

Elijah

It is late November when I realize that I lack absolutely nothing. I am healing from the chemo, and I feel great, considering. My head is bald, and my normally soft, dark skin is pale and gaunt. Anyone's eyes would count me pathetically sick. Jubilee is burning some spicy autumn-scented candle and stirring the stew she has on the stove. Licking a finger, then returning that hand to the unmistakable bump on her belly with a smile. Hakim is playing checkers with Bennett and our gas fireplace is on. Just a normal, quiet evening. There are dishes and homework to be done. But I wouldn't dare insist on any of it. I'm seeing everything perfect all at once, despite complete weakness being my current version of "great."

"Lord, if I'm going to die, let it be tomorrow. Because I'll have seen the best of life tonight."

Jubilee sighs, exhausted, and even though I'm weak, she still leans on me in spirit, proven by the way she curls up against me on the couch like I'm completely whole and well. Kissing my cheek. It takes all my strength to put my hand on her belly to touch the baby, whose gender we've decided will be a surprise. Incentive for me to live, Jubilee had said. She looks over at Bennett.

"Ben, did you decide what you want for Christmas yet?" she asks him.

"A brother," he says, like always.

Hakim laughs. "You know there is a 50 percent chance the kid is a girl, right?"

"I know. That's why I'm *asking* for a boy. Nobody else cares, so I wanted to vote," Bennett reasons and suddenly I find the strength to laugh along with my wife and brother-in-law.

"Well, either way, Christmas would be a little early for the baby to come. Can you think of anything else you want? Something fun. I have the practical stuff covered." Jubilee yawns. A mother from birth, I suppose.

"I want Dad to live," he says to the heart sinking of us three adults. Until he speaks again. "And Uncle Hakim to stay forever...and a toy pirate ship."

The pirate ship set he wants costs three-hundred dollars. We can't afford it. But since I can't guarantee his other demands, I find my strength.

"Done." The voice is raspy, and Jubilee looks at me like I'm insane. You only live once. Me, maybe not too much longer. And there is only one Bennett. Jubilee reads all that on my face.

"Maybe it's cheaper somewhere online." She sighs into my ear. "I'll do my best to find a way."

Bennett and Hakim burst into laughter about something with their checkers game, and they start throwing checkers at each other. Jubilee starts to quiet them, but I put my hand on her leg for her to stop. I want her to see what I see. To find joy in what she might think is stressful and mundane. After a moment of laughing we join in, Hakim sighs contently as he collects stray checkers.

"Jubilee, this is nothing like our childhood. You're doing a great job. There's so much joy in this house." He feels her belly once as he passes, looking slightly troubled like he always does. But smiling nonetheless. He whispers, "I already got him the pirate ship. Don't worry."

Thirty-Four

Jubilee

"Don't let them notice. God, please don't let them notice."

I'm not due for five weeks. And it is Christmas Day at my parents' house. All my brothers and sisters are in town to criticize my birth choices and husband and family choices. They ridicule our choice to be joyful, despite all the "solemn" things in my life like terminal cancer and a disabled child. The baby is supposed to come in the sweet spot between Elijah's chemo recovery and decline when no one is in town. But he's not that strong yet. The baby is not developed enough. If this baby comes tonight...

"God, please don't let this baby come tonight."

Another contraction hits me. After the first two, I sent Bennett to the barn to quietly retrieve his dad where Elijah is conversing with my brothers. The women and children are inside, knitting and chit-chatting, and I am sitting in a chair along the stairs, pretending to be fine. I hear Elijah's boots on the hardwood, and the fox enters the hen house. He crouches at my side. Hair so thin under that hat. Face so pale. No. *"Not tonight, Lord. Not tonight."*

His hand runs along my hair. His whisper rumbles into my spirit. "Tell me what's goin' on."

"I've just had a few contractions," I whisper back.

"Braxton Hicks?"

"No. Painful ones." I sniffle and realize I may be close to crying.

"It's still early yet. We should call your doctor and see if we need to go in and get you checked out. How much water did you drink today?" I don't care if he looks thinner and older and sicker than he did a year ago when I married him. His eyes still comfort me like balm.

274

"I drank plenty like always, Husband." I whine. "I don't know what's going on."

"I'll call your doctor," he says, and disappears up the stairs.

Hannah glances over a few times, her now fifteen-month-old Mary on her hip. She chooses a moment when no one is looking to make her way over.

"You having contractions?" She whispers, understanding the delicacy that is peace in this family, even though our parents pride themselves on a peaceful home.

I nod. Whisper. "Elijah's calling the doctor."

"If you need to go in, I'll watch Bennett," she offers without hesitation. "That way he'll be in town if he's gonna be a brother soon."

I shake my head. "It's too early…and even if not, I want you there. Thank you for offering, but Hakim will watch him." Then I cry out, not having expected the sharp pain in my abdomen.

"Something is wrong, Jubilee," Hannah says calmly, but the mob of women heard the shriek and begin opining until Elijah comes back downstairs and speaks over their "concern."

"Hospital." He knows I am only listening to him. "I'll go let Bennett and Hakim know. Hannah, will you get her in my truck please?"

The drive is silent and the pain is intense. When we arrive, the emergency department does an ultrasound. There is a problem with the placenta, and they prep an operating room for an emergency cesarean.

"It's okay. It'll be okay. We're meeting this baby today. Focus on that." Elijah keeps me steady after I call my family, who drives into town. But not without reminding me that an emergency cesarean is certainly not a drug free home birth.

When we chose baby names, we wondered how many times the names in the Bible can be repeated before we forget where they came from. Sure, they have meaning. But do they have relevance? The Word of God is always relevant. His blood always saves. Why then, do we settle for names that cause more of a yawn than a whisper?

I have always loved my name, because I felt like maybe my parents finally understood that the Bible is alive and well. Jubilee. The year when all is restored and debts forgiven. Then there was Judah, the son of Leah, that made me realize they were still stubbornly old-fashioned. But for my own child, I wanted to bring the Lord to life, as He is, using His greatest feat.

We hadn't found out the gender. We hadn't shared the potential names with even Bennett. They numb my pain and cut the baby out. And Elijah blubbers shamelessly when they hold the crying little girl over the curtain.

"It's a girl!" The doctor announces.

The whole room erupts in applause that our daughter's cries cover in song.

"What is her name, Dad?" One of the nurses asks after she's been weighed.

"Scarlett. Scarlett Liberty Bering."

Because what is more beautiful than a scarlet cord out a window or precious blood spilled on a cross? Red is the traditional color of a wedding dress where I was born. Of my family's hair. Maybe sins are as scarlet. But not after the liberty of the cross. It is liberty we want her to experience every time she writes her signature.

She has lots of dark hair and bright eyes like mine. They put her in the NICU because of her early arrival. When they come to visit, my family first passes Elijah, who is glued to the NICU window, before coming to my room with disdain on their faces.

"Scarlet?!" Priscilla whispers. "Like the *letter?*"

"Like Jesus' blood, just with two t's to match Bennett." I clarify with a smile. "Scarlett."

"Did your husband choose that? That's almost inappropriate, Jubilee," Mom says.

"Almost." I shrug. "But not quite."

Hannah smiles. "Elijah looks *so* happy."

"He is." I nod. "We weren't sure he'd live to see this."

And then I cry because of confused hormones, then I see that Hakim is coming in the room.

"Where's Bennett, Hakim?" I nearly jump from my own skin with worry.

Hakim smiles. "With 'Husband,' staring at his sister. He was only mad for like five minutes when he found out she was a girl. Then he saw her and now he's in love."

Elijah

Standing at the NICU window all the time and holding Scarlett whenever they allow it certainly brings back memories of the same with Bennett. He'd been my son even then, as far as my soul was concerned. And I've always considered the soul to transcend the flesh.

But there is still something new about the way my daughter feels in my arms. It has nothing to do with two healthy arms and legs and ten fingers, ten toes. Bennett has always been whole to me. What's new is that Scarlett's skin is red, which they tell me will turn out like Jubilee's. Her hair is black. Sure, she came from me too. But that makes no difference. Bennett is plenty part of me. What makes the difference is that Scarlett came from the woman I love more than my own soul—and *because* of that love.

I only visit the baby when Jubilee is asleep in her room. Bennett is safely at home with Hakim, and I am here with my wife, helping her recover, waiting on her hand and foot. Because I'm a good man? Maybe. But more so because she took the 'in sickness and in health' part of things to the extreme, helping me battle cancer even while she was not at her strongest either. They all ridicule her for it too. Some family. But I can't let that get to me. The only thing I allow on my conscience is that I can never repay her. Because it keeps me trying until I can't anymore.

"Hey, I was worried. Where did you go?" She says groggily when I return to her room.

"Just went up to see Scarlett," I reply. "I just can't get enough of her, I guess. I hope you didn't need anything. Do you need something? Did you sleep okay?"

"I'm fine." She smiles. "How are you feeling today?"

Which she's been asking me daily.

"I'm fine. How is your incision and everything?"

"It's doing great. They say I might be able to go home tomorrow." She smiles. Then winces. "Without Scarlett, of course. She could be two or three weeks."

"It'll be hard, I know, Mama. But on the plus side, you'll have plenty of time to heal before we take her home."

Jubilee cries all the way home and all night long the first night. I can't even wrap an arm around to comfort her as we sleep because her belly is too sore. I'm so helpless, having no inkling of what to do for her. Then she rises early and asks to be driven to the hospital, Scarlett on her mind.

When we arrive, Hannah is already there with her brood. Outside the window, of course, because of little Bethany's sniffles. Hannah looks distressed, but Monroes rarely mention why without sometimes years of prodding.

"Hey," Jubilee says, eyes bright at the presence of her sister. She clutches a little thermal bag with her own pumped milk inside to give to the NICU staff.

"Hi. We have errands to run, so we came by to see her. She's so beautiful, Jubilee. I'm glad we finally have someone else who looks like the prettiest of us." Hannah rubs at her belly.

Observant Jubilee gasps. "Again?"

Hannah rolls her eyes in a smile. Then nods. "Number four. I think Penny's expecting too. But you know how she likes to wait so long to tell anyone."

"Y'all Monroes are just baby factories." I chuckle, glancing a warning look at Bennett, who is getting rowdy with Jonathan.

A nurse comes out with a smile. "Hey, Jubilee! I was just about to break out some of your reserves when I looked up and saw you."

Jubilee giggles. "There may even be enough in there to donate some again. I can't wait to get her home so I can nurse her all the time."

"Well, she's ready for you now, if you want to come in." Jubilee follows her behind the two sets of doors that create a soundproof barrier.

I grumble sarcastically with Hannah, "I guess I don't have the right equipment to be invited in. Nevermind the whole *father* thing."

Hannah giggles. "It may always be that way, unfortunately. People always favor the mother. James is a better parent than me sometimes, so I'm thrilled all the kids look just like him. People can't walk around denying his paternity. I bet my father would like to, otherwise."

I chuckle. "Then there's my little family that'll confuse anyone at first glance or even after a few. So, I should be glad little Scarlett looks like her mama. No explanation needed."

"Families are funny like that sometimes." Hannah smiles. Shrugs. "I'm a ginger and I have an Indian sister and an African brother. I love that about my family. Gives a little of God's view of things. Nevermind DNA. The blood of Christ is really our closest tie, right?"

I nod. She's a wise woman.

Bethany's sniffles turn out to be the full-blown flu, we find out after the last holiday dinner that sends off the far away siblings. The strain works its way through the children and then the adults of the family. Hakim has to deliver Jubilee's milk to the hospital because she's bedridden for two days, and I use Leah's remedies to get her on her feet quick—minus the oil, of course.

Jubilee is baffled that I don't get the flu first, considering my immune system is still substantially knocked down from the chemo and radiation. But she's only baffled because I don't tell her about the mild symptoms I have, and she's too sick to really notice. Needless to say, Scarlett's homecoming isn't going to happen this week.

I hear Jubilee Chandra Bering curse for the first time when I wake up to her ice-cold hand against my forehead. Then she jumps out of bed, healing incision, influenza, and all, to get *my* fever down.

"It's a low-grade," I tell her, feeling like death warmed over as we look at the thermometer.

"Because you don't have an immune system," she scolds. "I'm calling your doctor. This may be a hospital visit. Why didn't you tell me you were sick? You were coughing all night. That's the only reason I woke up to check on you."

"Was I?" My head swims and then pain courses through my body and I hear myself hit the floor. I'm wondering why my leg is kicking the nightstand, but I'm powerless to stop all such convulsions for the next three minutes.

Jubilee screams, "Hakim!" And that's the last thing I remember until waking up to a masked and angry flesh of my flesh at my bedside in the hospital.

"He's awake!" I hear Bennett say.

"When did I fall asleep?" I mumble.

"Just after your *seizure*," Jubilee says with fire. "Someday, Elijah Bering, you are going to stop making me worry about you."

I smile and grab her hand. "Someday."

Thirty-Five

Jubilee

A seizure. Never in his life, he says, has he had a seizure. The doctors tell me that with the flu and no immune system, the body will do strange things to compensate. They say he has a touch of pneumonia...again. *A touch*? They say my first instinct to bring him in was right, even without the seizure.

It's burned in my memory now. My husband, once so solid, falling to the floor in his dying-of-cancer state, eyes all white, his arms and legs jerking around. Burned there forever. And I'm furious at him for it. I couldn't even lift him because I had a cesarean not long ago and body aches for days from the flu. Why do we both always have to be sick? Why not one or the other? How can I properly care for a dying man if I'm not well myself?

With half my little family in the hospital, Hannah—three blocks from the hospital—opens up her home for Bennett and me to stay. Hakim stays back at the house. But I almost forget about all my misery and Scarlett's tininess and Elijah's relentless illness when the children sing a little song about joy after one of James and Hannah's soul-warming meals.

Joy.

My husband is alive. My daughter is alive. Bennett is well and smiling, singing about joy without his prosthetics on. What do I have to be miserable about at all? What is occurring that God has not already conquered?

Something of which I spoke far too soon. Because when I arrive at Elijah's room to see him, his oncologist is there.

"Hello, Jubilee. Come have a seat. I was making my rounds today and thought I'd stop in."

"He did an x-ray to see how we're doing," Elijah elaborates.

"How bad is it?"

"Well, with pneumonia on the x-ray as well, it's hard to say what's what. His lungs look like those of a miserable man. But it's still in his lungs for now."

I nod, kissing Elijah, then sitting on the foot of his bed. I sigh. This feels like what the beginning of one of my dad's lectures feels like.

"I'm in trouble, aren't I?" I ask.

The doctor chuckles. "Why would you be in trouble?"

"Because of what I've been giving him."

"No, I'm happy you're doing it. It can extend his life or improve his quality of life or both. I just can't *recommend* it. And I assume you brought it with you, but you need to wait until I'm gone to give it to him."

"That's understandable." I nod. "So why are you here?"

"I have alerted a counselor to come talk to you and put your wishes in writing, but I need to give them a recommendation for when things decline." He sighs. "Elijah is a nurse. So, I am going to take his wishes and use them as my recommendation."

"Okay?" I'm confused.

"They need to know if I want to die here at the hospital or at home."

"Oh." I clear my throat, begging God to give me strength.

"My first thought was at home," he says. "Because of the kids and all. And because people are supposed to want to die at home."

"But?" I hear it in his tone.

"But Bennett would have the trauma of watching his father die in his house. I'd rather he hate hospitals than hate the house he'll finish growing up in."

"But whatever time you have left, we wouldn't be able to see you much."

"This isn't *now*, Wife. This is later when I'll be bedridden and dying," he explains.

"Okay." I sigh. "So here, then. You're a nurse, so you'll be more comfortable in a hospital than most."

"Exactly. And you can come see me as much as you want, and you can bring the kids."

"Okay," I say with a squeak. Then tears start to come.

"I'll go make that recommendation." The oncologist rises, leaving to give us time. I wish he could have given us so much more, and so does he.

Elijah moves aside and I join him on the bed, where he encourages me.

"You know I'll fight to be with y'all till the end, whether that's tomorrow or a hundred years from now. I'll go down fighting," Elijah reassures.

And fight, he does. But instead of his inevitable decline occurring "later," the pneumonia triggers it, and this becomes the hospital stay where we will say our goodbyes. They revise their months to weeks, and Elijah decides it isn't worth it for us to try to go home.

He's too weak to visit the NICU, but I visit Scarlett and put Elijah on a video call. I leave after dark each day, after rubbing him down with oil that won't save him. Elijah even stays up into the night on the phone when I sit up in Hannah's guest bed so that we can discuss a future without him. But we've been down this road. If we discuss, he will go. So, we instead discuss our ability to talk on the phone late at night. My father never allowed that during the courtship, so there is blessing and joy even in this. One night, he is weak and sleepy and sighs a long sigh over the phone.

"Oh, to touch you one more time…" A week after the pneumonia began, and he is silent. My heart seizes and I dare not even say his name. I pray.

"God. I'm not ready. Don't take him from me without one last kiss. Or a million. I've not done near enough having or holding. Plenty of sickness, not enough health. I'm not done loving him yet, and he's not done loving me. Absolutely not. You can't have him!"

Then I hear him breathing. Then the voice of a nurse.

"Alright, Mr. Bering. No more late-night sexy talk with the wife. You need your rest."

I sigh in relief and hang up the phone.

After I drop off Bennett at school, I head to the hospital. Elijah is the sickest I've ever seen him. He greets me with a smile, then closes his eyes and lowers his voice as I curl my still-healing body next to his. "How are my kids?"

"Bennett is great. He keeps telling me to trust in God and we've been praying like crazy. And Scarlett can go home in the next few days."

"Oh, that's good. That's perfect," he rasps.

Then I awaken with a blanket on me, likely placed by a nurse. I only awaken because Hannah initiates her daily call to tell me Bennett made it safely to her house. How little I've slept without Elijah at my side. Even his sickness is no deterrent for the comfort of his presence.

"I'm gonna go get Ben and come back, okay?" I whisper and kiss him.

And when I return an hour later, Bennett and Hakim in tow, that same oncologist greets us.

"Oh no. What—?" I ask, exasperated. More addressing God than him.

"Your husband's vitals went a little sideways when you left. And his lungs are a little rattly." The doctor clears his throat. "We're running tests to see how long—"

I take a physical step back, barely hearing what the doctor says next as Hakim puts an arm around me. The narrative is long. But all I manage to glean from it is that Elijah will likely be gone within forty-eight hours.

"Can we still see him?" I sniffle and lose all strength of will as I sob into my brother's chest.

Just a few phone calls later, and Aaron is flying in. Priscilla is driving. And within several hours, all my family is gathered in the waiting room outside the ICU. I only learn it from a nurse, who whispers to me while Elijah is sleeping. I don't want to leave him, but the nurse assures me his vitals are fine for the moment. Bennett stays with his dad. Hakim follows me.

I drag myself out into the waiting room, realizing that I hadn't taken any pain meds for my surgical scar today. Every single embrace they give is painful.

"None of you had to come," I tell them in gratitude, my face probably a mess from crying all day.

"How long are they giving him?" Priscilla's question is gracious and gentle.

"Um..." But I can't answer for the tears. My mother embraces and shushes me.

Hakim answers. "They said it could be twenty-four hours or two weeks. But Elijah is fighting this like you wouldn't believe. His vitals are nearly perfect, and he wakes up from every nap. I think they forgot to tell *him* he's supposed to die now."

Which makes me smile a little and whisper, "He's so stubborn."

"How is Scarlett?" Hannah asks, trying to cheer me. But it only burdens me more, which I wouldn't ever tell her.

"Scarlett is perfect. They said they'll release her first thing in the morning, and I can bring her here so her daddy can hold her." I sigh. Sniffle. Then bear my bitter soul. "Then I can take her home and raise her and her brother by myself."

"You're a catch, Jubilee. I'm sure you won't be alone long." Adam Monroe crosses the line. I wonder if he is pleased with all this.

So I approach my father, then slap him across the face, to my family's horror.

"How *dare* you?" And then I buzz back into the ICU, followed by everyone but my father. We stand outside the window a moment, watching Bennett laying on Elijah's bed. Father stroking son's hair, speaking love and truth into his heart that we can't hear.

Dozens of them gather outside the room. Lucinda and Jessie and Garrett and Pastor Jordan. All my family. I know Elijah feels them there, but he's too busy talking to Bennett. I reenter Elijah's room.

"You understand?" He's saying to Bennett.

"I understand, Dad," Bennett says.

Then they both look up when I walk in. Bennett sits up and retreats to the corner, looking far too sad for a nine-year-old boy.

"Hey, Mama," Elijah says, sitting up with much effort. "Who called in the cavalry?"

"I just told them what the doctors told me, and they came." I sit next to him and he kisses me, then runs the back of his fingertips along my arm like he'll sometimes do before seducing me. I giggle at the familiar sensation, not ever caring that his eyebrows are gone and his hair is nothing like the thickness my fingers remember from our first few months of marriage. "I love you." Which doesn't at all capture exactly what I mean.

"Ben, go out there with your aunts and uncles for a minute?" Elijah requests. When Bennett is gone, Elijah smiles. "If your family wasn't looky-looing, I might use the last of my energy to dance with you one more time."

"I don't care anymore who sees when you dance with me." I giggle, thinking of the blizzard last year during which we moved all the furniture in the living room so he could teach me and Bennett to waltz. One of the memories I'll treasure forever. "But you save your energy. We'll dance again when they're doing it too."

He laughs, then lowers his voice in a way that stirs up my insides. "Oh, but given another chance, Miz Jubilee, I'd teach you to tango."

"You do *not* know how to tango," I call out in a giggle, glancing at my family that can almost hear. Then I see we are both solemn, knowing it doesn't matter if he can tango, and it doesn't matter if that's even what he meant. We'll never get another chance to do anything. I take to confession to save us from sorrow. "I hit my dad a few minutes ago. Like, slapped him across the face. I don't know what came over me."

Elijah laughs appreciatively. "What did he do?" His eyes light up like he isn't going to leave in the next couple days, and we converse as if leaning on elbows in our bed at home, not sitting cordially in a hospital room where he'll make his grand exit.

"He suggested that I could find someone else besides you when you're gone," I admit, trying not to let him see me cry. He's seen that so much lately.

"You could, you know," he says after wiping a tear. "I mean, as long as God and Ben and Scarlett approve of the guy, I wouldn't mind. And trust Hakim's judgment, too. You're not that difficult to fall in love with. Someone will, Jubilee. It wasn't your dad's place to say it, but it is mine. All a man needs to see what a treasure you are is a good set of eyes."

"But I want *your* eyes, Husband. No one else's. I didn't marry young because it was expected. I married young because I wasn't any older when I met *you*. I asked God to make me the woman you deserve. I guess that was never meant to happen." Then the tears flow and his arms wrap around me.

"Lord, who will comfort me when he is gone?"

"I will."

"I know, Lord. I know. Forgive me for doubting. But forgive me also, if only his arms will suffice. I'll take Your strength over a new husband."

And then peace overwhelms me.

"Rejoice. Take joy even today, and joy will forever come with ease. Rejoice."

I laugh aloud, shutting out that Voice. *"Not if You take him, I won't. Why should I?"*

"What?" Elijah asks of the bitter laugh.

"You wouldn't believe me if I told you."

Thirty-Six

Elijah

It is morning when Jubilee brings me my little girl to hold. I pity my daughter. Even if she has the best memory known to womankind, her only memory of her father will include a great deal of blubbering. All Jubilee's brothers can't believe how many tears can come from a grown man.

Family is in and out all day, despite the nurses telling me I should rest. Rest why? So I can be less weary in my last few days on earth? Not even. I take cat naps here and there, but right now I'm sitting with my wife, blubbering over my little girl. My arms barely have the strength to hold her.

But she is perfect. When she cries, Jubilee takes her and does her best to shush. But I like the crying. Why don't we all cry? Does the world get better as we age? Certainly not. So why when life is all love and nurture do we give ourselves to wailing and grief? And when life is hard, we hold it in.

"Let her cry," I say. "It's the only time I get to hear it."

And then I think I drift off to sleep because my dead mother comes in and my whole body seizes, which is always my response to her.

"There, there," she says, taking Scarlett from Jubilee, who panics. "Grammy's got you. You hush now."

And when Scarlett is quiet, she sits on the bed with me, with my daughter.

"Hey, Mom," I tell her. "Thanks for coming."

"Of course," she replies. "You make beautiful children."

"Well, I didn't make Bennett." I shrug. "That was all you."

"But you made him who he is. I'd have made him someone else," Patrice Bering confesses.

Then she grows taller. Her hair sets aflame, literally, and the ceiling sprinklers turn on. She hurls the baby across the room, and she screams horrifically as Jubilee desperately tries to catch the baby.

Then I gasp and sit up. The wet from the sprinklers is my own sweat. Jubilee is across the room shushing Scarlett, and all her family has chairs in the room. The nightmares are getting worse, and harder to distinguish from reality.

"Oh, Elijah. Scarlett woke you again. I'm so sorry," Jubilee says.

"I don't like sleeping. Don't let me sleep." I look around the room. "Where is my mom?"

"Elijah, your mother died nearly a decade ago," Jubilee soothes, worried. "Do you remember that?"

And I do remember, so I nod. "Don't let me sleep, Jubilee. Where's Bennett?"

"At school," she replies. "He insisted. Said you'd be upset if he missed because of you."

I look around to be sure my mother's hair didn't singe anything.

"Bad one, huh?" Jubilee whispers when her family resumes whatever conversation they were having when I'd been asleep. She sets Scarlett trustingly in my weak arms.

"They always are," I whisper. "Well, they *were*. That's why I used to drink not too long ago. So, you're taking her home tonight?"

"Yeah." Jubilee nods. "Pray for me. I'm glad I'm starting to heal. That'll help. I'm just worried I'll be a terrible mom. I haven't done this before. *You're* the one who knows what he's doing as a parent."

I laugh and raise an eyebrow, well, eyebrow muscle, at her. "I wish you could have met *my* mother and you'd understand why that's insane. If you completely fail at your standards for motherhood, you'll be ten times the mother she was. And God protected me still. Trust in God. He'll take care of you."

Jubilee's phone rings. She looks around and there is no one that would be calling that isn't here. Except her father, but they aren't speaking at the moment. I listen to her half of the conversation.

"Hello?. . .Yes, this is she…What?…What's the matter? Is he alright?..." Jubilee panics. "Oh…that doesn't seem right. Are you sure you called the correct parent?. . .Bennett Bering, that's right.…My daughter just got released from the NICU and I can't bring her to a school, so I'll have to make arrangements. I'm at the hospital right now. I prefer not to leave if I don't have to....I told several staff members at the school the situation with Bennett's father. I would appreciate a little more grace…Expulsion hearing?! Bennett is a good boy…I understand. I will make arrangements and get there as soon as I can. Goodbye."

"What was that about?" I ask when she returns, wondering if I'm dreaming again. "Did I hear something about expulsion?"

"It was Ben's school." Her face distorts. "He got into a fight. Has a black eye. The other kid…he sent him here to the hospital, Elijah. They have a zero tolerance policy and don't care that Bennett has never even been so much as reprimanded in class and his father is dying. But he's okay, Elijah. I don't want you to worry."

"Do you need me to watch Scarlett? I'll stay right here. Do you have any bottles I can give her?" Hannah offers.

"There's some milk in the diaper bag." Jubilee nods, fighting tears.

"Wife, let me call them. There has to be a mix-up," I offer.

"Elijah, I have to learn to do these things on my own," Jubilee snaps. "I'll be alone soon."

"I'm here *now*." All here. Heart too, in case no one noticed.

Jubilee nods and apologizes, taking a few minutes to say goodbye, then heading off to raise hell at Bennett's school. I wish I could see it. I wonder if *her* hair will light on fire.

Most of the family leaves too. For lunch, they say. But it is clear they are here for Jubilee, not me. Sweet Hannah stays back with Scarlett.

"I don't understand how they can say you're dying," she says. Hannah is the faithful optimist, and Jubilee's best friend besides me and Hakim. There is no one that doesn't adore Hannah, however naive they think she is. But I don't think she's naive at all. I think she gets it. All of it. Life and death and everything. Doing that with God gives you only peace.

"This cancer is serious," I tell her.

"Sure it is. I always is," she reasons.

"This is different, Hannah. I can't survive this. I've seen dozens of people die from this kind of cancer."

"I'm sure you have. But 'can't'? Really? What would you have done if my dad had said, 'No you *can't* marry Jubilee.'?"

I chuckle. "He sort of did. But that's different. That's love. This is scientific fact. Like two plus two equals four. This is impossible, Hannah. I love you for keeping hope alive. Jubilee will really need you and James after this is all said and done. But mostly because I won't be here."

" 'Behold, the Lord's hand is not shortened, that it cannot save, or His ear dull that it cannot hear,' " Hannah quotes from Isaiah. "He can heal you."

"Sure, He can. But that doesn't mean He will. It's pretty clear He wants me dead."

"This isn't about *you*, Elijah."

Then I open my eyes and sit up, and Hannah startles, having been contentedly rocking baby Scarlett, likely thinking of her own babies at home with James, and the one in her belly.

"Do you need anything, Elijah? Jubilee should be back any minute," she says.

"Were you talking to me just now?" I ask.

"No, you were sleeping." She smiles. "But I was praying impossible prayers. Does that count?"

"It might," I reply. And she seems to understand.

I swear Jubilee was born to be Bennett's mother. It doesn't matter what the world says, because no one would argue that Jubilee's hotly pursed lips and Bennett's drained scowl are the result of a thorough talking-to on the way from Bennett's school to the hospital.

"Sorry it took so long, Hannah," Jubilee says, taking Scarlett from Hannah's arms. "We had to stop in the emergency department to deliver a mediated apology."

"A court mediator?" Hannah asks.

"A judge, actually. I asked him to come. It's a conflict of interest for him to decide anything, but I just wanted him there. Had to do some apologizing of my own." Jubilee rolls her eyes. Which means Adam Monroe knows more about my son than I do at the moment. "Bennett's likely expelled, but the other kid's family isn't pressing charges. At least *someone* has compassion."

"Did the guy deserve it?" I ask Bennett. And Jubilee's eyes widen, her lips pursing again.

"He said Mama was a gold digger and wanted your insurance money. I didn't really know what that meant, and he was a sixth grader and bigger than me, so I walked away like you taught me. Then he said I was a cripple. Then I walked away again, because I'm not a cripple and I knew you'd be mad if I clobbered him." Bennett stops. And he's fallen short of explaining his swollen-shut eye.

"Then what happened?" I wonder.

"Then he told me if God loved me, he'd let my daddy live. I told him God does love me, because I got Mama to take care of me. He said you loved my sister better than me, which I knew was wrong. Then he said something I didn't like about Mama, and I'm not saying it again so you can't make me. But it was real mean and real bad, so I hit him. Then he hit me. But Daddy, I can't even feel how hard I kick with my legs. Think they can fix that on the next pair?" Bennett wonders. "Because Aiden has stitches in his head and I only kicked him the once after he was on the ground. I knew it was wrong, but I was real mad."

I laugh to hysterics, gladly spending likely hours of energy to do it. "He said something about your Mama?"

"Well, he said the first thing too, but I didn't know what insurance was and Mama don't dig for gold. But I mostly understood the last thing he said. I didn't like it. *At. All.*" Bennett enunciates.

"Aiden is probably expelled too." Jubilee winks at me. "And Bennett knows he should have kept his cool. But he's also pretty excited about homeschool. . .if that's alright. I'll have to see what I can do about work."

I sigh relief. "Jubilee, don't ever doubt that you are an amazing mother."

Thirty-Seven

Jubilee

He's comatose. So am I after my first night ever alone with a newborn infant, cursing God for making it the first of many. But I take Scarlett back to the hospital nonetheless—Scarlett and her expelled brother. And Hakim. Comatose means close to death, and the hospital called early to tell us it was time. Having to ready an infant makes me last to arrive in his room, where for once my family is seeing the gravity of the situation and requiring tissues around the barely breathing man. His skin is grayed, and if not for the monitor declaring otherwise, I'd say he looks dead already.

"Oh, Elijah." I sigh, setting sleeping Scarlett's carrier next to weeping Cindy and Jessie, and sitting with Elijah on the bed. I'm glad our goodbye last night had been thorough. Nothing left unsaid.

He should be serving. Asking me how last night went with Scarlett. Joking about dancing or rolling his eyes about my father. He should be laughing with his son. Crying over his daughter. But he's not even here. He's somewhere else that borders on death.

"How dare you, God?"

"There is a time to be born and a time to die."

"He's barely thirty and the most wonderful thing alive. It isn't time."

Then there is silence in my heart until hours later when I hear in his labored breaths the inflammation taking over. He's probably in pain wherever he is right now. And I'm here. Alive and well. And so selfish it sickens me. Sniffling when I realize it. Then I hear the impossible.

"Rejoice."

"NOW? Half of my heart is about to stop beating, God. How can I rejoice with half a heart?"

"Rejoice in the Lord always. Again I say. Rejoice."

"I can't do this alone."

"The Lord is with you, mighty woman of valor. Rejoice."

"I cursed you all night. God, I'm so sorry. Please forgive me."

"I forgive you. Rejoice."

"I'll die without him."

"I died for you. Rejoice."

"I won't be able to stop loving him. But Lord, please stop his pain."

"You were never required to stop loving him. I have loved you from everlasting to everlasting. Elijah too. Rejoice."

I sniffle, keeping wild notions inside my heart as it bends and folds. I begin to see that no matter what changes or dies here on earth, I will still be just as loved and treasured as when everlasting began and Jesus was on death row for my sins.

"Thank you, Lord. I will find my joy in You alone. Let Your will be done."

"Tell Me louder."

"My family won't understand."

"I am here. Tell them I am here."

"I don't know how."

"Who made your mouth, Jubilee?"

So I sniffle and clear my throat. And simply open my mouth.

" 'The Spirit Himself bears witness with our spirit that we are children of God, and if children, then heirs—heirs of God and joint heirs with Christ, if indeed we suffer with Him, that we may also be glorified together.' "

My tears overwhelm me, and speech becomes impossible.

But I think the next part needed to be in his voice anyway. Bennett picks up where I left off, speaking to his daddy.

" 'For I consider that the sufferings of this present time are not worthy to be compared with the glory which shall be revealed in us.' " He sobs, taking his daddy's limp hand, "I understand now, Dad."

But God isn't done with our rejoicing, and Pastor Jordan takes over, " 'For the earnest expectation of the creation eagerly waits for the revealing of the sons of God. For the creation was subjected to futility, not willingly, but because of Him who subjected it in hope; because the creation itself also will be delivered from the bondage of corruption into the glorious liberty of the children of God.' "

"Liberty." I sob, speaking my joy aloud. "From corruption to liberty. *Liberty* is the glory that will be revealed in us."

"That's what liberty is for," Pastor Jordon concludes, his voice trembling. "For God's glory."

Their family has had a difficult few weeks. We learned that Abuela Millie passed on to glory recently. Elijah had been sorry he didn't get to say goodbye. But here the family is, grieving again. From behind me comes a lovely voice that I hear from the stage on Sundays. Jessie, sobbing, but her tone clear and powerful.

"All to Jesus, I surrender
All to Him I freely give
I will ever love and trust Him
In His presence daily live."

Lucinda and Garrett join her.

"I surrender all
I surrender all
All to thee my blessed Savior
I surrender all."

Pastor Jordan then prays, "Lord, let this cup pass," then melts into his own sobs.

"Still, let Your will be done in Jesus' name," I whisper aloud.

I stay a few hours in silence, and my family disperses to wait on the call. Our joy and outpouring had been too much for them, I think. But the Durants keep a vigil with me until the hours wane and I must get my children home. One last time, my pastor watches as I rub fragrant oil laced with illicit substances into the chest of my husband. Leaving is an excruciating choice, knowing I've been promised Elijah won't survive the night. Hakim stays, not wanting his kindred spirit to die alone, or anyone else to give me the call.

The Monroe family meets at my house for breakfast when the night passes without word from the hospital. I had been glad all night to have a newborn—an excuse not to sleep. And then while my sisters are cleaning up after breakfast, my cell phone rings and everyone freezes.

"It's Hakim," I squeak. Sniffle. Staring at the silly contact ID photo of my brother on a horse until I nearly miss the chance to answer. Not ready to receive the news.

"Hello?" I finally manage. Barely.

A short silence stagnates inside my bones. And then:

"He's awake," Hakim says directly.

"I'm sorry?" I ask.

"Awake. Color all over his body. Jubilee, the pneumonia is what practically killed him last night, but he bounced back. They've done two sets of chest x-rays this morning. And they can see now that his cancer is a fraction of what it used to be. It's significantly decreased like someone who is finishing up chemo. His oncologist says that he still has cancer, but it's getting better. It is manageable. Maybe even beatable without chemo. Jubilee, he's eating waffles and asking for his wife and kids," Hakim says.

I pause. Stunned. Not even able to ask for clarification. My family assumes the worst and is in the same state.

"Jubilee, you there?" Hakim asks.

"I'm here." My spirit is in a state of stunned bliss that I haven't rehearsed a reaction for. Who has?

"Did you hear me? Your *old* man is going to *live*. The doctor just told him that this stage of cancer often results in men walking their daughters down the aisle and holding great-grandkids. They say he probably shouldn't go back to the nurse thing right away, but they think within six months his strength could be back up enough to work." Hakim lowers his voice. "Jubilee, every doctor in the hospital has come to talk to him. They've never seen anything like this."

"So, we can…we can *see* him?" I ask.

"Jubilee, by the end of the week, we can take him *home*. He's been talking about having a chance to tango, which I'm pretty sure is inappropriate. But right now, I don't even care. You need to get here *now*." Hakim is a marveling child.

"We'll be there soon." I nod, though he can't see it. "I'm leaving now."

My family still doesn't understand and begins to try to comfort me. I don't even know how to explain.

"He's awake," I tell them. Then I laugh and look at Bennett. "Get your legs, Ben. Let's go see Dad."

"What?!" Bennett asks.

I sniffle. "He's gonna live, Bennett. Dad's not dying today. Not from this."

Then Bennett bursts into tears, and no one shushes him.

"You serious, Jubilee?" Isaac asks, eyes narrowed.

"He's eating waffles." I laugh once. Cry more.

"Gosh, I've been craving waffles for days," Penny says.

Hannah bites her lip. Noah smiles. And Penny announces her pregnancy and steals the thunder of joy. Great joy. But garden-variety joy, which is easier for a narrow-minded, stifled-hearted Monroe to swallow. But I rush out the door with my children in pursuit of something much greater.

"I like riding back here," Bennett says from the back seat where he is staring at his tiny sister. "So I can know she's safe."

Which is pretty much Bennett in a nutshell. Hakim meets us at the doors of the ICU, and I am sure this is some cruel joke and Elijah is dead. As we walk back to Elijah's room, Hakim takes the heavy baby carrier that I'm not supposed to carry for another couple of weeks because of my cesarean. Then he winces.

"Should've mentioned…" And here it is. "Elijah died last night. No vitals at all for seven full minutes. He was about to receive an official time of death, Jubilee. I had you a tap away in my phone to tell you. It was awful. But since you were stubborn and wouldn't let him sign a full DNR, the CPR worked last second. I was pretty mad, because he was still in his coma, fighting for six hours. Could have been brain dead. I just wanted the pain to be gone. I fell asleep in the horrible chair and woke up to Elijah removing his own breathing tube and calling a nurse, asking her why she put it in when he 'expressly requested not to be hooked up to life-sustaining machines.' "

I giggle. "He removed his own tube?"

"Yeah, he had to tell them he'd done it a thousand times on patients. They started doing the tests…He beat it, Jubilee. God. God beat this. He must've decided Elijah had more work to do."

We arrive at the room, and Elijah looks up. That light in his eyes again.

"Hey, Mama." He tilts his head, speaking a little sensually. "You ready to dance with me?"

I bolt to his side and begin savoring maybe a hundred deeply resonating open-mouthed kisses, and he doesn't protest.

"You two and your kissing. That is so vulgar." Maren, of course, showing up just in time with the family.

Elijah has that narrow-eyed ecstasy in his eyes. I see his jaw clench to fight the sensations in public eyes as he looks into my eyes with some sad sort of hunger.

"I'm so glad I don't have to leave you," he whispers, and the others are silent as they watch.

"You'd have been better off," I admit. "I certainly wouldn't have. But I hope you didn't make some deal with God to stay with me."

"If I did, I don't remember." He laughs. "Best nap I've had in a long time. No nightmares. I wanted to go home today, but they said I can't."

"They have to make sure you're really okay, Husband." I run a thumb along his cheek and look him over. Whisper. "Your eyebrows are starting to come back."

Then Bennett jumps onto the bed with his parents and curls into his daddy's arms.

"I was waiting for Mama to be done kissing you. I hope it's okay."

I realize my selfishness to have stolen a child's reunion with his dad.

"I should have let you hug him first." I wince. "Sorry, Ben."

"Well Lord willing, I have time to spare now, so it doesn't matter who I see first or last. But where is that little girl of mine?" Elijah asks.

I look back to see that most of my family is in the hall securing flights and making travel and work arrangements. Apparently, a miracle isn't a good enough reason to stick around.

 Thirty-Eight

Elijah

I arrive home like I'm walking on holy ground, touching the couch and kitchen counters as if caressing fine gold. Looking at Jubilee's wall decor as masterpieces in an art gallery. I'm walking with the confident air I did the day I married Jubilee. Not at full strength yet, and I may never be. But I'm no longer dying of cancer. I'm just living with it.

There is a note from Jubilee's mother that she left a casserole in the fridge. She does so a couple times a week, as promised. We enjoy dinner as a family, and I am more than delighted to help put my children to bed. Bennett can hardly get to sleep and keeps poking his head out to the living room to make sure his dad is still at home.

Us three adults sit together rejoicing, fellowshipping, and laughing about what has been and what wasn't—beyond speaking relief over what could have been. Late in the evening, Hakim sighs.

"I'm really gonna hate going back home. I love the way your house feels. It's so real. The past year has been awful, but this still feels like home," Hakim says.

"This *is* your home," I offer. "You can stay with us as long as you want and then buy your own house when you get sick of us. You're a grown man. You don't have to be married to fly the coop."

"Our parents like us to be," Jubilee shares with a wince.

"So you married me to get away from home?" I joke.

"Yeah. Exactly." She snickers.

"And no prospects for the 'acceptable' path, I'm guessing?" I confirm of Hakim.

"The only girl I'm interested in right now is my horse." Hakim laughs. "If God sent one along, I wouldn't mind having a wife. But if He doesn't, I'm okay with that too. I think God has something else for me right now." Hakim smirks. "I've been thinking about Africa a lot lately."

"Africa? Where you were born?" I confirm.

"Yeah," Hakim shares. "Normally when I think about it, it just hurts. But lately I feel, I don't know. Empowered? Like maybe…maybe I could do something about, you know, *something*."

"You'd really go back there?" Jubilee wonders.

"One of my counselors suggested it once. Face my fears or whatever. I never considered it until…you know almost losing one of your favorite people gets you thinking about life," Hakim says. "That counselor might have been right."

"Okay, counselors?" I ask and Jubilee winces.

"Yeah, to deal with stuff from before I was adopted. I guess it helped. I saw biblical counselors that used God's Word in a way I couldn't see myself." Hakim smiles a little.

Jubilee seems glad when Scarlett cries and she must rise to retrieve her from the bedroom.

"She remembers," Hakim whispers.

"Yeah, she's mentioned that." I nod, then whisper, "She ever seen anyone about it?"

"I think she's much better at coping with it than I am. She's seen the worst and doesn't like to talk about it. She copes by just being *better*. I'd say she's improved the world quite a lot with that philosophy. Wouldn't you?"

Later, in our bedroom, I hesitate when I reach over to hold my wife.

"How is your incision?"

"It's mostly healed. I'm even going back to work next week. Hannah says she'll take care of Ben's schooling," she tells me, and she's running fingers along my arm.

"That's sweet of her, but it's hopefully not for long," I whisper and kiss her shoulder. "I know you'd rather be home with the kids, and I should be back up to snuff soon."

"Take your time getting better, Husband. I don't mind my job in the meantime."

"I want you to love what you do, not 'not mind' it."

"I know." Jubilee sighs. I change the subject.

"We need a bigger house, don't we? I'd rather add on to this one. I have some equity in the house. We could add a bedroom or two. I'm sure Hakim knows someone who could help me build it. I'll ask him in the morning."

I'm talking about plans. About the future. Tomorrow. Something that last week we didn't even have together, and I certainly didn't have the strength to be talking like this. But our bed becomes a big grateful spoon drawer of planning an addition to the house.

Jubilee

The very next day, Hakim comes home from work at lunchtime, which is welcome, but unprecedented. He immediately unloads.

"God sometimes talks really loud, and works really fast, doesn't He?" Hakim laughs some bittersweet laugh.

"That He does," Elijah replies. "Tell us what's going on."

"He's been telling me to go to Africa, especially after we talked last night. I stayed up late looking into some things and found out this organization is looking for people to help run a center for children. I prayed about it. God already answered, but I figured I'd give it some time. Then I went to work this morning...and got laid off."

The whole room gasps. At the loss of a seemingly stable job. At the power of the Almighty. Then smiles at Hakim's smile. He continues.

"I immediately went over to the church, just for a place to pray about it. Jessie was there. She helped me fill out all the applications, since she just did something similar for Mexico. They called not ten minutes after I submitted it. I've already done a phone interview. Pending a visa, kissing Mom goodbye, remembering Amharic, and some other logistics, I'm moving to Africa."

"That's quick!" Elijah notes. Already missing him. "Are you ready for this? Psychologically, I mean?"

"I wasn't," Hakim admits. "Let's just say that a certain sister of mine has inspired me to experience liberty and serve in ways our parents might find disturbingly unconventional. It doesn't really matter if I'm ready. I've been called. God will be with me as I answer."

"I'm serious. I'm…I'm going. I'm even a little excited," Jessie says with a smile days later.

"What convinced you?" I ask in wonder, bouncing fussy baby Scarlett in the fellowship hall of the church.

"Among other things, Elijah almost died." Jessie laughs once.

"Elijah seems to have inspired quite a few people recently."

"It wasn't *Elijah* who inspired me." Jessie crosses her arms. "It was you, Jubilee."

"Me?"

"You were at his side as much as you could be. And the rest of the time, you were taking care of a newborn and helping Bennett get through a difficult ordeal. And you never complained. Not once. It's like you're not even capable of thinking of yourself. I saw that, Jubilee. And then…" Jessie sobs suddenly. Then composes herself. "I saw that, and then went home to Garrett and gave him a tongue lashing about taking me to Mexico. And my heart just shattered. And I realized that serving in a foreign country with my healthy, loving husband is nothing compared to what you've been through. I also talked to Hakim when he was deciding to go to Africa. Which I suspect you *also* inspired."

"But you were there to help him. Thank you, by the way."

"I haven't stopped thanking *him*. He helped me understand how powerful *Garrett's* call is to Mexico. How awful of me to question it…" Jessie smirks. Cradles herself. "The final push was last week when I found out that I'll most definitely be giving birth in Mexico. That's how I told Garrett. In…in Spanish. I've been trying to learn. Abuela Millie would have been proud. She begged me all my life to learn Spanish."

"Oh, Jessie. How adorable! And congrats on the baby!"

"Well, it wasn't exactly an 'on purpose' thing," Jessie admits. "But it's fine. We're getting used to the idea."

But I ignite. "*'Fine'*? Jessie, it's not 'fine'! Your baby has a name and an individually crafted soul and a *purpose*. Babies aren't blessings just for people who *want* them and planned for them. God isn't giving you a *burden*.

By His grace, He is giving you a *person*. *You*, Jessie, have been called to this as much as to Mexico. It's not 'fine.' But that's just…that's just my thought."

"Prim and Proper Jubilee. You are so wonderful, you know that?" Jessie compliments through tears. "We'll miss you for sure."

Hakim has been gone for three months. Since then, the household has transitioned from how it was before, with Elijah not well enough to watch the children and me working full time. He eventually insisted on keeping the children home with him. The house was a constant disaster, and he was frazzled by the end of each day, but Bennett did seem to focus on his schooling better with his father than with Hannah. Three weeks ago, Elijah was cleared for work, and I gladly put in my two weeks' notice.

I worked with other women; career women who loved working *and* their families. I understood them. But I knew it wasn't my calling when I spent the better part of my first morning at home holding onto Scarlett in tears of gratitude. Elijah had come home from work smiling. We know the roles suggested from my upbringing were not purposes that everyone must fulfill. But for us, they glorified God immensely.

In addition to changes in the household, there have been changes in my family. There are differences of opinion about Hakim's choice to move to Africa; differences divisive enough that we have not attended any family meals to avoid the conflict. Much of the family has chosen to support him. The rest chose to treat his departure as a banishment. While the many branches of the family have not fallen out of communication, we tend to avoid one another's presence wherever possible.

One morning in late summer, Bennett engages me in conversation while I feed Scarlett some mess of mushed up leftovers. A sloppy, unsavory transition from milk to solid foods in the eyes of anyone who watches. But Scarlett bounces happily as each bite fills her belly more.

"I miss Uncle Hakim," Bennett begins. "When is he coming back?"

"He isn't. He wants to be there as permanently as possible. But he hopes to visit. You know that," I explain yet again. Then with a twinge of painful understanding, I sigh. "I know. I miss him too. He and I were best friends growing up."

"That's what Aunt Hannah said when I went to see Jonathan that day you went with Daddy to the doctor," Bennett recalls. "She said you miss him, but that when God calls someone to do something, we need to be okay with it. We need to respect it even if you don't want them to do it."

"That's right. I know Hakim is doing this for God's glory, so no matter how we miss him, we need to support him," I confirm for the boy.

"Like Jonathan says his mommy and daddy were worried when you married Daddy. But that God asked you to, and now they are happy you did."

"That's right." I love to watch his heart connect the dots and extract meaning from his life, as always.

"Yeah. And like how you don't like what Grandpa thinks sometimes. But how he loves God and does it for Him, so you respect him. Right?"

I don't answer readily. Instead my pause gives way only to a knock at the door which I must answer. It's Judah, with a delivery of a frozen meal and a basket of apples. I let him in.

"You can tell Mom we're back on our feet and she doesn't need to make us food anymore." I laugh, putting away the meal.

"I've tried to tell her." Judah shrugs with a smirk. "The apples were simply extra, as always."

"Does Dad still buy them faster than he can use them?"

"Not anymore. I have a dear friend who supplies me with apples. More than the three of us can eat." Judah rustles Bennett's hair, pausing, then stating some unexpected business. "I'd like for you to come to my birthday celebration. The four of you. I know that in recent times you've been avoiding being in our father's company because of some differences regarding Hakim. But I'd like for you to come. Please."

"Thank you for the invitation, Judah. And for the apples." I avoid his eyes. "I'll have to ask my husband, of course."

"Of course." Judah nods, making his sad exit knowing Elijah's attitude toward those who live at the Monroe Homestead.

I consider my little brother Judah—a young man barely beginning to find his own opinions. But willing, still, to deliver apples and messages among the branches of the family.

"Yes," I state at random while cleaning dishes from feeding my baby girl.

"Yes, what?" Bennett had long forgotten the conversation.

"Yes," I answer the previous question. "We sometimes disagree with Grandpa. But that doesn't matter. He is my dad and a member of the body of Christ. For that alone, whether or not he changes, he should receive our love and respect."

Thirty-Nine

Elijah

"I'd rather not, Jubilee. I love them just fine, but I'm not going to support this anymore. They ridicule everything we do. Their legalism is suffocating. I don't know how you can't see that," I rant, arms crossed on the Sunday morning in September.

"But Uncle Judah is having a birthday party," Bennett begins, gently bouncing his giggling sister on his legs.

Scarlett doesn't know or care that her brother is different. She's enjoying being bounced back and forth between his legs as one lifts and tosses her to the other, which catches her.

I interrupt my son, practically at full throttle intensity. "So you just bend to their will, once again? You're a grown woman with a family of your own, Jubilee. They can't expect you to just show up whenever they ask."

"Why not?" Jubilee reaches her volume limit, which is still within the peace of our home. "Why can't they expect that? I know it's all completely different and crazy sometimes the way they think. But what if that's okay? What if how they are never changes and there's nothing actually wrong with that?"

"What are you saying, Jubilee?" I raise shrugged arms. "Are you saying the way God grew you these past two years has all been—"

"Wonderful." Jubilee sits on the couch and sways her half-up hair and one member of her collection of long feather earrings and crosses her denim-covered legs. "This has nothing to do with the liberty God required *me* to use. I'm grateful for the way He's transformed me."

"So what exactly do you mean?" I join her on the couch.

"That liberty goes both ways. The point of liberty was never to break away from God-honored tradition if that is the place He wants us. It was to have the ability to serve God the way *He* wants us to serve. Any person who uses liberty to sin is in the wrong. Likewise, for any person to take their own convictions and use them as a standard for everyone is sinful." Jubilee explains, allowing my smirk and the sweep of my fingertips to move a hair from her face.

"Your dad has been doing that to us for years. To everybody, actually," I point out.

"He has. But honestly, his profession requires him to sometimes. That's God's purpose for him. But we've done the same to *him*, Elijah. Why should my dad bend to *our* convictions?"

"I'm not asking him to. I only want him to accept them."

Jubilee, in all her wild beauty, shrugs her modestly covered shoulders and stares intensely from her golden eyes into my black ones. "Maybe he will. Maybe he *never* will. But that isn't ours to judge. Our only job is to love him and support the work he does for Christ. He has always welcomed us into his home. His final judgment has always been to love us. We are called to be at peace with our brethren and to fellowship with them and be unified in Christ. We have answered that call. Perhaps we should leave the rest of it alone?"

"Will Jonathan be there?" Bennett asks, knowing his poor dad's will has crumbled at Jubilee's gentleness, once again.

"Of course." Jubilee nods. What she doesn't say, but clearly means, is that Hannah has never allowed personal convictions to stand in the way of loving and serving her family in the name of Christ. Much like Jubilee.

Jubilee

"I still have cancer," Elijah answers my mother with a laugh. "But that's to be expected. The way we're treating it is slower than their poison, which almost killed me."

"And how are you treating it?" Mom blinks confusion, turning to me.

"A strict diet, avoiding carcinogens whenever possible, and the oil for another few months." I shrug. And since it doesn't matter, and love will abound in any case, I speak the truth. "When you give me the oil, I always add a hefty dose of CBD, which is shrinking the cancer slowly over time."

"Cannabis?" Dad asks.

"Yes." I sigh, then smile as I deliver the rest. "And it was working, but with lung cancer sometimes the cancer doesn't shrink fast enough to save someone because the lungs aren't open enough to accept the treatment. Mom, your oil? With all that fragrant eucalyptus and peppermint and everything else? It made what I added *able* to work. The oncologist says he thinks that oil saved his life when he had pneumonia at the beginning of the year. Not just the CBD. *Your* oil, Mom. He told us that at our last appointment."

"So you're on drugs?" Dad, of course.

Elijah rolls his eyes at Dad and then sighs. "You're a big man, Adam. You're telling me you aren't on any drugs for hypertension or blood sugar at your age?"

"Medications, not drugs."

"My treatment is being monitored by a medical professional, and I don't use it for recreation. Mine is medicine too. And Jubilee is right. Thank you, Leah. Mom. For spiking it for us." Elijah leaves it at that, save a wink that makes my mother blush.

"Have you spoken with Hakim?" Mom changes the subject cheerily over freshly grilled cheeseburgers and hot dogs and a big salad. The avid gardener clinging to the last breath of summer.

"We did a video chat last week, and he seems to be doing well. I think he's finally getting settled into a routine at the center," I share.

"He mentioned that in his last letter. I know he loves his technology. It's so good of him to write letters to his old-fashioned mom." Mom smiles.

"I heard rumors that another construction company was hiring laid-off employees from Hakim's former employer," Isaac promotes. "In case that will change his mind about this whole Africa nonsense."

"He's not interested in working construction anymore, Isaac," James says inside a laugh.

"And this Africa move isn't what I would call 'nonsense.' " Elijah supports.

"What would you call it then, Elijah?" Dad booms, probably seeing Elijah as a drug addict now. "When a child's well-being is fought for, and his faithful upbringing is a hard-won victory and then that child grows and returns to the place from whence he was rescued?"

"If you hadn't rescued him, he might have died there. It might look like a loss to you that he's going back. I get that, trust me. God allowed me to rescue my own son from a similar situation," Elijah explains to the hurting father. "But it's a victory, Adam. If you hadn't raised him to love the Lord, strong-willed spirit and all, he'd have nothing to take back with him. I call it God using your obedience, and Hakim's, to His glory."

"Hakim has the tools to have done anything but what he did and use *that* to God's glory." Dad works through it aloud. "He had the freedom to do anything. Why did he choose that?"

"Dad…" I speak up. "What Elijah is saying is…the same liberty that made you choose to adopt Hakim from Africa is the liberty that sent him back. I miss him, and I wish I'd had a little more warning. But I'm content knowing that he's doing God's work. That's enough for me."

When supper is cleared and conversation lightened, the room rejoices as Mom and a couple of the older children bring in dessert—a few homemade apple pies and dollops of ice cream. I look to my little brother, who is preoccupied with Scarlett's smile. I smile the comment at Elijah.

"This is like heaven for Dad and Judah." The smile is then for Judah, who has looked up at the sound of his name. "You two just love your apples. These are McIntosh, I assume. Good for a snack *and* for pie."

"Delicious in any form," my father concurs with an endearing smirk.

First, Judah smiles, then looks to Dad, then to me, deciding something.

"Something wrong, Judah?" Mom asks of the pie.

"Not at all," Judah reassures her. "However, Jubilee is only slightly correct. I don't really prefer apples to other fruit. And honestly, I prefer green apples in pie, and honeycrisp for eating raw. McIntosh is suitable for both purposes, but isn't ideal, in my humble opinion. But the pie is lovely, Mom. Not to worry."

"Judah, you brought these apples home. I asked you to get apples for today's pie. You chose these yourself after having requested apple pie for dessert," Mom reminds him.

"I didn't *choose* them, per se," Judah explains. "Nor would apple pie have been my first choice as a birthday dessert. But one must always be willing to accept what one is given. I was given McIntosh apples. I accepted the need for less-than-ideal apple pie. As I mentioned, I knew your skill in baking said pies would surpass the quality of the apples, as it has."

Mom takes the compliment with a smile, but I am puzzled. Some storehouse in my heart is breaking open. It couldn't be.

"Who gives you McIntosh apples? You always have them here. I thought you bought them at the market," I wonder.

Our father responds, "Given our abundance of apples, I've pardoned Judah for consistently refusing to answer that question."

Judah smirks a little, looking to me. He shrugs. "I can show you, if you like. All of you. It's a wonderful evening for a walk."

"Walk?" Now I'm doubly suspicious.

Judah nods. "You may ride, if you like. I often do."

"To the market?" Dad asks.

"I don't..." Judah begins, then gains confidence. "I don't get the apples from the market, Dad."

The family—those vehemently adhered to tradition, along with those in vibrant skin and denim; parents, siblings, and the younger generation—set out from the house together.

"Where we headed, Judah?" Isaac asks.

"Just go around the barn and follow the path with the white stones," Judah answers as he heads into the barn.

"You enjoy your ride with Judah," Elijah says, kissing me at the barnyard fence, then strapping his daughter into a baby carrier normally worn by a woman. "We'll see you wherever it is we're going."

Judah emerges from the barn suddenly, with a box in his arms, calling out. "You'll need this!"

But as he draws nearer to Elijah, it is clear. It isn't a box. No. It's a cooler.

Elijah takes to full laughter. I gasp.

"I always wondered where it went! I always assumed you took it home while we were courting," I say to my husband. "But then I've never seen it at home."

Judah winces, handing the cooler to Isaac's older boys to carry. "Oh. Is it yours, Elijah? I've been using it for...well you'll see. But I can get something else if—"

"That cooler helped me snag a wife I still don't deserve. Why don't you keep it, Judah? Maybe it's still lucky." Elijah winks at his younger brother-in-law, who returns to the barn with a warm nod.

As the family begins their unknown trek, Judah leads the horses from the barn. Then, when he has them out, he removes their leads.

"I thought we were *riding* them," I express my confusion.

"We are." Judah nods. "Lightning injured herself on some barbed wire the second time I rode her. She missed Hakim and was out of sorts. The injury was where the saddle strapped on, and I wanted it to heal while still getting her used to me. So, I rode her bareback. Just the once, I thought. But she took to it well. Then I tried Thunder the same way. They both seem to prefer it."

"I've never ridden bareback. That doesn't seem safe, Judah. Since when do you go around lying to Dad about apples and riding the horses bareback?"

"You've often overlooked many of the things I do, Jubilee," Judah says, putting a stool under Thunder for me to mount him.

Suddenly, I get a spark in my heart. I'm dressed for it. Maybe I've become it. So I follow the spark.

"Wanna ride?" I whisper to my horse. With cancer, a new baby, and Hakim leaving the country, it's been many months. Still, I know I needn't ask.

I step onto the stool and grasp his black mane, swinging myself onto the gelding. I find myself at home on a horse without the stability of a saddle. In jeans, hair loose, maybe even a little messy. I can't even consider now that once upon a time I was so scared of everything. Scared to opine and feel and hunger and love. I'm so at peace, I barely hear Judah speak to me from Lightning's back.

"I'm only sorry Hakim can't join us today."

"He'd have a fit knowing you rode her this way." I giggle.

"No, not...not the horse," Judah clarifies. "But because of where they're taking us."

Today, at the point in the trail where the gallop normally begins, I'm not scared of anything, even as Judah points to where the gallop will cause us to graze the limits of some man's boundary.

The horses turn and gallop another way. Not on the beaten-down trail in the safety of the center of the land. No. Right along the fence. Safely inside, but not having wasted an inch of space to run. Pure adrenaline and adventure rush over me as we gallop past the walking group of family.

I assume from Mom's gasp that she is worried over our riding bareback at this speed. It's unsafe.

But from Elijah's wild, Texas yee-haw, I wonder if I have finally been released from the cage he began to tease at years ago. My hat flies free from my head, and I gallop on without it. Without fear. With only joy—earned joy I'd have missed had I kept to what was trodden and safe. To trees near the Tree.

Today, I laugh as it approaches, and Judah begins to slow Lightning. Thunder reluctantly follows suit. We stop at a tree not too far from the very barbed wire edge of the property. I dismount and reach up and touch the fruit. It's not forbidden, of course, just wild. Likely for over a decade, an apple tree has been hiding along the fence after the land slopes—where no one ever goes.

I know because I planted it myself, unaware of the work God was doing all along.

Judah dismounts and draws my attention to a smaller tree a few feet away.

"White-blossom crab apple," he says. "Lovely in the spring. But the fruit is practically inedible. However, when I discovered that one of the seeds you planted was beginning to become what you see here, I did research and discovered that it would need a pollinator if there was to be any hope of it producing fruit."

It wasn't enough for the tree to be close to the fence alone. The seeds needed tending, and the flowers needed pollinating. Someone had to be willing to step close to the fence repeatedly. And because they did, the tree that had been placed here through no choice or fault of its own, could thrive.

"You knew about the seeds? I'd forgotten, Judah. Dad said we couldn't come over here, so we couldn't tend them," I explain.

"I didn't have a horse, but I saw where you went that day. I came out here the next day, because Mom only said I had to stay inside the fence. I was too young then to participate in your trail rides. But not too young to tend this tree when you couldn't." He laughs. "Well, perhaps, I suppose. It's practically wild I neglected it so often. But it was obviously a work God wanted to complete. Now I have more apples than I can manage. I don't really even like apples..." Judah trails off with a smirk. "Lucky Dad does."

"I underestimated you." I sniffle. "Severely. I thought you were a brat."

"I was. Then you met Elijah and I started to wonder if Dad's version of Jesus was the truth. I hadn't been to this tree in years, but God asked me to tend it. I don't know what else He has for me. But for now, I ride bareback to a wild tree and bless our traditional father with its fruit." He chuckles. "Actually, all of the fruit is from the same source, unbeknownst to all of you."

"Wasn't it always?" I ruminate.

Judah smirks his understanding as the family approaches and hears of the tree and the apples. And they all share in its joy, climbing limbs and biting apples and laughing, regardless of age or denomination. They take joy in that same source of McIntosh apples, filling a forgotten cooler.

I'm eating an apple off the tree and feeding one to my horse. I'm mounting again and taking Thunder through tall grasses and the unknown, instead of that old path my father taught me to keep. It's all completely unsafe. Uncharted. But a life of purpose isn't about safety, keeping traditions, or even happiness. It is about God's glory. And there is nothing safe about an apple from a mostly untended tree in a fallen world. Or, depending on your loyalties, a pitcher in the hand of Gideon.

"The Monroe Series"

Update 2026: The Trees of Eden can be read as a standalone, complete story, and it may remain that way. For now, the remaining installments of The Monroe Series are on hold. See Acknowledgements page (front matter) for further explanation.

Get in Touch

My website: https://www.rebekahtynemckamie.com

Instagram: @rebekahspelledlikethebible

Facebook: https://www.facebook.com/rebekahtyne

TikTok: @rebekahtyneauthor

For book editing: https://www.repriseeditorial.com